LIVE FROM MOSCOW

CHAPTER 2

"Damn it!" I snapped the phone shut and stomped to Camille's car.

She cocked her head, but said nothing.

"They expect me to go to the back of beyond to check on some old coot who forgot to turn the page on his calendar. If he even *has* a calendar. Probably figures the date by the length of the moss on the north side of the trees or the width of a snail's slime."

"Can you do that?" Camille asked without a trace of a twinkle in her copper-brown eyes.

"Who the hell knows?" I snatched up the shirt and thrust my arms into the sleeves.

She laughed. "You're cute when you're cranky." Stretching, she laced her fingers at the nape of my neck and brought her lips to mine. I resisted for a second, then closed my eyes and leaned into the kiss, letting her suck the venom from my mood. "Mmm." I ran my hands along her back and cupped her against me.

Her lips curved into a smile and she pushed away. "My car bottoms out in four-inch ruts. You better take the SUV."

I cursed once more to demonstrate I still had an ounce of free will, then we wrestled the trailer loose from the hitch. "I don't know when I'll be back."

"Take the lunch I packed for us." She stashed a brown paper sack and a jug of water in the back seat.

"What will you eat?"

She nodded at the trailer. "I'm quitting when that sucker's full. Gonna go back to the Brocktons' place, take a long, hot shower, and make you a peach pie."

I could almost smell the brandy and nutmeg, taste the flaky crust that was her specialty, see her bronze skin gleaming in a sluice of water from the showerhead. "There's nothing I like more than a clean woman and a fresh pie."

She bounced on tiptoe, kissed my nose, and patted my butt. "Then get gone so you can get back."

Jefferson Longyear sat in the doorway of the old schoolhouse he called home, his feet resting on steps built from blocks of dark stone. Generations ago, Hemlock Lake men hewed those blocks from quarries at the north end of the lake and dragged them seven miles on sledges pulled by draft horses. As a kid, I would stare at sepia-toned photographs and imagine riding one of those huge horses, fingers knotted in its mane.

Jefferson ran a hand across his gray brush cut and stood, tall and straight, still a Marine to the

10

LIVE FROM MOSCOW

a novel

ERIC ALMEIDA

Published by Cove Rock
First released in digital format in 2010

ISBN-13: 9780692730256
ISBN-10: 0692730257

www.ericalmeida.com

CHAPTER 1

Peter Bradford was certain he'd done this for Claire. Not because she'd asked him. The initiative was all his.

She'd propelled him. And he'd almost gone the distance.

He lay on his back. Straining his head forward, he looked down the length of his body and clutched both hands over his stomach. Under flat moonlight he saw that his fingers were dark with blood, which was soaking through his shirt and coat, pasty and warm on his skin. Temperatures were mild but now felt sub-freezing. He shivered and noticed that his breathing and pulse were rapid and increasing. An unmistakable precursor, he'd once read.

His hearing was acute. In the distance he heard the sound of single automobile, reversing north. Its two occupants…the idiots…had concocted their rash and unsophisticated plan over a laptop computer…. They'd unzipped the case and grown confused, then angry, arguing with wild gestures. Bradford didn't understand a word of Tajik; he'd just stood by. Now he realized the two had been debating his fate. Without warning one broke off the discussion, strode toward him in the clearing, and fired two gunshots at short range to the stomach: *thwack, thwack.*

He turned his head to one side. The laptop still lay on the hardscrabble surface, several yards away. Nearby was its companion case. Both left behind like surplus baggage.

Sound from the motor faded, leaving the forest quiet. He looked up. Stars shone. Signaling what came next? Instead of grappling toward last-minute answers he thought of Claire. Somehow she softened the unknowns.

His breathing quickened further and his heart began to pound. Lucidity gave way to dizziness. He felt himself slipping away, disconnected from his surroundings and enveloped by warm liquid. Swimming and sliding into a long tunnel.

CHAPTER 2

Arthur Gallagher cleared his throat and scanned the faces of the congregation. There were occasions when compassion trumped other considerations. This was one.

He concluded his eulogy for Peter Bradford on a sublime note.

"In the journalistic profession pursuit of facts---of the truth---often requires sacrifice. Peter clearly lived by this credo. In his work he was willing to do whatever was necessary. Even risk his life. For all of us his passing is premature, and tragic. And the violence with which he died carries a certain senseless quality. But I would suggest that we find another interpretation. Peter was engaged in a moral undertaking, serving all of us. What higher calling is there than the quest for truth, especially on behalf of others? At this difficult moment, I would hope that we can take some small solace from this feature of Peter's time on earth, however shortened."

Gallagher folded his notes and re-beheld the 300 or so mourners. With care he descended two steps from the altar and headed back toward his seat in the second row. He was still a few years from retirement, but advancing age and an old football injury already imposed certain limitations, and these were only compounded by jet-lag after the flight from Boston.

In the aisle he received an appreciative nod from Harrison Whitcombe, the publisher of the *Boston World Tribune*. Whitcombe wore his usual stoicism---almost. He was also Bradford's uncle. Gallagher, as Managing Editor, had supervised Bradford's final assignment---the first in which a reporter had died during the 153-year history of the newspaper.

There was a short pause. The church fell quiet, except for a couple of muted coughs that reverberated off the high ceilings. In the row ahead of Gallagher, Bradford's widow, Claire, reached into her purse. Her shoulders convulsed as she extracted a handkerchief. She dabbed her eyes with a quivering hand looked forward again. Her shoulders squared---a show of determination.

Gallagher's acquaintance with her was meager---a few conversations at social gatherings in Boston a couple of years earlier, when Bradford was based there. Her French accent was strong, he remembered, but she'd left an impact for other reasons, even if she didn't mean to. A combination of idealized mediums: middling height, light brown hair of shoulder length, green eyes---average lengths and colors, rendered in curves that were just short of voluptuous. Also...how would Gallagher describe it? She threw off live energy.

Oriented around her husband's career. No children yet. As far as Gallagher knew she had just part-time work in Paris. With Bradford gone where would she look for new direction and purpose? Where would that energy go?

Gallagher wondered.

The fact was he didn't believe his own lofty rhetoric. The assignment had seemed worthwhile at the outset. But Bradford had taken it too far; his death had been needless. Gallagher felt disquieting responsibility. Was there a way to give her true solace? He wished there were.

It was rather late in the game for new lessons. Reporters sometimes did have to take risks. But he could at least prevent another tragedy on his watch. That was something. He focused his gaze on

Bradford's casket, which was open. The priest, a tall, gangly man in his 30s, returned to the center of the altar. The funeral mass resumed, in the French language.

Yes, Gallagher told himself. This would not happen again. Certain assignments had to be kept under tighter control.

CHAPTER 3

An eight-oared crew swept by 20 yards off the riverbank, under insistent shouts from the coxswain. The rowers' faces were concentrated, and written with pain. Other boats followed in close succession, displaying the same aching resolve.

"What drives those guys?" Steve Conley asked.

"You did a sport in college," said Thom, referring to Conley's four more-or-less respectable years on the swim team.

"So?"

"You should have some idea."

Disinclined to ponder the question, Conley laughed and drained the rest of his beer. Their group consisted of four couples, late 20s and early 30s, sprawled on blankets on the Cambridge side of the Charles River. The occasion was the annual Head of the Charles Regatta---for them and most others, rowing as pretext for an afternoon in the October sun. He placed a languid hand on the back of Jenna, who was sitting cross-legged next to him. She had not participated in an analogous outing the previous year. Indeed, at the time they had not even met. Thom observed the gesture.

"Remember last year's Head of the Charles?" he asked.

At once Conley felt some of his lightness dissipate. It had been a stressful juncture. Just weeks before, he'd seen his career derailed.

Hints of scandal. An abrupt transfer from London back to Boston. From fast-track international correspondent to backwater features writer. To counteract the recollections, he hooked his palm around Jenna's waist and drew her closer.

"This year's better," he responded. "In more ways than one."

"That occurred to me also."

Jenna understood the implication, and reacted with a slight, prolonged smile. She was even-tempered and tolerant, features which Conley appreciated after preceding events. Her smooth complexion, auburn hair, and arresting figure only compounded her pluses.

There was a break in the procession of crew shells: a brief interlude between race events. Conley sat up. Lunch had already come and gone, while the Boston skyline and foliage of Back Bay still glistened across the river. He proposed another round of beers, to which everyone assented. He stood and began gathering empty cups and the discarded bags and wrappers from their picnic.

"I'll give you a hand," Thom volunteered.

They dumped the refuse in a nearby trash can, then strolled toward several tents that alumni organizations had set up about 75 yards away along Memorial Drive. Their path was winding; people lounged everywhere on blankets or on the grass. Scents of autumn leaves and alcohol permeated the air. Sunglasses and semi-drunkenness were motifs of the day.

About halfway, Thom asked, "How *are* things at work these days?"

"Tolerable."

"What about other newspapers?"

"More rejections. From *The LA Times* and *The Washington Post*, most recently."

"Too bad…Tough times in the industry, I've gathered."

"That's an understatement. The Internet continues to take a huge toll, especially on classified advertising. No one's hiring. If anything, they're laying reporters off."

"Maybe you should be grateful you still have a job."

"I am. And I prefer Boston anyway."

"I'm sure Jenna helps."

"She does."

They rounded the corner of the joint Brown/Dartmouth tent, now out of sight of their group, and joined a queue. In an open area to their left they spotted a tall, conspicuous blonde, early to mid-twenties, with low-cut jeans that emphasized the spread of her hips and a swath of luminous skin around her midriff. She was in conversation with two friends, but her large eyes settled at once on Conley. They held contact for a few seconds.

"Wow," Conley exclaimed under his breath.

Thom shook his head, aware that Conley's exemplary proportions and thick hair often provoked this kind of spontaneous interest. The girl's two companions also shot glances in their direction. Some seconds later the girl herself looked again. There was no mistaking the signal.

"Don't even think about it," he said.

Conley looked down: a bout of self-regulation. It was fleeting, thanks to the beer.

"We have to walk by them anyway. Harmless. Doesn't have to lead anywhere."

Thom shook his head again.

Passing by the girls, beers in hand, they stopped. Ensuing banter was true to form: offhand quips from Conley, polite questions and suggestive giggles from the girls. Thom stood to one side and participated only to the extent necessary, reluctant to abet the undertaking. When the repartee was spent Thom shifted on his feet: a show of impatience. Conley was looking for an exit line when the girl pulled out her business card.

"Why don't you call me?" she said. "…I mean, if you want to." She held a smile.

Conley hesitated for a second and offered a sheepish grin.

"Sure…why not?" Transferring the beers inside one forearm, he took the card, gave it a once-over, and saw that she was a paralegal downtown. He thrust it into his back pocket, and thanked her. On the way back through the blankets and bodies toward the riverbank, he felt a little giddy. When they were out of earshot of the girls, Thom let loose.

"Why are you still doing that?"

"What could I do? I had to be polite."

"I hope you won't call her."

"Well…no. Of course not."

Conley realized his tone was unconvincing. Thom did too.

"Jenna's a good find, Steve. I'd think you would have learned."

The remark hit home. Dislocations from London still stung. Conley took a deep breath to clear his head. They were almost upon their group. Thom studied Conley's profile and sighed.

"Let's just forget it," he suggested.

"Good idea."

All the same Conley decided Thom was right. Time had really come for self-restraint.

CHAPTER 4

Disorientation engulfed Claire between the fourth and third floors of her apartment building in Saint-Germain-des-Pres, during her descent to street level. This morning the precipitant was ordinary---the control buttons in the elevator. Those buttons…Peter's fingers had pressed them almost every day, just weeks earlier. All of a sudden the tight space became hot. She broke a sweat and started panting.

The elevator door opened and for a dizzy moment she braced her arms against the frame. Though the building was well-appointed it didn't have a concierge; the small lobby was empty. She made her way to a bench against one wall and sat down. Her breathing echoed off the marble surfaces and amplified the void. Could this really have happened?

The past week seemed surreal.

She caught a reflection of herself in a mirror across the lobby, leaning back against the wall---skin flushed scarlet, knees thrust forward and apart. Gaze vacant and half-wild from lack of sleep: almost another person. In response she closed her eyes. The lobby was cooler. Her breathing slowed and she refocused on the mirror. That was *her* image: haggard but still alive and present. The reality of *being* fortified her. She had to marshal forward. She owed that much to herself and

Peter. She set her jaw, shot to her feet and strode out through the front door. The fresh autumn air evaporated her dampness and cleared her head; she kept her chin up, marching through the morning pedestrian traffic toward a nearby parking garage.

Driving was part of the plan. Relatives or friends had shuttled her around for the past week. Getting behind the wheel would be an important step. Parisian traffic would be a test. She'd always thrived on the disarray and confusion of the city's boulevards and narrow side streets. Not because she relished disorder---the opposite. Her satisfaction derived from mastery.

Two levels underground she spotted her car, a green Peugeot sedan, and dug the keys from her purse. The familiar vehicle boosted her pace. She managed a polite nod to an elderly man...before she stopped in her tracks and stared. There, just a few spaces from her own car, was Peter's silver Audi. Somehow she'd forgotten...he'd left it there before flying to Moscow. She'd driven him to the airport... So tangible! Only the screeching tires of a car at the other end of the garage jolted her out of her fixation. She'd have to deal with the Audi later...

Her keys trembled in her hand as she unlocked the door of her Peugeot. Before the tremor had appeared just on stressful occasions: university examinations, job interviews, her wedding. Now the condition seemed permanent.

Seconds after disgorging from the exit ramp onto the Boulevard St. Germain, she was westbound along the bank of the Seine in the late-morning flow. Traffic, as usual at this hour, was fast and unforgiving. She drove with both hands on the steering wheel, leaning forward. With a glance in her rear-view mirror she executed a quick lateral move, which provoked honks from two cars behind her and a quiver of satisfaction. Her capacities were intact...She was not a helpless victim...She could still bend chaotic variables to her will.

Skirting the Seine on the Quai d'Orsay, the Eiffel Tower swept by on her left. Straight and tall: a galvanizing point of reference. Her foot pumped the clutch and she jammed the stick shift into higher gear. Additional confidence came with a rare and unexpected parking spot on rue Franklin. Notre Dame de Passy was just around the corner. Minutes later she was seated on a divan inside the rectory. The salon around her was ornamented in Napoleon III-era gilt frames and red-velvet curtains. A crucifix hung over the carved marble fireplace.

The room already felt a little stifling. Claire wondered what she'd gain from this.

Francois, the priest who'd officiated at Peter's funeral, entered with a sympathetic expression, accompanied by a nun carrying a silver tray. Once the nun served coffee and withdrew, he settled into an adjacent armchair. Claire thanked him for his orchestration of the funeral. Short notice. Peter's Protestantism and long-pending conversion had not been an obstacle.

"Veronique suggested I come to you for advice," she said.

They were both aware of the premise. Veronique had set this up---Claire's closest friend and Francois' cousin. Francois now cradled his cup and saucer and crossed his long legs. He seemed unsure what to expect. Claire was hardly a regular at mass. She made an effort to keep her voice steady.

"With Peter gone, I feel…I don't know where to go or what to do next."

"That's natural, Claire."

"Everything points me back."

She described her disorientation in the elevator, and the shock of Peter's car.

"Perfectly normal," Francois responded. "It's just been a week."

Claire spotted a Bible on the small table next to Francois' armchair. Several bookmarks protruded. She opted for preemption.

"I do believe in God, Francois."

He eyed her over another sip of coffee.

"…Jesus…the lessons from the cross…everything you mentioned at the funeral."

No movement yet toward the Bible.

"It's just that...I need something more immediate."

His eyes narrowed with new concern.

"...What I need is a goal."

Francois' voice became gentle: an attempt to understand.

"Goal?"

"Something to point me ahead. An objective...one that's connected to Peter somehow."

He paused and looked into his cup. "Everything doesn't happen according to our earthly designs, Claire," he said. "Sometimes we have to wait."

"I can't wait, Francois."

"Here..." he said, slowing the tempo. He set down his saucer and reached for the Bible. "Let's try to find some answers in the Scriptures."

Claire shifted on the divan. She had nothing against the Scriptures. But she was already eager to go.

CHAPTER 5

Bradford's death still hung on Gallagher like lead ballast, and jet-lag only weighed him down further. He'd revved himself with extra caffeine this morning to keep going. Halfway across the newsroom, clutching paper cup in one hand and notepad in the other, he repeated his resolution.

No more calamities.

When he huffed into conference room Janet Larson, the editor-in-chief, was already seated. With characteristic efficiency she reached for the phone at her end of the long table.

"Hello Harry? We're ready down here."

She replaced the handset and stared at notes through her reading glasses. This was a special meeting. Called by Harry Whitcombe late the previous afternoon, from a first-class plane cabin over the Atlantic, during a delayed return flight from Paris.

The subject was Bradford.

Gallagher was taking his first sip of coffee when Whitcombe strode into the room. Face still bearing strain from the funeral. Otherwise pressed and erect, despite the travel. Purposeful set to his Brahmin jaw-line. Straight to his customary place at the end of the table. There was reason to worry. Much about Bradford's death remained unresolved. More might come from the same pipeline. Gallagher got right to it.

"I've exchanged several more e-mails with the U.S. official based in Moscow---Franklin Stanson, the same one who organized the transport of Peter's body to Paris."

"Diplomat, right?" Larson interjected.

"Not exactly."

Larson eyed him over her reading glasses.

"Anti-terrorism. His main focus is Tajikistan."

Gallagher pressed on.

"Stanson believes the original claims of the Tajik government, and of Prime Minister Shakuri. Peter was killed by two of Shakuri's bodyguards. Their own plan: a botched robbery. They thought Peter was carrying a lot of money."

Whitcombe shook his head, still not buying it.

"I queried Stanson about the robbery angle," Gallagher elaborated.

"And?"

"Apparently Peter spoke Russian during his dinner with Shakuri. The bodyguards figured he was an arms dealer."

"An arms dealer?" Whitcombe's normally stoic features roiled. "Why in God's name would they think that?"

"We're talking about a corrupt part of the world here, Harry. Roles and rules are pretty fast and loose." This remark made Whitcombe mull for a few seconds.

"...Stanson says that Peter's laptop computer and wallet went missing," Gallagher continued. "It's consistent with the robbery explanation."

"Anything ever recovered?"

"No. Even after the bodyguards were arrested."

Whitcombe joined his fingers into an inverted "V" and stared down through the space underneath.

"What happened over the weekend was more troubling," Gallagher added.

Whitcombe brought his gaze up over his co-joined fingertips. Larson's head snapped up from her notes.

"...The two bodyguards were themselves killed. Some sort of prison disturbance. Stanson and the other American official never got a chance to interview the suspects."

"While awaiting trial?" Larson asked, incredulous.

"Yes."

Whitcombe's inverted "V" crumpled. After a moment the set returned to his jaw.

"That settles it," he said.

Gallagher felt additional weight descending. The week was not unfolding as he'd hoped.

"I had some ideas on the flight back," Whitcombe said. "I want to run over various angles in my own mind...during lunch. But I'll want to move forward. Let's meet again this afternoon."

CHAPTER 6

At times Conley wished he had become a sports writer, rather than a news reporter. The atmosphere in the sports department was juvenile and uncomplicated, like the locker room of a high school or college athletic team. Energies were channeled into games; writers kept one foot in the halcyon of pre-adolescence.

Every time Conley saw Joe Banacek he was reminded of these traits. This morning Conley spotted him in the green-marble, ground-floor lobby of *The World Tribune*. Banacek wore a jocular grin, as usual.

"Good time at the Charles?" he asked Conley.

Their encounter on the Boston University Bridge had been brief. Banacek had been heading in the other direction; there hadn't been much time to talk. Conley said he'd enjoyed himself. Also that he'd been surprised to see Banacek on a Sunday; Banacek's fall beat was pro football.

"The Pats played Monday night," Banacek noted, laughing.

"I know. Still…" Conley laughed as well.

They passed through the glass door at the rear of the lobby and stepped onto the escalator to the newsroom. "I skipped out after that," Banacek added. "Caught some games on TV. Rowing can be boring, after a couple of hours."

Indeed the crew competition, for Conley also, had been mostly a backdrop. In the corridor down to the newsroom they didn't hurry. Neither one of them was on deadline. In addition Banacek was divorced, with plenty of free time---always ready to share a beer during later hours if opportunities arose. On the bridge he'd given Jenna an appreciative once over. A woman had accompanied him; there'd been compulsory introductions. Conley could not recall seeing Banacek with the same woman twice.

"You're lucky, with Jenna," Banacek exclaimed, slapping Conley on the shoulder.

Conley mustered a vague smile.

"Have a good day, buddy," he said, then turned and headed toward the sports department.

About 15 reporters and editors were scattered across different desks in the newsroom. There was little noise except for murmur of phone conversations and light clicking of computer keyboards. Most reporters were out on assignments. Activity would pick up in the latter half of the afternoon.

Conley's desk was in the Sunday/Features Department---a holding pen for accomplished reporters who didn't quite fit anywhere else. Since London features had become his main stock in trade.

Conley booted up his laptop and remembered Sunday.

Images of Jenna came back: tight sweater and jeans, the curves of her back and behind, the shades of her hair enhanced by the sunlight. Also the scents that permeated the stillness of her bedroom late that evening…He took a deep breath and ran one hand through the hair on the side of his head. Nothing in her was lacking. Educated, sociable, considerate… So what if she traveled on business two or three days most weeks? Banacek was on the mark. He *was* lucky.

Why did his attentions still ramble?

The girl from the alumni tent re-entered his mind; Samantha was her name. Conley remembered he'd stashed her card in his wallet. He extracted it, re-examined it for a moment, and threw it in the wastebasket. The issue was now definitively settled. Nothing would develop from the encounter. He logged into the network with his laptop, ready to get to work.

The phone rang on his desk.

"Hello, Steve?" The voice was female---at once familiar.

"Yes?"

"This is Samantha."

Conley's heart pounded a few hard beats. The exposed skin of her midriff came back to him, full-center.

"Hope I'm not surprising you by phoning at work. You mentioned you were at the *World Tribune*. I also saw your by-line in yesterday's paper. Excellent article."

Conley thanked her and said he didn't mind the surprise.

"Anyway, you never telephoned me after Sunday. Thought I'd take the initiative."

Her firm was one of the more prominent in Boston, and occupied offices in of the city's premier skyscrapers. Conley inquired about her workweek, which yielded an enthusiastic response. Peasantries soon ran their course, much like Sunday. The girl had now twice put herself forward. Now she fell silent. Waiting for a suggestion.

"I'm flattered you called, Samantha, but…How to say this? My situation is such that I can't go further than our talk at the Charles…I'm seeing someone else. It wouldn't be fair all around."

After a pause she recovered. "Well, you're right to tell me up-front, Steve. That's not so usual these days…I'm glad we connected anyway."

"Me too."

A tactful exit…When Conley hung up the receiver his disquiet was gone. Such contacts did not have to develop further. Restraint was within his powers. As it should be---at last---by age thirty.

Jenna was due to return from a business trip that afternoon, and dinner was slated for evening. He looked forward to seeing her with a clean conscience.

CHAPTER 7

Woods and rocky hillsides shone in the headlights as the Mercedes wound fast along the two-lane road. Bradford tried to ignore the bodyguards in the front seats. They were annoyances---set pieces in a much larger story. He was operating with sweep and scale that they couldn't begin to understand.

This evening had been pivotal: a culmination of a month of planning and weeks more of execution.

Shakuri had been forthcoming. Even beyond expectations. Out of pragmatism, mainly. Aware of the power of American media and the leverage possessed by a lone and determined reporter. Ready to open up. All that Bradford had surmised about Central Asia---and about Tajikistan in particular---had turned out to be true. U.S. initiatives in the region were having all sorts of secondary effects.

This assignment had developed as planned.

Some aspects of the evening had been distasteful. As dinner had worn on and the main business had been concluded Shakuri had become too familiar. Made altogether too many references to Claire.

"I could tell there was an exceptional woman behind you, five minutes into our interview this morning," he had said.

Bradford had eyed him over the top of his wine goblet.

"And that she's the main priority in your life," he'd added. "I'm also a devoted husband."

Shakuri's wife was nowhere to be seen. On extended vacation in the Maldives, he'd explained.

"To the health and happiness of your wife," the Prime Minister had concluded, raising his goblet.

Bradford had managed a smile and reciprocated the toast.

The Mercedes rounded a hard curve and Bradford grabbed the handle over the door for stabilization. With the other he held his laptop case in place on the seat. Woods and hillsides continued sliding by in darkness. For all Shakuri's crude edges, the man was perceptive. He'd guessed right about priorities, and about Claire. Still, why was that his business in the first place?

Though now was no time to dwell on small intrusions. There were reasons to be satisfied. Even to celebrate.

His timing had been perfect.

A massive new U.S. aid bill was imminent: the latest installment in the war on terror. Other Western reporters were not yet on the trail. That left the field wide open. And rich with provocative story elements: terror, heroin, and high-stakes international politics. Within a week his stories would get front-page play in the *World Tribune*. Picked up by the wire services and re-published around the world. Discussed in the corridors of government in Washington and elsewhere. True sweep and scale.

Top journalistic prizes seemed within his grasp. Even a Pulitzer. Why not? Wealth and status beckoned. He'd have the kind of life he'd always wanted for himself and Claire...a proper apartment, for starters...wherewithal to take her along on assignments... close access to her at all times...

His reveries were interrupted when the car abruptly slowed. The driver's eyes showed nervousness in the rear-view mirror. The other bodyguard turned backward; his eyes first flitted over the box of spices on the seat, then to Bradford.

"Maybe problem…with tire," the man said in crude, heavily accented Russian. "Need to check."

Their Mercedes pulled over onto the narrow shoulder with a crunching of gravel. The road remained empty. Nothing about the car seemed out of order. Bradford became suspicious and alert, while in the front seat the two men exchanged another nervous glance. The bodyguard in the passenger seat got out and walked toward the back of the vehicle. Bradford watched the man's burly torso pass by the window.

In a flicker the door jerked open and Bradford was staring into the barrel of an automatic pistol.

"What the hell?"

"Move over," the man scowled, teeth half-bared in his beard.

As Bradford slid across the seat the man slid in after him, jabbing the gun barrel into his ribs. The driver gunned forward again with a churning of gravel. His cohort with the gun shouted several words in Tajik and pointed to a turnoff a short distance ahead. The Mercedes careened off the main route onto a narrow dirt road, just wide enough. They ascended: up a hillside into rock-strewn woods. Bradford felt the gun barrel stick harder into his ribs.

"Give me that case," the man said.

CHAPTER 8

Outside the soundproofed windows of the conference room, the newsroom was revving higher. Reporters were materializing with varying degrees of dispatch, bearing laptop computers and notepads. Inside, at the head of the ovular table, Whitcombe sat tall, in his hereditary and natural place of command. His straight spine suggested he had reached a decision.

"Art's eulogy gave me some ideas..." he began. "And not just because Peter was my nephew."

Gallagher buttressed his elbows around his notepad several chairs down, his gray hair tousled. Lunch was over-compacted in his stomach; preoccupation had made him eat too much. From the opposite end of the table Larson peered over her reading glasses. Gallagher could almost hear her mind whirring forward, reconnoitering the variables ahead. Gallagher gave a worried stroke to his beard. This had not been his intention with the eulogy at all...

"The State Department investigation was not enough," Whitcombe continued. "Too many questions remain."

"We haven't gotten Stanson's final report," Gallagher noted.

"True. But we can't wait. That wouldn't be worthy of Peter."

Larson asked Whitcombe what he had in mind.

"Re-trace Peter's assignment from the beginning. Then...when he gets to Tajikistan...get some answers."

"The whole trip?"

"Yes."

"When?"

"As soon as possible."

This urgent tone made Gallagher fold his arms across the top of his stomach in a defensive reflex. "Harry, are you sure we shouldn't wait?" he suggested. "Let the dust settle? The final report from Stanson might answer more questions."

"I'm afraid not, Art. We need immediate answers."

"What about the safety of the reporter?" Whitcombe was sympathetic but unflinching. Something they'd have to manage, he said. Gallagher glanced out into the newsroom. Standard afternoon patterns, although today was shaping up to be less than routine---a launch-point for new unpredictability. "And what if we don't learn anything new, Harry? Will it be worth the risk?"

"We can still do Peter's original story on the heroin pipeline out of Afghanistan. Let's not forget...That's what brought him there in the first place."

Larson struck a pose of quiet observation. Little surprise: she always employed careful tactics with Whitcombe.

"I'm thinking of another angle, too," Whitcombe added.

Gallagher braced himself.

"...By reconstructing, Peter's final assignment, we can pay tribute to him. Elevate his sacrifice. He died on the job after all. In the pursuit of truth, as you said, Art."

Gallagher almost winced. An obituary had led the front page on Sunday, and run into two inside pages, complete with extensive biographical detail, testimonials and photographs. His eulogy had been included.

"...This isn't just for the paper, Art, or for me. This is also for Claire. She deserves more."

Still with arms crossed, Gallagher leaned back, provoking a loud squeak from the undercarriage of his chair. He remembered Claire's trembling hand in the church pew, and felt further clutches of responsibility.

"I can't argue there," he said, before releasing a long exhalation through his nostrils.

"Knew you'd see it that way, Art."

Gallagher's next breath was heavier---more like a sigh.

CHAPTER 9

Paris was in exuberant transition from daytime rigor to evening indulgence. Twilight had passed; cafes and boulevards were now glittering with light. Streets were jammed and sidewalks humming. Departing office workers mixed and merged with pleasure-seekers. The city was pulsing with renewed vitality. Claire even felt a flicker of that this evening. She had wondered if she ever would again.

From her seat at the outdoor café she had an unobstructed view across the Quai de la Megisserie to the Pont des Arts. The bridge was brightly illuminated. Amidst the heavy pedestrian traffic she spotted her friend Veronique, striding along with bright scarf and designer handbag. Veronique glanced at her watch with a worried expression, then in the direction of the café.

Claire always spotted people from far away. Nervous energy, she supposed, even with her best friend. Moreover this was only their second meeting since the funeral. So other emotions held sway. As Veronique approached her table Claire stood and struggled to suppress tears. Veronique's eyes moistened as well. She kissed Claire on both cheeks before they sat down, and placed a hand on Claire's forearm with a look of mild alarm.

"I came as fast as I could…"

Claire thanked her.

"I mean…you're holding together, aren't you?"

"As best I can," Claire answered, dabbing her eyes.

Veronique gave her a sympathetic inspection. "With our lunch plans tomorrow, and all, I didn't think you'd be ready for an evening outing."

"I just wanted to see you sooner."

Veronique gave her another worried examination. "But there's no emergency?"

"No."

Veronique showed a bit of relief.

A waiter appeared. His cheerful *Bonsoir, mesdames* gave way to a more subdued expression when he noticed Claire's red eyes. They ordered two *diablo menthes*. After the waiter left Claire finished composing herself.

"I wanted to tell you…I actually got excited about something today," she said.

Veronique looked surprised. "Going back to work?"

Claire worked as a part-time assistant at a fashion conglomerate---a position with modest prestige and little future. The firm had given her a one-month leave at the news of her husband's death.

"No, it's not that."

"Francois?" Veronique responded, with a rise of enthusiasm. "Was it something he told you?"

"No. That was…helpful, Veronique. Thank you again for arranging it. I'll tell you more about it later…"

Their waiter came with their cocktails and Claire was hit by a wave of apprehension. What if this project didn't go forward? Were her hopes already too high? She took a generous sip of her drink before resuming.

"Peter's uncle called me last night," she resumed. "Remember him from the funeral?"

Veronique nodded.

"He's the executor for Peter's estate. He wanted to talk about a few of those matters. All that's beyond me. It's too complex."

Veronique nodded again. Her *haute bourgeois* background gave her ample acquaintance with wills, trusts and estate complexities. She appeared puzzled, although active inquiry about such matters was out of the question.

"...But that's really beside the point. His call had mostly to do with the newspaper."

"The *Boston World Tribune?*"

"Yes. He told me the paper is doing some additional stories on Peter."

Veronique leaned closer, to be sure she heard Claire above the growing din in the café.

"There's going to be a kind of tribute," Claire continued. "This will include...as far as I understand it...a re-enactment of Peter's final assignment. It will be a way to honor him...to elevate his memory. Maybe it will even produce more answers concerning his death."

"How?"

"They're sending a reporter out along the same trail. Same cities, same interviews...everything."

Veronique considered this development for a moment, unsure how to react.

Claire's excitement welled up along with new tears. "Can't you see, Veronique? It's great! This will be something lasting...for Peter's sake. Maybe it will make his death seem less senseless. And it's just what I need right now...a goal."

"You mean you can help with this?"

"I think so...That part is still unclear."

*   *   *

The elevator whirred and whooshed up the long shaft toward Jenna's office, a reliable trajectory and an emblem of new serenity and order. Alone in the compartment, Conley leaned against the back railing.

He felt responsible, mature, settled. Maybe his usual undisciplined impulses were behind him.

Jenna's public relations firm was on the 25th floor. Conley greeted Nancy the receptionist, a jolly woman in late middle age who was preparing to go home. Nancy had grown acquainted with him over the past few months. Now she represented an amiable and comforting fixture. From there he ambled down the familiar carpeted corridor to Jenna's office, a place, by now, where he felt he belonged.

Time was 5:40: a period for loose ends, winding down, final e-mails. However when Conley poked his head in the door, Jenna sat immobile. Her elbows were on her desk and her eyes straight ahead. She didn't brighten when she turned and saw him. Conley's first guess was that she'd had a bad day, or an unpleasant flight back from New York. He gave her a kiss.

"Everything okay?" he asked.

"Fine."

Jenna's controlled manners could sometimes make her hard to read.

Conley kept his hand on her back. "Thought we'd head to Newbury Street for dinner," he said. "That Italian place we've noticed a few times. Sound good?"

"Sounds great." Gracious, as always. But something was off.

The weather was nice. They agreed to walk, and return for their cars later.

She dashed off a few remaining e-mails; he stepped toward the plate-glass window. Night had fallen over downtown Boston. Surrounding skyscrapers sparkled with light. Signals changed at intersections; traffic stopped and started. Across Boston Harbor a plane was landing at Logan and another followed on a path of descent. Constancy, regulation, progress: a view of civilization.

Tonight Conley felt more integrated. On track toward full membership.

Behind him he heard light clicking from Jenna's computer keyboard. He resolved to cheer her up----overcome whatever unpleasantness had arisen at work or on the road. Part of his new duty.

At reception Nancy had gone. From a closet Conley helped Jenna don her light overcoat.

"You can stay at my place tonight, if you'd like," he said.

Her head tilted: neither pleased nor displeased. Detached. "I don't know," she said. "I was just there last week. We'll see."

Outside the building Conley held her hand. No resistance, though somewhat limp.

They crossed Beacon Street and entered the Commons. To their right loomed the illuminated façade of the Massachusetts State House. Crisscrossing the lighted pathways were office professionals, workers, students, vagrants: the whole buzzing cocktail of urban America. Air was crisp, clear and still. Most autumn leaves had been raked away.

"Sure everything's okay?" Conley asked.

Jenna stared forward and didn't answer right away.

Whatever was amiss, Conley was fairly certain that he was not the cause.

CHAPTER 10

Larson, editor-in-chief for little more than a year, had been brought in from the outside: formerly of the *Minneapolis Times*. Gallagher had been passed over for the top job. Age had been a factor. Gallagher had been gracious, Larson pragmatic. Their resulting relationship had been cordial and efficient, not close. With an obvious backdrop: Gallagher's retirement was not far off.

Gallagher often suspected that Larson preferred an earlier exit to a later one. This suspicion was on his mind this morning as he watched Larson at one end of the conference room. She was standing next to a whiteboard. A list of bullet points. Giving her due to both sides of the equation, in her usual subtle fashion. She was also preparing to place responsibility for the assignment squarely onto Gallagher.

"Safety is a critical concern," she said.

"By all means," Whitcombe agreed, immaculate in tailored suit and silk tie at the other end of the table.

Gallagher sat hunched over his notepad between them, and listened as Larson enumerated various guidelines for the assignment that would minimize risks to the reporter: no lone interviews, no night-time excursions, no meetings with known criminals, special care with Shakuri. Whitcombe endorsed every one, without hesitation. Larson returned to her chair.

"Art and I have talked this over," she continued. "Art will supervise the reporter. Okay with you, Harry?"

"Art supervised Peter. Makes perfect sense to me."

Larson leaned back: one piece in place. "That brings us to the choice of reporter."

"Yes," Whitcombe said.

"Art came up with the short list. I'll leave the rest to him."

Gallagher took a gulp of coffee and set down his paper cup. Why did he sense he was being set up? "Harry, you know that this story... has unusual demands," he began. "That limited the field."

Whitcombe nodded and folded his tanned hands on the tabletop.

"...The reporter has to be single. With international experience. Without a critical beat, at present. In short, not tied down and ready to go next week."

Whitcombe's eyes narrowed somewhat.

"I'll cut right to the chase. I think Steve Conley is the best resource available right now."

For all his in-bred civility, Whitcombe couldn't conceal a flare of distaste. He took a deep breath...seconds passed before he regained his equanimity. "Frankly..." he said, holding a cold, even tone. "...That was one name I'd hoped you wouldn't mention." Gallagher glanced over at Larson. Her eyes were locked over her reading glasses and down the length of the table on her boss.

"Art is confident Conley can do the job, Harry."

Whitcombe didn't react. He stared at his hands on the tabletop.

"However...if you're opposed, we can return to Art's short list."

More seconds passed. Gallagher became aware of the advancing second hand on the clock face over Whitcombe's shoulder. Hadn't London receded by now, after more than a year? Gallagher had thought so...

Then some insight brightened Whitcombe's features. His hard expression dissipated and he nodded to himself. "On second thought," he said. "Conley is probably a very suitable choice."

CHAPTER 11

There were probably reasons why most people visited cemeteries during daylight, Claire realized. Brightness offset the darkness of mortality. Gave clearer perspective.

She refused to be bound by such conventions.

Night was falling and there was a chill air. The Cimetière de Passy was empty. She'd chosen to come at this moment. Her will was what mattered.

She stood in front of Peter's grave. New sod had been overlaid but earth was still fresh in several places. Bouquets of flowers stood against the headstone. Hers was freshest among them.

On earlier visits she *had* come during morning. Now though, privacy and isolation made her feel closer to him than ever. She remembered his voice, his laugh…his consuming fervency in intimate moments.

What on earth drove him into such hazard? Tears erupted and streamed down her cheeks. Then she closed her eyes and reminded herself why she had come. Tonight was different. *She now had a goal.* She would understand. *She would elevate his memory.*

She stood straighter.

An idea came to her and she opened her eyes. What better way to start than with a place they'd shared? Not just any place. Very special, and just a short walk away. She took a step forward and touched the headstone. A slight smile formed amidst the tears.

On the path toward the gate her bearing became purposeful. Her shoes generated a staccato friction on the fine gravel. Yes, this was a new phase. Acting, not waiting. Once out of the cemetery she turned right. Her car was parked in the other direction. It didn't matter. She was in *motion*. By the gate of the church she caught a glimpse of the rectory. Light emanated from several windows. Francois was probably inside enjoying his second or third drink of the evening. She had no urge to stop for a visit. Faith was well and good. But she required more immediate solutions.

Pedestrians on the sidewalk observed her fast pace and parted in front of her. Several men attempted eye contact. She kept her gaze straight ahead.

When she reached the bookends of Palais de Chaillot her stride slowed. Through the opening the Eiffel Tower rose up in full illumination. She took a deep breath. Recollections crystallized.

Yes…she and Peter had walked exactly here. They'd had dinner around Alma and strolled to Trocadero afterward. Their third date. Autumn, just like now. They were still tentative with each other. Both students: Peter in the first year of graduate studies in Paris, she halfway through her six-year struggle at the Sorbonne. Claire remembered Peter stiff and proper and wearing a raincoat, keeping a comfortable distance as they walked. Hesitations issuing more from his side than hers. Not because he was withdrawn or uncertain, but because he was deliberate and systematic. Trying to assimilate Claire into this outlook for the future. Claire remembered him walking across the terrace with his hands clasped behind him, contemplating an attraction that was new and consequential, but in the manner of an older man already confident of his place in the world.

He had attracted her like a force field. His energy was controlled and directed. He saw a way forward.

She remembered his words as they had approached the end of the terrace and stopped at the stone banister. His voice had been smooth and modulated, even in French: "Are you sure you want to continue seeing me? Given my plans after this?"

Claire hadn't answered. She had just smiled.

Now she stood in the same location and closed her eyes for a moment. They'd stood here, a couple of feet separating them, then leaned forward and rested their forearms on the banister. They'd gazed across the Seine at the Eiffel Tower, illuminated then just as it was this evening. Claire didn't open her eyes. The memory was vivid enough. She'd looked at his profile. He was reflective, earnest. It was evident to her what he was thinking, even if the context was distant, contingent, and uncertain. He was thinking ahead. Restraining his impulses.

He could be relied upon. The recognition had released an emotional charge inside her.

She'd turned toward him and stepped closer, so that her body was almost touching his, then tilted her face upward and clasped the lapels of his overcoat. What happened next seemed foreordained. An awakening of closeness and understanding drew them into full embrace. Their lips met without effort. Afterward Claire couldn't say for sure whether she'd kissed him or he'd kissed her. Their kiss had just happened.

And been attended by the first, unmistakable upwelling of... another part of him. From that moment forward his restraint had gradually fallen away. A surprise, at first. But what woman would complain? Control continued to reign in other domains of his life...

Now, back in the present, Claire opened her eyes. The same nighttime panorama lay before her. To her left lay one of the stairways that led down to the fountains and park. They'd descended these same steps, still holding hands. That's what she'd do now. She didn't want this aura to be broken...

At the top of the stairs a voice sounded from her left. Unintelligible, at first...followed by louder repetition. Claire roused herself and refocused on here and now. A young man in disheveled clothing stood next to her. His hair was long and unkempt and his face unshaven. He was close---too close. His manner was aggressive.

"Can't a beautiful *mademoiselle* like you spare any change?" he said. Half grin, half sneer. He thrust his had toward her.

Anger exploded inside her. At this place, at this moment, she felt intrusion...violation of the worst kind. She clenched her fists.

"Get away from me!"

The young froze in place, surprised. Still wearing a half-grin, not sure whether to mock her or retreat. With a quick movement Claire reached into her purse and grabbed a collapsible umbrella. She raised it over her head like a weapon.

"I mean it, you bastard!" she shouted.

The man recoiled downward and away, anticipating a blow to his head. Across the terrace near the Palais a policeman took notice and ran toward them. With a frantic look in his eyes the panhandler looked over his shoulder then fled down the stairs. Out of breath, the policeman drew up to Claire.

"Are you all right, Mademoiselle?"

She nodded. The policeman continued his pursuit down the stairway.

She replaced her umbrella in her handbag, and noticed that her hand was shaking and her body was coursing with adrenaline. She took several deep breaths. After a moment she collected herself. Still standing at the top of the stairs, she made a determination. This episode would be an example. There was no room for such inanity. She would not tolerate distractions.

Nothing would stop her.

CHAPTER 12

Fire dwindled in the massive hearth, mingling wood scents with the aromatic haze of cigar smoke. Shakuri sat embedded in his armchair and ready to launch into another superfluous discursion. Bradford tilted his snifter and finished the rest of his cognac.

"Care for some more?" Shakuri asked.

"Nyet spasibo." *No thank you.* They'd been speaking Russian all evening.

Bradford edged forward on the low-slung sofa. He glanced over his shoulder. The thuggish bodyguard hovering near the entryway made him uneasy; otherwise Shakuri's company would have been more tolerable. Nonetheless he'd gotten all he'd wanted. Nothing would be gained by staying longer.

"I should get going," he said. "It's late."

With overdone regret Shakuri stubbed out his cigar. "I understand."

"I'll just collect my laptop."

"Fine. I'll have my men get the car."

Bradford traversed the sunken living room, climbed a few steps and proceeded down the corridor to Shakuri's study. His laptop remained set up on a large reading table, connected to the villa's wireless network. He reread material he'd downloaded from the Internet an hour earlier---the main reason he had brought his computer---then checked for new e-mail messages. There were none. He shut down and packed laptop into zippered case.

In the entry hall the maid was waiting Bradford's overcoat, along with Shakuri. One bodyguard returned from outside.

"Did you use the chance to send e-mail to your wife?" Shakuri asked.

Why did Shakuri persist with this theme? Bradford told him he intended to call Claire back at the hotel. Morning interview and evening dinner had been long. Bradford did not expect Shakuri to say a quick goodbye. His expectation was correct.

"I appreciate your resourcefulness, Mr. Bradford," Shakuri said, as they stood near the doorway. The maid was holding the door open.

Bradford set down his laptop, preparing to shake Shakuri's hand. "Resourcefulness?"

"You're the only Western reporter to come here in months. You've taken time to delve into the situation in our country."

"I've tried."

"You see the big picture. Unlike most."

"I appreciate the compliment."

"And…even more important…you're not a mouthpiece for the U.S. government. I didn't know what to expect when Franklin Stanson organized your visit. Turns out you're your own man."

"It goes with my profession."

Shakuri concluded with a handshake that was too long and intimating for Bradford's comfort. "I'm glad we found a common language," he said.

"Don't forget, Mr. Shakuri. I still have to write my stories."

Shakuri reacted with an overlong laugh. He wasn't through. "You do all this for her, don't you?" he said, pointing at the laptop case hanging in Bradford's hand.

Bradford tilted his head, not sure what he meant.

"I mean your work," Shakuri elaborated. "Your ambitions. What we did this evening."

Bradford contrived a polite smile. By now he had had enough. Outside on the oval of the drive, Shakuri's Mercedes was already waiting. The bodyguard from the hallway reached toward the laptop, ready to pack it in the trunk.

"It's small," Bradford said in deliberate Russian, in order to be understood. "I'll take it in the backseat."

The backdoor was already open. By the side of the car, Shakuri said, "Roads here can be dangerous at this hour. But you're in good hands. My men are armed." He offered a last handshake before Bradford got inside, then waved as the car pulled away.

The Mercedes descended through woods abutting Shakuri's long driveway. In front, the two bodyguards exchanged meaningful glances, uptight for reasons Bradford couldn't discern. At the bottom of the driveway, before they merged onto the main road, the driver examined Bradford in the rearview mirror.

"K moi gastinitse, da?" Bradford said. *To my hotel, yes?*

"Da."

The road was empty. Another nervous glance passed between the two men before the driver turned right and headed in the direction of the Dushanbe.

CHAPTER 13

Gallagher liked giving reporters challenging new assignments. There was a sense of fresh purpose. Pending discovery.

Not this time. Round one had yielded barbaric murder in a far-off country.

Granted, Claire Bradford deserved answers...some kind of redress. But there were limits. Pressures from Harry Whitcombe or not. Another reporter was on the line. Worst of all, he was starting to worry that the Whitcombe, along with his desire for a tribute, also saw this as a means of reversing dismal financial trend-lines at the paper.

With a grunt Gallagher stood and reached across his desk for his notepad. Though his glass wall onto the newsroom he spotted Conley's shock of hair out in the features area. Most interlocking reporters' desks in the surrounding expanse were empty. A fitting tableau---Conley in internal exile. Today he was putting finishing touches on his latest article: an investigation into grade inflation in Boston public schools. Worthwhile reporting, but hardly glamour beat.

Even through recent turmoil, Gallagher had persisted as one of his advocates. Most important: his top-notch writing and solid journalistic work, rendered consistently within deadlines. No sick days and unfailingly punctual. Beyond that there was certain common ground, despite gulfs of generation. Though Gallagher was from South Boston and Conley the suburbs, Conley had always struck Gallagher as uncomplicated---just an ambitious young guy from Boston trying to make his way up. A contemporary variant of a long-standing prototype that had once encompassed Gallagher himself. What happened in London, as far as he was concerned, was not relevant.

After winding through the newsroom maze he sat on a desk adja-cent to Conley's and crossed his arms over his stomach. Their usual rapport remained on key, even when Gallagher tugged his beard and indicated he had something important to discuss.

"Not a transfer to the Worcester bureau, I hope," Conley joked.

Gallagher tried to laugh. Instead he got right to his point. For Conley's next assignment, he said, he would be supervising editor. Conley was plainly surprised. His surprise grew when Gallagher told him the subject.

"Bradford? Even after all the articles this weekend?"

Gallagher had to suppress a sigh.

"Yes, Steve. The paper wants to do more."

*   *   *

Ninety minutes later Conley sat across Gallagher's desk, more upbeat than Gallagher had seen him in quite a while. He'd forwarded all relevant e-mails. Conley now scanned down Bradford's itinerary and interview schedule.

"Prague, Moscow, Dushanbe...This will be quite a trip."

"Those are just the basics," Gallagher explained. "Bradford's lap-top was never recovered in Dushanbe. And he operated on a long leash."

Conley didn't have to inquire. Bradford had been unique among field reporters with his direct supervision by Gallagher. Prerogatives of blood-line. There was an assumption among news staff---well founded---that

Bradford was destined for the role of Managing Editor, once Gallagher retired. Hence the special arrangement.

"Don't forget about Paris," Gallagher added.

"Right. That drug bazaar outside the city."

"Actually…you should allow a full week there."

"A week…?"

"Claire Bradford has agreed to help."

This provoked another slightly surprised look. Gallagher elaborated.

"She's volunteered to help fill the gaps I mentioned. Also to give some personal insights…especially as to why Bradford threw himself into this heroin story the way he did."

Conley paused, mulling this information.

"Peter Bradford…now Claire as well," he said. "I can't figure it out, Art. This story has to be important to Harry Whitcombe. Why would he agree to put me on it?"

Gallagher's gaze wandered to a pile of local editions on one corner of his desk. He possessed scant knowledge of what had transpired between Whitcombe and Conley in London. And he'd asked himself the same thing. However that ranked least among his concerns. More pressing was another question. Where should he draw limits, this time round?

"Harry approved your selection, Steve," he said. "Let's leave it at that."

"Okay."

"I'd prefer to focus on something more important."

Conley gave him a quizzical look.

"…Your safety."

Conley had apparently considered this already. "Don't worry, Art. I'll make sensible choices."

"I hope so. This assignment will be high profile…with extra pressures. Especially at the end, in Dushanbe."

"I know."

"If questionable situations come up…significant risks…will you consult me?"

"Given what's happened, of course."

CHAPTER 14

The scene was still vivid in Conley's memory. Early autumn sunlight streamed into the small conference room. Central London hummed outside: the bustle of mid-morning. Harry Whitcombe was pressed and groomed and sat with his hands folded in front of him. No obvious signs of turbulence from the previous day. Anger detectable, but contained. Little showed in his eyes except determination to address a most unwelcome problem---of which Conley was the root cause.

"Tracey is only 20 years old," he'd said.

"Yes, I know." Conley couldn't justify himself. So he stopped and waited for Whitcombe to continue.

"Tracey and I have open communication on most matters," he said. "But in this instance, I told her I'd prefer not to hear details."

Conley took a breath before reacting. Whitcombe held up his hand.

"The fact is I didn't come here to delve into her romantic life. Therefore I asked her just one question. That was whether she had a relationship with you that went beyond professional boundaries. She said that she did."

The patrician publisher waited a long downbeat before breaking the silence. His stare was like granite.

"Would you acknowledge that that's the case?"

Conley paused. Nuance seemed pointless.

"Yes."

Whitcombe eyes narrowed briefly but he retained his cool. "Whatever the exact circumstances, the situation is unacceptable. Tracey is an intern, and you're her immediate superior in this bureau."

Conley remembered thinking: Whitcombe's hand is on the lever and he appears disinclined to waste time. The pull will come before this meeting is over. In the next instant, however. Whitcombe had paused and looked toward the window. His thoughts seemed to drift out of the room. His face acquired a softer, less businesslike cast.

"However in this case I am not disposed toward extreme measures."

Conley raised his head slightly, surprised.

"...Precisely because Tracey is my daughter."

Whitcombe had then turned back and refocused. "You'll be transferred back to Boston."

And that was that.

"What are you thinking about?" The question came from Jenna. She was at the wheel of her Saab, speeding along under the bright lights and white walls of the Ted Williams Tunnel toward Logan Airport. It was mid-afternoon on Sunday and traffic was light.

"Sorry," Conley said. "I was thinking about Harry Whitcombe."

"He's given you another chance."

"True."

"If I were you I'd be grateful."

"I am."

Jenna offered a distracted smile and redirected her attention onto the tunnel roadway. Distraction or nor, Conley was relieved she was still in his corner. He hadn't been sure over the past few days. Since dinner on Newbury Street, something had been off. What, exactly? He couldn't say. Most significantly, was that he was turning a new page

Misadventures like that in London were now part of the past. In that sense he was departing on an upbeat.

Daylight broke ahead at the end of the tunnel. They emerged onto the up-ramp: a long smooth curve. Without obvious precipitant, Jenna grew hard-faced and intent. Conley assumed she was focusing on the signs and routing to Terminal E for Air France. Instead she pulled off into a breakdown lane.

"Something wrong?" he asked, looking around. He hadn't noticed car trouble or inadvertent wrong turns.

She sat staring ahead, both hands fixed on the steering wheel. Self-control was her norm; this seemed a pause for verification. Conley studied her from the side, now concerned.

"I decided now might be a good time to raise this," she began.

"Raise what?"

"An issue that's been on my mind."

"Something serious, Jenna?"

"Yes."

"But I'm leaving for Europe."

The circumstances didn't give her pause.

"I'm going to interview for a job in New York next week," she said. "It's another firm. A position with more responsibility and more money. They're very interested in me."

"I don't know what to say...I thought you were happy in your current job."

Her hands remained on the wheel.

"...And that you liked Boston."

"I do."

Conley thought for a moment. "What about us?"

"That's why I want to talk. It means we need to reconsider where we're going. Maybe step back."

"Step back? You mean break off?"

She took her hands off the wheel and turned to look at him. "Yes."

"Can I ask why?"

"We've been together now for almost five months. Long enough to know each pretty well." She paused, weighing her words. "You have a lot of what I've always wanted in a guy. Smart...I'm even amazed sometimes. Good-looking and athletic...you stay healthy. And you're considerate, in your own way."

Conley assessed the last phrase. "So what's the problem?"

"Sex."

"Sex?"

"Not the sexual component of our relationship. That's fine. Sex in a more general sense."

"What do you mean?"

"I'll speak openly, Steve. Are your desires are limited to me?"

Conley was caught off guard. "I've never been unfaithful, Jenna. I hope you know that."

She observed him closely. "That may be, but is that enough? Don't you think I'm sensitive to the way you are in public? Anytime an attractive woman...from teenager right up to early 40s...gets within 100 yards, it's as if you go into high alert. You're like a hound with its tail up."

"Please, Jenna. I think that's an exaggeration." He paused. When her face didn't soften he continued. "Anyway...to the extent that I have those impulses, I try to control them."

"You *try*."

He nodded.

"When I'm around, you mean."

"Yes. Of course."

She gave him a frank stare. "And what about the rest of the time?"

Conley didn't have an immediate answer. Jenna averted her eyes, showing disillusion that was deep-seated and impervious to repair, a sort he had never glimpsed before.

"Look, Steve," she said, looking back at him. "You've told me what happened in London. And at first, when you told me the details, I gave you the benefit of the doubt. But now I have my own experience to go on. And that's made me see it in a different light. These propulsions of yours…they're just too overpowering. You can't ever really contain them. Consequently I'm never entirely confident what will happen next."

"Really? Your doubts are that extreme?"

"Yes, I'm sorry to say. I'm still not convinced I can always count on you to do the right thing."

Conley stared back. Her words stung.

Sudden pity crossed her eyes.

"Don't take this the wrong way, Steve. I know you mean well. Your intentions are good. If not for this particular factor, I wouldn't be taking such a step."

They both fell silent, staring out the windshield. The only sound came from cars passing by outside on the ramp. After a moment Jenna put a hand on his knee. "I do still like you," she said, in a benevolent tone. "…a lot. And I really hope this assignment goes well." She shifted the automatic transmission into *Drive* and glanced in the rear view mirror, preparing to re-enter traffic.

"Well, that's something, I suppose," Conley said as they pulled out and headed toward the terminals.

*   *   *

Forty-five minutes later Conley had passed through security and was sitting at the Air France departure gate, his laptop and overcoat draped on an adjacent seat. Tall windows looked onto terminal docking stations and the western reaches of Boston Harbor, which was dappled in late-afternoon sunlight. The landscape had a unreal quality; Conley felt shell-shocked. He pulled out his cell-phone and called Thom. Thom was in his living room watching a football game; his girlfriend had gone to the supermarket. He had to mute the television before Conley told him what happened.

"That's too bad. I really thought you had a chance with her."

"So did I."

"How are you taking it?"

"This isn't the first time I've heard this. I'm starting to wonder if she's right."

There was a pause on Thom's end. Compassion kicked in.

"Forget it…Hey, look on the bright side. You're going to Europe. You'll be on your own. You can run free for a few weeks. Let off some steam. And you won't encounter any interns, right?" Thom laughed.

"No."

"And no relatives of your publisher?"

"Well, that's not exactly true."

Thom's laugh subsided. When he spoke next his voice was thick with worry.

"Good Lord….I'd forgotten about that…"

CHAPTER 15

Sunday dinner at the Gallagher household was winding down. Denise Gallagher stood and prepared to serve dessert to her husband, two daughters and their spouses, and four grandchildren. Art Gallagher sat at the head of the dining table, his progeny arrayed along both sides. As he aged Gallagher relished such moments more than all others.

"Who wants ice cream on their pie?" Denise asked, directing her question at the grandchildren.

"I do!" the four said in almost in unison. They were two boys and two girls, aged four to seven.

"Not too much," cautioned Gallagher's daughter Cathleen.

Denise distributed the desserts to the four children. Though she'd grown plump in recent years, she still radiated the healthful beauty that had first attracted Gallagher when they were both students at Boston College. She was in perpetual good cheer.

Cathleen and Ann and their husbands all declined ice cream, and asked for narrow slices of pie, which Denise served along with decaffeinated coffee. "The usual, Art?" Denise asked Gallagher.

"Sounds great." Gallagher's diet, such as it was, did not extend to Sunday evening meals at home. He addressed himself to the eldest of his grandchildren, aged seven. "Been reading lately, Neil?"

"Yes," Neil answered. "I just read a book about Abraham Lincoln."

"He really likes history," Cathleen explained.

Gallagher asked him some questions, then said. "Keep it up. Reading is very important." After dessert Denise took the children into the living room to play a short board game, while Gallagher stayed at the dining table to talk with the adults.

As the visit concluded Denise retrieved jackets from a hall closet, and Cathleen and Ann prepared the children for departure. The Gallaghers' dog, a slightly graying golden retriever, shuffled nearby with wagging tail. After final farewells and embraces the young families walked down the flagstone path in front of the house and back to their cars on the street.

The time was about 7:30. "Can I help clean up? Gallagher asked Denise.

"No thanks. I'll manage. Just go and relax, Art."

Gallagher made his way to the family room, followed by the dog, where tall Georgian windows opened onto the darkness of their back yard. He plopped into his favorite chair, a leather recliner while the dog settled on the floor nearby with a snort. With children and grandchildren gone, he lit a cigarette, relishing the after-glow of the meal. The afternoon had been idyllic: needed respite after a demanding week.

Their cat soon entered the room, jumped on the couch and curled up with an air of contentment. A minute later both dog and cat had closed their eyes. The room was quiet except for the faint sounds of Denise loading the dishwasher on the other side of the house. Gallagher took a deep drag and leaned his head back. When he finished smoking he stubbed out his cigarette in the ashtray by his armrest and picked up the remote control. He tuned in to "60 Minutes," keeping the volume low so as not to rouse the pets. It was broadcasting a segment he'd seen before so he switched to CNN. There he found a report on political and religious strife in the Kashmir. A British journalist had been taken hostage by Islamic extremists the previous week. He leaned forward in his chair and turned up the volume. The dog moved its ears and furrowed his brow. The cat half-opened her eyes.

This is a video that the terrorists released of Terris three days after they abducted him…

The footage showed a man in his 30s, unshaven and with several bruises on his face. He was holding a newspaper and looking toward the camera with a blank expression.

Terris' abductors demanded the release of five Islamic militants from Indian prisons…This demand was not met…The day after this video was taken the terrorists executed Terris by slitting his throat…The terrorists filmed the execution; we cannot show the footage because it is too graphic for television….

Denise returned from the kitchen, carrying a mug of hot tea. Before she sat down she noticed Gallagher's demeanor. "What's wrong?" she asked. "You look worried all of a sudden."

"This report," Gallagher said. He pointed at the television.

Denise settled onto the couch, next to the cat. With her husband she watched the rest of the report in silence. When the segment concluded Gallagher grabbed the remote and switched off the television. He'd lost his appetite for news---at least for this evening.

"Thinking about Conley?" she asked, tilting her head in sympathy.

Gallagher pursed his lips and shook his head. "He left this evening. In a few weeks he'll be in the same part of the world. Back to where Bradford was."

Denise released a sigh. "Let me get you a drink," she said. She rose and walked over to their liquor cabinet. "…What would you like?"

"Cognac, please," he answered. "A rather big one."

The room was quiet again, but both dog and cat were now awake and alert. From the floor the dog raised its head and gazed at Gallagher with worried eyes. On the couch the cat sat tense and upright and looked back and forth between Gallagher and Denise, trying to determine what had changed. Denise crossed the room and set a snifter of cognac down next to Gallagher.

"It will be all right, Art," she said, placing her hand on his shoulder. "You'll just have to keep this one under closer control."

CHAPTER 16

Claire slammed the door to her Peugeot and turned the key in the lock with a trembling hand. Then she thrust the key-chain into her purse and strode across the parking garage, heels snapping on the concrete and raincoat billowing up behind her. This rendezvous was too important for foul-ups. She had to communicate the seriousness of her intentions. The week had to start right. She couldn't be late.

Halfway to the elevators she glanced at her watch: 7:45 a.m. Conley's flight was due 10 minutes earlier. She broke into a run. When she reached the elevator she stabbed the button with her finger. Through clenched teeth she cursed the morning traffic. She was still out of breath when she emerged in the terminal. She checked the arrivals screen. Next to Conley's Air France flight was the notation *Vol Arrivé*.

The arrival hall was crowded. She half-ran, half-walked to the gate area, dodging people along the way. She'd met Conley once, at a *World Tribune* employee barbecue several years before. Tall, light-brown hair...athletic shoulders, perhaps...holding a beer...that was about all she remembered.

She spotted him standing in the middle of the hall next to a luggage cart. Unshaven, though dressed quite presentably in dark knit shirt and unbuttoned gray overcoat. Looking around---waiting.

"Steve?" she said as she drew up, still out of breath.

"Yes. Claire? "

"Yes. Hope I'm not too late." She spoke in English.

"No, I just came out of customs."

His face bore polite sympathy. Claire mustered a half smile. She was determined not to play bereaved widow. There was too much they had to accomplish. She had to bear Peter in mind and steel herself. "My car's this way," she said.

Two minutes later they were standing by the back of her Peugeot. She opened the trunk and cursed to herself. "Let me clear some space here," she said. She bent over and pushed a couple of small boxes further back. With her arms extended her spine arched...at the same instant she felt a twinge of discomfort. She sensed that Conley's eyes were on her...Not so objectionable under different circumstances, however...With a jerk she stood up and whirled around. She gave him a frank stare.

Conley startled, then recovered his blank sympathy. His eyes bore dark circles after the all-night flight. Now Claire felt embarrassed. Probably an inadvertent glance.

"Should fit now," she said.

With luggage stowed and Conley strapped in beside her Claire nosed the car up the ramp and out of the parking garage. When they emerged outside rain splattered on the windshield and she turned on the wipers. Through the maze of ramps leading from the airport she tried to collect herself. She remembered what Harry Whitcombe had told her on the phone the day before. Proven reporter, with international experience. Suffered some kind of setback and transfer last year, though that didn't reflect on his abilities. Now entrusted with a coveted assignment. Would be raring to go. Would do Peter justice.

She hoped so. She would accept nothing less.

Conley told her he already had an interview plan for the week---a good sign. She reminded herself about her end. Hospitality was essential; he had to be comfortable in order to be productive. Optimal results. For Peter. That was what she wanted most.

"I'll take you straight to your hotel," she said.

"That would be great."

They were on the A1 heading into Paris. Despite wet conditions Claire gunned the car along in the passing lane. She took her eyes off the expressway for an instant to glance at Conley.

"I want this week to be worthwhile," she said.

"I'm sure it will be."

"This story is important to me. Maybe more than you realize."

CHAPTER 17

Conley had not been overseas for more than a year. And he was traveling alone. Maybe Thom was right. Sunday afternoon in Boston had changed certain parameters. This was a chance to throw off restraints. At least entertain possibilities. Though with one caveat.

Anyone but Claire. He had to remember that.

Nine hours of sleep had restored his energy. He was standing by the front door of the Paris Hilton, waiting for Claire to pick him up and conduct him to another location. It was a crisp fall morning. A half-day of interviews lay ahead: the first session about Bradford.

A new workday produced a steady emission of guests from of the hotel. Cars pulled up; businesspeople emerged with briefcases; the doorman hailed cabs. A team of young stewardesses emerged, wearing uniforms and pulling small carry-on suitcases. Conley tried to guess their provenance then heard their accents as they passed. Australia or New Zealand, he figured.

The women proceeded to a waiting van and began climbing aboard and sliding onto the long seats. Several skirts rode up. Conley had a direct view.

One of the affected stewardesses sensed his gaze and whirled around before getting fully settled. She caught him…and smiled. No ramifications: just a nod at forces of attraction. Conley smiled back. Doors closed and the van pulled away down the semi-circular hotel driveway.

His mood elevated. Attractive women were everywhere. Why entertain unsuitable possibilities? There was no need.

A honk from across the drive re-directed his attention. It was Claire; she waved from inside her Peugeot. Once he was strapped in she maneuvered out of the drive.

"Where are we going?" he asked.

"St. Sulpice. I have a café in mind."

Conley noticed a slight quiver in her voice, but no other outward signs of distress. His first impression from the airport was reinforced. She had stayed remarkably strong through her trauma. They headed east Avenue de Suffren. Claire drove fast again, weaving through heavy morning traffic. Conley steadied himself with the handle above his door. Her gaze was resolute. She seemed anxious to get started.

"Do you like Paris?" she asked.

"It's one of my favorite places."

The remark seemed to please her.

Ten minutes later they were seated in a café off Place de St. Sulpice, at a table under a windowed canopy. There were only a few other patrons, alone and reading newspapers. The space was quiet except for occasional clinks from the kitchen and pigeons flapping their wings in the square. Conley set his notepad on the table. They ordered two café-au-lait, which arrived in short order.

"I've prepared some notes, too," Claire said. She pulled a sheaf of papers from her purse and placed them in front of her. The stack contained at least 15 pages, some handwritten, some computer-printed.

Conley was a little taken aback. Claire noticed his reaction.

"I hope I haven't overdone it," she said.

"No, of course not."

Fact was, Conley was impressed. He'd half expected her to be incapable of full-bore interviews. Could he proceed in French, he asked?

He'd done a few interviews before in the language, when he'd been based in London. He'd read *Le Monde* on the plane to bone up.

Claire looked doubtful. "Are you sure?"

"Let's try."

They switched. Conley began with by reviewing Bradford's impetus for doing the story, which he had gleaned from Bradford's e-mail correspondence with Gallagher. It stemmed from the war on terror.

Opium production in Afghanistan had boomed since the U.S. and allied invasion in late 2001---an unintended consequence of the ouster of the Taliban. Now ninety percent of the derivative heroin from Afghanistan that reached Western Europe transited through Tajikistan. This destabilized Russia's southern borders and frustrated Western attempts to choke off the financial base of Islamic terrorist groups like Al Qaeda. Hence the U.S. interest.

Bradford had sought to trace the pipeline from Europe back to Tajikistan and explain the link to terrorism. Claire confirmed these details. However Conley didn't want to get too bogged down in geo-politics. This was more about Bradford.

"Tajikistan is obviously a dangerous place," he observed. "Did that worry Peter?"

"Somehow it didn't," Claire said, her eyes watering a little as she recalled.

"Why was that?"

"He seemed to have a clear plan. He said lots of elements were coming together at once in Tajikistan…and that he might be the only reporter to understand them."

For now Conley was inclined to agree. Bradford had been on to something. The country's role in the global heroin trade was important---and largely overlooked.

With one finger Claire brushed away a tear. However she didn't falter.

"He believed this was his big opportunity."

CHAPTER 18

As a rule Gallagher didn't spend lengthy periods on the Internet. He employed it mostly for breaking news. This afternoon was an exception. He was at his desk digging into Tajikistan. What he was finding didn't make sense. Recent U.S. State Department bulletins, released in January and re-affirmed in July, presented a confusing picture:

This Public Announcement replaces the Travel Warning dated December 20. It is being issued to reflect the decrease in incidents of political violence in Dushanbe and the rest of the country. The Department of State reminds U.S. citizens, however, that the potential for terrorist actions against Americans in Tajikistan remains. U.S. citizens should evaluate carefully the implications for their security and safety before deciding to travel to Tajikistan. The political security situation in Tajikistan has improved in the last two years. Nevertheless, terrorist groups allied with al Qaeda, such as the Islamic Movement of Uzbekistan (IMU), remain active in Tajikistan and still pose risks to travelers. In the past, the IMU has been responsible for hostage-takings and border skirmishes near the Uzbek-Tajik-Kyrgyz border areas. The U.S. Embassy in Dushanbe continues to observe heightened security precautions...

Was security improving or not? How could the country be getting safer despite the persistence of "terrorist actions against Americans," not to mention "hostage-takings and border skirmishes"? Gallagher located the current State Department "Advisory" on Tajikistan and found similar contradictions.

Security personnel may at times place foreign visitors under surveillance. Hotel rooms, telephones, and fax machines may be monitored, and personal possessions in hotel rooms may be searched. Taking photographs of anything that could be perceived as being of military or security interest may result in problems with the authorities.

From time to time, the U.S. Embassy may suspend or otherwise restrict the travel of U.S. Embassy personnel to Tajikistan and within Tajikistan. The Department of State relocated U.S. Embassy operations from Dushanbe, Tajikistan to Almaty, Kazakhstan in 1998 due to instability in Tajikistan, threats against Americans and American interests worldwide, and the limited ability to secure the safety of U.S.

Embassy personnel in Dushanbe. For the time being, American diplomatic personnel officially reside in Almaty, Kazakhstan, but spend most of their time in Tajikistan. This situation is likely to persist at least through 2007...

Bradford had said there was no permanent State Department presence in Tajikistan. And that Bill Hermann, the U.S. intelligence "liaison" whom Bradford had interviewed, was based in Almaty and visited Dushanbe only several days per week. Franklin Stanson was based in Moscow but had said much the same thing.

Gallagher remembered Bradford's characterization of U.S. policy toward Tajikistan. "In flux," he'd had said during a phone call before his departure. What was U.S. policy? It struck Gallagher as confused and ambiguous. Next he turned to independent news media. He knew Western coverage of Tajikistan was meager, but did a search of recent bulletins from wire services. There were no indications of newfound stability:

March 27-Three French Medical Aid Workers Slaughtered

Three French doctors from the French organization Médecins Sans Frontières were found decapitated yesterday along the main road east of Dushanbe, Tajikistan. Local authorities said they suspect Al Qaeda operatives...

May 2-Chinese Road Engineers shot in "Random Attack"

Five Chinese road engineers were gunned down on Saturday in a remote region of northern Tajikistan. According to Tajik officials, the attack was conducted by a team of four masked gunmen, who later escaped in an all terrain vehicle. They have described the attack as "random." Four of the engineers died during or shortly after the attack; the fifth is in critical condition in a Dushanbe hospital...

July 3-German Student Missing in Dushanbe

Dushanbe, Tajikistan-Jorgen Klein, 21, a student from Munich, Germany, was reported missing Thursday from his hotel in the center of the capital. Local law enforcement sources said they are investigating the disappearance. Klein's family in Munich has appealed to the German Foreign Ministry for further answers...

In October there were several headlines about Bradford, which Gallagher read with a nauseating sensation. He leaned back in his chair, removed his glasses and held the bridge of his nose between thumb and index finger. Why hadn't he done this research earlier? He'd relied on Bradford to make informed choices. And now he was sending Conley into the same murk and anarchy.

"Art?"

Gallagher startled and turned toward the door of his office. Larson stood there, holding the stem of her reading glasses in one hand and wearing her usual expression of cool appraisal.

"Heard from Conley?" she asked.

"Not yet. His first interview with Claire was just this morning."

"Anyway...Glad I caught you before you left."

Gallagher turned full around with a loud squeak from his chair. Something about her tone added to his unease.

"Harry wants to have another meeting tomorrow," she said.

"About Conley?"

She nodded.

"Did he say why?"

"Only that he wants to expand the scope of the assignment. Give it more importance."

"What does that mean?"

Larson begged off with an open palm. "That's all he would say."

Gallagher stroked his beard and released a long exhalation. This assignment already suffered enough pressures.

"Nine o'clock tomorrow," she said. "Right after the editorial meeting."

"I'll be there," Gallagher answered, giving her a worried look.

*   *   *

This was already their second day of French. For Claire, the slow pace was getting a little frustrating. She listened as Conley formulated another question---this one about Peter's investigation of smuggling circles in Prague. Conley's grammar was more or less correct. But he searched for words. Her impression was that he hadn't utilized his French in quite a while. At last he reached a punctuation mark.

"He called around lunchtime on those two days," she answered, referring quickly to her notes. "In the evenings he ventured into cafes and bars where these Albanian criminals are supposed to congregate."

"What was he hoping to gain?"

"He didn't attempt any direct contacts. He just wanted visual impressions."

"Did he succeed?"

"As far as he told me, yes."

Claire reviewed scenes and people that Peter had described, then took a deep breath while Conley scribbled on his notepad. The two of them were camped at another window table, this one in a cafe along the Champs Elysees. They'd each had several cups of coffee. Vehicles hummed outside along the wide boulevard.

Today the void inside her felt more acute. Comparisons came to mind. Peter's mastery of French had been so complete, almost to the point where she'd taken it for granted. Just one of the ways in which he'd been exceptional…such a scholar, so many languages…

She and Conley devoted another hour to Prague, then the second half of the morning to Moscow. She endured the session with her best cheer, but was glad when he wrapped up around 12:45 and signaled for the check.

"I'd invite you for lunch again today, Steve," she said. "However I'm meeting a friend."

"I'm monopolizing your time as it is, Claire."

He smiled, appearing satisfied with the interview. Claire smiled back, as best she could. They'd gotten through another day.

"I chose this café because it's near Peter's office," she said. "Peter got it because our apartment is rather small. I'll take you there now, and give you the keys. You can work there the rest of the week, if you want."

Minutes later they were striding up a broad sidewalk of the boulevard, toward the Arc de Triomphe. Conley bore his laptop case in one hand. Claire grew eager to recount her progress to Veronique, over lunch.

Conley was tolerable in half-day allotments. And he did seem committed to this assignment, in his own methodical way. Still, why couldn't he show a bit more drive, like Peter?

CHAPTER 19

Overall Conley felt upbeat. He'd held his focus and re-activated his French. Nonetheless being alone in Bradford's office was unsettling.

He was seated at Bradford's desk in an upholstered chair. Everything appeared preserved since Bradford's last visit---the Friday after Prague and just before the next leg to Moscow. Bradford's personal effects were all around: on the desk a photographic portrait of Claire, on one wall a framed Harvard diploma with a summa cum laude notation, on another a large map encompassing Europe and the former Soviet Union. Furnishings were modern, standard-issue stained-wood, supplied by the office leasing company that managed the floor. Conley swiveled around. A tall, two-paned, French-style window looked out on Avenue Wagram. By leaning forward and looking and looking to his left up the street, he could see one corner of the Arc de Triomphe.

Underneath the window were a low file cabinet and a small bookshelf. Another photograph stood on top of the cabinet, which he picked up and examined. It showed Bradford and Claire sitting on the deck of a large sailboat, wearing foul-weather gear. The vessel appeared to be of racing variety. Conley guessed the photo was taken in the U.S., but he couldn't tell for sure. There were whitecaps on the water and the boat was heeling. Claire held her hair away from her face with one hand, curves obvious even in her gear. Bradford held his arm around her. Both of them wore contented grins.

On the bookshelf there was a small collection of books, mostly on history and politics, in both English and French. Several books in Russian as well; Conley couldn't read the titles but assumed they fell in the same category. On the lower shelf was a small stack of academic journals from the Russian and Slavic Studies Department at the Sorbonne. More evidence that Bradford wasn't some scion dilettante, biding his time in the field until he assumed a higher mantle. Bradford strove. He was serious.

Next Conley opened the top drawer of the file cabinet and looked inside. Bradford's paper files were meager. There was a slim hanging folder marked "Heroin Trade", which contained photocopied newspaper and magazine articles from the European press. All other printed materials were related to previous stories. These were also sparse; it seemed Bradford had preferred electronic storage.

He turned and dropped the heroin-related folder onto the desk, for later perusal. His attention fell next on a plastic case of back-up CD-Rom disks on top of the cabinet---small and unlocked. He flipped open the cover and looked at the first disk in the rack. There was a list of dates, scrawled by hand. The last was September 27th---the Friday Bradford returned from Prague. Conley set up his own laptop on the desk. After boot-up he inserted the CD and viewed the disk's contents.

One master folder was labeled "World Tribune," and contained a sub-folder entitled "Heroin trade." Conley opened it and saw about 30 files; reports from governments, law enforcement agencies and the United Nations, along with some newspaper articles in HTML format. He copied the entire folder to his hard disk.

There were about a dozen other master folders, with labels including "Finances," "Academic", "Claire," "Family," and "Legal." No need to delve into these, he decided---not his business.

However he couldn't help but notice dates of last access.

"Finances" and "Legal" had been opened on October 19 and again on October 23. How could this be, more than a week after Bradford's murder? Conley thought for a moment. Perhaps Claire or some other family member had accessed them in connection with Bradford's estate. Other master folders had remained un-opened since backup. Conley removed the disk from the drive and placed it back in the rack on the cabinet.

Next he opened a file on his laptop and pulled out his cell-phone. He spent much of the afternoon lining up and confirming interviews in Prague and Moscow.

As evening approached opened his e-mail program, in order to send a message to Gallagher before dinner:

Art,

Tried calling earlier but just got your voice mail.

First two days with Claire have gone well. I had worried that talking about Bradford would be a strain for her. But she's composed and businesslike. Also well prepared. She even assembled a bunch of notes before I arrived.

So prepared, in fact, that we went into more detail than I had originally planned; the sessions lasted longer than I expected. Yesterday we talked mainly about Bradford's expectations for the story. The session lasted the whole morning and included lunch. This morning we covered Prague and Moscow.

Bradford did a lot of preliminary research on the heroin pipeline. I now have access to those files in his former office. Claire's letting me work there this week.

Bradford explored---albeit in a limited way---the Parisian heroin scene as well, as you know. Claire told me about that at length. He went to a suburb called Argenteuil, where dealers and users congregate. I'm aware of your concerns about safety, but I'm inclined to venture out there tomorrow or Friday, probably in the evening. Bradford did, and came to no harm. Obviously safety will become a more pressing concern when I reach Dushanbe.

As you know Bradford had a very broad vision for the story. He saw the heroin trade as an embodiment of several geo-strategic conflicts: the poverty of

Central Asia versus the prosperity of Western Europe, Islamic terrorism versus the West; chaos in the former Soviet Union versus efforts by Russia to re-establish control. Really does make an interesting subject.

Appointments are already falling into place for Prague and Moscow. I should have my schedule for meetings finalized by the end of the week. I'll aim to reach you by phone tomorrow.

Steve

There was a high-speed cable connection in Bradford's office. Conley connected and sent the message, then perused the on-line edition of the *World Tribune.* Before disconnecting he considered writing an e-mail to Jenna. Instead he disconnected and powered down; he could write her later. Paris beckoned. He was eager to find a café and have a beer or two before dinner.

*   *   *

The red-faced and affable personage of Mike Fallon appeared in the conference room before Harry Whitcombe. That gave Gallagher an immediate notion what this gathering was about.

"Not much of a hello Art," Fallon said, grinning. "You blanched when you saw me."

"Sorry, Mike. Just didn't expect you."

"I'm as in the dark as you are," Fallon explained in apologetic tone as he sat down.

Normally Gallagher liked collaborating with Fallon. They were friends, with a relationship that extended outside the newspaper. From one end of the table, Larson observed them over the tops of her reading glasses. She offered Fallon a polite greeting before she returned to her notes. All other editors had departed after the morning's news conclave.

Whitcombe materialized in short order and took his usual place of command. Gallagher expected to start with a quick summary of

Conley's progress in Paris, and pulled out a printout of Conley's e-mail. Whitcombe preempted.

"No need, Art. I spoke to Claire last night."

"Oh? How's she finding it?"

"Very positive. She said Conley is deliberate and thorough."

Paris is the easy part, Gallagher thought to himself.

"Moreover I could tell," Whitcombe added. "This is giving her a boost. You can't imagine, Art...It means a lot to her."

Gallagher offered an uncertain smile. A new knot formed in his stomach.

Whitcombe pressed on. "I must say I'm gaining confidence in this project. That's why I've asked Mike here this morning." He nodded at Fallon. "We all know Peter was the first *World Tribune* reporter to die on assignment. The effect has been felt all the way through our news organization, through the whole company, in fact. Therefore Conley's assignment is important--a way for us to complete our mourning...and to regroup. It also presents an opportunity, it has occurred to me... to reconnect with our readers. Affirm our continuing commitment to news that matters. And show what this newspaper stands for."

Gallagher waited for the other shoe to drop. Indeed, Whitcombe announced plans for an advertising campaign. Reconnoitering his intentions, Larson asked what he had in mind.

Much more than the usual, Whitcombe answered. Half or full-page ads. Accompanied by radio and TV. Fallon was already intent; he was vice president of marketing. This really grabbed his attention. "To start when, Harry?" he asked.

"Next week. I want to ramp this up fast."

"And there'll be money budgeted?"

"More than enough. Specifically for this campaign."

Whitcombe elaborated. Fallon was to take personal charge. Formulate the ads in cooperation with Gallagher. And business motives? Everyone at the table knew that circulation had been in slow decline for a decade. Competition from the Internet on classified advertising had savaged the bottom line. Was this an attempt at resuscitation? Gallagher frowned and cleared his throat.

"Harry, I hate to offer a note of caution. But might we consider waiting a bit…until Conley's assignment gets further along?"

Whitcombe studied him. "Why would we do that, Art?"

Gallagher glanced down at Larson. She was impassive, obviously disinclined to help on this one.

"The outcome is still uncertain. We don't know what Conley will find out."

"Conley's got my complete confidence," Whitcombe said, matter-of-fact.

"Yours also, I hope Art?" Larson queried, with a penetrating gaze over her glasses.

"Well, yes. It's that I'm wary of rushing ahead with things like this. Don't forget we're talking about Central Asia. That means unpredictability, just as it did with Peter."

"I appreciate your prudence, Art," Whitcombe said. "We'll keep that in mind as we go forward."

CHAPTER 20

When he was alone in European cafes and restaurants, Conley generally found he could meet women under two conditions.

---Tables were in close proximity.

---There was no language barrier.

Both had applied the night before. He'd struck up conversation with two French university students. The girls were a pair; that had helped minimize their reserve. One had given him her mobile number. There was even vague promise of an outing on Saturday evening. Conley had returned to his room, energized by the possibility and pleased about his French.

Time in Paris was short. So what? At least he wasn't isolated in his room, moping over Jenna.

Now he sat in the breakfast café of the Hilton, situated below street level with a view onto a courtyard with tropical plantings. He took a bite of croissant and surveyed other tables. Most other breakfast goers were middle-aged businessmen. His eyes gravitated to a woman breakfasting alone, at a table along a partition. About his age, dressed in a female business suit---gray and conservative, except for the tautness against her breasts. A translucent white blouse was visible underneath.

Straight blonde hair, falling halfway to her shoulders. Slender ankles crossed under the table.

Probably English, Conley guessed. He'd spent enough time in London to recognize the type. She registered his attention, then looked up and dabbed her lips with a napkin. Her eye contact was measured, but carried a charge that prompted Conley to return cup to saucer.

The woman noticed; merriment flickered on her face before she returned to her breakfast and that day's edition of the *Financial Times*. Conley checked his watch. Claire was due to pick him up in 10 minutes.

Five minutes later, as he gulped the rest of his coffee, the woman re-established eye contact with a polite smile, then refocused on her paper. Tables had been too far away. An amiable conclusion to a meaningless vignette...Or so he thought, until she materialized alongside him in the lower lobby while he waited for the elevator. He smiled and pressed the "Up" button to keep the door open. She thanked him; her accent was indeed English. Both of them faced forward as doors closed.

"In Paris long?" he asked her.

"Until tomorrow morning."

Her glance fell on him for a calibrated instant as her floor approached.

"See you at breakfast tomorrow?"

"Maybe," she answered, as she stepped out of the elevator.

Conley still carried a buzz of excitement when he returned downstairs and settled into the passenger seat next to Claire. She noticed his smile, but seemed to have other priorities in mind---first of all, speaking English.

"Why, my French not up to standard?"

With a courteous expression she put the car in gear. "I though I'd drive you up to Montmartre today," she said, maneuvering out of the drive. "The weather's clear. I also know a nice restaurant there where we can have lunch, after the interview."

As the Peugeot shot onto Avenue Suffren with a squealing of tires, she leaned into the turn and inadvertently splayed open her silk blouse.

Conley looked away. His encounter at breakfast gave him something else to think about. He kept his mind on the English woman all the way down the Seine.

Around the Place de la Concorde, with its distinctive Egyptian obelisk at the center…Claire twisted and maneuvered between different lanes in the rotary, her attention occupied. "*Zut!*" she exclaimed, jamming the brakes.

Both of them lurched forward against their seat restraints as they came to a stop. A car shot across their front end, missing Claire's Peugeot by inches. "*Imbécile stupide!*" she shouted, gesturing at the other driver with the back of her hand. She leaned back from the steering wheel, eyes half closed, and took a deep breath. At once honking horns erupted behind her; she released the clutch and started forward again. "Pardon my language, Steve," she said, her voice jangled. "You okay?" She reached across and placed a hand on his knee.

There was a tremble in her fingers. He assured her he was fine.

Anyone but Claire, he reminded himself.

*   *   *

The worst part about that last day," Claire said, describing Dushanbe, "was that I missed Peter's phone call. It was before he left the hotel. I was at work, wrapped up in a meeting. He left the message on my voice mail."

They were sitting outdoors in a café in Montmartre, just down a quiet side street from *Sacré* Coeur. Sunlight was warm but both of them wore overcoats and scarves because of the seasonal chill. There was only one other outdoor patron, an elderly man reading a book and smoking. Conley ran his fingers through the hair on one temple, with traces of self-absorption. He looked up behind his sunglasses. Even in English, this interview was proceeding at slower pace than Claire would have liked.

"What did the message say?" he asked.

"That he had a dinner engagement with Salimjon Shakuri, the Prime Minister. "His message was brief. He said he'd call later with details."

"And he never called later?"

"No, and I was worried sick," she said. "I hardly slept that night… and I stayed home from work the next morning." She heard her voice crack. "The next call I received was around lunchtime, from the U.S. Embassy…"

She choked on the words. Tears formed and she drew a hand up to cover her face. She had vowed to avoid such small outbursts today, but couldn't help herself.

"I'm sorry, Claire."

"No…please go on."

Conley took a sip of his café-au-lait and waited a moment before continuing. "Let's get back to that last message, before Peter had dinner with Prime Minister Shakuri. Did Peter say anything else?"

Claire hesitated. This was somewhat personal.

"Well, yes…"

"If you'd prefer not to say…"

"No. I guess I don't mind. Peter said, 'I'm doing all this for you, Claire. For us.' "

"He meant his assignment, or the dinner?"

"Both, I think."

Conley looked puzzled. "The dinner? Why would that be connected to you?"

"He often told me I was the main reason he worked so hard. And this dinner was a conclusion to a long project. Peter described it as important to his ultimate success."

A heavy pause ensued as Conley studied his notes. The old man sitting nearby closed his book and signaled inside for the check. To

Claire Montmartre seemed as always: a hilltop oasis amidst surrounding urban bustle. It also felt a world apart from the brutality and unknowns of Tajikistan.

So did Argenteuil. Even that now seemed tame by comparison. She'd fretted when Peter had ventured there as part of his early research. It was Conley's destination that evening---a repeat of Peter's foray. She started to worry about it.

But the locale was French, she decided. And Conley was experienced. He would manage.

The check arrived; the old man placed money on the table and slowly rose from his chair. Claire wondered if the man was a widower. If so, he appeared to have found peace, a way forward. Through reading? Whatever worked. Each person had to choose his own means.

She'd learned that from Peter.

CHAPTER 21

From a viewing plateau on one side of the valley, Claire and Peter gazed out. The Pont du Gard was a stunning work of Roman engineering. Construction was all in stone. The structure had endured 2000 years, from around the time of Christ. Claire had visited once before, when she was 12 years old with her parents, an only child and the beneficiary of lavish attention. They'd tried to communicate historical and architectural details to her from a guidebook. Because of her age she'd been oblivious.

On this visit she'd also brought a guidebook. There was no need for it. As usual Peter had done his research.

He started with history. The Roman general Agrippa initiated construction in 19 BC; it was completed several decades later. Building materials consisted of limestone: blocks weighing up to six tons each, hauled into place by massive pulleys and slave labor.

The edifice served two purposes, Peter explained: bridge and aqueduct. Claire followed his finger downward as he indicated six large arches rising from the River Gardon and adjoining, rocky banks. These supported the first level, which included a bridge roadway wide enough to accommodate ancient horse-drawn traffic. Now it was reserved for pedestrians and bicyclists, and accessible from the viewing plateau. From the bridge level rose eleven more arches: identical in size to the base arches but more numerous because they connected a wider expanse. These in turn supported 35 much smaller arches on the uppermost level, which under-girded the aqueduct. It spanned 275 meters and soared 50 meters above the river---the highest bridge in the ancient world.

In Roman Gaul, the enclosed canal transported water a total of 50 km from the springs at Uzes to the city of Nimes, 18 km to the southwest. Flow came from subtle use of gravity. Over this 50-km distance the total downhill gradient was only 17 meters, or .4 percent. Such propulsion was more than adequate. During a period of 400-500 years, the conduit provided the main water supply for Nimes: about 400 liters per person per day to city residents.

"Amazing," Claire said.

"Yes," Peter answered. "Especially given the technology of those times."

"Shall we walk out on the bridge? Maybe take some photographs?"

"I have another suggestion."

Claire smiled. "I'm listening."

"Why don't we take that trail and climb higher." He pointed to a craggy walkway that wound up the hillside from the viewing area. "That will bring us to the aqueduct level. We can walk across that to the opposite bank. From there we can descend another trail and return over the bridge, which will bring us right back here. And we can take photographs along the way."

She glanced first at the trail, visible at various points but hidden at others by trees and brush. A few small groups were making the climb. Most other tourists meandered toward the bridge or down to a picnic area on the riverbank. Then she gazed further up, shielding her eyes from sunlight. She spotted some small human figures at one end of the aqueduct, where it joined the hillside. No figures were visible on top.

"Are you sure we can cross up there?" she asked. "I don't see any-one doing it."

"The practice isn't encouraged. But the authorities don't intervene."

A year earlier, Claire might have hesitated. No longer. This one of the features that thrilled her about Peter. He was controlled and directed. But she'd learned; that didn't preclude the unconventional.

"You're on," she said.

He returned a smile and reached for her hand. They crossed the viewing area to the trail and began ascending the hillside. Sweet and fertile scents permeated the air. The morning sun warmed their faces and spirits. They were at the beginning of their first real vacation together, a four-day, April escape to Nimes and Arles before year-end academic rigors of May and June. Claire's mother had gently suggested such a trip was premature. Wouldn't it be better to wait for a honey-moon? Claire had gone anyway. What was the point in delay?

Passion had exploded between them just after the New Year and grown more powerful since. Claire expected Peter would propose to her by early summer, once her exams were over.

Their future together seemed foreordained.

Nonetheless a certain issue had entered her consciousness in recent weeks. Not a doubt, really. More a question of causes and effects. As the two of them strode up the trail, hands still joined, relishing each other's company and contemplating the adventure that Peter had out-lined, this question came up again.

Peter's devotion was unmistakable. He'd placed her at the very center of his life. But sometimes she wondered if his physical attrac-tion was subsuming everything else…The previous night in their hotel had been a prime example. In most respects she was flattered. After all Peter's desire was concentrated on *her*. No one else. It was a catalyst, a plus.

She just needed to be reminded of the reasons he'd fallen in love with her in the first place.

When they emerged from the trail at the top, he drew her closer to the limestone blocks that formed the opening to the aqueduct, then released her hand. The interior canal where water had once flowed extended into the edifice: narrow, but large enough to accommodate a person. Sunlight was visible further inside the passage, penetrating from an opening on the ceiling. He peered inside, retreated, and jumped up on a brace of side-blocks for an outside view. His first glance was downward, then along the top surface.

"More or less what I expected," he said. "Do you want to take a look?"

Claire came over and found a foothold. Peter helped hoist her up.

The surface of the stone slabs was rough and weathered: treacherous footing. Width was just a few meters. At the point where she'd glimpsed the interior sunlight, some slabs were missing, leaving a gap they would have to hop over, or navigate around by balancing on the vertical sidewalls. There were no railings. When her gaze descended, she gasped. The river was a long way down. Picnickers along the banks appeared tiny. The valley yawned on both sides.

"Good God, this is high up."

"Almost 50 meters. The equivalent of an 18-story building."

Claire became a little dizzy. Peter helped her down.

"Do you still want to walk across?"

She thought a moment. If she could quell her fears, the risks were manageable. Three meters was wide enough. But she needed to confirm something first. She looked around. Other tourists had departed the area. They had the spot to themselves.

"Before that, Peter, can I ask you a question?"

"Sure."

"What do you believe holds us together?"

Even in this setting, her sudden question didn't surprise him. His expression, as usual, was mature and certain. He stood facing her, and clasped both her arms.

"We share the same orientation, Claire. The same outlook on life."

"You've said that before. But how can that be? You're so accomplished already. Your future seems clear. Meanwhile I don't know where I'm going. I'll even be lucky to get through all my exams this semester."

"Oh, that's just a question of timing, circumstance," he said, smiling into her eyes. "And I'm a few years older...at a later stage than you."

"Do you think that will ever change?"

"Maybe, maybe not. But I'm talking about something more fundamental."

"What?"

"We're both willing to think for ourselves."

They'd visited this theme two or three times before, back around Christmas, but in different contexts. Peter did not mind another elaboration.

"...We're both from circles where expectations can be rigid. Certain rules, fixed patterns. Right?"

Claire nodded. That certainly described *her* circles.

"...And that's true of society in general, wouldn't you say?"

"Yes."

"Well, we're both prepared to throw off norms. To disregard what others tell us, when necessary. We want to make our own choices. And act upon them."

His declaration stirred her.

"...I saw that in you from the beginning, Claire...it's perhaps the main reason I fell in love. Now, even more than physical attraction, I believe that's what binds us."

For a moment Claire felt overwhelmed. Then, gradually, her head cleared. Peter was right. He seemed to understand her better than she understood herself. As usual he had explained everything.

And she had the reminder she needed.

She took a step toward him, raised herself on her toes, and delivered a long kiss to his lips---part gratitude and part tenderness. When she pulled back she beamed at him.

"Still ready to walk across?"

"Of course."

Both of them wore jeans, warm-weather hiking boots, and light-weight pullovers. Their clothes did not impede them from mounting the side-blocks and scrambling up on the aqueduct. There the sun felt even brighter. Peter donned his sunglasses, and Claire put hers on as well, then looked down. From a full standing position the drop looked even more vertiginous than it had before. She raised her head and hyperventilated a few breaths, while he offered counsel. Stay square in the middle. Concentrate on surface footing. Avoid looking out to one side or the other. He would lead the way. She nodded.

They set out.

Their progress was deliberate, but unhesitating. She soon realized that clumps of moss and undulations in the stone presented the greatest hazards. This fact helped her concentrate. Deep panoramas on either side became blurred. Forty meters out they reached the first gap, where several slabs were missing. Distance was several meters across: too far to jump. That left the two sidewalls, each less than a meter thick, as the only means of traverse. Peter inspected one, then the other, and stopped near the right one. He pivoted and searched Claire's face as she drew up. There was still opportunity to double back.

"I don't want to stop and think about it," Claire said, forcing herself not to look down. "I'll come right after you."

"Remember, Claire. Concentrate on your footing."

"Right."

Peter proceeded across by even steps, holding his arms out for additional balance, in the manner of a tightrope walker. Claire watched him, keeping the backdrop out of focus. Once he completed the traverse, she paused, took a deep breath, and followed his example, keeping her eyes riveted to the stone surface. Halfway across, feeling suspended in air, she felt a bolt of panic. An instinct for survival kept her moving until she reached him. Shaking, she told him to keep going. They finally stopped 100 meters further ahead, at about the halfway point, when her legs grew weaker and she needed a break. Dropping to their knees on the rough surface, he scooted closer and embraced her, smiling. At last, over his shoulder, she suppressed her fog of adrenaline and allowed herself to re-gauge height and distance.

The valley sprawled far underneath on both sides, awash in sunlight. They were so high and alone she sensed they were flying. Peter leaned back and looked her in the face through his sunglasses. She felt bound to him like never before.

"How's this for choosing our own way?" he asked her.

She was still shaking. She could hardly catch her breath.

"It's not easy," she answered. "But it's what I want."

"Me too."

Three weeks later Peter had proposed. She'd known her answer in advance.

CHAPTER 22

Gallagher never brought his cell phone to editorial meetings---an example for other editors. Today he half-wished he'd made an exception. He was awaiting a call from Conley. Thankfully this particular conclave was almost done. Sunday's layout had been more or less decided, barring important breaking stories. Several editors had already left the room, including Larson. Only the business section remained. Phil Marcello, the Business Editor, suggesting leading with the bankruptcy of Telelogix, a Route 128 high tech company.

"How many people out of work?" Gallagher asked. "Fifteen-hundred or so?"

"Closer to two thousand."

"Big number. Let's go with it."

Gallagher glanced at his watch. Time was nearly noon. He adjourned the meeting, a little earlier than usual. Marcello and two other remaining editors didn't look surprised. They knew Conley's assignment had risen to the top of Gallagher's priorities. And that Harry Whitcombe was the precipitator.

Gallagher huffed his way down the side of the newsroom, at a pace that dampened his armpits by the time he reached his office. At once his desk phone rang. He thudded into his chair and picked up. It was Conley. He wanted to talk about Argenteuil. There was a charge in his voice. Gallagher recognized it at once. Male reporters and threatening environments. Impulses toward excess daring. Sometimes needing to be tamped down.

Bradford had already provided the basics about Argenteuil: northern suburb, mostly public housing, heavy concentration of poor immigrants, main market for hard drugs in Paris---especially heroin. Bradford had gone there, by his own account, to chronicle "the end of the pipeline" and "the human toll."

"Why go there at night?" Gallagher asked Conley.

"That's when most of the dealing takes place. And Bradford went there at night."

He sighed. "Look Steve, I know that's the thrust here. But as I've said, you have some flexibility."

There was a pause on Conley's end. Gallagher sensed another factor was involved.

"I hope you don't feel pressured, Steve."

"Pressured? How?"

"I mean because of Claire."

"Not at all. In fact she seems to have misgivings. She even suggested I might back out…that the rest of the assignment is more important."

"She may have a point."

"No need. I think it'll be worthwhile."

"Okay, just be careful."

"Will do."

Before the call concluded Gallagher remembered the advertising campaign that Whitcombe had conceived. Before he could tell Conley about it Larson appeared in his office doorway.

"A bomb exploded at a beach resort in Indonesia," she said. "A tour group from Boston is there. We're trying to find out more." She pivoted and headed toward the conference room.

"I'm afraid I've got to go, Steve," Gallagher said into the handset. "Send me an e-mail after this is all over and tell me what happened."

After hanging up he huffed around his desk and headed out toward the conference room. His mind was already shifting toward the new story out of Indonesia, though knots in his stomach persisted.

CHAPTER 23

There was a general rule about narcotics trade, Conley knew. Harder the drug, greater the violence and mayhem.

And this was heroin. What drugs were more potent? Perhaps only crack.

He sat in back of a taxi, headed north into Argenteuil along a desolate, trash-strewn boulevard. Grim, 1970s-era apartment blocks passed by outside. Time was nearly 10 o'clock. The driver, looking wary, reached for his door panel and activated the locking mechanism. *Thunk.* Now Conley was beginning to understand why Claire had wavered from her original single-mindedness. Reconstructing Bradford's assignment was one thing. What had possessed him? Simple follow-through? He started to second-guess himself.

"This intersection is the one you specified," the driver said, pointing ahead.

"Sure you can't wait here near the corner? I'll be 20 minutes, at the most."

Worried eyes rose to the rear-view-mirror. "I'm sorry *Monsieur.* Not a place I would choose to remain for any length of time."

Conley asked to be let out at the curb. At once the driver performed an abrupt U-turn and gunned back toward central Paris. Left alone on a broken sidewalk, he became more alert. Surrounding apartment buildings were set back across dirt and scraggly trees. Rhythmic music emanated from a parked car. Low, aggressive-sounding male voices were audible from an opposite building. Clustered around a shadowed doorway, he spotted a half-dozen human shapes, wearing baggy pants and hooded sweatshirts. Heads pointed in his direction.

Several years earlier Conley had done an investigative story on drug markets in Boston. From that experience he knew it was best not to stand idle. He should glimpse some dealers, see how business was conducted, and get out. A phalanx formed as he approached the assemblage.

"I'm looking to buy," he said in French, scanning the darkened faces to make eye contact. "This the right place?"

"Aha…a foreigner," said one, in guttural tones.

"That's right."

The spokesman exchanged amused glances with his cohorts.

"Where from?"

Conley didn't answer. "Can I buy heroin here or not?"

Inside his baggy sweatshirt the spokesman seemed to bristle. "We've got a place inside," he said, gesturing over his shoulder.

"I'm just buying, not shooting."

"We do business in there."

Several smirks were distinguishable under the hoods as Conley followed the man through the door. There was a bank of battered mailboxes, with a half-stairway illuminated by low-wattage bulbs. Graffiti dominated the walls. Five knocks by the dealer brought access to a run-down, first-floor apartment. Another man, bigger, re-latched the door behind them. Were there any actual residents in this part of the building? Conley's heart began thumping. Off the entryway lay a small kitchen. Through a half-closed door he glimpsed piles of cash and heard voices.

"This way," the dealer said. His hand swept toward a wide doorway, into an erstwhile living room. Conley took a half step forward and looked inside.

Four people. Representing three or four races, like the dealers themselves. Shabby furniture. Vacant stares. Faint stench. One was preparing to shoot up. Two others displayed bloody, bandaged arms. Conley absorbed impressions, as best he could, then recoiled and re-addressed the dealer.

"I told you. I just want to buy, not shoot."

"Why rush?" the dealer sneered.

Conley glanced around. The large man from the door stepped closer. Another emerged from the kitchen and adopted a threatening stance.

"Don't like our facilities?" The dealer, though shorter than Conley, brought his face up close. Conley held his ground.

"I'd just rather shoot up elsewhere."

"You are a first-timer, aren't you?"

Conley didn't answer.

"We always help our new customers. Shoot here, then we'll let you go."

"I don't have a needle," Conley said, trying to buy time.

"I'll get you one."

The dealer's chuckle yielded a gold front tooth. A shudder ran through Conley, as he considered ramifications. Could he make for a window? The living room faced street and hoodlums out front.

"It's crowded in there," he said. "Is there another room?"

This provoked a suspicious glare. Then another chuckle as the dealer pointed toward the other end of the entry corridor. Conley went first. A toilet lay ahead, along another small corridor perpendicular to the entryway.

"Take a left," the dealer said from behind.

"Just go on in?" Conley asked when they reached a closed door.

"*Oui*. Hurry up. Quit wasting my time."

There was no handle, and Conley pushed the door open to reveal a cramped room, a soiled twin bed along one wall. One window, masked by a tattered red curtain. Cheap table in the center. Syringes

and spoons scattered on top, around an ashtray. Single, battered easy
chair arrayed alongside. The dealer grinned and picked up a syringe.

"These look clean to me. Sit down and get ready."

"Shouldn't I buy first?"

"Wait here. And I said...*sit down*."

With a pretense of compliance Conley settled on the easy chair.

Before turning away the dealer displayed a triumphant sneer, and
Conley watched him down the corridor toward the kitchen. He didn't
squander any seconds. In three quick steps he bounded to the door,
slammed it shut, and slid the deadbolt. Shouts erupted outside. Then
angry pounding. Sprinting across the room, he threw open the ragged
curtain. His airways constricted. The window was encased on the outside by a metal grill.

A crash came from the door, producing splinters on the hinges.

With a violent tug Conley ripped the curtain from the rod, wrapped
his fist in the fabric, and smashed the glass. Most shattered away; he
punched out remaining shards. Reaching through, he grasped two
narrow metal bars and shook as hard as he could. Loose at the bottom. At once he bounded back to the easy chair, grabbed its armrests,
and hoisted it to his chest. Then, after a deep breath, hurtled himself
across the room, chair first. At the final instant he lowered his head
and drove his shoulder forward into the backrest of the chair.

A clang filled the room and jarred his insides. The grill gave way,
but didn't break loose, and he bounced backward and landed with
grunt on the floor, the chair tumbling back upon him. Shouts from
the hallway grew more intense; with another crash, the hinges started
to break and detach. Cursing, Conley struggled to his feet, then picked
up the chair for another run at the window. In his second short sprint
he sought maximal speed and with his last stride launched himself
and the chair again toward the window with concentrated force. The
impact yielded shearing steel and crumbling concrete, as the bottom
of the grill gave way and the latticework swung outward as if on a
hinge...His momentum carried both the chair and his body out into

the darkness, the sensation of sailing through a void...Wood snapped as he broke through branches of bush...followed by a violent, thudding impact. His nose and lips drove into hard, wet dirt. Pain throbbed in his midsection and knifed through his knee. He scrambled to his feet and looked up. The lighted opening was eight feet above. Muffled shouts gave way to splintering as the door to the room finally gave way.

Conley turned heel and sprinted away into darkness. Despite his injured knee, he ran faster than he had run in a very long time.

Several blocks he came spotted a police car, parked near a well-lighted taxi stand. He also made a vow. He would set aside compulsions like the ones that had propelled him here, whatever they were.

There would be no more misadventures like this one.

CHAPTER TWENTY24

Cars were backing up behind Claire's Peugeot in front of the Hilton. Apprehension took hold of her. What if some misfortune had befallen Conley in Argenteuil? She turned off the ignition and grabbed her cell-phone. Her call was ringing through when Conley emerged from the hotel's sliding glass doors. *"Mon Dieu,"* she gasped. She jumped out, keeping the phone to her ear. Over her roof she took in a frightful picture. Conley was limping. His face was scraped in several places, his lips swollen. He stopped and reached inside his coat to answer.

"What on earth happened?" she blurted in French. At first Conley appeared fazed, then spotted her and gave an awkward wave. "I'm coming over," she said, clicking off and rounding her car.

On the sidewalk her jaw slackened. Every other footfall made Conley wince---apparently an injury to his right leg. A uniformed doorman observed his fitful progress, and offered to take his laptop. Conley declined the offer and started down the steps. She bounded up, grabbed an elbow, and helped him to the bottom. There he straightened himself with a droopy smile.

"I encountered some trouble in Argenteuil last night…Nothing serious."

Claire stared at him, still open-mouthed. Nausea rolled through her. She thought these worries would arise later. Not in *Paris*.

"Just a hyper-extended knee, along with few scrapes and bruises..."

"But you have trouble walking!"

"Actually my knee is worse this morning. It stiffened up."

"Why didn't you call me?"

"I evaluated it myself before breakfast, based on my sports experience. Really, Claire...There's nothing to worry about."

Nausea turned to mild panic and hyperventilation. She'd hardly considered the possibility that Conley's assignment would get derailed, especially so early. She managed to sputter a question.

"Have you eaten?"

"It's not that bad. I was able to take the elevator down to breakfast." He read her expression. "...Nothing's changed, Claire. I'm continuing my assignment. I just have to go easy for a few days."

"Are you sure? I mean...you're in tough shape."

"Really. I'm sure."

Her breathing slowed, as she sensed her alarm was overdone. Eager to get off his feet, Conley moved toward the car, and she grabbed his elbow again to help. He had to extend his right leg as he lowered himself in the seat, while her mind raced over his remaining two days in Paris. She'd wanted to take him to the cemetery that afternoon to see Peter's gravesite...

By time she scrambled back around and behind the wheel, she re-focused on his injuries. She leaned toward him and held his chin between her thumb and forefinger, turning his face from side to side to inspect abrasions and swelling.

"Anything I can do, Steve? Buy you some medicines, maybe?"

"Maybe a temporary knee brace. Also Ibuprofen for the pain."

Claire jammed her key back in the ignition. Out in traffic Conley gave a brief account of his encounter with the heroin dealers. Minutes later they were double-parked in front of a pharmacy on a side street. He reached for the door handle.

"Don't be absurd, Steve…you can hardly walk. Stay here."

Inside, waiting at the counter she overran with self-rebuke. How could she have been so nonchalant, letting him go alone? She'd just been at home, reading magazines. She couldn't let this sort of mishap happen again. Through the windows of the pharmacy she gazed back toward the street. Inside her Peugeot Conley had lowered the visor and was inspecting his face in the mirror, touching his scrapes with tips of his fingers. She felt sudden pity.

For now she had to bolster him.

Several minutes later, items in hand, she opened his passenger door and squatted alongside. "I got what you wanted, Steve. The pharmacist suggested you try this brace on before we leave." He took the box from her and read the directions. "…Why don't you stick your legs out? That'll give you more space." She shifted to one side, keeping her upright crouch on the asphalt.

Conley winced as he swung his injured leg outside the doorframe. The brace bore Velcro straps; he unfastened them and leaned forward. Constriction from his overcoat hindered his reach.

"Here, let me help," she said, taking the brace. She put it on, taking care not to apply excess pressure. "That's not too tight?" she asked, examining from both sides.

"No, not at all. It fits fine."

She looked up, alert to indications of discomfort. Instead Conley appeared dazed. Even embarrassed. When he looked away, she thought fast. What adaptations were now in order?

"Do you have any plans for tomorrow afternoon and evening, Steve?" she asked, still her upright crouch.

"Tomorrow's Saturday…" He glanced at his knee. "No, I suppose not. Why?"

"I'd like to invite you to my apartment for a home-cooked dinner. After all…we should conclude the week on a more positive note than this."

He paused, his expression reluctant. "But you must have other plans, Claire. I don't want…"

"I insist."

He agreed, still looking a little worried. She guessed the reason.

"As for the afternoon…I'll have to come up with a creative plan," she told him. "One that takes account of your knee."

CHAPTER 25

The icepack had been on Conley's knee for about an hour, and his hotel room already felt confining. That was a problem with reduced mobility. Accumulations occurred. Energy went into surfeit.

An outing with the French female student was now impractical, thanks to his knee. Meanwhile the woman he'd noticed at breakfast---he'd never even learned her name---was likely now back in England, following her business trip. He flicked off his TV by remote control and dropped his icepack into a bucket. Fighting stiffness, he hobbled to the sliding glass door of his balcony, where his ninth-floor vantage afforded a view across the Seine to Palais de Chaillot and its bracketed, floodlit fountains. He remembered an evening walk there, about two years before. Just transferred to London, covering a meeting between Chirac and Bush. Dinner afterward with a German female reporter...followed by a stroll across Trocadero terrace. Later a weekend rendezvous in Amsterdam. An unintentional, combustible romance which hadn't lasted.

Then more immediate recollections took over: Claire squatting on the sidewalk, fingertips lingering on his lower thigh, adjusting the brace...knees and haunches jutting forward and back...

These drove him through the sliding doors into fresh air.

Out on the balcony nighttime traffic along the river became louder---a rumble with frequent honks. Voices rose from the hotel drive below. He placed his hands on the railing and took a deep breath, contemplating her dinner invitation. Prudence told him he should bow out, avoiding the potential for trouble. His knee gave him a viable excuse. No, he decided. Just the weekend remained; he was leaving Paris on Monday. For such a short period, he could avoid impulsive blunders.

There would be no more career demolitions. His maxim would hold. *Anyone but Claire.*

Fortified, he hobbled back inside, extended his right leg and lowered himself into the chair in front of his desk. A click of his mouse got him onto the Internet. He'd already sent a conciliatory message to Jenna. Now he composed one to Gallagher:

Art,

As I said in my brief message this morning, my visit to Argenteuil proved worthwhile. I gained a vivid picture of the consumer end of the heroin pipeline, and Bradford's starting point on the assignment. A grim world, as I expected. I experienced a tense encounter with some drug dealers had to make a quick exit. However I emerged intact. More details later.

Today I wrapped up my interviews with Claire, focusing on Bradford's personal side.

Basics I knew already: old-line family, stellar academic record, self-discipline, talent with languages. Claire added depth and dimension. Another quality emerged: his devotion to her. Claire has described how he called her daily while on assignment, wherever he was.

I asked her: how could Bradford---usually so measured and sensible---proceed into hazard in this case? Or was it just bad luck? Despite their closeness, Claire herself is uncertain. She's eager for more answers.

That's one question I'll try to figure out as I press forward.

Steve

CHAPTER 26

Ferocious crunching of shoulder pads and helmets ended with a screeching referee's whistle. When Gallagher's cell phone rang from inside his jacket he removed a glove and answered.

"Excuse me dear," he told Denise, clasping her knee. "...Be right back." He then huffed to his feet, negotiated down the steps of the bleachers and disappeared.

Bundled against autumn chill with scarf and mittens, Denise re-directed a modicum of attention toward the lighted field. She didn't relish high school football, in part because games fell on Friday evenings or Saturday mornings. More appealing were Saturday afternoon contests at Boston College---where she and Art were both alumni---with their warmer temperatures and better halftime shows. However she did consent to one or two games per season at Boston Latin. For her husband the games were a tenuous link to a more athletic youth, when he'd played at Latin as a mid-sized offensive guard. During intervening decades, sedentary regimes of the newsroom had taken a toll. She liked to remind him, though; he'd kept all his hair---albeit gray now---the same thick thatch that had captured her fancy in college.

Minutes later Gallagher thudded back onto his seat, out of breath from the climb, head tousled from the outdoors. "Sorry. That was

Reynolds, calling from Washington." He was interrupted when the Latin quarterback scrambled and threw a pass downfield. Latin supporters in surrounding bleachers leapt to their feet. The pass sailed beyond the fingertips of the receiver, and the fans sagged back.

"Remember Salimjon Shakuri?" he continued.

"The Tajik Prime Minister?

"Right. He was the one who invited Bradford to dinner just before Bradford was murdered. Anyway…Reynolds learned that Shakuri visited Washington about 10 days before he met Bradford in Dushanbe."

Denise looked at him, intrigued.

"The visit wasn't publicized," Gallagher added.

"Did Bradford know about it?"

"If he did, he never mentioned it."

A booming punt arced across the field. Higher than usual for high school: the punter was bound for college-level ball. Play concluded with more hurtling bodies and crunching equipment. Gallagher elaborated. The Administration was proposing a half-billion dollar military aid bill for Tajikistan: for airfields, reconnaissance aircraft and helicopters, much in the form of cash subsidies. The aim was to cut back the opium flow from Afghanistan.

"Sound like Bradford's timing was good," Denise observed.

"That's for sure."

On the field a running play produced numerous cutbacks and missed tackles. Typical chaos for high school football. To Gallagher all the random variables seemed apropos. After the whistle Denise was ready with another question.

"Do you think there's any connection between this bill and what happened to him?"

"That's not what the State Department concluded."

"But you think otherwise?"

"Too early to say."

A section of students nearby broke into a chant: "Stop them cold. Stop them cold…" Gallagher waited for the boisterous chorus to subside before adding a footnote about the Chechen drug lord. When he'd finished, Denise reached toward a canvas bag at her feet, pulled out a thermos, and offered him some hot chocolate. Gallagher didn't hesitate. She filled two plastic mugs, and gave one to him. His first sip tasted good and warmed his insides. Both turned their attention to the field as the opposing quarterback threw a long pass downfield. It fell incomplete, punctuated by another cacophony of whistles. First half was over. Players from both teams trotted off the field to their respective locker rooms. On the sidelines the bands readied themselves with instruments and formations.

Denise wrapped an arm around Gallagher's shoulders and squeezed. "You can just do your best, dear."

"You've said that since college, Denise."

"And I'll continue to say it," she said, laughing.

The visiting band marched onto the field, drums pounding. She squeezed tighter and looked out. "For now let's try to enjoy the half-time show."

CHAPTER 27

A determined and tactful young woman, Claire recognized, could achieve small wonders. In France especially. Claire's chin was up and her hands were high on the steering wheel. She and Conley cruised slowly down the tree-lined lane, pedestrians parting before them.

"I had no idea private vehicles could drive in here," Conley said.

"I wanted to surprise you."

Out of one eye she could see that Conley was impressed, and smiled, her mood continuing to lift. "I drove out here yesterday afternoon and spoke to several administrators," she said. "I explained that you were an American reporter, and described how you'd been attacked in Argenteuil."

"Well, it worked." Conley looked forward again to see where they were going.

They'd been permitted special entry into the Gardens of Versailles, through the Porte Saint Antoine on the northern perimeter. Now they were proceeding toward the center of the gardens along Saint Antoine Allée, fine gravel crackling under their tires. A body of water came into view at the end of the lane.

"The Grand Canal?" Conley asked.

Claire nodded, still smiling. "I still can't believe you've never seen it."

"The one time I visited Versailles, it was pouring rain."

She gazed upward through the windshield. Gray skies, but no pre-cipitation was forecast until evening. So far her plan was on track. At the end they reached a basin which formed the top end of the canal. To their right the waterway stretched off, long and straight, over what looked like a kilometer or more. Straight hedges of trees abutted both sides, along with sculptures at precise intervals.

She drew the car to a stop and turned off the motor. Ahead, at water's edge, was a float. Tied to it were about a dozen rowboats; an attendant was helping a young couple into one. She gestured with an open palm. "This activity is outdoors and doesn't require walking, Steve...just what you wanted."

He looked a little unsure.

"Don't worry... I'll help you get in and out. You just have to do the rowing."

Less impeded than usual because of slacks and casual shoes, she clambered out and hurried around to his side of the car. With both hands she clasped his right elbow as he eased up to a standing posi-tion. During their traverse he endeavored not to lean into her, as if proving he could walk unaided. That was a good sign, she figured.

"Take this one," the attendant said as they reached the float. "But watch your footing. Those boards are wet." The man bent down to draw the vessel closer, causing the float to shift slightly.

Claire tightened her embrace on Conley to make sure he didn't slip. Climbing in, he supported himself on the gunwales and lowered himself into the middle seat, between the oarlocks. She followed, grasping his shoulders as she climbed around and settled in the stern. His right leg was splayed straight out, brushing hers, with his foot under her seat. "How's your knee?" she asked him.

"A little pain...not bad. The main problem is that I can't bend it."

She leaned forward and placed her fingertips on his good knee. "That's the last thing to be concerned about. Let's start!"

The attendant shoved them off.

As Conley maneuvered out of the basin, a wind kicked up. Small ripples appeared on the water's surface. Claire grew concerned, but was relieved to see that Conley was not put off.

Instead, with sudden fixation, he aimed the bow straight down the canal.

His first several strokes launched the vessel forward with startling force that she had to tighten her neck muscles to prevent her head from whiplashing back. Where did that come from? At least he was enthusiastic...

Once their momentum was established, he found a smooth rhythm, his arms and shoulders rocking forward and back. Oarlocks thunked and rattled at the conclusion of each stroke, sending vibrations through the wooden hull. Water gushed off the bow and gurgled along the gunwales.

Claire relaxed her neck but continued to grip the forward edge of her seat for stabilization.

"You're a good rower," she said, noting the large surface puddles he was generating with the oars. "But you don't have to go so fast. Take it easy, if you like. There's no rush."

"I have a lot...of pent-up energy."

His powerful strokes and high tempo persisted, and she made no further objection. Most important to her was that he seemed to have forgotten about his injuries. "If you don't mind my asking," she said, raising her voice over the racket. "What did you tell Art Gallagher about Argenteuil?"

Conley was not winded, though he was taking deep, regulated breaths, like an athlete in an endurance event. The question seemed to rouse him---as if he had half-forgotten about his assignment.

"I told him basic facts..." he said during the recovery portion of his stroke, straightening his arms and leaning forward. He dug the oars into the water and drove his back toward the bow, producing another surge forward, then exhaled as he twisted the oars out of the water and started the cycle again. "…But I didn't tell him much…" he paused for another cycle, "…about my injuries."

"Did you talk about Prague and Moscow?"

"I told him…" *surge, thunk, rattle, exhalation,* "…that all my appointments are set."

That was just what Claire wanted to hear. She released her grip on her seat and placed her palms on the transom behind. After straightening her elbows for support she leaned back, more relaxed. Some distance ahead they neared an intersecting waterway. "This is the Petit Canal," she half-shouted. "Why don't you stop here?"

After an additional pull and surge Conley lowered the oar handles to his knees, lifting blades above gunwales. They coasted over long meters, silent except for the gurgling of water. Finally he dropped the oars with a splash.

Claire noticed traces of perspiration around his neck, and suggested he relax a moment. Conley pulled off his scarf.

"Enjoying it, Steve?"

"Very much."

"In the mood for a little detour?"

"What do you propose?"

"We can take the Petite Canal that way," she said, pointing to her right. "That will bring us to Grand Trianon."

Conley looked along this somewhat narrower passage. The Trianon gardens and palace were visible at the end.

"Some people think Trianon palace is just as magnificent as Versailles itself," she added.

Just then a gust of wind swept across the water and splattered raindrops on the surface. Claire looked skyward. A bank of threatening clouds had formed.

"Oh no…"

Conley also looked upward. Another gust swept a sheet of rain over them, heavier this time. Drops splattered on their faces.

"We may not get the chance to do either," he said.

"I agree. We'd better turn around and go back."

When they were up to speed in the other direction, rain became constant. Claire raised her coat collar, re-gripped her seat, and hunched forward to stay warm. With new disquiet she observed rain-drops exploding on the scabbed-over scrapes on Conley's face. His wool overcoat was already soaking moisture.

"We should dry ourselves and warm up after this," she half-shouted, her body rocking with the hull. "I know an old café in the town of Versailles with a big fireplace...built before the Revolution. We have plenty of time before dinner. We can go there."

Conley nodded, but didn't break his rhythm. He gazed over Claire's head and shoulders down the Grand Canal. "Too bad...," *surge, thunk, rattle, exhalation,* "...we didn't at least..." *surge, thunk, rattle, exhalation,* "...make it to the end."

"I know. It wouldn't have taken much longer."

CHAPTER 28

In subsequent days, Conley tried to determine when he'd taken leave of his full faculties. Front to front in the rowboat, Claire close-by in the stern? Before blazing hearth at the inn, Claire with slacks plastered dry and face lustrous from heat? Hobbling out in tandem after goblets of brandy?

At least one feature was clear. By time he found himself sitting alone on a marble bench in her lobby, back in Paris, while she parked her car, his maxim had flipped.

Anyone but Claire no longer applied.

It had become something like: *Claire is all that matters just now.*

Conley caught his image in the lobby mirror. Hair windblown from the Grand Canal, then dried into a wild thicket at fireside. Eyes shiny and euphoric.

"It just won't stop," Claire said as she entered.

Rain drummed on the sidewalk outside. The iron and glass door clanged shut as she shook the rainwater from her umbrella.

"…Anyway…we're back indoors."

Conley propelled himself to his feet before she could help. She looked at him, curious.

"It suddenly feels better," he said.

She formed a smile.

However when they entered the elevator compartment and she pressed the floor button, lingering rose drained from her cheeks. She averted her eyes. Several seconds passed before Conley remembered why. As they ascended, elevator whirring and clanking in keeping an earlier epoch, his impulses gained a sudden and fatuous rationale. Simple human closeness. That was just what she needed.

When the door opened on the sixth floor there was no going back.

"This way," she said, leading him out and around a corner at a slow pace because of his limp. Her apartment stood alone at the end of a side corridor. When they reached it she lowered her head and fumbled for her keys in her purse. Conley stepped closer and clasped her upper arms with both hands. She looked up---surprised.

"I know this week must have been challenging for you, Claire..."

She studied him, unsure what to make of this.

"...And you've been exceptional..."

Words were irrelevant, he decided. He placed both hands behind her back, then drew her into embrace. Her body stiffened, as she managed a measured response.

"What can I say? Thank you."

She glanced at her door and back, as if this could still benign.

Instead he brought his lips down onto the side of her neck: gentle but unambiguous. Immediately she shook free. Startled, Conley retreated and re-focused. Tears materialized as she steadied herself against a wall with one hand. They were short-lived.

In their place rose a boil of anger.

"Why did you do that?"

Conley couldn't answer. His move hadn't seemed that forceful. Part of it was also surprise. He'd been rebuffed before, but very seldom.

"I was just widowed...It's been a matter of weeks!"

"I'm sorry, Claire. That was completely out of place. Some impulse took over..."

"Impulse? This is your work!"

Conley could only look back with wide eyes. Her glare made him cringe.

"There's no excuse…Perhaps I should go…"

She paused. By degrees, her anger appeared to recede. A more analytical expression emerged. She reached into her handbag again, as Conley wondered what would come next. Was she going inside to call Harry Whitcombe? Past dislocations replayed themselves. His own recklessness astonished him. Her hand trembled as she clicked the deadbolt free---though this seem to indicate determination rather than trauma. Before opening the door she turned back toward him. Her hard gaze brooked no further nonsense.

"I invited you here because of what you went through in Argenteuil," she said. "That was the *only* reason." She paused again: one last re-consideration. Then she added, "We've gotten this far. Stay for dinner anyway."

"Are you sure?

"Yes. This is a good point to talk some things through."

CHAPTER 29

Gallagher handed his keys over. The fellow looked like a college student.

This was a consistent virtue of Whitcombe's parties. Valet parking. No need to search for a vacant spot on the streets of Cambridge on a Saturday evening.

"I never figured out where they bring the cars," Denise said, as she took Gallagher's arm. They were in front of Whitcombe's Georgian mansion, in an elegant, tree-lined neighborhood. The valet was already driving off.

"We could ask, if you're curious."

They passed through a small gate and mounted several stone steps to a red brick walkway. Clusters of people were visible through the lighted living room windows: top-level editors and managers from various departments of the *Boston World Tribune*. These affairs usually numbered about 50 people, including spouses. Cocktails and hors d'oeuvres. Whitcombe and his wife held them twice a year: in spring and autumn. The autumn gatherings, Gallagher had noted, never fell on the same weekend as the Harvard-Yale game.

Denise inclined her head and spoke in an undertone. "I'm still surprised they're having it this year."

"Already been a few weeks. These Brahmins move on."

Inside a maid took their coats. Whitcombe and his wife Elizabeth greeted them, gracious as usual. Elizabeth was a tall, slender woman with immaculate courtesies from another era. Both husband and wife were products of a vanishing New England WASP establishment.

Indeed, grief was not on display.

Gallagher and Denise meandered into a spacious, high-ceilinged living room, with traditional furniture and light gray carpet. About 20 people milled about, drinks in hand. Denise and Art opted for white wine presented by a roaming waiter.

"My fellow marketer!" Gallagher felt a meaty hand on his shoulder and turned to see the red face and jovial grin of Mike Fallon. Gallagher responded with a beleaguered smile, remembering the ad campaign.

Fallon gave Denise a hearty kiss. "You know, Denise…I've never spent as much time with your husband as I have this past week."

"Does he have good marketing instincts?"

"Unsurpassed among newsmen."

Gallagher shook his head and took a sip of wine. Fallon reacted with throaty laugh and a gulp of scotch. Across the room Gallagher caught sight of Larson, standing in front of the fireplace. Head bowed forward, in a confidential-looking exchange with Nathan Frick, the new Deputy National Editor. He'd followed her to Boston from their former shared employment at the *Minneapolis Times*.

"Art's too modest, Denise" Fallon continued. "Even more space is being allocated."

Gallagher startled. "What?"

Fallon lowered his voice and nodded sideways toward the entry hall, where Whitcombe was still greeting guests. "Harry wants to ratchet up the campaign. The first ads have been moved up to Wednesday."

Gallagher stared back at Fallon, speechless.

"Look on the bright side, Art. If your man Conley comes through, you'll be a hero."

"That's not my aim here."

"I'm just trying to make the best of all this."

After Fallon moved on Gallagher and Denise made their way over to Larson, for obligatory hellos. When Larson turned to greet them she showed her usual smoothness.

"Good to see you and Art in a social setting again," she said, placing a solicitous hand on Denise's forearm. "It's been a difficult few weeks."

Recent political maneuvers didn't help, Gallagher thought to himself. He noticed Larson and Frick were both drinking mineral waters. Couldn't they relax and suspend their plotting for one evening?

"And how are you enjoying Boston, Nathan?" Denise asked, trying to be inclusive. "Settling in?"

Frick shifted from foot to foot. He was taut and wiry---an avid runner. "We like it, thanks. Finally bought a house here, In Quincy. Our daughter will start kindergarten there next year."

The four of them contrived some more strained small talk before Larson pulled out her cell phone, glanced at the display and excused herself. Frick beat a prompt exit to the hors d'oeuvres table, bypassing a nearby waiter with a tray.

"Janet does seem a little different than earlier," Denise observed, in an undertone again, as Gallagher helped himself to a small toast with prosciutto and cheese. "Sure it's not just because of Bradford?"

"It's more than that."

They began a circumnavigation. Part way along Denise lingered with Megan Fallon. Gallagher continued on his own. Later he cut through the adjoining dining room to the hallway bathroom. On his return a young woman passed him near the long mahogany dinner table.

"Mr. Gallagher?"

Gallagher's drew up. She was tall and slender like a model...Long hair and high cheekbones ...Young...He smoothed his tie over his stomach...

"Tracey?"

She gave him an awkward smile. Gallagher remembered she'd been shy. He hadn't seen her now for almost two years. Her summer internship had been followed by a year at the University of London. As far as Gallagher understood she'd spent the previous summer traveling on the Continent.

"I'm back at Wellesley now," she explained. "I'm in my senior year."

Another shy smile. Gallagher looked at her. She had never seemed the wild type. Whitcombe had handled the Conley episode; details had always been vague. Her work in London had been solid---short news bulletins and occasional human-interest pieces. Not just a spoiled rich girl. She'd gotten good reviews from her supervising editor. Her work had continued part-time through the academic year.

"First time I've seen you since your internship, Tracey."

"I should have come to the newsroom, Mr. Gallagher."

"Remember? It's Art. Anyway...this is my chance to hear more, first hand."

Her shyness receded. "Best summer I ever had," she began, more animated.

Gallagher was taking a sip of wine. He swallowed hard.

With minimal prompting she recounted highlights. Conley came up at several junctures, always in favorable light---willing to bring her along to press conferences, give her advice on assignments. What had been so traumatic?

Gallagher was startled by a voice over his shoulder. It was Harry Whitcombe, all courtly bonhomie.

"I'm hearing all about Tracey's London experiences," Gallagher told him.

Whitcombe didn't bat an eye. He cast an apologetic glance at his daughter and placed a hand on Gallagher's shoulder. "Please excuse my interruption. Art...I'd like to discuss my trip to Washington before you leave tonight."

Gallagher assured him that he would. On Whitcombe's meeting schedule next week in the capital were several high-ranking Congressional and State Department contacts---potentially privy to further information on Bradford's murder. Whitcombe's next remark sounded free of residue.

"Anything we can do to help Conley, right, Art?"

"By all means, Harry."

Twenty minutes later Gallagher rejoined Denise. He described his conversation with Tracey and this latest example of Whitcombe's inexplicable, newfound enthusiasm for Conley.

"Maybe it doesn't matter any more, Art."

Gallagher reflected for a few seconds.

"…It was more than a year ago, after all."

"You're probably right, Denise. Just a sidebar."

CHAPTER 30

Claire glanced at her watch while they sat in a coffee shop in Terminal 2 of Charles de Gaulle Airport. Conley was already checked in, and measures were in place to ensure he reached his gate on schedule. His face still bore scabs from his misadventure in Argenteuil, and he winced once when he flexed his knee. Despite that he looked relieved. And how would she put it? Obliged.

He was proceeding onward with certain new understandings. Parameters, she could say. Most gratifying? Impetus for them had come from his side.

After his ill-conceived overture the previous evening, she'd been standing in her kitchen, stirring a saucepan on the stove. Trying to stifle her irritation and discuss his plans for Prague and Moscow. What had happened in the hallway, she'd told herself, was just a product of surging hormones and brandy on an empty stomach. Granted, his advances had been inappropriate. Appalling, even. But didn't he still deserve some dispensation because of his injuries? And what was he worried about? That she would thwart his assignment, by complaining to Harry Whitcombe? Didn't he yet understand?

For now, this was her way forward.

"Can I make amends, Claire?" he had asked from her small dining table.

"Amends?" She'd been perplexed. "What you have in mind?"

"I wish I had some ideas."

He'd fallen silent and she'd studied his profile over the serving counter. Hair still wild from Versailles. Expression out of whack. As if dismayed by his own behavior...Then she'd considered wider context while finishing her cooking. By time she brought over the first course and sat down, she was ready to explore this further.

"I don't wish to be out of place, Steve..." she'd begun, trying to moderate the edge that remained in her voice.

Conley had listened with full attention.

"...Or intrusive. It's your assignment."

To this point he looked amenable to whatever she might propose.

"What I'd like most of all is to remain involved."

"In my assignment?"

"Yes."

"You are involved."

"I know. What I mean is...on an ongoing basis. So we can avoid problems like Argenteuil."

From there she had proceeded by tactful increments. Not that delicacy was required. Conley hadn't needed much persuasion; worry appeared to weigh on him. She remembered Peter saying something about a stain on his record---an unspecified association with Tracey Whitcombe in London. Was that what lay behind his apprehension? By the second course she brought her notion into starker relief. She mentioned staying in the loop. Almost like Art Gallagher.

This had caused him to lean back from the table---first indications of caution.

"First of all," she continued. "I want to stay in contact by phone."

"I planned to do that anyway."

"I mean every day, at least once."

He'd cleared his throat. "And discuss what?"

"Everything. How each interview is going...additional discoveries about Peter...the overall direction."

Another pause: Conley had stared at the table, a crease forming between his brows. "This is my story, Claire, even if it concerns your husband. I can't let you write it for me."

"Of course...*naturellement.* I just want to stay informed. Is that too much to ask?"

He'd reflected again. Accountability appeared to settle over him. "No. It's manageable, I suppose."

"We're agreed then," she had said quickly, raising a toast. The glass had trembled in her hand. After an instant of hesitation Conley had raised his as well.

Now, at the airport coffee shop, she didn't sense that he was leaving. More that she was sending him off. Her sympathy came back to the fore.

"Do you have enough Ibuprofen for your knee?"

Conley nodded.

"In Prague, please wear your brace. Your knee needs to heal. We want to avoid problems the rest of the way."

He chafed slightly at the first person plural. She checked her watch again.

"Your flight boards in 30 minutes. I told the cart driver to meet us here. In fact here he is now..."

An electric cart pulled up, adjacent to the coffee shop. While the driver waited Conley hobbled across to the passenger seat. Claire deposited his laptop in back and came up alongside him. He seemed afflicted by another impulse to hug her. It passed; he extended his hand instead.

"Don't forget, Steve. Every day."

"I'll try."

"I'm counting on it. Good luck." She waved as the cart beeped and moved off toward passport control.

Yes, she determined...Argenteuil had probably been a fluke. This would turn out fine---as long as he took suitable precautions when he reached Tajikistan. Her efforts on behalf of Peter would continue. Greater meaning would come out of this. She raised her chin and strode back across the departure hall toward the parking garage.

CHAPTER 31

The soaring atrium lobby of the Prague Hilton echoed with sounds of morning: clinks of cups and plateware from the ground-level restaurant, receipts printing at reception, luggage loaded onto trolleys, doors sliding open at the front entrance. Conley had already eaten breakfast and was sitting in the lounge area next to a gurgling fountain.

It was impossible not to notice. Even at this early hour there was an improbable circulation of riveting and slender young women. Every other female seemed in the same exalted class as Tracey Whitcombe. He'd had heard that about the Czech Republic, and after Paris he was glad to see its reputation confirmed. Anything to take his mind off the travesty with Claire; just watching would be salutary. And if something, by chance, went beyond that? Here there were no innate hazards.

He checked watch and pulled an e-mail printout from his leather case. In one respect he wouldn't be able to follow Bradford's lead in Prague. Bradford had spoken passable Czech; in Conley's case he needed language assistance:

Dear Mr. Conley,

Milena Janikova will be your interpreter. She has been informed of your nationality and occupation and will look for you in the main lobby at 8:30 on

Monday morning. If she has trouble locating you she will have you paged from the reception desk.

Thank you for using our service. I will also thank the U.S. Embassy for putting you in contact with us...

An announcement aired over the hotel public address system: *"Mr. Steven Conley please come to reception. Your party is here to meet you."*

Conley rose and limped across the lobby. When he drew closer to reception he inhaled and didn't breathe out...Only one person stood nearby: a tall girl in high-heeled boots and black leather jacket...and in-between, legs that extended across an improbable distance. When the girl saw him limping toward her she made brief eye contact, then turned away. The girl had a thick main of curly, strawberry blond hair and wore glasses.

Conley identified himself to the receptionist. The girl, hearing this, seemed surprised.

"I'm sorry. I'm Milena Janikova. I saw you, but..."

Bright blue eyes behind the glasses. Fair, slightly freckled skin. Notably younger than he was. He introduced himself.

"Let's go sit down," he suggested.

"I saw you...but you didn't look like a journalist."

"What did I look like?"

"An athlete, maybe."

She looked at his facial scabs and then at his leg brace, her face reddening. But by the time they sat down she'd recovered her composure. Her eyes were cheerful and she tilted her head to one side when she listened to him. Her glasses gave her face a scholarly quality. Conley could hardly keep his eyes off her exposed knees, which were jutting toward him.

"What's your background?" he asked.

"I've done English translation work for a couple of years..." Here he noticed she had a very slight lisp "...part-time, mostly for business visitors. I graduated from the Linguistic Institute of Charles University last spring."

That was good enough for him.

He proceeded to summarize his assignment. They would seek to duplicate Bradford's interviews: the Czech Deputy Interior Minister in charge of drug enforcement, a Prague-based United Nations official, the Prague Chief of Police, the head Interpol Liaison in Prague, and a Czech journalist who'd investigated the heroin trade.

"All these people probably speak English to one degree or another," Conley said. "But I'd like to have you along as a backstop."

"Did you say the Prague Chief of Police?"

"Yes. Ivo Klucar is his name."

"My future father-in-law."

This set back Conley back a notch. He'd gotten way ahead of himself. "Father in law?"

"I'm getting married in April."

Taking in this disclosure, Conley re-focused, filling out details of the interview schedule for the first two days. That left Wednesday and Thursday:

"I may decide to venture into some criminal haunts. Certain Albanian restaurants and cafes---ones Bradford visited. Maybe it will be a waste of time. We'll see. I can assure you, though, we won't take unnecessary chances in such places."

Milena shrugged as if the outings would amount to harmless fun. Conley gained the impression that she was not the cautious type.

His cell phone rang inside his coat pocket. He answered. The caller was Claire.

"Steve, I just wanted to make sure you made it to Prague okay, given your injuries and everything." Her voice was businesslike but tremulous---testing their new arrangement.

"I'm briefing my interpreter now," Conley said. "We're about to leave the hotel."

Claire was already apprised of the schedule; Conley reviewed objectives for each meeting. She seemed on the verge of asking additional questions when he checked his watch and interrupted.

"Can I call you back this evening, Claire?"

On her end Claire paused for several seconds before they concluded the call.

"Your editor in the U.S?" Milena asked, looking at her watch with some confusion, aware of time zones.

"No."

"Your wife?"

"No. I'm not married."

Milena looked even more puzzled.

"I'll explain in the taxi," he told her.

CHAPTER 32

Gallagher considered himself adept at setting priorities. Larson, though, was a master of the art. Now Conley's assignment had risen to top rank.

"I feel I should make more time for this," she said, elbow on her desk and a stem of her reading glasses in one hand.

Gallagher sat across from her. Monday, about an hour after lunch. Whitcombe's displacement to Washington had not brought calm at home base. The opposite.

"Any particular concerns, Janet?"

"The aid bill adds a new dimension. The paper's got a lot riding on this. And it's obviously important to Harry."

Could he provide such summaries at the morning editorial meetings, Gallagher asked? Other editors had been curious and inquired. Her reaction made clear that she had another mechanism in mind: daily briefings in her office…"at least until Harry gets back."

"Daily?"

"Just ten or fifteen minutes."

"Okay. Just you and me?"

"No. I'd like to include Nathan Frick."

In the plate-glass window behind her traffic hurtled by on Morrissey Boulevard---a normal backdrop for an unusual request. However Gallagher had seen this coming. He shifted in his chair, producing a loud squeak.

"Why Nathan?"

"He's interested in a broader role, down the road," Larson answered, in an even, reasonable voice. "This will give him some exposure to international reporting."

Gallagher stroked his beard. He found himself looking forward to Whitcombe's return.

CHAPTER 33

The rectory of *Notre Dame de Passy* was not a disagreeable place, even with musty air. Just not one where Claire expected to advance her goal. In truth she was here as a courtesy to Veronique. Also as another show of appreciation to Francois. She couldn't forget; he'd gone to extraordinary lengths in the organization of Peter's funeral.

"Maybe you're getting too wrapped up in this, Claire," Francois said, in a gentle, worried tone, lanky frame inclining forward from his velvet armchair.

Claire's cup trembled as she took a sip of coffee. Did Francois have a point? Was she pushing Conley toward some disaster…a repetition of what happened to Peter? The thought unsettled her. She decided caffeine only added to her turmoil and put cup and saucer back down on the low table fronting the divan. "Remember last time how I said I needed a goal?" she said.

"Yes."

"This is it."

"Hmmm." Francois considered this. "Still…asking this reporter, Steve Conley, to call you every day. Isn't that rather demanding?"

"Maybe…On the other hand, if I can help him avoid more problems, and keep abreast of his progress, isn't that good? I mean…what's wrong with it?"

Francois considered again. She hadn't told him about Conley's inane overture on Saturday evening.

"Goals are fine," he finally answered, choosing his words with care. "But in our pursuit of them we have to be considerate of others. That's clear in Christ's teachings."

"I respect the Church and its teachings, Francois. You know that." At that moment she noticed that his clerical collar was askew. A well-meaning but disconnected *haut bourgeois*. She also noticed, with some apprehension, the Bible that lay again on the table next to his armrest.

"There are other ways of coping with grief..." He began, reaching for the text.

"Before we get to that..." she interjected. "I was reading Voltaire yesterday evening..."

Francois tensed at this pronouncement.

"...And he had an interesting perspective---one which I related to Peter and to Steve Conley's assignment. That was...'To the dead we owe only the truth.' I decided that's the minimum we owe Peter."

Francois' eyes narrowed; his lips became more severe. Her citation of Voltaire---in the rectory, moreover---was obviously not pleasing to him. "The *philosophes* of that period were great thinkers," he said. "Frequently misguided, though."

Wouldn't those centuries-old antagonisms ever subside? On the divan Claire straightened and set her jaw. Francois studied her. After a pause his pastoral duty came back to the fore. "Let's walk over to the sanctuary," he said, gently again, as if that venue offered protection from unwanted influences.

Whatever his stratagem, Claire was relieved to get up and move. She preceded him out of the salon and across a small courtyard to the church. They entered through a side door that came out near the altar, which they rounded to the center aisle. The sanctuary was empty and mid-morning light filtered through the high, stained glass windows. There was a lingering scent of incense from early mass. Snapping from her heels echoed off granite walls.

Francois slowed their pace: an endeavor toward calm. Though bent slightly at the waist, he towered over her. His long, slender hands were clasped behind him.

"Francois, it's just that I want these stories about Peter...to come out the best they possibly can."

"Don't you trust the reporter?"

"Well...he's smart enough. But he can make mistakes."

"We're all fallible, Claire. You have to allow for that."

"Of course. That's why I want an active role."

Francois gave her a worried sideways glance. A few steps further---about halfway down the aisle---he drew to a stop, causing Claire to do like-wise. He folded his arms, lowered his chin and reflected for a moment.

"Just be careful," he said. "...That the *philosophes* don't lead you to excess."

CHAPTER 34

"Your father-in-law seems like a tough and capable official," Conley said.

"My future father-in-law."

This was day two. As usual Milena was smiling---clearly enjoying her translation work. They were on a street outside the Prague Police Headquarters. Sparkling autumn afternoon. Conley opened the back door of a taxi. Milena angled her bare legs and climbed in.

Conley had convinced himself: her status made this week simpler. It was easier to focus on his reporting. He slid in beside her, deliberate because of his knee-brace.

"My impression is that he's a formidable adversary for these Albanian gangsters."

"I don't doubt it."

Next stop was the Interior Ministry, situated in the Hradcany section of Prague: a hilltop on the other side of the Vltava River. Their route skirted the narrow streets and picturesque squares of the old city. Church spires loomed around every corner. Streets were full of pedestrians. To Conley it was an enchanting, civilized place. Though not without dark undercurrents; he remembered comments by the

Interpol liaison the day before, a stout, middle-aged German with a bushy handlebar mustache.

"You'd be surprised at the drug-related criminality that goes on here," he had said, in German-accented English. "It's brutally violent."

Such a remark was discordant with carefree scenes outside the taxi. On a bridge over the Vltava Conley noticed a young couple getting photographed. He'd read that Prague was a popular destination for honeymooners. This dissonance was still on his mind 15 minutes later when he and Milena were ushered into the expansive, high-ceilinged office of Jaroslav Forman. Two windows behind Forman's desk afforded spectacular views across the river toward Old Prague.

"I read about what happened to Peter Bradford…just a couple of weeks after he was here," Forman began in professional, competent English, while still standing. His eyes flitted down to Conley's brace, with no comment. "A tragedy. I give you my sympathies."

"…In fact he sat in that very chair," the official continued, gesturing behind Conley. "I was surprised. He spoke very passable Czech."

Forman presented an even gaze and a modest, reasonable manner. He was Deputy Minister of Interior, with drug enforcement his main portfolio. As the interview got underway he lit a cigarette. During the next 45 minutes he smoked about five more.

Milena was called upon to assist at occasional intervals.

Forman provided a recent history of heroin in Prague. The fall of communism had spawned a freewheeling drug sub-culture. In the early and mid 90s Czech authorities adopted a semi-tolerant attitude, and Prague acquired a reputation as a minor drug mecca. However usage never reached alarming proportions. Mostly marijuana. Heroin addiction existed around the margins.

Until this laissez-faire approach attracted drug interests from outside the country.

Albanians and Italians arrived about the same time. To the surprise of Czech authorities, the Albanians soon prevailed over the

Italians in the local market, though the Italians had ruled heroin distribution elsewhere in Europe for decades.

"These Albanians employ savage methods," Forman said. "Perhaps because of their deprivations back home. There were scores of gangland killings in the mid- 90s. Pulverized bodies. Slit throats. You name it."

Overland smuggling routes through the Balkans made Prague a distribution hub. From there the Albanians developed retail networks in Amsterdam, Hamburg and other West European cities, in further competition with Italians. By late 90s the Czech government began to get serious about the problem. However intensified enforcement efforts coincided with an increase in supply, mainly from Afghanistan. Prices dropped all along the pipeline, creating more retail demand and bigger wholesale business for the Albanians.

"It was always an uphill battle," Forman explained.

There was a brief respite in 2000-2001 when the Taliban regime undertook a poppy eradication campaign in Afghanistan. But that ended with the American military invasion. Production soared again: an ironic outcome for the West. Europe was flooded anew with cheap heroin. Now that the Czech Republic was a member of the EU, the Czech government was under increasing pressure to choke off the pipeline. Albanian Mafia clans had proven difficult to penetrate. So the authorities had resorted increasingly to immigration crackdowns and expulsions, rather than arrests.

"It's a struggle on many fronts," Forman admitted, blowing a plume of smoke toward the high ceiling.

Afterward, Conley and Milena made slow progress across a cobblestone square surrounded by other government buildings. Though his knee was less sore, he still walked with a limp, while Milena clasped his elbow. He recalled what Klucar had said about Albanian restaurants and cafes that Bradford had visited. Such places were always hazardous. Never mind with limited mobility.

He told Milena. "I'm still considering our plan for tomorrow and Thursday. I haven't decided yet."

"Whatever you say." She laughed. "I'm ready either way."

On a nearby street they'd seen a taxi stand. Their plan was to drop her off at her apartment before he proceeded on to the Hilton. He was startled when she wrapped his arm and drew closer.

"Why don't you let me show you some of Prague?" she asked, in a singsong voice.

"I don't know…My knee is still stiff."

"We won't walk far. And I'll help."

"What about your fiancé?"

"This week he's at a medical symposium in Brno…part of his training," Milena said, tilting her head with the same bright excitement she showed toward the Albanian venues. With her everything seemed a lark.

Conley thought for a moment. He had no work planned for the evening. It would be simple companionship. What harm could come of it?

"Okay. I'll just have to make a phone call or two," he said, pulling out his cell phone.

"Claire?" Milena asked.

He nodded.

"You're really nice to do that for her," she observed, leaning close enough so that her curls brushed his face.

CHAPTER 35

Gallagher was cutting across the newsroom and passed the desk of Jerry MacPherson, city columnist, whom he'd known for almost two decades. MacPherson had a half-eaten sandwich within reach, and was scanning a late edition.

"Hey Art," MacPherson said, lowering his paper. "These stories are getting quite a buildup."

A full-page advertisement had appeared that day. Gallagher had tried in vain to mute any hyperbole, in cooperation with Fallon and the marketing department:

*Boston World Tribune reporter Steve Conley is now on assignment overseas, retracing the steps of reporter Peter Bradford, who was murdered in Tajikistan on October 17th. Through Conley, **The World Tribune** is carrying on the work that Bradford never finished: investigation of a heroin pipeline that stretches from Europe back to Central Asia. Conley is also reconstructing the tragic events that led to Bradford's death.*

*Details to come next month in **The World Tribune.***

Below, in one corner, was a head and shoulders file photograph of Conley, wearing a tie and blazer. Opposite was a similarly sized portrait of Bradford wearing a pinstriped suit, with the sub-caption *Peter Bradford, 1977-2006.*

Gallagher slowed and stopped, feeling beleaguered.

"Quite a resurrection for your boy Conley," MacPherson observed.

"That's the good part."

"And the bad part?"

Gallagher sighed. "I'm due for a meeting Jerry. Maybe another time...over lunch."

"You're on," MacPherson said, rustling his paper back up.

When Gallagher entered Larson's office Nathan Frick was already present, and by all appearances had been for quite awhile. Taut and nervous, as usual. He frowned when Gallagher lowered himself into the other chair with a light thud.

"Before we get to the briefing, Art..." Larson said.. "I've scheduled a conference call with Harry. On events in Washington."

At once Frick flipped his notepad open to a page of pre-prepared notes. Larson's phone rang, and she activated the speakerphone. Whitcombe sounded as if he was calling from a busy lobby.

Gallagher felt ambushed.

"I'm sitting here with Art and Nathan Frick," Larson said. "Nathan's here for edification. And to stay informed."

Whitcombe sounded a little surprised about this but didn't delve further. Foremost on his mind was the aid bill. He'd inter- sected with Reynolds earlier in the day, then proceeded with his own back-channel contacts. "Timing is striking, no doubt," he said. "Is there a connection to Peter? My contacts don't know any more than we do." He recounted conversations he'd had with Senator Knowlton, senior senator from Massachusetts, and a Deputy Secretary at the State Department. Next day he was scheduled to visit two other Congressmen, but didn't expect much. After that he had some pri- vate business.

Gallagher provided a quick update on Conley's activities in Prague.

"I hate to say it," Whitcombe responded. "But that Chechen drug lord may represent our best hope for a breakthrough, at least until Conley gets to Dushanbe."

Gallagher was not surprised when Frick spoke up next.

"This is Nathan speaking," he said. "I've become well enough acquainted with Peter's case to offer a suggestion."

Frick referred to his notes. "A lot seems to depend on the Russians here. With this drug lord, for example. They also interacted with Peter in Tajikistan. Why not contact them, even before Conley gets to Moscow? That way we're not just depending on the State Department and other parts of the U.S. government for information. I'd suggest a meeting with the Russian ambassador, if you can arrange one."

Gallagher had not thought of this. He had to admit that Frick's idea was a good one.

"The Russians may at least have some theories," Frick concluded.

"Excellent suggestion, Nathan," Whitcombe said over the speakerphone. "I'll pursue it."

Afterward Gallagher noticed that Frick made insinuating eye contact with Larson.

"Complexities in this story keep growing," she said, with her elbows on her desk and her usual calculating detachment. "It's a good tutorial for you, Nathan."

Good idea or not, Gallagher thought their scheming was getting out of hand.

CHAPTER 36

East European journalists were even more cynical than their West European and American brethren, Conley reckoned. They remained worn out by the half-truths and repression of the Communist period, as well as the ensuing corruptions of the 90s. They assumed their battles were half-futile.

Jiri Hodac had been a university student when Communism fell in the "Velvet Revolution" of 1989. Nonetheless he had a grayish pallor and dark circles under his eyes. Burdens of an earlier time.

Conley and Milena sat with him in an Albanian restaurant near the Prague train station---ensconced in a side booth. Décor was expensive but gaudy---red velvet and brass. Most tables were full. Air thick with smoke. They had just ordered. Hodac worked for a Czech weekly news-magazine. He was explaining his investigation of the heroin trade.

"People at the top try to hide the problem," Hodac said between drags on a cigarette.

"Officials I've spoken to have been pretty frank," Conley said.

"Oh…they may admit the problem is big," Hodac continued, brushing his longish hair away from his eyes. "What they don't admit is that lately the problem has gotten beyond their control. It's huge… enormous."

"They've mentioned a few successes."

"Immigration crackdowns? Those are more symbolic than real. They're just scoring points with the EU---aiming for more funding."

Hodac spoke excellent English. Milena's presence wasn't really necessary, but by now she'd become as much companion as interpreter... Conley took mental notes. This was not a place for notepads.

"And Klucar?" Hodac added. "He's worried about keeping mafia-related violence out of the center of town. So as not to damage tourism."

"Looks to me like he's succeeded."

"He has. But certain outlying areas have become trading bazaars."

Milena tilted her head with interest---a bookish girl on a lark. Her short skirt and high heels matched the attire of the other women in the restaurant. Conley assumed most of the latter were hookers.

"Same thing I told to Peter Bradford a month ago," Hodac added, shaking his head and stubbing out his cigarette. "Here, right in this restaurant...sitting over there." Hodac gestured toward a nearby table.

The waiter came with their main courses.

Hodac had been investigating the Prague heroin trade for more than two months. His sources were varied: police, drug enforcement, Czech criminals on the periphery. He was due to file his story the following week. After that, he said, he would probably leave Prague for a while. His story might kick up dust. Not just with the Albanian mafia. Certain institutions in Czech government were also bound to be unhappy. Of course the mafia was the bigger worry.

"This restaurant is safe, more or less," he said. "...Until my story comes out."

Wholesale heroin business in Prague was compartmentalized in a way that stymied authorities, he continued. Two different locales in central Prague served as business venues. The restaurant they were in, with the bland name *Restaurant Centralna Praha*, was where deals were negotiated and final terms agreed. Cash exchanges were not allowed.

Nor were weapons. Both rules were followed---despite violent disposi-
tions among participants.

Conley gave the restaurant another discreet survey. Hookers
aside, the clientele was mostly male. Europeans---dark-haired and
swarthy---most under 40 years old. Lots of bulging muscles. Not many
cheery faces.

Hodac said sellers were all Albanians. They controlled inflow. Most
buyers---those who smuggled heroin on to various European cities and
retail networks---were also Albanian. However a significant contingent
of Italians remained; the longstanding "pizzeria" distribution system
was alive and well. Italian retailers weren't averse to tapping into a new
wholesale source.

In parallel there was an Albanian-owned casino outside the city,
called the *Lunar Eclipse---w*here buyers and sellers met to carry out
the deals. Only cash changed hands there: no drugs. Transfers of
product occurred outside of town, deep in surrounding forests. Big
cash meant big weapons. Patrons of the *Lunar Eclipse* packed heavy
firepower. Both sides waited in the casino while product transfers
proceeded outside of town. If deals went bad guns blazed---usually
in the parking lot.

"Here in the *Centralna Praha* they tolerate outsiders like us," Hodac
said, "It gives the place...a normal air."

"And the *Lunar Eclipse?*"

"Outsiders are not welcome. They're known to go missing and
turn up dead."

They finished their food and ordered coffees. Their waiter conveyed an unspoken message. *This is not your habitat. You can eat here.
But stay within appropriate boundaries.* Ignoring him as he turned away
toward the kitchen, Hodac lit another cigarette, and watched the
smoke dissipate with an air of pessimism.

"Therefore I was surprised that Bradford wanted to go there," he
said. "I told him he would have to go on his own."

"What did he hope to achieve?"

Milena leaned forward on her elbows: bright eyes behind her glasses. A counterpoint to Hodac's weary resignation.

"He said something like 'Journalists have to get up close and observe. To see their subjects.' He wanted some vivid material to weave into his story."

Conley crooked his index finger under his lower lip. "And the risks?"

"Recklessness seemed out of character for him," Hodac observed. "My impression was that he was a serious and responsible guy."

"He was."

Hodac squinted and took another drag.

"Did you hear what happened?" Conley asked him.

"He called me from the airport the day after. Said he just showed up at the casino, played electronic blackjack, walked among the gaming tables, took in the scene, then left."

"Hmmm."

"He talked as though the danger never worried him…Almost like he was immune. I just thought he was lucky. At least until I read what happened to him in Dushanbe, about two weeks later."

Conley folded his hands, formed a V with his thumbs, then drummed the V on the tablecloth a few times.

"Are you going?" Hodac asked, referring to the *Lunar Eclipse*.

"Probably not," Conley ventured another glance at nearby tables. "I've seen these people here. That's enough."

*   *   *

Hodac's car, an aging *Skoda,* was parked a half-block from the restaurant on a dark side street. Without explanation, Hodac crouched and pulled a small flashlight from his coat pocket. He craned his head close to the asphalt and inspected the car's undercarriage. "Can't be too careful," he said, standing up. He clapped dust from his hands and brushed his hair back from his eyes with a sleeve.

Bomb check? Conley asked. Hodac responded with a grim nod.

The Skoda's interior was cluttered with magazines and music CDs. The journalist got behind the wheel and rolled down his driver's side window, lighting another cigarette.

"You've got my number," he said to Conley. He nodded at Milena gunned the low-horsepower engine and sped off down the narrow lane. Conley and Milena watched the car disappear.

"*Wenceslas* Square is only two blocks from here," she said, taking his arm. "Let's walk."

Conley still suffered a slight limp; he shot several glances over his shoulder as they made their way to the top of the square. There they stopped facing the statue of King *Wenceslas* on horseback. The rectangular expanse was mostly empty: small groups of students and younger tourists. Milena stayed close by his side.

"What's wrong?" she asked. "You still seem tense."

"I'm just thinking about the casino."

She tilted her head, hair framing her face. "You need to relax. Why don't you take a night to decide?"

"Good idea."

"What are your plans now?"

"I'll drop you off. Then maybe watch a movie in my room."

"In English?"

"Yes. Why?"

"Can I watch? I love American films."

Her inflection was amiable and innocent: no more suggestive than an invitation to the library. Conley visualized the queen bed and tight furniture arrangement. "In my room…?"

She smiled. "It's just a movie."

Conley reflected for a moment.

"Still wondering about my fiancé?"

"Well…"

"I caught him at a restaurant last week…with a nurse. He'd told me he was at the hospital. Yesterday I learned the woman is with him this week at the medical conference. It seems they're sharing a room."

"I'm sorry."

"Don't be. I plan to break it off when he gets back."

Milena nudged a breast into his ribs, yielding a whiff of perfume. Energies from Paris swelled back, sudden and hard after the buildup with Claire. He rotated her so that they pressed front to front, moved his hands to her hips, and pulled her tighter. This met no resistance; she tilted her face upward, her hair spilling everywhere…

His cell phone rang. He exhaled and stepped back. The caller was Claire. She said she'd gotten his message.

Conley tried to focus, glancing first at Milena then at his watch. Better to talk now; Claire would not be stayed. Collecting himself, he recounted the interview with Hodac. Also his doubts over visiting the *Lunar Eclipse*.

There was a tense silence. As if new worries were rising on Claire's side.

"The last thing we want is a repeat of Argenteuil. Would it help if you went with someone else…maybe a bodyguard?"

"No, that would just invite more trouble. I'd go with my interpreter. But it's not fair to put her in that situation…"

From Milena came a shake of the head. She gestured toward the phone. "Can I speak to her?" she asked.

Conley hesitated then passed the device over. Milena pulled one side of curls back, listened intently, answered "Oui," then proceeded in French: "Yes, I participated in the interview…I know where that casino is…No, I've never visited…A little dangerous, maybe…But I wouldn't worry about it." Claire spoke at length on the other end; tears welled in Milena's eyes. "…I understand. On my side I just want to help…"

Conley stood by, perplexed.

"She wants to speak to you again," Milena said, handing phone back.

"I talked it over with Milena. She convinced me. Please, if you can, call me back later."

Conley clicked off the connection, and looked at Milena for an explanation.

"I'm ready to go with you, Steve," she said.

"I appreciate that Milena, but…"

"Please don't worry about my safety. I want to contribute. And Ivo Klucar might be able to give us some extra police protection."

Conley was taken aback, given what she'd just told him.

"He knows everything about his son," she said, seeing his reaction. "He disapproves. And he's still fond of me."

"Are you sure?"

"Yes. So why not use his help?"

Conley shifted on his feet and gazed down the square.

"Let's do this for Claire," Milena urged.

"I don't know…"

His body was now slack; she grabbed his arms and brought him back face to face. She looked up with an expectant smile---prepared to wait.

"All right," Conley said, after a moment. "We'll go."

Her eyes brightened. She released a shriek of delight and planted a kiss on his cheek. "I knew it. I was right about you."

Conley looked at her, uncomprehending.

"Your motives aren't typical…" she said. "I mean they're not the ones that usually drive men in these situations, with women. With Claire you've assumed a kind of responsibility. You're acting for reasons that so…*noble.*"

They were still in a half embrace. Conley cleared his throat.

"Still interested in that movie?" he asked.

To his surprise she placed her hands on his chest, new purpose in her eyes.

"Our plans for tomorrow night are too important," she answered. "That can wait."

CHAPTER 37

Harry Whitcombe issued from austere Brahmin aristocrats who demanded steadiness and efficiency from their own and others. His decisions held. He seldom entertained second thoughts.

Therefore Gallagher was stunned when Whitcombe materialized in the conference room, minus his usual purposeful stride. Drooped shoulders. Dark circles. Wrinkled suit. Fleeting eye contact. Even his "good morning" sounded ragged.

There was no precedent for this.

Once seated, the publisher began. "By accident or by design, Peter ended up in Tajikistan at peculiar time…"

Had late facts emerged in Washington, Gallagher wondered? Whitcombe hadn't mentioned any by phone. Nothing new from Reynolds, either.

"… I knew about the aid bill, of course. What I didn't appreciate were the geo-political complexities behind it."

Gallagher shot a glance back at Larson: perched in her usual end position, opposite Whitcombe. Today Frick coiled at her right. Her usual comprehension was absent. She studied Whitcombe over the tops of her reading glasses before floating a careful prompt.

"What…geo-political complexities, Harry?"

"Let's say the Russian ambassador opened my eyes."

Reactions from both Larson and Frick suggested this had not figured in their calculus.

"...The ambassador indicated that the Tajik government is corrupt...complicit in heroin smuggling. Including Salimjon Shakuri."

"Did the ambassador say that Shakuri was responsible for Peter's death?" Larson asked.

Whitcombe shook his head, as if the question carried unsustainable burdens. "The Russians don't know for certain. However they suspect Peter stumbled across evidence of corruption, and died as a result."

"We talked about that possibility before," Gallagher noted. "Remember, Harry...Franklin Stanson dismissed it."

This provoked another pang of discomfort. "I trust Senator Knowlton, Art, as well as Undersecretary Marston at the State Department. I have no reason to disbelieve this fellow Stanson, either. In my view...there's no cover-up."

Gallagher recalled that Whitcombe's maternal grandfather had been Governor of Massachusetts. A paternal uncle had served in the U.S. Senate. Patriotism was hard-wired. Gallagher, for his part, had maintained a healthy skepticism toward U.S. foreign policy since Vietnam.

"The Russian ambassador said the U.S. is new to Tajikistan," Whitcombe explained. "...And has poor intelligence there. They're eager for a new strategic foothold. The ambassador also implied...that obsession with terrorism blinds the U.S. to Tajiki corruption."

To Gallagher this was entirely plausible.

"...Do I believe him? Tajikistan is a former Soviet Republic. So the Russians have their own agenda. But many pieces fit together..."

Whitcombe choked on these words. Okay, Gallagher thought...but why such distress? It was way out of character.

"Are you sure your contacts in Washington are fully informed, Harry?" Larson asked.

"Perhaps it's a question of competence, Janet...The U.S. may be in over its head there. And Peter ventured in alone..." Whitcombe's voice choked again. "...I'm now worried that we're sending Conley into a situation...with dangerous variables. Something for which I've been at fault.

Heavy silence ensued. Government incompetence? New dangers? Did this mean Conley's assignment would be cancelled?

"I admit I now have a certain impulse to pull back," Whitcombe continued at last. "...But...there's still the matter of the truth in all this. Peter went to Tajikistan looking for that in the first place."

He fixed a pained gaze on Gallagher.

"For now, Art...Please just ensure that Conley stays safe."

CHAPTER 38

Milena's lark now had a moral dimension. Cheerfulness combined with altruism.

She was sitting beside Conley in their rented Opel, Conley at the wheel, winding along a two-lane road through forest. A gaudy red and gold sign loomed up on their right, incongruous in the darkness: *Lunar Eclipse Casino.*

"Turn here," she said, with no detectable apprehension.

Conley didn't share her calm. This bore hallmarks of a dangerous farce.

They curved downward though thick woods to an unremarkable concrete building, which resembled a small swimming facility except for its red color. About 20 cars occupied the lighted parking lot, mostly BMWs and Mercedes. As Conley climbed out he spotted three late-model, gray Skoda sedans parked away from other cars, next to an embankment. A cigarette glowed in one, revealing two silhouettes. Conley walked around and opened the passenger door for Milena.

"Let me guess," he said in a low voice. "Plainclothesmen sent by Klucar?"

She smiled. "You were concerned about safety, weren't you?"

The *Lunar Eclipse* lay outside city limits, and therefore outside Klucar's formal jurisdiction. To Conley these plainclothesmen were just as likely to arouse suspicion and volatility. He was starting to wish he'd heeded Gallagher.

Milena merrily took his arm as they crossed toward the casino. Tonight her pending bust-up with Klucar's son seemed last on her mind. Two burly doormen flanked the front entrance, which consisted of heavy double black doors. On edge, with unwavering gazes. One had a hand inside his overcoat. Conley could guess why. It had to be the police presence.

"Lord help us," he said under his breath as they approached.

Milena spoke Czech to the pair. "They're asking what we want here," she told Conley.

"Tell him we saw the sign on the road and are interested in gambling."

Conley's use of English provoked surprise. One spoke Albanian into a walkie-talkie and became suddenly friendlier. He opened one of the heavy double doors and beckoned them through.

That was odd, Conley thought. *Thud. Click.* They were inside.

Around them was a small lobby, decorated in red and black, with a garish gold-colored chandelier and stale odors of cigarettes. Double doors to the gambling salon lay straight ahead. Another security man was already opening one, all hospitality. Conley still couldn't read the dynamic.

"Don't forget that we're doing this for Claire," Milena said, still smiling.

He frowned. Something about this wasn't right.

When they got through his misgivings were confirmed. He pulled Milena up short. Through a haze of smoke he surveyed the room.

They'd walked into what looked and felt like a hair-trigger. Most gambling activity was suspended. A patchwork of swarthy faces---from card tables, roulette wheels, cash booth, all corners---turned in their direction. Muscled bodies under flashy suits, lots of stubble and open collars. Tense stares…shifting back and forth, between Conley and Milena and another object of interest on one side. Conley turned and saw what that was. At last he understood what was wrong. Two clean-cut Czechs in dark trousers and flashy blazers---unmistakably Klucar's men despite their apparel---were seated at the bar. Two others at a small table against the wall. No Albanians were nearby except for the bartender. The plainclothesmen caught Conley's glance. They tried to appear cool. They obviously weren't.

He whispered in Milena's ear. "You didn't tell me Klucar's men would be *inside* the casino!"

Her smile had gone. Her only response was to dig her fingernails into his bicep.

An Albanian-looking man approached; his tie identified him as a manager.

"We welcome English customers to our casino," he said in heavy accent.

Conley didn't rectify the misidentification. Options were limited. For now he decided to go along. After a detour to the cashier's booth for chips he and Milena sat down at a blackjack table in the center of the room. At once Albanians congregated behind them. With a wrenching sensation Conley put remaining elements together. They supposed that he and Milena were tourists, there by chance. They were anticipating gunfire with Klucar's plainclothesmen. He and Milena had become human shields.

He could hardly believe they'd blundered into this situation.

Milena stayed close on the stool beside him. Her back and neck were now stiff with fear. Her lark had become something else altogether.

Conley placed a 50 Euro chip on the betting square, and when the dealer gave him ten and seven, with seven showing, he held. The dealer turned over a queen and nine and swept the chip away. Two similar, perfunctory games followed, before Conley held up the palm of his hand.

"This is absurd," he said in an undertone to Milena. "Let's get out of here."

He gathered up his chips and helped Milena off her stool. The manager re-approached with an air of protestation.

"There's too much attention," Conley told him. "We just want to relax."

The manager nodded with contrived sympathy. Other Albanians reluctantly...with deliberate slowness...cleared a path so they could leave the table.

"Don't make any sudden moves," Conley whispered as they crossed back to the cash booth. Milena's neck was still tense and her eyes straight ahead. When they got out the front door quiet prevailed behind them---a continued standoff. He sucked in some fresh air. Neither he nor Milena looked back.

"That's a lot more color than I needed," he said, as they reached their Opel.

No sooner had he spoken than a clang rang out behind them. They whirled around to see two older-looking men---one with a mustache whom Conley had not noted earlier, emerged from the front door, ignoring hard words from the security pair. They strode straight toward him and Milena, eyes fixed forward and glaring. A loud exclamation emanated from the embankment, and Conley pivoted and saw Klucar's men outside their Skoda, drawing pistols. The two older men accelerated their strides, fumbling inside their coats. Behind them the two casino security employees went into half crouches, also reaching inside their coats.

"Get down!" he shouted, pulling Milena into the narrow space between their Opel and the next vehicle.

In mid-movement a shot rang out from the embankment, followed by a *thwack* in the direction of the casino. There was a cry of pain, a heavy thud, and then the zip of another bullet passing nearby.

Milena emitted an "aagghh" as she hit the asphalt.

Several seconds passed without more gunfire---nothing but frantic shouting and rapid footfalls. Conley raised his head and saw that Milena's face was contorted in pain.

"Are you hit?"

"Yes…my foot, I think."

He glanced down and saw that the top of her boot was torn. Blood showed through a hole. Two of Klucar's men from the casino appeared at the end of the opening between the cars, out of breath. One bent down and examined her wound. His partner spoke in urgent tones into a walkie-talkie.

"Keep her laying down" the first plainclothesman said in halting English.

Conley cradled Milena's head and shoulders on his lap, to keep her off the asphalt, which was wet and cold. She continued wincing, but showed no other signs of trauma. Nearby were the sounds of man moaning and angry protests in Italian. He turned to one of the plainclothesmen.

"What happened?" he demanded in English.

"They were going to you and we told them to stop. One of these reached for his gun. We shot him. When he fell his gun fired. The shot hit Milena."

To Conley it didn't make sense.

"They're Italian," the plainclothesman continued. "We're still trying to figure everything out."

Two police squad cars screeched up, sirens wailing. Klucar got out of one, wearing a trench coat and with his thick neck straining against his tie and shirt collar. He strode straight over to Milena, bent down, and asked her several questions in Czech. His relief was fleeting; he stood and barked orders. An ambulance arrived; Milena was loaded onto a gurney and then into the back.

Klucar cast a reproachful glance at Conley, turned heel and jumped in the passenger seat of a squad car. Ambulance and squad car sped out of the parking lot with sirens re-activated, while Conley surveyed the aftermath. One Italian was sitting on open asphalt, clutching his arm. His compatriot was in handcuffs, attended by an uniformed policeman. Assorted Albanians and the two security guards were observing the scene from the casino entrance, keeping their distance. The English-speaking plainclothesman drew alongside.

"There's your explanation," Conley said, pointing to a vehicle two parking spaces down from his rental car. The vehicle was an Alfa Romeo with Italian plates. "They were just going to their car."

"This got more complex than we expected," the plainclothesman said, shaking his head.

"That's an understatement."

"You'll have to come with us to the station."

CHAPTER 39

It was only 8:15 and Claire---who'd risen early since Peter's death---had been on a knife's edge for two hours. Four cups of coffee had exacerbated her strain. After each cup she'd gotten up from the table and paced back and forth. Conley was taking too long. Ten more minutes and she'd call him. Again she reassured herself. Milena seemed astute. The police were there. Conley had help and protection. And Peter had gone the casino alone without incident, after all.

Her cell phone chortled on the dining room table; its tones reverberated inside her rib cage. She leapt forward and snatched it up. Her chest tightened. Conley sounded strained and tired. Something had gone wrong.

"We ran into some problems last night."

"Mon Dieu...What happened?"

"Where should I start?... We visited the casino as planned. The police protection was a little clumsy. Milena was shot in the foot...an accident. I should stress it's nothing serious..."

Claire's right hand trembled, holding the phone. She pressed the device hard against her ear. "...Shot?...By whom?"

"By a heroin trafficker. Now she's in the hospital. I'll visit her again in about an hour. Again, Claire. It's nothing serious."

"Are you sure?"

"Yes. Just a superficial wound."

"Where are you now?"

"I'm at the Prague Central Police Station. In fact I'm back for a second visit. I was already here half the night."

Claire had to sit down as he provided more details. Dread took over. This was even worse than Argenteuil. An early-stage calamity she never expected. She remained astonished that Milena had been shot. Was this a forewarning that Conley was heading toward a violent outcome, similar to Peter's?

"Turns out the man who shot her was an Italian."

A misunderstanding, he explained. Two Italians had chosen that night to confront the Albanians over disputed retail territory in the UK, and had mistaken Conley and Milena for dealers. The rest was too confusing for Claire to follow...

"A big mess. I'm still helping the police with follow-up reports. I've had to postpone my departure to Moscow."

Claire pressed the cell phone harder to her ear. She couldn't think straight.

"I now expect to leave on Sunday, if all goes well."

His contingent phrasing made her shudder. On the other hand, should she still be urging him on?

"I'm not looking forward to telling Art Gallagher," he added.

"Will you call me from the hospital later?"

Conley said that he would.

After the call Claire dropped her cell phone, sending it clattering on the table. She closed her eyes and held her head in her hands. All she'd wanted was to honor Peter. Now Conley's assignment seemed to be spinning out of control. She felt helpless.

Her disquiet drove her to her feet and over to her dining room window. Morning light provided some equilibration. She spotted a workman on the other side of the interior courtyard, standing three stories up on a tall ladder, installing a new drainpipe. His face was half-turned in her direction. He appeared content, absorbed.

The workman gave her a cue. She took a deep breath. Her usual determination re-stirred. Yes...that was exactly what she needed. Hands-on involvement...action. Real engagement. Not sitting in Paris waiting for phone calls, but *moving...doing something*. She just had to figure out what.

CHAPTER 40

Somehow Conley had gained an impression---without ever visiting the country---that Czech health care was first-rate. Milena's hospital room supported this notion: large, clean and airy, with a high-tech, adjustable bed and other state-of-the-art furniture. Or had Klucar commandeered one of the better rooms in Prague?

Fortunately she'd only been grazed. She was due to check out soon, and now reposed in a sitting position, with her foot bandaged and resting on a small pillow. Her hospital smock was flimsy and revealed most of her long legs. She was already back to her cheerful norm, and asked Conley if he could accompany her home.

"The police are sending a car," she noted.

"Will Klucar be in the vehicle?"

"Don't worry about that. My mother's fixing lunch. I want to invite you."

"And your fiancé?"

"He won't be back in Prague until tomorrow."

Conley thought a moment. "Okay…I should just call Claire first."

This had the same effect as before. Milena tilted her strawberry blonde mane and smiled. Claire answered after just one ring. Her voice was still fraught, and had a new quality that put him on guard.

"I've decided to come to Prague. I'll try to get a flight later today."

"Prague? Why?"

"First of all, I feel responsible for what happened to Milena."

"Claire, I told you she's fine."

"She was shot! And I encouraged her."

"She's right here, Claire. I'll let you speak to her."

Conley suppressed the "mute" button as he passed his phone over. "She's upset. Try to reassure her that you're okay."

Milena switched eagerly to French. Empathy welled again in her eyes, unaffected by their misadventures at the casino: "...I'd love to meet you sometime, Claire...But there's no need to rush here today...I don't think you could help us with the police...I'm really fine. Next week, maybe...or even in Paris."

When Conley took back the phone Claire didn't sound placated. She asked him about reactions back in Boston.

"I reached Art Gallagher about an hour ago," he answered. "Unfortunately I caught him in the shower." Conley had imagined Gallagher standing with towel wrapped around his ample midsection, beard dripping wet. "He was shocked...until I assured him that Milena was okay."

"And?"

"He remains worried...that's for sure. He also mentioned that Harry Whitcombe has become more concerned about my safety, for reasons having to do with the aid bill. However for now the assignment is still on. Any changes will probably be around the margins..."

Klucar stormed into the room, again wearing a trench coat. He shot Conley a pugnacious, dissatisfied glance before turning his attention to Milena at bedside. Conley moved toward a far corner and turned to face the wall, placing his index finger over one ear. Claire was still unsettled.

"Will you at least call me again before you leave Prague? Update me about Milena and keep me abreast of any changes in Boston?"

"Of course."

Upon disconnection Conley attempted a polite retreat to the corridor. Klucar stood up straight, folded his arms in front of his barrel-like torso and made hard eye contact. He addressed Conley in Czech.

"Before he leaves, he wants to say something about the article," Milena translated.

"The article?"

"He said he hopes you'll go light on last night...Prague has a positive image in Europe and the U.S....He wants to keep it that way."

"I'll report the facts. I can't soft-pedal what happened."

Upon hearing the translation, Klucar seethed, holding his chin in thumb and index finger. Only additional remarks by Milena---in Czech---cooled him down. He stepped forward with his meaty hand outstretched and only half a scowl. Abruptly he was gone.

Conley gave Milena querying look.

"He's always had a soft spot for me," she explained.

"Does he know yet about...?"

A nurse breached the doorway with a wheelchair, interrupting him. After a courteous nod she collected some folded clothes from a side dresser, then slid curtains closed around Milena's bed. He stepped aside. After Paris he had yearned for a more straightforward, conventional week here in Prague. It hadn't turned out that way.

"Will you wheel me downstairs to the police car?" Milena asked, from inside the sashes. "You can also get a ride."

He walked to the window. The semi-circular drive of the hospital was visible five stories below; a Prague Police squad car was parked there, waiting. In short order Klucar's bald head and burly shoulders materialized; an intense conference followed with the uniformed policeman/driver.

"I'm happy to wheel you down," Conley said. "But it's probably better if I go separately, by taxi."

CHAPTER 41

Harry Whitcombe's spacious, wood-paneled office on the top floor was his refuge. Visits by Gallagher and Larson were rare. The publisher preferred to meet his managers for different departments---news, advertising, circulation, and production---in other parts of the building, in their own domains.

This habit was emblematic. Whitcombe was not haughty. Just patrician. Better to descend from the heights than blur lines.

Gallagher and Larson now sat in front of his massive, mahogany desk, while a secretary served coffee on cups and saucers. This morning Gallagher would have preferred the conference room. Conley's mishap in Prague didn't need amplification.

He also would have preferred the standard Harry Whitcombe.

The publisher sat in a high-backed chair padded in burgundy leather. Again with sagging shoulders and wrinkled suit. He sat mute, hands folded, and listened to Gallagher's account of the evening at the *Lunar Eclipse*. His well-bred features were even more pained than before---as if all this was moving toward tragedy.

Nathan Frick was absent. When things got unpredictable Larson flew without cohorts.

"Fortunately the Czech interpreter is expected to recover completely from her wound," Gallagher concluded, finding himself in the unaccustomed position of downplaying risks to life and limb. Anything to mitigate the pall. "And it was an isolated event. There's no connection to what happened to Peter in Dushanbe."

"Are you sure, Art?"

Gallagher thought this question odd.

"Absolutely, Harry."

For a moment the only sound was metronomic ticking of a grandfather clock against one wall...an heirloom. Gallagher half-wondered if Whitcombe would take his face in his hands.

"Are you inclined to change anything, Harry?" Larson ventured.

Whitcombe closed his eyes and took a slow, deep breath. Several seconds passed. Eyes remained closed. Again, Gallagher wondered. What was this all about? The publisher held his next breath at the point of maximum expansion. His eyebrows rose...as if he'd glimpsed a resolution. Some of his torment seemed to dissipate. His shoulders straightened somewhat as he opened his eyes.

"I'm removing myself from further involvement in this assignment."

Gallagher was too stunned to react. Larson spoke first.

"Why, Harry, if I may ask?"

"It's gotten...beyond me. This military aid bill has muddled the whole picture. I can't stay objective. I'm too directly affected."

She shifted and scrutinized him from a slightly different angle. "But you still want it to go forward?"

"Yes."

"Along the same lines?"

"Well, maybe less emphasis on Peter and more on straight news aspects..." His voice trailed off. "...But from this point forward I think you and Art should make those decisions."

Larson waited for more.

"...Conley's safety has to be respected. But everything else...the character of the stories, the advertising...I'll leave up to you."

"Can I confer with you if I need to?"

"No. I'm taking two weeks of vacation."

Larson's eyes widened. "Two weeks?"

"Yes."

She brought one stem of her reading glasses to her lips and recalibrated herself. "Should Art still supervise Conley on a day-to-day basis?"

"That makes sense to me."

She turned to Gallagher.

"Art, please make sure that nothing like this happens again. I want to give safety higher priority." Her eyes flicked over to Whitcombe, to make sure he'd heard.

Larson was badgering *him* on such issues, Gallagher thought? This was even more bizarre.

"With all due respect, Janet, I've been emphasizing safety all along."

Larson responded with a cool look. Gallagher crossed his arms and gazed back across the desk at Whitcombe, whose eyes appeared vacant, thoughts already bearing him elsewhere. This office now seemed more way station than refuge.

"Where are you going on your vacation, Harry?" Larson asked, still struggling to map this out.

"My ski lodge in New Hampshire."

It was still early November. Gallagher had never known Whitcombe to go there off-season. But today all bets seemed off.

"No snow yet," he added. "But I'll benefit from the peace and quiet."

CHAPTER 42

"A shame your mother had to leave so soon," Conley said. "She went to such trouble with lunch."

Milena shrugged.

"Back to work," she said, in a singsong voice.

Her apartment in central Prague was in a high-ceilinged, pre-war building. Early afternoon light filtered through tall windows. Plates and half-empty platters remained spread before them. Milena stretched her arms overhead. Conley stood and started to clear away dishes.

"Just put those platters in the refrigerator," she said. "I'll do the rest later."

"Don't be ridiculous. You've got a bullet wound."

Her smile implied that it was harmless. Her face shone.

"Would you like some tea?" she asked.

"Great idea."

Conley ignited the gas stove to heat the kettle and transferred empty plates to the sink. There was no dishwasher---a legacy of communism, he supposed. He opened the tap and began washing by hand.

"While you're doing that I'll go into the living room."

Milena reached for her crutches, which were leaning against the wall. When Conley scrambled over to help, she waved him away and hobbled out, unfazed. Near the sink he glimpsed a wall clock: almost two-thirty. Still early afternoon: a languorous time on weekdays. Many hours stretched ahead before dinner. Most of the world around remained at work. He and Milena were secluded…crisis over, all labors behind them…

Circumstances were quite different than in Paris. Out in the hall-way with the tray, he passed a window that looked toward the street. The squad car was long gone.

"There you are," Milena said when he rounded the corner into the living room.

She was sitting on the couch with her legs crossed, forthright and natural. Some buttons undone on her blouse, but not too far down. Only her foot bandage was incongruous. Conley set the tray down, poured the tea, sat down and leaned back next to her. The living room was quiet. Windows faced an interior courtyard, where last, golden-hued leaves of autumn hung on tall branches.

"I'm relieved to get clear of Klucar," he said, taking a sip. "I worried he'd detain me before I get to the airport."

"On what grounds?"

"I don't know. It wouldn't be difficult to come up with some pre-text. Foreign nationals were involved. It was a mess."

She chuckled. "Don't worry about Ivo. He's not as hard as he looks."

"I hope so. For your sake, too."

This remark somehow pleased her. Without a word she placed her cup and saucer on the coffee table and leaned toward him.

"Let me take that," she said, transferring his teacup as well. Rising to her knees and gripping his shoulders, she kept her bandaged foot stable swung the other across him into a straddle. In an instant Conley found his face enveloped in her mane of curls. "You'd probably do the same thing again," she said, rocking back and looking him in the eyes.

"I'm not sure about that."

"I am."

Pent-up energies propelled Conley's hands under the fabric of her skirt. His fingers found a gossamer-like thong, and a total absence of resistance…

A doorbell buzzed in the hallway.

Milena disengaged, moving upright on her knees. Her face drained.

"Oh no."

"Should I get it?"

"No I'd better."

The doorbell buzzed again. Conley fetched her crutches and helped her up. With a worried expression she hobbled out in double-time, while he followed behind. At a hallway intercom, she pressed a button. A young male voice answered. Her worry became panic.

"It's my fiancé," she said, her words hoarse. "He's back early."

"What should I do?"

The buzzer rang again. Milena hesitated, then activated the de-locking of the door downstairs.

"He's coming up. You'd better go."

Conley was already re-tucking his shirt. His overcoat hung nearby. He grabbed it and snared his shoes from the floor. For her part Milena eyed the peephole, in an awkward position on her crutches. Her breathing was quick; she turned the deadbolt and flung open the door. The elevator lay opposite, enclosed in a metal cage. Machinery whirred. Compartment on the way up. Milena pointed left, toward the stairway leading to the sixth floor, barely getting words out:

"There! Up to the next landing…"

He darted across the threshold and bounded up stairs two at a time---shoes in one hand and overcoat draped over his other elbow. At an intermediate landing he slipped on his stocking feet and almost fell. A bolt of pain went through his knee before he clenched his teeth and bound up remaining steps to floor six. The elevator clanged to a stop below. He could climb no further. Floor six was topmost in the building. He crouched in a far corner stayed quiet while wooden doors rattled open.

Milena and her fiancé exchanged tense words. Her apartment door closed with a bang.

Still in his socks, Conley padded back down, alert and careful as he rounded the fifth-floor landing. Prague suddenly felt like Paris. It had not been corrective at all.

CHAPTER 43

During his adult life Conley had passed through passport controls often enough to take them for granted. He shared a conceit common among Americans: that he was welcome to come and go from most countries as he pleased. Who could object? Therefore he was taken aback when a Czech customs officer scanned the barcode of his passport and stiffened with attention. The officer studied a computer screen and picked up a phone.

Klucar, Conley guessed. Who else could be behind this?

Another officer entered the booth by a rear door, and gave him a grave appraisal. The two men returned to the screen---in no rush. Conley glanced over his shoulder. Other passengers in the same line grew disgruntled and peeled off to other queues. His *Aeroflot* flight was scheduled to leave Prague for Moscow in 90 minutes.

"Come with me, please," the second officer said, coming round front, Conley's passport in hand.

"May I ask what's wrong?" Conley asked, keeping stride as he followed, still with a slight limp.

The officer stared straight ahead and gestured toward a side room. Inside there was a three-foot high counter manned by another uniformed agent, and a small table with two chairs. A camera on a tripod stood facing the far wall.

"Sit down," the senior officer said, closing the door. "...And fill this out." He placed a one-page form on the table, with pen. It was in English and required information was standard: passport number, date, next destination, airline and flight number.

"I have a right to know what this is about..." Conley objected.

"You've appeared on our list of 'persons of interest,' per order of the Prague Police. Our job is to confirm that you leave the country."

Indeed, a parting jab from Klucar. Conley picked up the pen.

Twenty minutes later he was sitting in the departure gate for his *Aeroflot* flight, exit stamp finally in his passport. Seated around him were most burly, middle-aged Russian business types, conversing with each other or talking on cell phones. Intermingled among them were several striking young women, tall and slender and provocatively dressed, reading books or magazines. Conley had never been to Russia but he had read about freewheeling sexual mores in the post-Soviet epoch...

He pulled out his cell phone and called Milena---energetic and cheerful, despite the week's turmoil. When he related his travails at passport control, she was unconcerned.

"It's nothing," she said. *"I know Ivo. He just wants to be aware of every-thing."* She laughed. When she spoke again, her tone became more profound. *"You know you made my step yesterday easier...I mean breaking off my engagement. Can you believe my fiancé expected to proceed to bed as if nothing had happened? Doctor or not, he's crude and one-dimensional. You're an example of better...what women should aspire to."*

"Milena, I think you're giving me too much credit..."

"No...Claire made that clear to me. She's a widow, looking to you for rein-forcement...And she couldn't have chosen better..."

"Really, Milena..."

Conley leaned forward in his seat and ran his hand through his hair. This notion was already so far advanced that he'd given up protesting. He regretted that Jenna never found the same perspective.

"Look, Steve. Somehow this week our romance never really got started. When can I see you again?"

"Well, thanks to Klucar, I doubt Czech customs will let me back in."

"Oh…we'll think of something. Meanwhile, please call me from time to time from Moscow and Tajikistan…when you get a chance. Keep me updated. I feel involved in this story now."

"Of course, Milena."

This assignment, despite all the mishaps, had a way of attracting partisans. After saying goodbye he leaned back and folded his arms across his chest. Several of the girls he had noticed earlier cast interested glances in his direction. With luck, he thought, he would sit next to one of them on the plane. Otherwise, if reputation held, he might encounter others like them in Moscow. Perhaps that was just what he needed, after the ups and downs and near derailments of the past two weeks. Release.

Just before boarding he called Claire. He decided not to tell her about his customs difficulties. She answered on first ring.

"I've been up for four hours. I've been waiting for your call."

Conley checked his watch: almost 10 o'clock, the same hour as in Paris. He summarized what Gallagher had told him about the meeting in Boston, including Harry Whitcombe's recusal and abrupt departure on vacation. Across their connection her breathing quickened.

"Withdrew? That doesn't sound like Uncle Harry. What do you mean he withdrew?"

"That's all I know. Art Gallagher said he thinks Janet Larson won't cancel the story, but the emphasis may change…" As soon as the words exited his lips Conley wished he had employed different phrasing.

"Oh God…" Her voice rasped. *"Larson? I've never met her. What do you mean by…'a change in emphasis?' "*

He hesitated. "It's still preliminary, Claire…Nothing definitive."

"Steve, please just tell me."

"Maybe more straight news emphasis. That is, on Peter's original story. And perhaps…somewhat less on the tribute. But I should underline, Claire…" She cut him off.

"Right after this I'm going to call Uncle Harry."

CHAPTER 44

This Saturday morning, like most others in New England in early November, was ideal for walking. Though most foliage had fallen from trees, autumn lingered. Crisp, still air prevailed---a benevolent lull before onset of winter. Welcome outdoor tranquility after indoor stresses at work. Instead Gallagher was struggling to hold the leash. Something had excited the dog.

"Trajan!" Gallagher commanded in a loud voice. "Calm down!"

This name grew out of Gallagher's interest in Roman history.

"What's gotten into him?" Denise asked. "I haven't seen him like this for a while."

They were walking along a quiet, tree-lined street in Belmont, about a mile from their house. Residential, with little traffic. Most yards were wooded and landscaped. Small wildlife were not uncommon. They scanned the yard ahead, expecting to see a rabbit or a squirrel scurrying among the dead leaves. Gallagher noticed red markers for an electronic fence.

"There's another dog there," he said, yanking the leash in frustration. Both Gallagher and Trajan were now panting from exertion.

A few paces further they spotted a tall, lean Collie, previously concealed by bushes. One sight of Trajan and the other dog started yelping. It ran back and forth on a small patch of lawn, kicking up fallen leaves---agitated, though seeming neither aggressive nor frightened. Trajan barked in return, and surged forward with more determination.

"Probably a bitch in heat," Gallagher observed. "Better double back. Let's cut down along the pond."

They reversed direction. He gave the leash several harsh tugs, but Trajan wouldn't relinquish interest, continuing to bark and strain toward the collie. He was glad for his leather gloves, which gave him a firmer grip.

"I thought he was past that sort of thing," Denise said.

"Hardly. In dog years he's only in his 50s."

"Fifties? He's behaving like a randy teenager."

As they retraced the street this struggle continued. Every few paces Trajan lunged the other way. Soon Gallagher broke a sweat. He wanted to unbutton his coat and remove his scarf. But one hand held the leash.

"Dammit, Trajan!" he said, almost growling.

Denise tried speaking to the dog in soothing tones. When that didn't work, she scolded him. At last they rounded down a side street toward a small pond, as yelping from the collie receded. Trajan finally relented, though drool dripped from his mouth and his chest continued to heave. Gallagher also endeavored to catch his breath.

"Thank God humans have more control than that," Denise observed, eyeing the dog. Then she laughed. "Otherwise the world would be in chaos."

"A matter of…degrees, maybe." Gallagher was unable to complete a full sentence without gasping for air.

"I assume you're talking about men."

"Men more than women, I suppose. Luckily most men find… other outlets for that drive…Work, sports…and of course marriage." Gallagher wiped his brow with his handkerchief.

"And if they don't?"

Gallagher made fleeting association with Conley and Tracey Whitcombe in London. Somehow that context seemed different. "A few of our younger, unmarried reporters seem to lead variable romantic lives," he answered. "But not to the point where it disrupts their work." He looked down again at Trajan, now loping obediently alongside. The theme continued to interest Denise.

"Which do you think is more important for a man...as an outlet, I mean. Work or marriage?"

"Hard to say. Both are vital."

"What about Clinton?"

Gallagher laughed. "A rather unique case."

Denise removed a glove from one hand, and reached across and smoothed out her husband's forelocks of gray hair, then encircled his waist with an arm. Her message was unspoken: he was lucky that he'd married her early in life. He didn't doubt she was right. They reached the end of the side street, pond ahead, fronted by a small park with well-kept grass and scattered trees. Several benches stood halfway down to the water. They walked across the grass and sat down on one to rest.

"We'd better keep him on the leash today," he said of Trajan. For now the dog's energy had subsided; he sat alongside the bench, tongue drooping from his mouth. Before them the pond's surface was gray and glass-like. A half-dozen ducks floated on the other side. For Gallagher, it a placid scene after a stormy week. The shooting in Prague...Whitcombe's abdication...He wondered if the publisher was already up in the mountains of New Hampshire.

Denise divined his thoughts. " You still can't figure out what's gotten into Harry Whitcombe, can you?"

"No. Not really."

"And neither can Janet?"

"She seems as mystified as I am."

At once he imagined Larson and Frick huddled together---perhaps in Larson's office at that very moment---analyzing and recasting their strategy. The newsroom was quiet on Saturday morning. Perfect for intrigues. He shook his head and tried to banish the thought.

He and Denise sat in silence for a moment, gazing at the pond. Perspiration under his beard and around his neck evaporated in the dry, calm air. The weather would also be ideal for the BC football game they planned to attend that afternoon. But that was several hours away. "Let's stay here a little longer," he suggested, finding no objection from Denise. He reached into his jacket pocket for his cigarettes and lit one---not even shielding the flame of his lighter because of the calm conditions---and glanced down at Trajan. The dog glanced back, observing his repose, then settled snout onto front paws.

"I should look on the bright side," he said, expelling a plume of smoke toward the sky and watching it dissipate. "I don't expect any new misadventures next week. Moscow should be low-key."

CHAPTER 45

The sanctuary of Notre Dame de Passy was a long way from Boston. And from Moscow. Too distant for material influence. However Claire had come here seeking intervention from higher up.

So far she wasn't getting it.

Eight o'clock mass on Sunday morning, to which she'd gravitated after waking at 5:45 with a tense jolt, drew mostly elderly parishioners. Now she guessed she was the only communicant under fifty, in two lines stretching up center aisle toward the altar. Most were ladies 75 and older, way beyond calls to action. Meanwhile Francois' exhortations had struck her as empty platitudes, handed down from Rome. Church, at least today, was not a place for answers.

She wondered what to do next.

In recent years she'd made only rare appearances at Mass, with her parents. Her excuse had been that Peter was Protestant. Now she clasped her hands in front of her and bowed her head as she shuffled forward along the stone floor. She tried to concentrate. Maybe the act of communion would illuminate some path...

She kneeled along the left railing, second from end. Her hands trembled slightly; she folded them and opted to receive the wafer in her mouth. In her peripheral vision saw Francois---tall and lanky and dressed in his priestly robes--- moving down communicants to her right, administering the sacrament. When he reached her he paused in surprise. A hopeful expression crossed his face as he placed wafer on her lower lip and tongue and pronounced the liturgy. When she stood up with other communicants she felt...exuberant in a way she had never experienced in church before. She sat down again in her pew, straight-backed and gripping the forward edge of her seat with both hands.

An idea exploded in her brain and caused her toes and fingertips to tingle.

Further decisions were centered in Boston. She had to go there, while there was still time.

During Francois' final prayer and benediction, she continued sitting bolt upright, and hardly heard him. Her mind raced...How to organize such an expedition? On what basis? She'd tried calling Uncle Harry the day before but he'd left Cambridge for New Hampshire. His cell phone had been out of range. Francois dismounted the altar and with an assistant priest and two altar boys made slow procession down the aisle. After he'd passed, she was eager to get out. She'd received the inspiration she'd wanted. Now she had to develop the plan and take action.

In the aisle, to her frustration, she got caught behind a gaggle of slow-moving but well-meaning old ladies. When she finally reached the door Francois excused himself from a conversation with a white-haired man and took several steps toward her with his long arms outstretched.

"So happy to see you here, Claire," he said, clasping her above both elbows. He looked curious.

"Yes...I'm glad I came."

"Can you wait 10 minutes? Meet me in the courtyard?"

With reluctance she agreed.

The courtyard was small and lay between the church and the rectory. Trimmed shrubs, and empty flower beds, due to the season, intersected by gravel paths. Secluded from the city around, and partly sheltered from cold, damp wind. There were two stone benches; Claire remained standing. She paced back and forth, her heels grinding and scraping the gravel.

First she had to determine who was most important at the *World Tribune*, now that Uncle Harry had disengaged. She knew Art Gallagher, but not very well. Larson was a big question mark. Would any of them listen to her? What pretext could she manufacture? Questions became jumbled…Maybe if she just got away from church. She glanced at her watch. Already fourteen minutes had passed. Francois was typical *haut bourgeois*. For all his consideration and courtly manners, she remembered, he was often late. She sighed with frustration.

A moment later he rounded the corner, robes billowing. He was full of apologies. He asked if she preferred to talk in the rectory.

"Let's stay here, if you don't mind, Francois. Fresh air does me good."

"I understand." He studied her again. "How have you been?"

"Much better. I think I've found a solution."

He looked in her eyes, his expression growing worried. "Solution?"

In hurried cadences she related recent events in Prague and Boston. And her sudden revelation following Communion. As he listened, Francois crossed his arms and held his chin in one hand, staring down at gravel.

"This didn't come from the *philosophes*, Francois," she told him. "It came during Mass."

"Communion is a sacrament, Claire, an affirmation of faith. It's about forgiveness and redemption, not plans of action. I would be careful."

"The way I see it, I was inspired."

His priestly robes billowed with a slight gust of wind, and he lowered his hands to hold garments in place. "Inspiration is not always divine, Claire. Maybe this idea just came to you by accident."

"I came here for Peter's sake…to find a solution," she said, her eyes flashing with defiance. "God gave it to me."

Francois fell silent for a moment. He exhaled---a sigh almost---then asked, "Will you at least delay awhile before going to Boston? Maybe pray about your decision?"

"Maybe I'll pray for additional inspiration, Francois. But I haven't got time to wait."

CHAPTER 46

The Cold War was long over. Conley had been in middle school when the Berlin Wall came down. Still, certain associations lingered.

One was that the U.S. Embassy in Moscow was a nexus of espionage and intrigue, under constant surveillance by the Russians. A proxy in a dangerous global rivalry. Imbued with high-stakes glamour.

In reality he found a dilapidated building that seemed left behind by history. While a security perimeter kept pedestrians moving and cars from jumping the curb---anti-terrorism measures---there were few indications that the place remained important. Russians waiting for visas---an emblem of the 90s that Conley had seen on television---numbered just a dozen and didn't conform to old stereotypes. Several applicants spoke on cell phones. From heavy traffic on Bolshoi Deviatinsky Prospekt, another materialized out of a chauffeured Mercedes.

Light snow was falling, with temperatures just below freezing. He passed by the Consular entrance and into the Embassy gate. Inside the guardhouse anteroom, he stomped his boots and brushed snowflakes from his overcoat. Up on the fourth floor, American diplomats he passed in the corridor appeared glum and jaded. Open doorways revealed cramped, shabby offices with copious stacks of paper. Except for computers on desktops, the building seemed stuck in 1975. A relic from another era.

Enthusiasm was apparent only among staffers who looked Russian. And from Franklin Stanson, who seemed cut from a different cloth than his American colleagues.

"This is mine," Stanson said, gesturing into a doorway with down-home informality. "Come on in."

His office was bigger than others, with evidence of renovation--- two-toned walls, new furniture, and a double-paned window onto the Prospekt. "I'm a recent arrival," he explained as they sat down, with a vague drawl that evoked the central-southwest---and that some- how sounded to Conley more adopted than inbred. "Part of our new priorities."

Conley already had an idea about those, based on previous phone and e-mail contacts. Stanson's State Department title was "Special Coordinator--Central Asian Security Issues." Despite this lofty title the official was unpretentious. Mid- 40s and moderately overweight. Wire- rimmed aviator glasses. Photographs on a cabinet behind his desk: one of Stanson astride a miniature all-terrain vehicle wearing goggles and surrounded by open scrub-land; another with wife and three kids on a back-yard patio, all big smiles, Stanson holding a barbecue spat- ula. Not at all consonant with the more strait-laced, academic proclivi- ties of the State Department.

He reiterated his condolences over Bradford, which sounded sin- cere, and in fact he had been immensely helpful with scheduling and logistical matters. These included setting up meetings with Russian officials, transport to Dushanbe by Russian military plane and enlist- ment of an interpreter who spoke Russian and Tajik---male this time, to Conley's slight disappointment---named Oleg Mikhailov.

What to make of the cautionary notes sounded by the Russian Ambassador in Washington to Harry Whitcombe? Conley realized he would have to wait and see.

"Any more developments in the case from Dushanbe?" he asked, opening his notepad. He remembered that Bradford had occupied the same chair five weeks earlier, during his interview of Stanson.

"None, I'm sorry to say."

"And the Chechen?"

"Same as last week. Just hot air."

Stanson provided more detail on his role in Moscow and Central Asia. Since the mid-90s the Moscow Embassy had had a FBI representative cooperating with the Russians on law enforcement matters---the Russian mafia at first, then mostly terrorism after September 11th---and a DEA representative working on joint anti-narcotics actions. Both of these concerns loomed larger starting from 2002, when Afghan opium exports re-surged following the U.S. invasion. Hence more intense U.S. cooperation with governments of Tajikistan, Uzbekistan and Turkmenistan on anti-drug initiatives. This was new terrain, Stanson acknowledged. The Russians were not always comfortable with American inroads into former Soviet republics. Stanson was their main U.S. liaison on these issues and attempted to allay concerns.

Conley came to understand that Stanson did not speak Russian.

"I'm new to State," the official explained. This is my first overseas assignment. I came straight off the Vice President's staff. Before that I was in the military."

Was Stanson CIA? Incongruous: based on Conley's assumptions about that crowd. He wasn't the type for ponderous distinctions and shades of gray. Indeed, Stanson spoke with stark conviction about his role. Though nuclear disarmament ground on in obscurity, and joint space missions made an occasional splash, drugs and terrorism now overshadowed other aspects of U.S.-Russian relations. The war on terror was where the action was.

And wars required allies. Ones like Salimjon Shakuri. Conley asked Stanson straight out. Any worries that Shakuri was corrupt?

"None. I know him personally. He's a good man...and always accessible. It helps that he speaks excellent English."

Any new concerns, after what happened to Bradford?

"Absolutely not. As I told Art Gallagher by phone, Shakuri was furious when Bradford got killed. All the more because the killers were his own bodyguards. He caught them immediately. As far as I'm concerned, it was no big loss when they were killed in that prison disturbance."

"Were you satisfied with your own investigation?"

"Yes. When I went down there Salimjon bent over backwards to help me."

Conley's further probes about Shakuri and about the investigation yielded similar answers. Shakuri was above reproach. An ally in the war on terror. What more important measure was there?

There was another one Stanson saw fit to mention.

"As far as Salimjon told me, he and Peter Bradford found a common language, that last evening before Bradford died. That says something, doesn't it?"

CHAPTER 47

The green-yellow ball sailed a half-meter past the baseline, kicking up clay dust upon impact. Veronique reacted with a muted *"Longue,"* trying to be gentle.

"Ras le bol!" Claire muttered cross-court. Club decorum demanded she keep her voice down. Also that she not hurl her racket onto the red-brown playing surface.

Her problem, even after all her recent dislocations, was the same as usual. Plenty of velocity but no control.

They were in the indoor tennis complex on the Quai d'Orsay, just north of the Eiffel Tower. Claire held service: down *Love-30*. She stomped back into position. *Focus…*she told herself…*Positive energy… More topspin.* She took a deep breath, coiled and tossed the ball straight up. *Thwack.* Her serve arced down and sideways into the far corner, just where she intended. Veronique sprinted across the baseline, short white skirt fluttering up around her waist, ball just within reach, managing to stab a backhand.

Due to the original speed of serve, her return came back low and hard; only location was favorable for Claire: down the center. Begging for an aggressive forehand. She planted her feet and wound up… *Topspin…Come over the ball…Thwack.* Her contact unleashed an arcing, spinning buzz-saw that landed five centimeters inside baseline and rocked Veronique on her heels. It came in tight, and she fought it off with a cramped, defensive forehand. A lame floater arced back over the net and bounced high. Perfect for an overhead smash.

Claire surged forward. *No mercy...*She bent her knees, shifted up on her toes and brought her racket back. *Eye on the ball...Eye on the ball...*Veronique's backhand corner beckoned; there was no chance to chase the ball down... Claire's short skirt swirled up over her undergarment...She powered her racquet over and down...*Thwack.* Ball left strings like an air-to-ground missile, producing an instant of exhilaration....

Smack. It hit the tape and dropped straight downward.

She came out of her follow-through and watched in disbelief. The ball took several impotent, faltering bounces along net before stopping dead. A final mockery. *"Absurd!"* Her voice reverberated in cavernous tennis dome. She placed hands on hips and glared.

From cross-court Veronique observed this outburst with an expression of quiet sympathy. Then looked away. On the next point, still roiling with exasperation, Claire sent two serves long. Her double fault ended the match. Final score: 6-2, 6-1, Veronique.

They met at courtside to collect towels and tennis bags, and sat down for a moment. Claire stared forward, still simmering, a towel draped over her bare thighs, while Veronique zipped a cover over her racket head.

"I wouldn't worry about it, Claire. You haven't played for a month."

"It's frustrating. I expected better."

"You're too hard on yourself...especially after all you've been through."

"I guess I'd wanted this to set a tone."

"You mean after Peter?"

"No, for my trip to the U.S."

"Let's go drink some mineral water. You can tell me more about your plans."

They traversed the court area and climbed stairs to an open balcony with a café, where twangs of racquet strings and thuds of balls echoed around them. They sat down at a table that overlooked an expansive collection of courts, and ordered. Veronique wore a look of concern.

"I've already got my ticket," Claire blurted, eager to get her mind off tennis and refocus on her mission. "I'm leaving on Wednesday."

"This is all rather sudden, Claire. You said the idea came to you in church?"

Claire described her revelation just after Communion.

"I went to the later Mass," Veronique said. "Afterward Francois mentioned he had seen you. He seemed worried."

Claire set her jaw. Veronique meant well, but had a subtle way of nudging her away from bold undertakings. This pattern went back to their university years. Veronique and Francois were of the same ilk.

"We talked," she said. "I told him I was confident about what happened."

Veronique's worry appeared to deepen.

"...That afternoon I finally reached Peter's Uncle Harry. He's in New Hampshire now." She described what she knew about Whitcombe's retreat from Boston and his flight north. "He was evasive. Like he'd rather not talk to me."

"Maybe he just needed to recover, after all this stress. It happens."

"No...it's not like him."

"Still, what can you do?"

"I can't sit around here trying to figure it out. There's too much at stake."

Veronique took a deep breath, as if minor catastrophe was taking shape.

"When I hung up," Claire continued. "I was desperate. I didn't know what pretext I could use for going over there. I thought for a while..." She remembered herself panting, alone, at the kitchen table in her apartment. "Then I received another inspiration."

Veronique had to refrain from wincing. "What?"

"Peter's estate. I called him back."

"Peter's uncle is the executor, isn't he?"

"Yes."

Now Veronique listened with a more acute, analytical air. For *l'haute bourgeoisie* this was essential indeed. *Le patrimoine.*

"I told him I also wanted to talk about the estate," Claire recounted. "That I hadn't heard anything in a while."

She recalled his exact words. On his end Whitcombe had paused, as if caught off guard. "He said some complications had arisen...that the settlement was going to take longer than he expected."

"Problems like that aren't uncommon."

"But why would he be evasive? Not just about the estate, but about Steve Conley's assignment?"

Veronique adopted a discreet tone. "Have you familiarized yourself with Peter's estate?"

"There are complicated family trusts. I have some of the documents. The Whitcombe branch was just one side---Peter's mother is Harry Whitcombe's sister. Peter's father came from money also. I still don't understand how it all works."

To this point Veronique had forgotten to sip her Perrier. For Claire the estate was more means than end. She quenched her thirst before continuing.

"I told him I wanted to fly to the States to discuss it. He sounded shocked. He tried to dissuade me."

Veronique was now riveted; both of them were oblivious to tennis action below, despite line calls and ball/racquet contacts. Claire remained keyed up, even while frustrations from their match receded, and pressed on.

"I said, 'I'm coming anyway, Uncle Harry.' He was speechless. He still doesn't know when I'm arriving."

Veronique gave way to astonishment. "What are you going to do when you get there?"

"The first thing I'm going to do is insist upon seeing him. I'll drive to New Hampshire if I have to. Beyond that…" She pursed her lips and shook her head. "…I'm still developing my strategy."

In fact her plan remained vague.

"…Art Gallagher would agree to meet me…out of courtesy. I also want to be introduced to Janet Larson somehow."

Veronique reached across the table and put her hand on Claire's forearm. She'd abandoned any notions of dissuasion. "You're facing so much uncertainty, Claire…I wish I could help." Just then Claire's cell phone chirped from inside her tennis bag, on an empty chair. She yanked open the zipper and rummaged through her gear. Since Sunday she'd been so preoccupied with her pending trip to the U.S. that she'd been absent-minded about other matters…

"Excuse me, Veronique…*Bon sang!* I should have left the phone out." She found the device and answered. Indeed the caller was Conley, wanting to describe his interviews. She said she was keen to hear details, and asked if she could call back in 45 minutes.

"Steve Conley is in Moscow now," she explained, readdressing Veronique and placing the phone down.

"It's nice that he's calling you every day…keeping you informed."

"Thank God for that," Claire said, taking a sip of Perrier with a slight tremble. "When he called yesterday he was in his hotel room, working. I worried that he'd waver…but the shooting didn't affect him. He seems even more eager than ever to bear down…to thrust ahead with the story.

"This week Conley should be fine," she added. "The main question marks are in Boston."

CHAPTER 48

After Stanson, Conley had done two more interviews at the U.S. Embassy, with representatives of the DEA and Department of Justice. Now he held a slip of paper that contained two addresses: printed in Russian with English alliterations. The first was for a bookstore next to the Frunzenskaya Metro station. The second was for the Luzhniki market, on the southern edge of city center.

"I recommend one of those Russian fur hats," Stanson had told him at the end of their interview, in his informal, self-assured twang. "In this cold weather, I swear by them."

Even with Latin characters the names were long and difficult to pronounce. Conley showed the taxi driver, who nodded and eased onto the Prospekt. Light snow was still falling.

The driver, a rugged man of late middle age, spoke little English. "From what country?" he asked in a thick accent, glancing in rear view mirror.

"The U.S."

"America?"

"That's right."

Conversation stopped; the driver was a stoical type. On the dashboard Conley noticed a small photograph---an anonymous, well-endowed, blonde model---wearing a bikini. A universal little icon...free of language barriers.

He didn't expect the same at the marketplace. This despite Stanson's declaration that English sufficed---"the traders understand numbers, and that's enough."

After navigating through dense traffic, the taxi pulled up to a curbside where snow was piled a half-meter high. "*Vuot*," the driver said, pointing at a block-like, multi-story building. There was a large sign in block Cyrillic letters, beginning with a "K." Window displays identified the ground floor as a bookstore. The driver agreed to wait, and Conley climbed out and scrambled over the snow bank. In a series of four double doors, only one was open---the rest locked. People in their late teens and early twenties squeezed in and out in steady streams. He guessed there was a university nearby.

Inside was a long, single high-ceilinged hall, parallel to the street. Packed with students. Stiflingly warm, in contrast to the frigid temperatures outside. Information signs all in Russian. He wandered to his right, dodging students and scanning shelves for Latin characters or sections that looked like language reference, and stopped a passing clerk.

"Where can I find English-Russian dictionaries?"

The girl pointed toward a far corner.

Conley located the shelf and selected a dictionary that was pocket size. At the closest service counter and pulled out his wallet to make the purchase. Instead, an attendant pointed to a cash register booth about 10 meters away. There an older woman sat, in an elevated position above the floor.

"I don't understand..."

From his right came a youthful female voice: English with a Russian accent: "I'll help you, if you like."

Conley turned. Next to an adjacent bookshelf, with open book in hand, stood a tall, slender girl, about 20. Her eyes were a startling green gray; when they connected with his he swallowed hard. Eye color aside, she bore an exceptional likeness to Tracey Whitcombe. The girl took a couple of steps closer, at once assertive and shy. "You have to pay there," she said, gesturing toward the cashier's booth. "Then you bring the receipt back here and pick up the book."

Conley was still orienting himself. "It's my first time in Russia."

"I'll go with you to the cashier," she volunteered.

There was a line of several purchasers at the booth. The girl stood next to Conley, quiet and self-conscious. He observed her more closely. Same high cheekbones as Tracey. Same straight, red-chestnut hair parted in the middle. Tracey's eyes were blue and her skin probably got more sun, but otherwise...a Russian facsimile of Tracey.

"Do you like it here?" the girl asked, with polite shyness that differed from Tracey's only in accent. Her grammar was fluent. Conley told her about his limited foray into Red Square the day before. It had been cold. After he paid she walked back with him toward the service desk.

"Why do you need a dictionary?" she asked. "Don't you have an interpreter?"

"Not today. He starts tomorrow."

At the service desk he exchanged the receipt for the dictionary, while the girl appeared to consider the situation.

"Are you doing some shopping?" she asked.

"In fact I'm going to buy one of those Russian fur hats."

"Really? A *chapka*? Where?"

Conley pulled out his slip of paper and showed her the name of the market.

"That's a 20-25 minute walk. Do you know how to get there?"

"I have a taxi waiting outside."

"You could have trouble. Not many sellers there speak English."

She looked at him, waiting. Tracey's improbable beauty, minus career-decimating complications. A quirk...Just the corrective to Claire that he still needed...

"My name is Steve," he said.

"Mine is Lilya."

CHAPTER 49

Oleg Mikhailov walked out of the Interior Ministry onto Zhitnaya Street in a state of extreme disillusion. Conley couldn't understand why.

They'd just interviewed the Deputy Interior Minister in charge of drug enforcement---a lean, modern-thinking official named Sergei Zhukov. Zhukov was unlike sclerotic and blindered Soviet *apparatchiks* of yesteryear, or self-enriching cronies of Yeltsin's era. One of Putin's disciplined, westernizing breed. Part of a new Russia on the move.

"These problems are destroying us," Oleg said.

"Really?" Conley answered, donning his new fur hat. "Zhukov seems to have a logical strategy in place."

"Logical? How can it be? Heroin addiction is growing fast."

"It's still lower here than in Europe."

Oleg snorted, unimpressed. They moved along a wide sidewalk toward Gorky Park. Grim-faced pedestrians around them were bundled with heavy overcoats and fur hats. Snowfall had stopped, though temperatures had plunged to minus 12 Celsius.

His accent in English was negligible. His only grammatical weakness, if there was one, was an excess of idioms. "They sing a good tune," he continued, adjusting his scarf against a bone-chilling gust. "But it's still just boilerplate. It's just more polished than it used to be."

In his view, heroin was emblematic of the corrupt deluge that arrived from the West since the fall of the USSR. This surprised Conley somewhat. Oleg was only 32, little older than Conley himself. Minimal baggage from Soviet times, Conley would have thought. Ample youth for fresh perspectives.

"Our country is a mess," the Russian added, in a hopeless tone.

Conley glanced around as they approached a large square. Renovated buildings, fancy new shops, expensive German cars. On his way in from the airport, on the city's outskirts, he had seen perhaps two dozen new luxury high-rise apartment buildings. Indications were everywhere: Moscow was booming.

Oleg divined his ruminations.

"Don't let Moscow fool you. You haven't been to our villages."

"Less improvement there?"

"Improvement? Conditions are worse than in Soviet times."

Conley noted that heroin was primarily a big-city problem. Villages were little affected, according to Zhukov. To which Oleg responded with a faint grimace.

"Westerners can't understand our situation. Russia will never be normal by your standards."

Hard-pressed to advance the optimistic case, Conley dropped the subject. He'd been in Russian just a few days.

Otherwise Oleg had already proven himself a capable interpreter. Reserved and focused. Of medium height and build, dark hair. Married, Conley had learned, with a seven-year-old son. Nondescript except for intense, light-blue eyes that belied his intelligence. It was easy to suppose that he'd been a diligent, serious-minded student.

A towering statue of Lenin dominated the square. Fighting a gust of wind, Conley asked about Oleg's view of the Communist leader.

"An important figure in our history, for better or worse. We're still affected by the course he chose."

On that score Conley agreed.

At the entrance to Gorky Park there was a small flower market: a half dozen stands in the open air. Sellers were all elderly women: bundled in multiple layers of clothing, and thick, felt-lined boots. Conley marveled at their ability to stand outdoors for long periods in such frigid temperatures. Transferring his leather case to his shoulder, he straightened his new hat, made of beaver. Its warmth was remarkable. Lilya had taught him the Russian word.

"These *chapki* are superb."

A little surprised by Conley's use of Russian, Oleg turned and scrutinized the acquisition "That's not a bad one," he said. "Where did you buy it? Your hotel?"

There were a couple of luxury clothing shops in the lobby of the Radisson, which Conley had visited briefly on Sunday. Prices were outrageous. "No. Luzhniki market, near the Olympic stadium. Franklin Stanson told me about it."

"And you went down there by yourself?"

"No."

Conley encapsulated his acquaintance at the bookstore with Lilya, and their subsequent foray to the market. At first Oleg frowned. Then his face gave way to a sardonic smile.

"A familiar story," he said. "You're not married, are you?"

"No."

"Are you seeing her again?"

"Yes. Don't leap to conclusions, though."

CHAPTER 50

Gallagher, Larson and Frick had convened for breakfast at the Harborside Hyatt at Logan Airport. Tall windows faced west across water. Sunrise glistened on the skyscrapers of downtown Boston.

Both the setting and early hour were unusual. Gallagher was growing unaccustomed to departures from habit; Conley's assignment had that effect. Larson was bound for a one-day national conference of editors-in-chief in Chicago; her flight left in an hour. In these conditions, she'd concluded that one workday was long to be absent from the newsroom. Moreover Moscow was eight hours ahead of East Coast time.

"I see no reason to alter Harry's main parameters," she said, taking a sip of orange juice.

"Meaning Conley should continue on to Tajikistan?" Gallagher asked.

"Yes."

"And the advertising campaign?" He raised a forkful of scrambled eggs from his plate.

"It should go ahead as planned."

In addition to eggs Gallagher's breakfast consisted of plump sausages that oozed cholesterol, and a stack of toast soaked in butter.

Larson and Frick ministered over sliced cantaloupe and melon. Their only beverage was juice. Gallagher bit off some toast, took a gulp of coffee and girded himself. He was expecting another ambush.

"Art, what new steps have you taken to ensure Conley's safety... since we talked about it with Harry?"

"There are no significant dangers this week in Moscow, thank goodness. So we've been reviewing plans for Tajikistan."

He sensed Frick tensing next to him.

"I'm glad to hear that...But I'm afraid to note that the results so far have been worrisome. The shooting in Prague was a wake-up call." Larson paused, a cube of cantaloupe suspended on her fork. "If I may say so, Art, I think you need some help on this."

"Help? No one's been more vocal about safety than I've been..."

Larson held up the palm of her free hand, implying that she hadn't finished.

"I don't really fault you, Art. You're a newsman, through and through. But first Peter Bradford, and now Conley...we can't place reporters in harm's way in our single-minded pursuit of big stories. Perhaps I should have stepped in earlier..." She finally placed the cube of cantaloupe in her mouth. After chewing and swallowing she resumed. "Moreover Harry was right about Tajikistan. All sorts of new complexities we didn't appreciate. I've had to consider those as well."

Frick's head was down. He was slicing one of his cubes into two smaller pieces.

"Until now Nathan has been an observer," Larson continued. "Now I'm assigning him a more active role. He's to advise you day to day on safety issues with Conley."

Gallagher put down his knife and fork. "Advise me, Janet? Is that really necessary?"

"I think it's best. None of us wants more mishaps."

Gallagher snorted and glanced out the plate-glass window. At a nearby marina only a few pleasure craft and sailboats remained at their moorings. Others had been dry-docked for the winter. Retirement suddenly beckoned...

"I'll do my best to help, Art," Frick added, his tone a little snide.

He gave Frick an irritated glance, picked up his knife and fork and stabbed at a piece of sausage. Then he remembered Conley and Claire and swallowed hard. For their sake, if nothing else, he'd have to see this through.

CHAPTER 51

Claire had visited New Hampshire before. While living in Boston she and Peter had escaped north for ski weekends at Loon or Waterville Valley. Once in summer they'd hiked the White Mountain National Forest.

On this occasion, at 6:45 a.m. she departed the Logan Harborside Hyatt in her rental car---a Ford Taurus. Despite early rush-hour bottle-necks on Route 3 North reached the Massachusetts-New Hampshire border one hour later. Her plan was to stop in Nashua for breakfast. Previously she and Peter had only exited there for gas. As she turned left onto Nashua's Main Street she raised her left foot and reached toward the stick shift. Her foot kicked into a void and her hand grabbed air, due to her habituation to manual transmissions.

"*Zut!*" she said.

Perhaps she just needed coffee. She hadn't slept well, thanks to time zone change and nerves. Again she wondered if she was going too far, chasing down Uncle Harry at his ski lodge. Until she reminded herself of her mission, on behalf of Peter.

To the dead we owe only the truth.

At City Hall she switched to the right lane and scanned for res-taurants. Main Street was lined with trees and clean brick sidewalks.

Architecture dated from turn of the century: storefronts, restaurants, banks and churches. A breakfast place came up on her left---a greasy spoon: not the croissant and coffee category she had in mind. Then two more trendy-looking restaurants on her right...but which just offered lunch and dinner. Several blocks ahead, at what appeared to the last major intersection, she spotted another eggs-and-bacon place: *Central Diner.* She pulled to the curb and parked.

Next to her on passenger seat lay several folders of documents: Peter's will and trust materials, which she'd brought from Paris. She'd spent much of her flight from Paris to Boston reviewing these, and found them tedious and incomprehensible, due in part to the legalistic English. She considered bringing them to breakfast, but left them behind.

The estate was a means, not an end. Over breakfast she would focus on more important questions.

Outside air was colder than in Boston: temperatures around freezing, although still without snow cover. While locking up she noticed a parking meter. *"Bon sang!"* she said, fumbling inside her purse. She didn't have U.S. change.

Closer inspection revealed that charges didn't apply until 8 a.m. She checked her watch: 7:41---probably enough time. She turned heel and strode toward the restaurant, heels snapping on the bricks. When she entered the diner a small bell rang. Faces glanced in her direction: mostly male. A few did double takes and watched her as she seated herself on a stool at one of the two horseshoe-shaped counters. A young waitress approached. "Coffee?" she asked.

"Yes. And a menu too, please."

The waitress caught her accent and looked curious.

Claire looked around and found other glances, before eyes got re-directed. Clientele was a cross-section: several business or lawyer types in shirts and ties, a half-dozen others dressed for more rugged outdoor work, several white-haired retirees in cardigans.

Hadn't they encountered a foreigner before? Or was it her dark gray suit ensemble and pearls? She tried not to get irritated. Her first sip of coffee almost made her wince. At once bland and bitter. She added cream. The waitress re-materialized and took her order: blueberry muffin and a bowl of fruit.

Her encounter with Harry Whitcombe would be in a couple of hours. She had to concentrate…She'd start with the estate…Just general questions about the trusts…Later, perhaps over lunch, she'd displace that with Conley's assignment…

"Here you are," the waitress said, placing down muffin and fruit and interrupting her train of thought. "More coffee?"

Claire's mug was only half-empty. She had forgotten about this practice, which didn't exist in Parisian cafes.

"Please," she said.

The waitress paused a beat. "Where are you from, if I may ask?"

"France. Just arrived yesterday."

"We had a couple of people in here from Europe last summer… German backpackers."

Other patrons had stopped talking and were listening.

Claire was at a loss. "New Hampshire is good for that," she said finally.

"Where in France are you from? Paris?"

"Yes, as a matter of fact."

"That's interesting…welcome to Nashua."

The waitress considered another question, but gave her a half-smile and returned to other duties. A few patrons stood to pay bills. Attention waned. Workdays beckoned. Just as Claire finished her muffin and fruit her phone rang in her purse. It was Conley.

"I just got out of an interview…at the Defense Ministry. I received your voice message and your new cell phone number."

On the other end of the connection there was a lot of background noise, as through Conley was calling from a car or taxi.

"Where are you now? Am I reaching you at a convenient time?"

"I'm in Nashua, NH…just finishing breakfast."

"Nashua?"

"Oh no…" Through plate glass at the front of the diner Claire spotted a meter maid, moving up the line of cars parked at the curb, pad of tickets in hand and already eyeing her rental car. She checked her watch: 8:05. "Steve, something's come up," she said, determined to avoid a fine. "Can I call you back in a couple of hours?"

Before he had a chance to say goodbye, she stood from her stool, and reached into her purse and asked the waitress for change for a dollar, her French accent amplified by the rush.

The girl understood what was happening and scurried to the cash register. In seconds she came over with four quarters. Striding out, Claire realized she was right behind her, and appeared to know the meter-maid. When they emerged onto brick sidewalk the latter was examining the license plate and flipping to a blank ticket.

"Wait, Debbie…she's French," the waitress proclaimed, as if that warranted blanket pardon. "And she just got here."

CHAPTER 52

The FSB press official was a lean, urbane man about Conley's age. Well-cut suit and English with a Continental accent. Another example of Putin's new breed. When he spoke about Movsar Felayev, however, his eyes became unmerciful and hard.

"We've had him for almost two months now," he said. "We've employed various methods to get him to talk."

Franklin Stanson had prepared Conley, in his Rocky Mountain drawl: "Terrorism and drugs are extreme problems. They require extreme measures."

The press official conducted Conley and Oleg along a subterranean corridor of Lubyanka, the infamous building on Derzhinsky Square that once housed the Soviet KGB. Its reputation was now more benign. Though that perhaps was a matter of degrees. A they reached a heavy steel door, Conley noticed Oleg's face was set harder than usual. From the other side, a young guard with a blond buzz cut slid open a window hatch, then unbolted the barrier. The press official ushered them into a windowless room, with concrete walls, about five meters by five meters. Rugged wire mesh split it in two. In the other half was another single, steel door. On Conley's side there were three chairs.

"Let's sit down," the official suggested. "The prisoner will be here in a few minutes."

The young guard remained standing at attention against the wall.

"I want to underline," the official said. "We think Felayev is lying about Bradford. But we thought you should hear him first-hand."

Conley nodded and pulled out his notepad. "Why would he make say such things in the first place?" he asked.

The official's face was impassive, his tone scornful. "He thinks he'll gain leverage. Or a respite. Typical mindset of a terrorist. He believes he can dictate the game. Just like the group that took over *Nord Ost*."

The episode in question occurred in October 2002. About 40 Chechen terrorists took over a theater complex and held more than 700 attendees hostage. After two days of standoff, elite *Spetznatz* forces gassed the building with a powerful knockout agent, stormed it, and dispatched the hostage-takers who were still conscious with automatic weapons, all in under 30 seconds. Most theatergoers were saved, although 120 died from effects of the gas.

On the basis of that response and others, Conley knew the Russians would not make accommodation. Now he asked a question he had already posed in his interview at the Interior Ministry on Tuesday: whether Felayev more terrorist or heroin smuggler. The official didn't equivocate.

"In Chechnya roles of 'warlord' and 'drug lord', as you call them, are intertwined. You can't separate them. Among other offenses, for example, Felayev was involved in a plot last year to explode a bomb at the main McDonald's in Moscow."

This McDonald's was not far from the U.S. Embassy and the Radisson. Conley had already eaten there once. It was crowded and popular.

Opposite, a bolt clanged and the steel door swung open. Two, massively built young guards escorted Felayev into the room, handcuffed. The Chechen was about 45 years old: dark, swarthy and bearded. Other features stood out, though. One eye was almost swollen shut. In the midst of a tangled beard, Felayev's lips were cracked and bloodied. A few teeth appeared to be missing. He shuffled along the concrete floor in bare feet, gaunt and pale. Conley glanced at Oleg and the official. Their reactions were the same: cold contempt.

The Russian guards maneuvered the Chechen in front of a chair, and forced him down. The Chechen focused his gaze through the wire screen. His dark eyes were hollow, but anger boiled up and flared in his pupils. He spat at Conley in Russian.

"He says you're a...lackey," Oleg said.

"A lackey of whom?"

"Of the Russian government."

Conley stated that he worked for a U.S. newspaper, and had no association with the Russian government. In Felayev this provoked curled lips, and another insult, translated by Oleg:

"He says America and Russia are now one pack of infidel dogs."

Felayev leaned forward in his chair, snarling. His handlers slammed him rearward, causing his face to contort in pain. Soon he recovered his glower.

"Do Chechens dominate the movement of heroin into and through Russia?" Conley asked him.

From within his tangled beard the Chechen responded with a twisted smile.

"Here's your chance to explain yourself to an audience in the West," Conley added.

The Chechen snorted a response.

"He said Peter Bradford asked him the same question a month ago," Oleg translated.

"And what did you tell him?"

Oleg winced before translating.

"He told him it was none of his business...and that Bradford deserved to die for asking him such a question."

The press official sitting next to Conley shook his head, repulsed, and issued an instruction. One of the guards swiped a massive backhand blow. When Felayev straightened, blood trickled out of one side of his mouth.

"Can he communicate with the outside?" Conley asked.

"He does have a lawyer, who visits once a week. Part of our legal reforms."

"So it's possible he ordered Bradford's killing?"

"Possible, though very unlikely. We listen in on all his conversations with the lawyer."

Blood now formed a rivulet that dripped down Felayev's beard and plopped down onto his striped prison tunic. Without prompting, he barked his next pronouncement in guttural English.

"We'll kill you, too..."

The official considered this for a few brief seconds then issued another curt instruction. The guards hauled the Chechen to his feet and hustled him toward the door. Before Felayev disappeared he struggled to look back over his shoulder at Conley, and made a final exclamation in Russian. The door closed with clang before Oleg translated:

"He said they'll find you in your hotel this week."

Conley was a little concerned. He glanced at the official.

"I wouldn't worry. We'll make sure he remains incommunicado. A least until you leave Moscow."

The three of them stood to go; the young guard let them out. As they retraced the long corridor, Conley asked the official when the Chechen was going to trial.

"In a month and a half. We'll have to lighten up on him before he appears in public. But not for a few more weeks." Both the official and Oleg remained stern. It wasn't meant as a joke. The official saw them off. Outside on the square, a light snow was falling. Conley turned to Oleg.

"With a figure like Felayev, to be honest, I can't say I disapprove of such measures."

"I would imagine the same happens at your base at Guantanamo," Oleg answered.

"Guantanamo? That reminds me...I promised to call Franklin Stanson, to tell him what happened."

CHAPTER 53

Mid-November is off-season in Northern New Hampshire, Claire remembered. Vibrant reds and oranges have disappeared from mountainsides. Foliage-seeking tourists have gone. Skiers have not yet arrived. Vistas are stark, dominated by bare branches and granite bluffs.

Interstate 93 was almost empty as she now cruised north. The freeway consisted of two lanes on each side---northbound and southbound---separated by a wide median strip of trees and rock formations. She swept forward on long, banked curves, no cars ahead or behind, gaining new sight lines around each bend. Skies were gray but clear. Peaks of the White Mountain Range were low at first, then grew larger. At the exit for Waterville Valley, where she'd skied once with Peter for a weekend, memories resurfaced…Laughter on the chair lift…Hot chocolate in the base lodge…A violent tumble trying to keep up with him on an expert trail…

With a gasp she looked at the dashboard clock. She'd promised to call Conley 15 minutes earlier. She cursed and grabbed her cell phone from the passenger seat, and hit the speed-dial number she'd programmed. It beeped; the display read: "Out of range--Cannot complete call."

"Incroyable!" she shouted, gripping the wheel.

For distraction she turned on the radio. It was tuned to a rap/
hip-hop station. Raw, pounding beats. Male vocalists. Energized, she
cranked it up.

Ride or die...Double R what...Better keep your hammer right by your side...

A female artist answered, with tough, inner-city inflections:

I'm a savage bitch...Ain't nobody getting close to this...

Claire swayed at the wheel and rocked her head. She was in the
States, free of Paris' stilted confines...from *la prudence* of Veronique
and Francois. On the road and taking initiative. This was just the sort
of empowering anthem she needed.

Plus I'm a purebred baby. I don't fuck with mutts...

She kept the station on; other tough, pulsating riffs followed as
neared deep valleys of Franconia Notch. Peaks soared higher. At
Lincoln she curved onto an off-ramp. Lincoln's main drag was how
she remembered it: shopping plazas with skiing and hiking stores, restaurants and condo complexes. On her left she noticed a restaurant
where she and Peter had often dined during their weekend getaways
at Loon, on several occasions with Harry and Elizabeth Whitcombe.

When she turned into the entrance for the mountain bare ski trails
came into view: all brown grass and rocks. Chair lifts snaked up slopes,
listless and empty. Atop a pylon near the gondola base station, two
ski-area employees performed repairs. Otherwise there were no souls to
be seen. She took a left and wound up an incline by the Mountain Club
Hotel. Several more upward bends brought her to Whitcombe's lodge,
which was set back from the road through a swath of forest. Twigs and
dead leaves crackled under her tires as she turned into the driveway.

This encounter would require tact. Underneath, though, she
would stay determined.

I'm a savage bitch...

The lodge was modern, two-and-a-half stories high and paneled in
red-brown cedar: one of the larger houses on the mountain, though
not ostentatious. A ski trail ran nearby, also obscured by forest. Over

low treetops on the down-slope, there were commanding views toward the base lodge and across the valley.

From double front doors Whitcombe emerged wearing corduroy slacks and a fleece pullover, and embraced her when she got out. Without reserve, but minus his usual outdoorsman's glow. Depleted. Just as he had sounded on the telephone.

Claire still couldn't identify what had gotten into him. She was determined to find out.

Minutes later they were at a large cedar table in the atrium living/dining area, vaulted with exposed beams. Sliding doors and plate glass windows displayed the panorama across the valley. Whitcombe poured two mugs of coffee. Her hand trembled with adrenaline as she raised her mug. Hip-hop beats still echoed in her head. She just had to stick to her plan.

"Uncle Harry...I hope I'm not out of line coming up here."

"You're family, Claire. You're always welcome. You know that."

"It's just...there were certain things I wanted to talk about right away."

He studied her with tired eyes. "Estate matters, you said."

"That's right."

"I'm happy to answer general questions, Claire. But as I told you on the telephone, I don't have all the materials here with me."

"That's okay. I've got trust documents in the car."

She moved to get up, but Whitcombe raised his palm, his long fingers outstretched.

"I suggest we at least finish our coffee."

"Okay."

He studied her again, new apprehension in his eyes.

"Claire, has something in particular got you worried?"

"Well..." she said, her voice quivering. "...I don't really understand some of the trusts...They're all so legalistic..." In an instant she decided her ruse was pointless. Her shoulders sagged. "I admit, Uncle Harry. I really came here about the newspaper stories."

"You mean Steve Conley's assignment?"

She nodded.

"What, exactly?"

"I've worried about where this whole project is going...that it's not going that well. And might even be abandoned."

"Don't worry. That probably won't happen."

"Probably...? What does that mean?"

"I mean it's largely out of my control."

Claire felt herself start to hyperventilate, and managed to check herself. "I'm sorry, Uncle Harry...I don't understand what's going on."

"There are extra hiking boots and sportswear here, Claire. I suggest we take a hike. Better to explain in the fresh air."

CHAPTER 54

They'd marched up North Peak for almost an hour. Loon's mid-mountain lodge came into view: two-stories with dark wood siding. Whitcombe crossed a small side deck and tugged a door handle. "Locked," he said. He cupped his gloved hands and peered inside. "No one here."

Through an adjacent picture window Claire glimpsed silhouettes of stacked tables and chairs. During ski season she'd stopped there with Peter… Stomping snow from ski boots on a grate at the door. Pulling off hats, goggles and mittens. Flexing stiff toes. Collecting bowls of hot chili in the cafeteria line. Happier times, not long ago.

These flashbacks bolstered her resolve. Her efforts, she reminded herself, were on his behalf.

She and Whitcombe gazed further up. Near the summit, an employee of the mountain climbed down from a lift pylon and packed his tools. He was a long distance away and his figure was very small.

"Would you like to keep climbing, Claire?"

She had traversed six time zones and slept little the night before. Nonetheless her adrenaline was pumping. "Fine with me."

"Those are expert trails. A lot steeper."

"I'm ready."

They set off across a gentle incline that fronted the lodge, matted with brown grass. Gradients soon became more demanding, and ten minutes later they attained the lower portion of the peak's main expert trail. Ascent became sharper. Cables and empty chairs dangled inert on their right. Rocks required them to concentrate on their footing.

"Those boots fit okay?" Whitcombe asked. They were Elizabeth's.

"A little big. But I'll manage."

Keeping pace with his long strides was a challenge. Claire panted a little, determined not to lag behind. Beside her Whitcombe began breathing in deep rhythm, like an endurance athlete. Exercise seemed to liberate him, to quell his demons. They hadn't discussed Conley's assignment since they'd left the house.

"We'll talk on the way down," he had declared. "Easier that way."

A hundred yards up-trail Claire's turtleneck collar became damp. She pulled off her knit cap and stuffed it in her jacket pocket. There were first indications of snowfall. Several flakes fluttered onto her forehead and eyelids.

Whitcombe noticed her glancing at the sky, which was a darker gray than before.

"Just the kind of dusting we get here in November," he said. "Nothing to worry about."

There was also no wind. And Claire had more pressing concerns. They continued their upward march, sometimes zigzagging in favor of better terrain. Her thighs started to burn, increasing her need for oxygen. Nevertheless she tried to moderate her panting. To her this climb had become a measure of will.

And she wouldn't relent until she was satisfied.

"Remember that part of the trail…?" Whitcombe said, pointing to the right and parsing his speech to accommodate his breathing. "… Where the mogul field is…during winter?"

Claire glanced there through the sparse snowflakes. An image of Peter in mogul mode came back: knees together, back loose, shoulders square down the fall line---precise, as with everything he did. She fixed her gaze forward again and drew a knit glove across her fore-head to wipe away perspiration.

In places, snowflakes were now sticking to the brown grass.

"Heavier...than I expected," Whitcombe acknowledged, not break-ing stride. He glanced over his shoulder; she put on a strong face.

To the dead we owe only the truth...

"Just to the...traverse...up there," he said. "...Then we'll head back."

Five minutes later they propelled themselves up onto a strip of level ground: a narrow lateral route carved into the mountain to allow skiers to cross between different slopes. They stopped. Whitcombe put his hands on his knees for before standing up to his full, angular height. He tilted his face skyward and allowed some of the flakes to strike more directly, as if relishing an instant of escape. His gray fore-lock poked out from under his cap.

Escape from what, Claire wondered? She faced him, hands on her hips, standing straight.

Up the trail near the peak, she noticed that heavier snowfall made the upper pylons less distinct. Still she made out that the workman was gone, having descended by another route. In any event she didn't care about such side items. She couldn't wait any longer.

"What's changed, Uncle Harry?"

This broke his aura of liberation. He stared down at brown grass before he spoke.

"Claire, did Peter talk to you about the U.S. aid bill? For Tajikistan?"

"A little bit."

"The one now under consideration by Congress?"

She nodded.

"There's a lot of money involved. A half-billion dollars, to be exact."

"Money? Are you saying money had something to do with Peter's death?"

"Claire, let me put it this way. Tajikistan involves more than just heroin."

Claire thrust her hands in her jacket pockets: part angry and part befuddled. In careful, patient tones, Whitcombe recounted what he'd learned from the Russian ambassador about corruption in the Tajik government.

"But Peter knew about that…He talked about it with me."

Whitcombe winced and shook his head, snowflakes fluttering around him.

"What are trying to tell me, Uncle Harry?"

"That this has gotten very complex, Claire."

"Okay… it's complex. My question is…what does that mean for Conley's assignment?"

"It means that commemorating Peter…may not be the main objective any more."

Claire's hand trembled as she brushed a snowflake from her eyelid. "Are you saying there won't be a tribute, Uncle Harry?"

"I didn't say that. I'm just saying I could no longer be objective about it. That's why I've had to take a step back."

"So you're leaving it all to Janet Larson and Art Gallagher? They'll decide how to remember Peter?"

His burdens appeared suddenly heavier. Why such torment? The aid bill? Pressures from Washington? To her there was still some element missing…

"I'm sorry, Claire," he answered. "For one thing, another reporter is now involved…it's a matter of safety."

They stood in silence for a moment. Snowflakes became denser around them, obscuring vistas through a filter of whiteness. Claire tried to assimilate what he had told her. He was withholding something; of that much she was sure.

"Better head back, Claire. Would you prefer to take this traverse around to an intermediate trail? Inclines are easier."

"Whichever way is faster."

As they stepped over onto the down-slope she was already thinking ahead to Boston.

CHAPTER 55

So far this evening Lilya had been polite and companionable. But she'd kept her distance. She was more like Tracey Whitcombe than Conley had realized. Which meant that his week in Moscow was shaping up fine---apart from the threat from Felayev. Just not the free-wheeling release he'd fantasized about.

After dinner they found themselves in the *Chekhovskaya* Metro Station.

"Here, I'll help you buy tokens," she suggested.

He gave her some rubles, and she detoured to the cashier before they passed through turnstiles and stepped onto a descending escalator. It was the longest he'd ever seen; it traveled deep below ground. When they reached the platform, he observed marble and chandeliers---a far cry from the gritty "T" in Boston. Wall murals depicted outsized, heroic figures striving toward a glorious socialist future. Moscow's metro dated from the 1930s, he'd read, with construction overseen by several of Stalin's henchmen. He'd also gathered that Soviet authorities had intended stations to double as bomb shelters, even before the war. He asked Lilya if that was true.

"I don't know for sure. That's what they say."

When a train came they stood in the aisle and held handrails. Crowding by other passengers compelled her to move closer, and she brushed against him as the car swayed. The inadvertency of the contact kept him from overreacting. During dinner he'd learned more about her: third-year journalism student at Moscow State University, the elder of two sisters. Parents both university professors: father in Physics and mother in English. Academia, though, was not the first milieu she brought to mind. More like elite runways and fashion monthlies, like Tracey...

They disembarked at *Universitet* station, also deep underground, and ascended a long escalator. Outside, he re-donned his beaver *chapka*. Weather remained below freezing, but stars were visible across the night sky. Minutes later they were walking on a well-lighted, tree-lined street dominated by student dormitories. Most windows were illuminated. Accumulated snow had a muffling, peaceful effect. Although cars were parked at curbside, there was no traffic. Snow squeaked under their boots. Lilya pointed down a side street.

"My apartment building is just down there. But first I want to show you something."

The Stalinist-Gothic spire of the Moscow State University's main building loomed on their left. They crossed an expansive plaza, snow-covered and deserted, then drew to a stop and placed their hands on a stone balustrade. A twinkling panorama of Moscow unfolded below them, and she pointed out landmarks: the Kremlin, the Church of Christ the Savior and the Russian White House.

"And that's Luzhniki Stadium," indicating the nearest point across the river, where the Moskva River bent in a half-loop. "The market we visited is just beyond that."

Stadium grounds were snow-covered and empty.

Conley had an impulse to draw closer and put his arm around her. However Lilya positioned herself elbows-out against the balustrade. He knew not to go further.

"When are you leaving?" she asked.

"Friday morning, early. Six-thirty flight."

"I'd like to invite you to a ballet at the Bolshoi Thursday evening... if you can come. Swan Lake."

He agreed, and after gazing a moment more at the panorama, she took a prudent step away. It was time to walk her home.

Notions of release which he'd entertained earlier, he recognized, were just fantasy. Maybe that was for the better.

CHAPTER 56

Whitcombe drank only in evening and held his alcohol well. Still Claire remembered that his self-containment could melt somewhat before a fireplace, cognac in hand. This evening that hadn't happened yet. Perhaps because he was only halfway through his first snifter. Or was it because he was worried about her intentions with Gallagher?

"I'm glad you agreed to stay for the night," he said from his leather armchair.

"Well, it was snowing."

Snowfall had stopped in mid-afternoon. More important had been Gallagher's inability to see her until two o'clock the next day. She was still unsure about Larson. For now she'd settled into one of five bedrooms---that usually utilized by Tracey. She planned an early breakfast and a 7:30 departure. In preparation she'd already brushed the snow-coat from her rental car.

The stone fireplace and hearth were large---half of one wall in Whitcombe's atrium living room. Big enough to accommodate roaring blazes like the one he'd built after dinner. She sat at one end of a long sofa, facing the hearth and nursing a small apéritif. There was a sudden burst of crackling and sputtering.

"This wood isn't seasoned enough," he complained.

"It's not quite winter yet."

With a heavy air he re-crossed his long legs and stared into the red-brown hues of his cognac. By degrees his real worry came to the fore.

"I hope you don't try to pressure them, Claire."

"Art Gallagher and Janet Larson?"

He nodded.

"No...No. Of course not."

He observed her, clearly skeptical, then re-scrutinized the fire.

"I really should have listened to Art from the beginning," he said. "His was the voice of moderation."

She listened closely.

"Art was right about the dangers," he continued. "We just threw Conley out there. It was reckless."

"Does that mean you regret the whole thing?"

Instead of answering he tilted his head back and drained the remainder of his snifter with one swallow, causing his Adam's apple to rise and fall within his turtleneck collar. After the liquid traveled down full he rose and walked to the bar cabinet.

"More Amaretto?"

"No, thank you."

Claire didn't want her mind dulled by alcohol. Parameters were now clearer. Also what she had to do. Intercede with Gallagher.

Whitcombe poured himself another generous snifter and returned to his chair. Alcohol and fire had made his face flush. She decided to make another run at answers.

"Uncle Harry, one thing I don't understand is your preoccupation about Conley. Dangers seem under control. And he's a reporter. It's part of his job."

"There's an underlying problem, Claire. I agreed to send him for... how shall I say this?...inappropriate reasons."

She was confused. "He'll do a good job...the choice was fine."

"I mean…private reasons."

"Private?"

He drew another indulgent sip, then rocked his snifter gently with cradled fingers. This act of warming seemed to comfort him. His face acquired a mellower, regretful caste. His tone became more confiding.

"My judgment got mixed up…with my role as a father."

CHAPTER 57

His nightstand clock read 6:55. With a groan, Conley stood, stretched and tilted opened the blinds. Dawn was breaking; pale light filtered into the bedroom of his London apartment. There was a knock on his door.

"Tracey?" he answered.

"Can I come in?" Her tone was hesitant.

"Uh…sure." He was still drowsy, wearing just boxer briefs.

The door swung halfway open, with tentative movement. Tracey leaned in, appearing embarrassed. She wore nothing but a towel.

"Hope I'm not intruding."

"No…of course not."

Keeping hold of the handle, she took a step inside. Her exposed shoulders and long legs jump-started his senses.

"Been up long?" His voice was still gravelly from sleep.

"About half an hour."

He remembered they were both due at work at eight-thirty for Saturday duty. Just the two of them---London bureau was small. That had been their pattern for a while.

"I've already showered," she added.

Her hair was still wet and un-brushed; her skin looked soft and clean. As close to feminine perfection as he could imagine so early in the morning.

"Thank you for being a gentleman last night, Steve."

In reality, he remembered, his behavior had more to do with self-preservation than manners. He'd already been resisting such impulses for five months, through joint travels and tutoring sessions at the bureau. There had been no sound reason to abandon his efforts at this stage. Misplaced keys or not.

He shrugged. "It was an accident. And we're co-workers, remember?"

She responded with a shy smile. "I came to ask if you have a hair dryer..." Her voice didn't hint at anything more.

"Sure. Let me get it."

He padded across to his dresser, then turned with device in hand. Courtesy brought her several steps forward, reaching toward him. Her movement was natural, but had the instant and unintended effect of loosening her terry-cloth towel. Despite her wide-eyed grab, edges separated, revealing the smooth curve of one hip. Adjustment carried more risks...She went still, blushing.

Instead of turning away---a polite reaction---Conley went into thrall. The cord went spinning off the dryer handle. Tracey watched the plug strike the floor, remaining immobile. The double bed was inescapably close-by.

"Let me wrap this up," he finally managed. "Meanwhile you can adjust your towel."

Re-winding required concentration.

"And if we weren't...co-workers?" she ventured, in a tremulous voice.

Conley looked up and met her eyes, aware that complications were somewhat greater than that. He stepped toward her and with one quick movement encircled her with his arms. Tight contact between them further dislodged her covering, though this time her efforts to hold it in place were symbolic. She turned her lips up to meet his.

A moment later he loosened his embrace so that the towel slipped from her breasts onto the floor. He let the hair dryer fall on top of it.

CHAPTER 58

Computer-generated presentations had crept into *World Tribune* editorial meetings in recent years. Gallagher didn't mind, within limits. On occasion he'd even used a few Power Point slides himself, if they were graphical and related to current stories. However this presentation was the most bizarre he'd seen. Even more, that Larson---paragon of function and efficiency---listened as if it was normal and appropriate.

Frick was the presenter. On-screen at one end of the conference room was a large digital photograph of an Ilyushin 76 military transport plane. Below that was a table of data.

"There's little public information on these aircraft," Frick said, standing alongside. "These safety and crash estimates are from the CIA."

It was the type of plane Conley would fly to Tajikistan on Friday---same as Bradford.

"Art, how would you characterize Bradford's flight experience on this aircraft?" Larson asked, placing the stem of her reading glasses in the corner of her mouth.

Gallagher was leaning backward, his arms crossed over his stomach. " 'A little rough.' That's all he said."

"Weather turbulence?" Frick inquired.

Gallagher swiveled back toward the screen, provoking a squeak. "He wasn't that specific."

Frick was all taut energy, even though he'd presumably run his usual five miles that morning. He eyed Gallagher for a moment, then pressed on, intent. He related that three such planes had crashed in the previous 18 years, according to U.S. intelligence data. Two had been operated by the Ukrainian military on a contract basis for foreign governments. One, Russian, had been carrying equipment only; no troops had been lost, just pilots. If there had been other crashes, particularly during Soviet times, they had gone unreported. For a military craft, Gallagher thought that was a decent safety record. He stroked his beard, growing impatient.

Frick was not convinced.

"One plus is that this same plane is used for dropping paratroopers," he said.

Gallagher stared, half in disbelief.

"That means there's a large aft door." With a concentrated expression, Frick pointed to a rectangular hatch, visible in the image. Larson followed with rapt attention from her end of the table. "Therefore..." Frick continued. "...If Conley wears a parachute he may have time to get out in an emergency."

Now Gallagher had really had it. "You've got be kidding, Nathan..."

Frick returned his stare, taut and determined.

"Nathan might have a point, Art," Larson said. "What's the harm?"

Arms still crossed, Gallagher snorted. It was bad enough that Whitcombe had veered off normal. Now it was permeating the rest of the organization...

"Better to err on the side of caution, Art. Especially after the earlier mishaps."

"Are you suggesting I instruct Conley to wear one onboard the plane?"

Larson gave a slight nod. Her face was sympathetic.

"It's a troop transport, Art," Frick said from the screen, implying the point had been settled.

With a slight shake of his head, Gallagher made a corresponding note on his legal pad. Next on-screen was a map of Tajikistan. Several lines and arrows originated from the Afghan border in the south and crossed the middle of the country in irregular patterns. West and south were several Russian flags; in the middle, a Russian flag and an icon that an appeared to resemble an armored personnel carrier. In small text at the bottom was another attribution to the CIA.

"These are the main smuggling routes," Frick said, tracing several arrows from south to north with his index finger. Then he extended all four fingers, in a more expansive gesture. "Along with principal Russian and Tajik troop deployments." He bent at the waist and leaned across screen, indicating Russian flags in south and west. "These are the bases for 201st Motorized Rifle Division: Border Troops. In 2003 they numbered 20,000. Since then they've been in a phased withdrawal. It's now almost complete. Replacements are Tajik border forces."

Straightening, he traced his index finger along one of the arrows. "Conley will accompany a Russian helicopter patrol from the 201st that will attempt to interdict smuggling along this route. As you can see, this one originates from a border area now controlled by Tajik forces."

"Same kind of patrol that Bradford went on?" Larson asked, directing the question at Gallagher.

"Yes, Janet. Same route."

Frick had a wireless control in hand; he clicked it to bring up another slide, which contained a table of estimated casualties in the 201st Division since its initial deployment in Tajikistan in 1999. In the country as a whole, the unit had sustained 37 fatalities, according to CIA intelligence estimates.

"Skirmishes are frequent on these patrols," Frick noted.

Gallagher's impatience grew. "Isn't that the point...to observe these interdiction efforts?" Hearing his own words, he couldn't believe he was now the one downplaying safety.

"We're just acknowledging risks, Art," Larson said.

Endorsed by his mentor, Frick was ready with his recommendation: "I'm recommending a helmet and a flak jacket."

This just about pushed Gallagher over the edge. "That's something I'd rather leave to Conley..." he responded sharply. Then sighed; there was no point in arguing. He made a note on his legal pad and promised to pass the suggestion along.

Next up was an aerial photograph of downtown Dushanbe. The capital was centered on a single broad avenue, running from railway station at bottom to bus station at the top. At intervals along this thoroughfare were a large mosque, a Russian Orthodox Church and an opera house fronted by large columns. The photograph had apparently been taken in summer; leafy trees shaded sidewalks.

"Prospekt Rudaki," Frick said, extending his hand toward the screen. "Looks peaceful here. But we know better, after Bradford." He stepped away from the screen and picked up some printed material from the table, giving stapled packets of several pages to both Gallagher and Larson. Gallagher had to refrain from rolling his eyes.

"A State Department Travel Advisory on Dushanbe," Frick said, clicking ahead to the next slide.

On-screen were several excerpts from the Advisory:

Sporadic violence, including bombings and shootings in public areas, is common, and it is largely the result of fighting between rival warlord factions competing for control of markets and narcotics trafficking. In addition, incidents between government troops and militia factions occur regularly. These incidents have included several spontaneous shootouts in public marketplaces...

Americans should avoid, in particular, the Green Market in Dushanbe because it has been the site of numerous skirmishes that have killed or injured a number of bystanders. Americans should remain inside during hours of darkness...There have been a number of pickpocketings, muggings, and armed robberies in the homes of persons perceived to have money, including foreigners. Travelers should not travel alone or on foot after dark...

"Pretty alarming," Larson said, glancing from screen down to printed material through her reading glasses. "Art?"

"I've read this before," Gallagher objected. "In fact I gave a copy to Conley before he left...Let's also remember that Bradford was killed in the countryside...not in Dushanbe."

Back at the screen, Frick was ready with his next recommendation. "I propose that Conley be limited to his hotel after nightfall." He stood straight and faced Gallagher.

Gallagher crossed his arms more tightly and stared down at the table. "Now wait just a minute, Nathan. In the field Conley's capable of deciding such questions himself. His judgment is sound."

"He almost got shot in Prague," Frick countered.

Gallagher looked back at Larson. It was clear where she came down.

"I can suggest it to him," he said. "But that's all I'm willing to do."

Frick turned off the overhead projector, nodded once at his mentor, and sat down opposite Gallagher. Battle lines established.

"In my opinion..." Gallagher said, now past glaring. "These safety measures are okay to a point. But we should be more worried about this fellow Shakuri."

CHAPTER 59

They approached the building housing the *Boston World Tribune* London bureau, just off Fleet Street. There were few cars and pedestrians. Early October Saturday morning: quiet central city.

Tracey wore the same jeans and sweater she'd worn to the previous evening's play. She fixed her eyes on the sidewalk, a little overwhelmed. Conley floated in hormonal daze. He'd vowed self-control. Now he realized it was futile.

She moved closer and squeezed his hand more tightly. When he reciprocated, she asked him, "What are we doing after work?"

"Picking up where we left off, I suppose."

Mutual impulse pulled them up short and into full embrace. Her gangly limbs and shyness only served to accentuate her beauty, as well as her youth. Conley forced himself to cut their kiss short.

"So this morning wasn't an accident?" she said, looking up slightly at him.

"No. Spontaneous, maybe, but no accident."

She smiled and emitted a rare giggle. "Not enough to outweigh your work ethic, though."

Conley smiled back. Her tone was clear; now that they'd crossed the threshold, she wanted him as much as he wanted her. For an instant he wondered if his punctuality and responsibility could have saved him. His search for contraception...a reconsideration of the clock... some self-suppression at the brink of consummation. All of which had proven insufficient. Later, after work, the rest of the weekend held immeasurable promise and excitement...

Revolving doors issued them into a brown marble lobby---empty, as usual on Saturday morning. The guard took more interest in them than was customary. "Mr. Whitcombe has already gone up," he said in his East London accent, leaning forward across the countertop. "I remember him from last summer."

Conley and Tracey skidded to a stop on the smooth floor.

"Good God," he said.

The guard observed Conley with a trace of concern, then added. "He said he had a key."

Conley looked at Tracey. Her mouth hung open.

"I thought he was arriving on Monday," she said, in a tremulous voice. She fumbled in her handbag for her cell phone, then pulled it out and examined the screen. Her eyes widened. "I turned off the ringer at the theater last night, then forgot...There are messages."

Conley shook himself alert and thought fast. Send Tracey up first? The problem now was that the street was visible from the 10-floor windows of the bureau. Whitcombe may have seen them entering the building together...

"We better just go up," he said. "Let's decide what to do in the elevator."

Clasping her elbow, he guided her toward the elevators. Her excitement dissipated; she looked suddenly overloaded. The morning was already momentous enough. With a concerned expression the guard stood and watched them disappear around the corner. At elevator bank, Conley pressed "Up", and a compartment opened at once. This was unfolding at head-spinning pace.

"Let's just tell the truth...what happened yesterday evening, and this morning as well," he said.

"Easier said than done."

Their elevator was passing the fifth floor.

"What do you mean?"

"I can't lie to him." Her tone became fatalistic.

"Then don't…"

Doors opened; they both hesitated. Conley made a determination: intentions were what mattered. There was no evading them.

He placed one hand on her lower back. "It's your decision. I'll stand by you."

She glanced into his eyes as if tactics wouldn't matter, then entered a trance-like state. Falling mute, they proceeded through the tenth-floor lobby and down a short corridor to the glass office door of the *World Tribune* bureau. It was lighted inside. Through glass Conley saw Whitcombe's long legs and elegant cuffs extending from a side chair in the waiting area. He opened the door and Tracey entered first. Whitcombe stood, revealing tailored blazer and open collar. His tanned, weathered face was a mixture of relief and bewilderment.

"Dad."

"Tracey…I tried calling…"

She stepped toward him, struggling to hold eye contact. They kissed and hugged each other lightly, with noticeable tension.

When they separated, he said, "I went to your apartment about seven a.m., after arriving from the airport. You weren't there."

She continued clasping his elbows, but cast her eyes downward for a moment.

Over Tracey's shoulder Whitcombe focused on Conley, who had hung back. Assessment didn't take long. His eyes flared for an instant, then became hard.

CHAPTER 60

The pastrami sandwich sat heavy in Gallagher's stomach. Portions were generous at *Nick's*, a small diner a short distance down Morrissey Boulevard. Next visit there, Gallagher vowed not to consume his entire serving of fries.

After parking, he walked along the front of the *World Tribune* building with Marcello, the Business Editor. At the front entrance he checked his watch: 1:35. Claire wasn't due until two o'clock. If he got to his desk by 1:45 he'd still have a chance to scan wire services beforehand.

"Big lunch," he said, placing a hand on his paunch. "I don't feel like getting behind my desk right away, Phil. I'm going to have a cigarette."

"I'd join you," Marcello said. "But this time I've quit for good."

Gallagher reached into his coat pocket for his cigarettes and lighter. Marcello shook his head and smiled.

"Okay. See you upstairs. Talk to you later about that real estate piece." A high-flying commercial developer in Boston had just declared bankruptcy.

At the bank of glass doors, an overhead canopy provided protection from weather, and Gallagher moved to one side and lit up. After consecutive days of outdoor calm wind now kicked up off the harbor.

He buttoned up his coat collar. His first drag was deep. When he exhaled smoke vanished in the wind. Smoking at his desk had once been ingrained; now it was a fading memory.

His enjoyment was spoiled by the approach of Frick---unaccompanied by Larson, to Gallagher's slight surprise, even though she usually lunched in her office. Reproach flickered in Frick's eyes at sight of the cigarette. He contrived an ingratiating bonhomie.

"Enjoying a smoke before the storm hits?"

"Storm?"

"Nor'easter. Freezing rain and snow. Due to hit later this afternoon."

"Oh, right."

Gallagher paid little attention to weather forecasts on weekdays. There was always more compelling news. He took another drag.

"May have to forget about my run tomorrow morning," Frick added, smiling.

"A shame." Gallagher snorted smoke out through his nostrils.

Frick stiffened on his wiry frame. Safety notwithstanding, he had become less sure-footed since Whitcombe's abdication. Fields of battle had become unpredictable.

"Any news from Conley?"

"A short voice message. That threat from the Chechen didn't amount to anything." For now Gallagher just wanted to finish his cigarette in peace. "Excuse me Nathan...I'm meeting Claire Bradford at two o'clock."

Frick snapped to attention. "Claire Bradford!?"

He explained what he knew about her visit. When he mentioned that Claire had seen Whitcombe in New Hampshire, Frick's eyes narrowed.

"Hmmmm."

"She's dropping by the paper as a courtesy. At least that's my understanding."

Frick's suspicion intensified. "I'll see you upstairs," he said, turning heel and hurrying into the lobby. Bound for his mentor, Gallagher guessed. Now his cigarette was already half gone. His last few drags didn't bring their usual pleasure. He ground the butt into the sand of an outdoor receptacle.

Inside the marbled lobby, he was looking straight ahead toward the escalator when the receptionist hailed him. He whirled around to find Claire rising from a leather chair in the waiting area.

"I'm early, Mr. Gallagher."

Empathy replaced Gallagher's irritation. He walked over to meet her halfway.

"I've told you before, Claire. Please call me Art."

CHAPTER 61

Claire's gray overcoat and high heels were conservative but announced her curves. Reaction across the newsroom was electric. Male heads lifted. A few reporters recognized her; decorum forced their gazes back to computer screens.

Gallagher warned off malingerers with hard glances, and in his office helped Claire off with her coat. Her hands trembled as she sat down, gripped the armrests and crossed one well-shaped leg over the other. She looked keyed up. He guessed why. The newsroom had to bring back painful memories for her. His guilt re-surged.

"I've thought of you often since Paris, Claire."

"I appreciate that, Art."

"Under the circumstances, it's remarkable you were able to assist Steve Conley to such extent."

"I'm eager to contribute."

Present tense, Gallagher noted. Her grip tightened on the armrests. Did that explain why she was here? In her eyes was the same determination he'd glimpsed in *Notre Dame de Passy* church a month earlier. Only now she seemed to have an objective in view.

Suddenly it became obvious. This was more than a courtesy call.

"How is Harry Whitcombe?" he asked.

"In good health, as always. Though a little preoccupied, right now."

Gallagher nodded, withholding further comment. Her ostensible reason for visiting Whitcombe in first place, he remembered, was estate issues.

"How long were you there…in New Hampshire?"

"Less than a day. I arrived before lunch yesterday and left first thing this morning."

"Rather short visit."

"Yes."

Over Claire's shoulder Gallagher spotted Nathan Frick circling the newsroom, apparently in search of Larson. Frick cast a worried glance toward Gallagher's office; his eyes narrowed when he saw Claire from behind.

Gallagher looked at her again.

"Plan to stay in Boston long, Claire?"

An even tighter grip on the armrests.

"A week or two…I haven't decided yet."

Her eyes became more determined. As if she feared resistance. Didn't she realize how much he'd agonized over her trauma and struggled for balance these past weeks?

Frick appeared suddenly in the doorway. His search for Larson had come up empty.

"If you're here about Conley, Nathan…" Gallagher pre-empted. "…I haven't had a chance to check my messages yet."

Frick continued hovering. Gallagher had no choice but to introduce him to Claire. Something about Frick seemed to make her wary. Trying to get rid of him, he swiveled toward his computer: no e-mail from Conley. A quick check of his voice messages revealed the same. "Nothing yet," he reiterated, making his impatience evident. "But let's not blow this out of proportion. I'm sure he'll send an e-mail message before he turns in. And He's flying out tomorrow morning, for goodness' sake. Let's talk later."

"Why not call him?"

"Can't this wait, Nathan?" He turned back to Claire. "Please excuse this interruption, Claire…"

"I really don't mind. Any chance I can listen in?"

Gallagher hesitated, sensing it wasn't a good idea. However compassion lowered his barriers. "I guess not." He exhaled and looked down through his bifocals at his speed dial numbers. To his surprise Claire interjected again.

"In fact I tried calling him a few times during the past couple of hours. No answer."

Gallagher glanced up and paused with his hand over the keypad. "You tried calling Conley…from here in the States?" She nodded, which made him worry that Conley had let her get over-involved. By now the purpose of her visit was becoming clearer…He released a half-sigh and hit the speed-dial button. A message came from the speakerphone, first in English and then in Russian: *The number you have dialed is temporarily blocked…*

"That's the same message I've gotten," Claire said.

Gallagher checked his watch. "It's almost 10 o'clock now in Moscow. Not that late yet."

Frick reacted quickly as a whip. "Does he usually turn off his cell phone in the evening?"

"No…not usually."

"Let's call his hotel room."

CHAPTER 62

Thanks to a program printed in both English and Russian, Conley had acquainted himself with the story beforehand. And like most ballets, *Swan Lake* was vivid and easy to follow. At the beginning, Young Prince Siegfried, the hero, is dissolute and self-indulgent. A passing flock of swans intrigues him, and turn out to be beautiful maidens in another form---consigned by a wicked spell to be swans during daytime and human at night. Siegfried becomes besotted with Odette, queen of the swan maidens, and vows to rescue her from her daytime purgatory.

During a ball in Act III Siegfried is beguiled by another princess, and temporarily forgets about Odette. By Act IV he regains his good senses and goes in search of Odette. A storm breaks over the lake, stymieing his efforts. The final, pivotal scene now unfolded onstage. Beside Conley Lilya sat attentive. Tchaikovsky's musical score soared toward thundering climax. Two wings of ballerinas, clad in white, swept toward one another from opposite sides of the stage, carrying Siegfried and Odette with them.

At last the pair united at center stage. The two formations of swan-maidens coalesced around them, in an orgiastic fusion of trembling limbs and white fabric.

While Conley joined in applause he glimpsed Lilya's profile. During the ensuing standing ovation and curtain calls she kept respectable distance, which she'd done all evening. Outside in the theater lobby, provocative young women were everywhere, and he tried not to be affected, by them or Lilya.

By now he'd recognized that Russian social mores were more restrained than advertised. Which, he concluded again, was probably for the better. The military flight to Tajikistan on which he and Oleg were booked departed at 6:30 a.m. the next morning.

As he and Lilya collected their coats and hats in the lower lobby he stifled his usual impulses.

"We'll take a taxi and I'll drop you off at home," he told her.

"Why don't you come up for tea? Before you head back."

Conley stopped with one arm in sleeve. He looked at his watch. "It's late. What about your parents?"

"They're in Ekaterinburg with my sister. Visiting my grandparents."

She was facing him. Her expression was polite, non-suggestive... He nonetheless tilted into fancy until a voice startled him from the side.

"Mr. Conley. I'm relieved we found you. Your phone was turned off."

Conley turned. The press officer from the FSB materialized with two plainclothes security men, bearing an air of urgency.

"Why? Something wrong?" Conley promptly cleared his head, pulled out his phone, and re-activated the ringer.

"Movsar Felayev had an unscheduled meeting with his lawyer this afternoon. There was some...unauthorized communication. We have concerns about your safety."

Beside Conley Lilya tensed.

"Is there a chance he got some instruction out?"

"Well...that's our worry. Therefore some guards will be posted outside your hotel room overnight. We called Oleg Mikhailov. He's been apprised of the situation."

Conley thought for a moment. "So what do you recommend now?"
"Straight back to the Radisson, I'm afraid. It's for your own safety."
"What about Lilya? I intended to take her home."
"We advise that she also receive protection, at least for tonight."

CHAPTER 63

"No need to go overboard, Nathan," Gallagher said. "Why don't we just try again in fifteen or twenty minutes?" Frick was hovering at the corner of his desk. Claire was puzzled about his role. Thus far Conley had not mentioned him.

"In the meantime…mind if I sit down?"

"Go ahead," Gallagher snorted, crossing his arms over his stomach.

Gallagher's phone rang, and he took a heavy breath before hitting the speakerphone button. Frick edged forward on his chair; it was Conley. There were honking horns on the Moscow end, as if he was in a moving vehicle:

"Sorry for the delay. I saw your number in my log. I was attending a ballet."

Claire caught Gallagher shooting a disdainful glance at Frick.

"Didn't mean to interrupt your evening, Steve," Gallagher said, leaning forward and speaking toward phone console. "…Claire's here, by coincidence."

There was a pause on Conley's end. "There? In your office?"

"Hello Steve," she interjected. Why did he sound so…*agité*…keyed up? His voice reminded her of another occasion…

Gallagher continued, "We know it's your last night in Moscow. We just want to make sure that nothing came of that threat from the Chechen."

"Well...I'm safe, first of all. Excuse me just a minute." Male voices could be heard in the background, conversing in Russian. Frick strained forward, his sinews tense. Prompting Gallagher to frown. "... But there has been a new development...I'm now being escorted back to my hotel in a car from the FSB. There'll be two guards outside my door tonight."

Claire's heart skipped a beat. Frick sat up, enlivened again, while Gallagher leaned closer to the phone console.

"What? Did you say guards?"

Conley explained developments surrounding Felayev's lawyer.

"Good Lord."

"Everything's under control, Art. And I'm leaving my hotel in six or seven hours anyway."

Frick interjected. "Is there a reason to pull back...postpone, Art? Until we assess this?"

Gallagher stroked his beard, staring at the phone console, ignoring Frick's vindicating stare. To Claire he appeared torn. "No," he said, finally. "That makes no sense. Ignore that comment, Steve. You should go ahead."

Claire sighed in relief. Gallagher was not her adversary after all. Tugged in different directions, maybe. And prodded by this annoying Frick character. But not her adversary.

Better chance he'd be her ally.

CHAPTER 64

This evening had taken a breathtaking turn. Conley sat on the edge of his bed. Lilya remained stunned.

"Who could have imagined? he said.

Lilya fell silent for a moment. These outcomes were sudden.

"Well…" he added. "We'll just have to adapt." He leaned forward, placing his elbows on his knees and running one hand through his hair. "Have the guards outside made you feel safer?"

"I suppose so. It's a new experience. They're quiet, though."

"Same here. I hope we'll both manage some sleep."

"What time are you leaving?"

He exhaled and pressed the cell-phone hard against his ear, not quite free of his earlier fanciful visions. "Car's picking me up at 5:30. I'm meeting Oleg at the airfield."

"Will we stay in touch when you're in Tajikistan?"

He could find to reason to say no---not least because she'd fallen under possible danger from Chechen terrorists and now had two guards posted outside her apartment overnight, and agreed to try, following his first few days with Russian interdiction forces. After the conversation concluded he called Milena. It was an hour earlier in Prague. She was bright-spirited and didn't mention her gunshot wound until he asked.

"Oh that? It's healing fast. I'm more concerned about what's going on with you."

Her ardor for his assignment remained undiminished, and he pledged continuing contact from Dushanbe.

When this call was also finished he sprung up and strode over to his window. Four stories below, at the main entrance to the Radisson, he saw two young women emerge. They were young---early 20s. Long legs beneath their overcoats, along with smooth skin and high, rounded cheekbones that Conley could appreciate even from a distance. Perhaps part of the casino or lounge staff, just getting off the evening shift. They were laughing. Puffs of condensation burst from their lips as they approached a taxi and conferred through the front passenger window, and climbed into the back seat, revealing titillating expanses of thigh before they slammed the door. Conley watched the taxi drive off, forlorn.

His energies kept building, with no release. The surfeit would have to go somewhere, eventually. Where was an open question.

Time was near midnight; he re-packed his clothes and prepared for bed. At the desk he noticed that his laptop computer was still on, and decided to check e-mail one last time. Clad in undershorts, he sat down and connected. There was only one incoming message. He started when he saw the sender: Tracey Whitcombe. His heart pounded as he opened the text:

Dear Steve,

This message probably comes as a surprise. We last communicated more than one year ago…in London!…what already seems ages ago. At that time, as you know, I made a bargain with my father. Not one you wanted, I remember. It was my idea and my decision. But it was the only way I saw for you to keep your job.

And so far I've upheld my pledge to him---not to contact you again until after I graduate from college. (It's been more difficult these past few months with my return to Wellesley!) Why am I now breaking my promise?

These are unusual circumstances.

I'm aware you're overseas. I've gathered you're now in Moscow. (Yes, I've kept abreast of your activities at the paper, and especially your current assignment.)

I'm writing for two reasons. First because I'm worried about you. Second because I'm worried about my father.

About a week ago he returned from a short trip to Washington in a state of extreme disconsolation. I visited my parents in Cambridge the following weekend, and I'd never seen him like this before. Sunday he left for our lodge at Loon Mountain, though ski season won't start for another month. Even my mother is perplexed. About all we were able to ascertain is that his withdrawal is connected with your assignment. He made statements such as "I set the whole machine in motion." And "I hope Conley doesn't come to the same end as Peter."

Naturally I've been disturbed by this. So I took the initiative of calling him last night. Oddly, Claire was making an overnight visit---apparently discussing Peter's estate. I begged him for further explanation. "Specifically, I asked: 'Why are you so worried about Steve?'"

"He's heading into an unpredictable situation," he said.

I asked, "But haven't you known that from the beginning?"

"New factors have emerged," he said. "I'll be able to tell you more in a couple of weeks."

It still didn't make sense. When I begged for further explanation, he admitted that he'd agreed to send you in the first place in part because of me. "To get him away from Boston."

You see, Steve, I'll graduate in May. My pledge will then expire. After that...I think he was worried we'd resume what we'd started in London. You may not realize this, but I think he saw this assignment for you as a prelude to another transfer overseas. By time I graduated, you'd be safely gone. Now he's distraught that he's put you in peril for self-serving reasons.

Naturally, this whole situation is distressing to me. I hope stability will soon return---that you'll be safe and my father will be back to normal. For now, I have only one request: don't place yourself in danger! I realize you've got a critical assignment, for you and the paper both. But most important is to come back to Boston alive!

With affection (and worry),

Tracey

P.S. - Please send me an e-mail or two from Dushanbe if you have the chance.

CHAPTER 65

Gallagher had just seen Claire off. On the up-escalator to the newsroom he stared down at humming metal and shook his head. She'd lost her husband just a month before. At minimum the paper now owed her sympathy and consideration. She deserved to be heard. Problem was…where to draw the line? How would he ever tell her no?

At newsroom reception, he turned left and skirted toward his office. Halfway along he encountered Jerry MacPherson at a water cooler.

"Who was that?" MacPherson asked.

"Claire Bradford."

"Thought so. She's not easy to forget."

Gallagher shot him an arched eyebrow. "No. That she's not." He stopped, extracted a paper cup and opened spigot, bending to see the cup below his paunch. MacPherson looked a little puzzled. "Doesn't she live in France?"

"Yes."

"What brings her here?"

Gallagher exhaled so that his mustache puffed out. He straightened and took a sip of water before answering. "I think I have an idea."

MacPherson became intrigued. "Something to do with the stories on her husband?"

"You guessed it."

"Uh oh. Sounds like a challenging situation."

MacPherson listened with cocked head as Gallagher summarized the development particularly intent on Claire's connection to Harry Whitcombe, and that she'd just been to visit him in New Hampshire. "Interesting," he observed. "Did she fill in any of those blanks?"

"Not really. I have no more answers than you do, Jerry." Across the newsroom he spotted Frick entering Larson's office, and snorted. MacPherson followed his line of vision.

"How did Frick get mixed up in this?"

"Another question I've been contending with."

MacPherson smiled. "Makes me glad I'm a columnist and not an editor."

Gallagher grunted and gulped his remaining water. Feeling beleaguered, he crumpled his paper cup and threw it in the wastebasket. MacPherson laughed, throwing away his cup as well.

"Just one request, Jerry," Gallagher said, turning to go.

"Yes?"

"Don't even think about making Claire a subject for your column."

MacPherson laughed again. "Right. Fascinating material. Just a little too close to home."

CHAPTER 66

Floodlights illuminated the airfield and surrounding snow-banks. Four uniformed Russian guards manned the gate, wearing flak jackets and armed with submachine guns. One collected Conley's passport and scrutinized Conley through the back-seat window. Another kneeled and inspected the Volga's undercarriage with a bomb-detecting device. Check complete, the sentries slid open concrete crash barriers and waved the car through.

Chechen terrorism necessitated extra precautions, even in pre-dawn Moscow.

The Volga crunched along a plowed roadway toward a two-story building. An enormous Ilyushin-76 transport jet stood on the tarmac nearby, engines idling.

Closer to the building Conley saw two figures waiting, wearing fur hats and bundled against cold. One was Oleg; the other was Franklin Stanson, squinting through his aviator glasses through the floodlight. When Conley emerged from the car Stanson displayed an easy, lop-sided grin---somehow out of context on a Russian military base.

"Heard about last night," he drawled. "Wanted to make sure you left Moscow in one piece." He escorted Conley and Oleg onto the tarmac. They reached another checkpoint, manned by a pair of soldiers shouldering automatic weapons. "This is as far as I go," he half-shouted over din of jet engines. "Good luck."

Conley thanked him again for logistical arrangements.

"Keep me informed from Dushanbe," he added, still half-shouting.

A Russian officer conducted Conley and Oleg through the rear hatch, which was open and formed a loading ramp. Soldiers carried in boxes of supplies, which they stacked along both sides of the fuse-lage. Just aft of cockpit there were two benches, one on each side. Four Russian soldiers sat on one, in winter combat gear. Conley caught their attention; they stared at him, glum and impassive. The officer indicated seats opposite, where harnesses hung down; he and Oleg strapped themselves in. Nearby he noticed parachutes fastened by net-ting to the fuselage's ceiling, and remembered Gallagher's suggestion over the speakerphone with Frick.

Oleg followed his gaze, informed of this exhortation from Boston. "They're there if we need them," he said over the noise, with a faint grin. Conley shrugged off the jab. He was still curious about Stanson's unannounced appearance. "Did you know Franklin Stanson was coming?"

"No. But I wasn't surprised."

"Really? Why not?"

"I've done interpretation work for him. My impression is he likes to stay on top of everything."

"Still...a pre-dawn sendoff? I'm just a reporter."

Oleg thought a moment. "Don't forget about Bradford."

"You think all this attention is because of Bradford?"

"Why ask me? You're the American."

"Still...you know Stanson better than I do."

"Not much. Don't forget he only brought me on his first trip to Dushanbe. After that he went there on his own..."

"Without an interpreter? Why was that?"

Oleg opened his mouth to respond just as hydraulic lifts activated for the rear hatch. Din increased; speaking became impractical. He leaned back, silent and inscrutable. Engines revved higher and the plane taxied toward runway. Based on Bradford's experience Conley was prepared for a rough flight. However takeoff was smooth and the jet roared upward along a clean arc to cruising altitude. By degrees the din subsided, replaced by a hum and constant, low-level vibration that resonated through all hard surfaces. Several soldiers across the aisle nodded into sleep, out of either boredom or fatigue. Conley realized there were no females aboard---his first flight under such circumstance.

Conley wished to discuss Stanson further. But Oleg's eyes closed and he also nodded into slumber.

CHAPTER 67

The former *Le Meridien Boston* had passed out of French ownership and was now the *Langham Hotel Boston*. To Claire's disappointment the new management had closed the *haute cuisine* Julien restaurant, which she'd often enjoyed with Peter. Otherwise, though, the essence of the establishment remained. The 1920's-era building had once served as regional headquarters for the U.S. Federal Reserve and retained its stately, Old World character.

A hotel made most sense, she'd decided. Peter's parents were at their vacation home in Nassau, Bahamas, still getting over their trauma. Elizabeth Whitcombe was heading north to New Hampshire and her husband for the weekend. And from the Langham the *World Tribune* was just a quick 10-minute drive south. Moreover she'd always liked the aura of the place--one she associated with Peter and also with the building's half-century at the master-switches of New England finance. Even if she didn't understand central banking, she'd gleaned some essentials. Deliberation. Power. Quiet control. Attributes she wished for herself during the next week or two. She now sat in the three-story back lobby atrium, in a Louis XIV armchair upholstered in embroidered silk. Elegant jazz filtered down from a piano in the *Café Fleuri*.

Problem was...this power-setting wasn't conferring desired effects, Her airway was constricted and her heart was beating fast. Janet Larson was arriving any minute. Accomplished, confident and unflappable. A model of professional success.

Everything that Claire knew that she was not.

Larson pulled up outside under covered rear entrance, behind the wheel of a large Mercedes. The valet hastened to open the door. There was little doubt. This was a woman who'd proven herself.

Claire's swallowed hard and rose from her chair.

After exchanging greetings, as they mounted the escalator to the café, she remembered her previous day's conclusions. Gallagher was central, but beset by conflicts from all sides. Frick was mere watchdog. Harry Whitcombe had abdicated. That left Janet Larson as the only other remaining force.

The maitre d' gave her and Larson a respectful once over. "This way, please," he intoned before ushering them to desirable table on the atrium balcony. After they ordered, Larson reiterated her condolences---followed by a suitable pause, filled by ranging melodies and soothing chords of the jazz piano. She then placed forearms on the table and got to what seemed foremost on her mind.

"We had so little time yesterday in the newsroom, Claire," she said. "I didn't get a chance to ask about Harry Whitcombe…Nate Frick tells me you visited him."

"Yes, at his ski lodge at Loon."

Larson's tones were measured. How's he doing, she asked?

"Well…He took Peter's death hard. I guess he needs time to himself."

Yes, haven't we all. Not many visitors?

"Just me, as far as I know."

For the first time Claire detected in Larson's eyes something she hadn't expected. Larson became immobile, rapt. Deferential, even.

Then it occurred to her. Uncle Harry was not taking phone calls in New Hampshire. Larson, for all her accomplishment and high status, was still a hired hand trying to divine the boss's intentions.

For now, Claire recognized, she was sole conduit to the top.

Misrepresentation was out of the question. But there were opportunities for nuance…certain emphases. Larson resumed, weighing each word.

"I'm sorry to say the stories we're doing on your husband added to Harry's strains."

"That was my sense, too."

"Did you happen to talk about them?"

"You mean Conley's assignment?"

Larson nodded.

"Uncle Harry said the situation is more complex now."

"Indeed."

"Especially because of this bill in Washington."

Larson offered another guarded nod, still waiting. Claire took a quick breath and plunged forward. She felt an exhilarating return of confidence. The Langham finally felt right.

"But I believe he still wants to see it through."

"Right through Dushanbe?"

"That was my impression. After all it's just one more week."

*   *   *

Roaring engines and a staccato *thump, thump, thump* of blades announced their presence up and down the valley. Helicopters were not ideal for interdicting smugglers. And this was daylight besides.

However this flight was one part reconnaissance and once part show of force. Nikolai, a lieutenant officer in an elite unit of airborne infantry, pointed out the side hatch over a rugged terrain of rocks, scrub grass and stunted trees. They were about 500 meters above the valley's base. Air was clear and cold, He shouted to be heard. "He says look there," Oleg interpreted, speaking close to Conley's ear. "Just below the ridge line."

Conley wore a harness with a safety cord; he braced himself against the doorframe with one hand before raising his binoculars. A few seconds later he steadied his sight line on the object of interest: a small caravan of heavily laden mules and bearded men. They were dressed in camouflage gear and Oriental head coverings. They numbered seven or eight and all looked up at the Russian Mi-17-IV, an armed transport aircraft similar to those deployed in Afghanistan by the Soviet Union in the 1980s. Nikolai shouted again to Oleg, who translated.

"They may have heroin. Or they may not. In either case they won't run."

Indeed the caravan-goers made no attempt to flee as the helicopter flew closer. They continued plodding forward, leading their mules and casting sullen gazes skyward.

"Tajiks, judging by their head coverings," Oleg said.

"Why aren't they afraid?" Conley asked.

"The Tajik government forbids us to fire from the air. And Russian ground forces are being drawn down here. In another 10 months even these over-flights will come to an end."

Their helicopter descended halfway and hovered over the caravan, kicking up dust from the hillside. The smugglers stopped in their tracks. None made any sudden moves, though their faces---partly concealed by their headscarves---held traces of defiance. From a rear turret of the helicopter a Russian gunner aimed a large, mounted machine gun.

"The idea is intimidation," Oleg translated. "We're not going to back off as long as we still have a troop presence here."

"Do they ever fire at the helicopters?"

Oleg answered the question directly. "Almost never. What's the point? Anyway these are small potatoes. The main heroin caravans travel at night, under darkness. And those usually hide in caves before helicopters can find them." The helicopter banked away from the men below and continued down the valley. "See that? Where they were walking?" He pointed toward the trail, four or five feet wide with a surface of broken rocks and dust---little more than a ledge in the hillside. "That's one of three of four main smuggling arteries coming north out of Afghanistan."

Conley studied the trail through his binoculars, following the snaking line---barely discernible even in daylight.

"An ancient route for contraband," Oleg added "These tribes have been smuggling along that path for centuries."

"Can't they be stopped at the border?"

"This route crosses into Afghanistan at a point where Tajik forces have assumed control. Therefore the best we can do is interdict further north."

They continued sweeping down the valley. About 10 kilometers further south they encountered another caravan, similar to the first.

"Do these caravans ever use motorized transport?" Conley asked.

"Jeeps and SUVs, sometimes, along other routes. But here---usually mules and horses."

"One would think the Russian troops here have a big advantage."

Nikolai shook his head and Oleg translated.

"When we can catch them. But there are just too many getting through the border now to control."

The helicopter hovered over the second caravan as it did over the first. At the rear of the aircraft Conley saw the gunner train his gun; he was 18 or 19 years old, dressed in bulky olive fatigues and a fur cap. Conley was the only one in the helicopter wearing a helmet.

"If you can't attack them from helicopters," he asked Nikolai. "How do you catch them?"

"Air-and-land missions. We wait in ambush. You'll get to go on one of those tomorrow night."

CHAPTER 68

Café Fleuri was illumined by optimistic morning light. Claire basked in new confidence. Upon finishing her breakfast and strode past a uniformed Air France crew sitting at a circular table, festooned with croissants, fruit and coffee. Males in the crew didn't hide their attentions. Even female flight attendants were appreciative and let their glances linger. The maitre d' came alive as she rounded his stand at the boundary of the café area.

"Thank you, Mrs. Bradford. Enjoy your morning."

Claire sensed his gaze upon her from behind as she walked toward the staircase and escalator. She didn't mind. Why not? He was human. For perhaps the first time since Peter's death, she felt like part of society again.

This venue suited her after all.

At the bottom of escalator she exited the atrium and crossed through an expansive hall with marble ceilings--- once the main entrance of the Federal Reserve. To her left was a grand staircase leading up to the Julien Lounge, a former adjunct to the restaurant, one of the most elegant in Boston.

The night before, she'd celebrated there with a spare but expertly-prepared three-course meal, accompanied by fine Bordeaux.

Content to savor her initial success in radiant solitude, and to remember earlier dinners with Peter. Her trip was proving worthwhile. Conley's assignment was going forward. And she was very much involved---just as she'd wanted. On Monday afternoon, she was scheduled to meet Larson, Sullivan and Gordon at *World Tribune* headquarters.

"We'll benefit from your presence," Larson had said, with her new and unexpected deference. "Especially without Harry there."

Claire glided into the lobby, chin and spirits up. From her room she planned to call old friends of hers and Peter's, including a couple who lived in Back Bay. Her weekend was free. Time for a little distraction. She hit the elevator button and was waiting for one to open when a voice sounded behind her.

"Good morning, Claire."

A familiar baritone...she whirled around. Her jaw dropped. Standing before her in blue blazer and gray slacks, overcoat folded over his forearm, was Harry Whitcombe. Her immediate impression was that he looked haggard...Something was wrong.

"Didn't mean to startle you, Claire... I drove down from New Hampshire."

Claire glanced at her watch: just after 8 o'clock. He must have left Loon at 5:30 or earlier.

"Uncle Harry. This is so unexpected...Is there some emergency?"

"Not an emergency, exactly. No."

She stared up at him because of his height, overcome by sudden shortness of breath. Her confidence evacuated her in an instant.

"...But I couldn't wait. I came down here for your sake."

His expression carried a pall. Hints of painful duty. What could this be about?

"This may take a while," he said, looking at her with tired eyes. "Might be best if we find someplace quiet."

Both of them look around. The lobby was becoming busy. She felt a stirring of panic. "My room's not really *présentable*...The bed's probably still unmade."

"Of course." He thought for a moment. "The park should be relatively empty on Saturday morning. Fresh air might also help. Would you object?"

Her hand trembled as she reached up to brush aside a strand of hair.

"I'll get my coat."

*   *   *

Two platoons of Russian soldiers hid behind rocks that overlooked a small, hillside plateau---about 70 kilometers north of the Afghan border, along the same smuggling trail Conley had observed the day before by helicopter. They'd been ensconced for two hours, starting shortly before nightfall, armed with Kalashnikovs, a tripod-mounted heavy machine gun, and two shoulder-fired bazookas.

"Firepower is our main advantage," Oleg had explained beforehand. "Along with communications."

A pair of all-terrain vehicles lay 50 meters up-trail; two others were hidden off about 100 meters south, ready to close off escape. All four vehicles had back-mounted heavy machine guns. Ambush was the goal. Encroaching darkness brought lower temperatures; already anticipated with gray-camouflaged cold weather gear and fur hats. In the dimming light Conley could see the faces of the Russians. Expressionless, despite their youth, with an air of fatalism---they were doing a necessary job. Nikolai was most active: surveying the trail through infrared binoculars over a jagged boulder. Every 15 minutes he communicated in a low voice through a hand-held radio. Otherwise the contingent was silent. Oleg sat next to Conley---impassive, leaning against the same rock, hands thrust in his pockets. Back at the base he'd translated questions and answers to Nikolai.

"We get some intelligence on these convoys," the squad leader had said. "Some good, some bad. We can't be sure what will happen tonight."

And what happened during a similar foray with Bradford?

"Nothing. Our intelligence was faulty. We sat in the cold for six hours. He seemed more interested in what I told him the next day, in an interview back at the base." When Conley had queried him further, Nikolai said, "We'll have time to talk tomorrow, after the operation." He'd then pivoted his bulky frame and strode away toward the divisional command building.

Now Conley crossed his arms and tried to stay warm. His helmet was back in the barracks. Gallagher's exhortations notwithstanding, his fur hat was warmer. This was his first potential exposure to military combat. He remembered what Claire had told him back in Paris, tears welling in her eyes:

"I was so relieved when Peter called me afterward. And to think...I assumed main dangers were past! If I had known what was to come, I would have flown to Dushanbe to be with him..."

Nikolai raised binoculars for another survey. Motionless silhouettes surrounded him, cradling weapons in the moonlight. Conley closed his eyes; his mind traveled back to the sidewalk outside the *pharmacie* in Paris...Claire's head was down, her compressed thighs and jutting haunches straining against the fabric of her skirt...He caught himself. Two weeks and seven thousand kilometers later, the image enthralled him more than a pending firefight. Maybe that pointed out his difficulty...

"*Vinimanie!*" Nikolai said in a loud whisper, raising his hand.

Conley re-focused and glanced at Oleg, who signaled with an open palm that they should be quiet. Soldiers raised weapons and assumed more alert postures.

In the distance he could make out the clopping of hooves. Faint at first, then more distinct---another mule caravan. Nikolai peered south through his lenses, then raised his thumb. Without a sound, soldiers lowered their infrared goggles. Clopping hooves came closer, and Conley wondered if the smugglers had sent out advance scouts.

The answer came in the form of *Rat-tat-tat* automatic gunfire, just north. Nikolai barked a command into his transmitter and swept his hand forward, compelling soldiers out from their concealed positions. On one side two machine gunners soldiers set up a tripod, while others scampered up and over. From below came shouts in Tajik, followed by the whiz of bullets overhead. At once the tripod-mounted gun responded with heavy fire, while the other Russians descended the hillside, guns blazing. Conley thought he heard the *thwap, thwap, thwap* of bullets hitting flesh, followed by screams. Two explosions filled the valley as the Russians unleashed bazooka rounds.

Oleg clasped his forearm, keeping him down behind their rock. Within seconds gunfire abated. Remaining shots seemed to shift beyond the plateau, further down the mountainside. After a pause they rose from their squats and peered down. Carnage on the plateau was evident even in the new moonlight. A half dozen bodies---in traditional Tajik nomadic garb---lay scattered across the flat surface. One smuggler kneeled with his hands on his head, guarded by two Russian soldiers. A wounded Russian soldier sat against a rock on the edge of the plateau, holding his shoulder, receiving help from a comrade. Further down the valley, gunfire continued, punctuated by commands in Russian.

"A few probably tried to get away," Oleg said.

Two mules were down, apparently hit by errant bullets; their baying filled the night sky. Three others---heavily laden---were running around squeaking and hawing. One soldier ran after the animals, shouting in Russian, attempting to corral them.

"They're probably packed with opium," Oleg explained. Gunfire receded further; the Russians were giving chase. "...I think it's safe now to go down."

They scampered over the rocks and clambered down the gravelly hillside. When they reached the plateau the Russian soldier had secured two of the three mules to a boulder; with an air of reluctance he then dispatched the two wounded mules with pistol shots.

Bodies remained scattered around; one nearest to Conley and Oleg was face down, his robes soaked in blood. One hand still clutched a Kalashnikov. Oleg's features were hard, as if this were nothing new.

"Let's go take a closer look," he suggested.

He crouched down and turned the body over. Mouth gaped open; eyes rolled back in their sockets. "That's unusual," he said, frowning. "This one doesn't have a beard."

From the other side of the plateau came a shout: *"Opium na vseh!"* Conley turned. A soldier displayed a cloth-bound bundle high in the air.

"Opium on all of them," Oleg translated. "Guess the intelligence was good."

Nikolai and a half-dozen soldiers materialized from below, weapons slung over their shoulders and two more prisoners in tow. He surveyed the scene and strode over to Conley and Oleg. When he saw the body he frowned, bent down and ripped the tunic away. What he saw made him shake his head in disgust.

Beneath the robe of the dead man was a uniform. "National militia," Oleg explained, hands on his knees and leaning over Nikolai's shoulder. "Evidence of government involvement." Nikolai raised his bulk to a standing position and shook his head. He didn't appear surprised. Oleg translated his remark from Russian:

"He says this is a real-life example of what he told Bradford."

CHAPTER 69

Post Office Square lies in the heart of the Boston financial district and contains a small, well-tended park. The park was almost empty this Saturday morning, like office buildings that loomed skyward on all sides.

The soaring towers and absence of humanity added to Claire's sense of surreal.

Just opposite the *Langham* she and Whitcombe entered a long, trellis-covered walkway, surfaced with red brick. There was a line of unoccupied benches within the enclosure. "I suggest walk a bit further...sit in the open," he said, as if vertical space would emancipate whatever burdens he was about to share with her. Claire fought her disorientation by gulping cold air. Additional oxygen didn't help. Why was this encounter already more disquieting than the one they'd just had at Loon?

They proceeded into a circular plaza with a tall fountain, topped by a half-sphere of water. She glanced upward at the converging streams and beyond. Skies were gray again. Clouds that churned off Boston Harbor looked more unpredictable than in New Hampshire. A granite bench by a bank of shrubs met Whitcombe's criteria. As they sat down she adjusted her scarf and crossed her arms. Not to ward off the chill air. More to stabilize herself against unknowns.

Whitcombe crossed his long legs and stared at the brick walkway. His deliberation was more alarming than reassuring. "Claire, I've had a couple of days to reflect since you left Loon…"

Claire tightened her crossed arms.

"…And there's something more you need to know…something I didn't tell you."

She fixed wide eyes on him.

"It concerns Peter's estate."

"Peter's estate? I thought that was just a question of sorting through details…trusts and so on."

Whitcombe evaded her gaze for a moment before turning toward her. "Claire, did you and Peter share your finances?"

"Well, yes. Those trusts were complicated. But we had joint finances and shared the income. We didn't hide anything from each other."

His tired eyes hung on her. "Did you know about a Swiss bank account, with Hoderer-Feltz Bank in Zurich?"

This only added to her perplexity. "No."

"Something I came across when I went through Peter's computer files just after the funeral, at his office in Paris."

"In Paris? Why didn't you mention it to me then?"

"I wanted to look into it first."

Claire kept her gaze level; to look up at the surrounding skyscrapers, she feared, would invite reverse vertigo. She remembered her expedition long ago with Peter on the Pont du Gard; her sensation now felt like the inverse.

"How much money is in it?"

"That's the thing. At the time, there was a zero balance. That's what Peter's records reflected."

"When was the account opened?"

"On Wednesday, September 27th."

"September 27th? That was the week Peter was in Prague."

"I'm aware of that."

Claire looked away and took a deep breath. Could Peter have taken such a step without her knowledge? There had to be some explanation. Above her the tall buildings seemed to spin and sway in the gray skies. She closed her eyes. When she opened them Whitcombe uncrossed his legs and leaned forward, placing his elbows on his knees. "Peter didn't mention a trip to Zurich during that time?"

"No. Nothing."

"The bank said he opened the account in person."

"Maybe he was just preparing something...I don't know. Some kind of surprise?"

Whitcombe winced and looked down at the brick walkway. Okay, this was odd...disorienting. But such gloom was hard to fathom. A sudden thought rallied her.

"If there was no money in the account, Uncle Harry...What's the problem?"

His next words were slow and measured:

"Money did appear in the account later. The day Peter died."

"The day he died? That doesn't make any sense."

"You're right."

Something in his intonation made her shudder. "How much?"

"One and a quarter million dollars."

Claire gasped. "What? From whom?"

"Swiss banking laws are secretive. It took me a while even to confirm what was in the account. So far my lawyers haven't succeeded in identifying the origin of the money."

"Even though...Peter was murdered?"

"This is Switzerland we're talking about, Claire. We may never find out."

"Do you have any ideas?"

"Some---just hypotheses. I realize this is all a bit much to handle at once. It has been for me. Let's get up and walk some more."

CHAPTER 70

Today Whitcombe's secret didn't propel him up a mountainside. His gait was slow and considered. He bent slightly at the waist, gloved hands clasped behind him. Release came through slow revelation.

They fell silent and began a slow loop around the park. Claire glanced sideways at his profile: mouth closed, eyes narrowed and gaze fixed forward. Determined to complete the task that had driven him back to Boston. To her his lordly pace was at odds with his message. Her high heels struck the bricks of the walkway out of rhythm. All constants in her life seemed to shifting…swaying. She avoided looking up at buildings.

They passed a vagrant with several plastic bags of possessions, re-settling on a bench after nighttime ousting, when the park had been brushed and scrubbed. Further on a middle-aged man---probably a hotel guest---sat and enjoyed a cigarette out of doors. Ordinary sights. To Claire they now seemed like live props in a make-believe set.

What Uncle Harry had conveyed didn't square with reality, with all she believed about Peter. She crossed her arms again, trying to retain the sureties she was losing, until they reached a pavilion at the far corner. The newsstand inside was closed. She raised her head, kept her eyes closed and took a deep breath. When she opened them Whitcombe was looking down at her with worn-out compassion.

"How can this be, Uncle Harry?"

"We don't know, Claire. That's what we have to figure out."

They retraced their steps, and when they returned to the bench, Claire was grateful to implant herself again in one position. Whitcombe leaned back and interlocked his fingers on his lap. "My first thought was that Peter was working for the CIA. And that the money came from them. Lots of foreign correspondents have worked for the CIA over the years. Maybe even *World Tribune* correspondents."

"Peter? The CIA? Doing what?"

"God only knows. But the timing was peculiar. He went to Tajikistan to research the heroin trade. He happened to be there just as this military aid bill came up."

She shook her head and squinted down at the wooden bench between them, trying to concentrate. "It still doesn't explain why he was killed. And you were just in Washington. Why didn't you just ask your contacts in the government?"

Whitcombe paused. "I hesitated to do that."

"Why?"

"What if the money didn't come from the CIA?"

"What do you mean?"

"What if Peter had been working for another government? The French, for example, or the Russians."

"French? *La Surete?* Uncle Harry, please…"

"Okay, but there are other possibilities…There's lot of money involved. In the heroin trade, in this aid bill, everywhere. Peter put himself right in the thick of it."

The backdrop of buildings behind Whitcombe was becoming a big, spinning blur. Claire's thoughts were more jumbled than ever. "I don't understand."

"The Russian ambassador was frank with me. Tajikistan offers lots of room for sidelines, Claire. Of various kinds."

"Sidelines? I don't know that word…"

"Making money in parallel with reporting work. Selling information back and forth. Acting as go-between."

In her disbelief she slipped partly into French. "*La corruption? L'espionnage?* Uncle Harry, you knew Peter. That makes no sense. His character was, how to say…*irreprochable…*"

"Money can be a powerful motivator, Claire. And Peter may have thought he was helping his country. This war on terror has caught people up in all sorts of ways."

"Patriotism? I guess so…But money? Peter was rich, Uncle Harry. You know that as well as anyone."

Whitcombe turned his well-bred features down the length of the park, back toward the *Langham*. "Rich…well. You mean the trusts?"

"Yes, I suppose so."

"Did Peter ever complain to you about them?"

"Complain? No, not really. He said they paid for a first-class education. They also supplemented our income in Paris. Though sometimes he said he wished the higher payments would start earlier."

Whitcombe winced. Claire guessed why.

"Many trusts are set up that way, Uncle Harry," she said. "I don't think it was such a huge issue for him."

"What about the incentives to work for the *World Tribune?* Were you familiar with those?"

"I know that income increased if he became managing editor or editor."

Whitcombe became sphinx-like, hands still folded on his lap. "They didn't just increase. They tripled if he became managing editor and quadrupled if he became editor. And that's not to mention additional shares of stock." He pursed his lips. "Those incentives can shape lives in powerful ways. Our Yankee forebears put us all in straitjackets. I realize that, just as Peter probably did."

Claire opened her mouth, but didn't have a coherent response. She still couldn't tell what he was driving toward.

"If you don't mind my asking, Claire...how was your financial situation with Peter? Strains of any kind?"

"Strains? No, not at all. We lived well. We dined out a lot, and stayed in fancy hotels when we traveled together. Okay...our apartment in Paris was rented, and we both would have preferred something bigger. It's just that prices have been going up so fast..."

Whitcombe winced, his pain more pronounced. Sensitive to his every reaction, she paused.

"These real estate excesses of the past five or six years are like nothing I've ever seen," he said, with slight shakes of this head. "It's become an obsession...People everywhere setting themselves up for ruin. The sort of pitfall from which Peter would have been immune, I'd have thought..." He looked down at the pavement in another moment of reflection. "Anything else?"

"Well, we also both wanted kids. We'd just been putting off some of those things..."

A gust of northerly wind blew through the park and ruffled his salt-and-pepper hair from behind. For all his pain---or because of it---he seemed oblivious to the chill. "Whatever the immediate reasons...even in an indirect way," he muttered, half to himself, "Those trusts may have driven Peter to this. To pursue some kind of reckless plan."

His phrasing caused her to breathe faster. More oxygen traveled to her brain but didn't allay the spinning. "Reckless...but Uncle Harry... This is Peter we're talking about!"

"Claire, please. We're just getting at the truth."

* * *

The Russians had been all business on their interdiction mission: tough, stoic, and efficient. Now, though, they were back at base, and their tone was altogether different. They sat around an open fire in a sunken, sheltered area away from main buildings: singing, making

toasts, and devouring spits of barbecued pork. Vodka flowed in abundance. Midnight had already passed.

Conley sat between Nikolai and Oleg on a bench of logs and stone,
smack in front of the fire and hatless. Across flames a soldier strummed
a guitar and sang Russian folk songs, accompanied by a flushed and
swaying chorus of four, still wearing mountain camouflage.

Bradford had missed such festivities, due to the fact that his operation had come up empty.

"I'm surprised they're on key after all that vodka," Conley observed.
He and Oleg had participated in four or five toasts---less than most of
the group, and he was already feeling effects. Not that it mattered;
Nikolai had insisted upon putting off their interview to morning.

"It's a way for them to relieve stress, to unwind," Oleg said. "These
young guys are out here in pretty harsh conditions."

One serenading soldier disentangled himself and sat down on a
nearby stone wall. He stopped singing but continued swaying to the
music, empty shot glass in one hand and cigarette in the other. He
looked about 19 years old. For a moment Conley thought he might
tumble backward onto the ground.

"This posting is also remote," Oleg added. "There are practically
no women here."

Conley nodded.

"Moreover the locals are basically hostile. It's not as dangerous as
Chechnya. But our guys do get killed from time to time. In skirmishes
with bandits, like those you saw today. A couple of dozen died last year."

They paused and listened to music. Next to Conley Nikolai
stretched his bulky frame toward the fire and tended skewers of pork
and onions. Morsels of pork oozed fat, which made the flames sputter.

"Most Americans and Europeans hardly know this place exists,"
Conley said. "Let alone that there are Russian troops here."

This comment made Oleg grimace. "The U.S. has taken an interest *lately*."

"You mean because of Afghanistan?"

He nodded and Conley looked south. Beyond the base perimeter, 100 meters away, a rocky valley yawned in darkness. Afghanistan was only 30 kilometers further. "Franklin Stanson and his ilk mean well," he continued, exasperation crossing his face. "But we've been here for centuries, in one way or another. They forget that."

Conley was eager to talk about Stanson again. He tried, through his mild haze of vodka, to formulate a question. Nikolai interrupted his thoughts.

"Eshcha shashliki?" He asked, holding out a plate heaped with skewers of pork and onions.

Conley had already eaten two skewers' worth. Meat sat heavy in his stomach. *"Nyet, spasibo,"* he said. Oleg declined also. Nikolai grinned and shouted across to the musicians.

"About that uniformed prisoner, Nikolai..."

The Russian released a gruff laugh and reached for a vodka bottle with his outsized fist. Oleg translated.

"He says there's been no time for interrogation..."

Singing stopped. Guitarist and chorus rounded the fire with empty plates and shot glasses. Conley and Oleg consented to one more toast.

"I forgot to ask you, Oleg" Conley said, as Nikolai filled their shot glasses. "When you were in the military, was your duty similar to this?"

"No. More like staff work."

CHAPTER 71

In her absence maid service had put her room in order. Claire hung out the "Do not disturb" sign and doubled-latched the door. With unsteady steps she kicked off her heels, threw her scarf and overcoat on the bedspread, and collapsed into a soft armchair by the window. Quietness and comfort restored a measure of equilibrium. Her thoughts became a little more coherent.

Until questions re-emerged and careened around her head…Was the money connected with Peter's death? Where had it come from? Why had he opened a Swiss bank account without telling her?

For her the estate had been only a ruse. Not a gateway to these sorts of riddles.

Uncle Harry's hypotheses struck her as utterly bizarre. Peter as some kind of clandestine intermediary? Mixed up in espionage, perhaps with a foreign government? It was ridiculous! Peter had often spoken of thinking for himself, of independent action, but espionage was the opposite of that.

Worst of all were Uncle Harry's further intimations. "Sidelines," as he called them? Whiffs of corruption? Such notions made her dizzy. She leaned forward and held her head in her hands. Part of her felt an impulse to sob. These revelations were too overwhelming. For a quarter hour she remained in this same position---shocked and immobile, with careening questions and no answers.

At last something clicked and she sat up straight, her color rising. For the first time that morning she felt *angry*. Angry that Uncle Harry would leap to such conclusions, and that the *World Tribune* would back away from the tribute. Peter had given his *life* in service of the paper... And Uncle Harry was family, for goodness' sake!

Then she remembered the money. How to explain it? She slumped against the backrest with her eyes closed. Meeting her friends this afternoon was out of the question now; she was in no condition for that. And that evening Uncle Harry had invited her to dinner that night in Cambridge; Elizabeth would be there. She'd accepted, and was obliged to go.

Meanwhile Conley remained right in the middle of all this, now out of cell phone range in the hinterlands of Tajikistan. So what if his intentions were good? He was oversexed and self-absorbed, without a full grasp of what he'd stumbled into. Maybe if she just concentrated... focused...tried to stay calm...she could work this all out...

She nearly jumped out of her armchair when her cell-phone rang.

Only four people in the U.S. had her number: Uncle Harry, Gallagher, Larson and Conley...She'd just spoken to Uncle Harry and Conley was incommunicado. She took a deep breath and grabbed the device from the adjacent table.

"Hallo?"

"Claire, this is Art Gallagher...Hope I'm not disturbing you."

She had already lost her composure. His call only disoriented her more.

"I realize you're staying in a hotel. ...If you have no other plans, my wife and I would like to invite you to our house for a home-cooked meal. We live out in Belmont."

Claire struggled to think. Could this be an opening from another quarter? "That's very kind," she blurted. "Unfortunately I'm having dinner with the Whitcombes tonight."

"Harry Whitcombe? He's back in Boston?"

"Well…yes."

On his end Gallagher seemed confused. Voices and laughter sounded in the background, as if he was at some sort of social event.

"Actually we were thinking of tomorrow evening. Can you join us?"

"Tomorrow? What time?"

"Say…five-thirty? We can have a drink beforehand."

Claire gripped the phone tighter and tried to control stress in her voice. "Okay, thank you, Art. Belmont, you said? I'll need driving directions."

*   *   *

Gallagher snapped his cell phone shut and held it near his chin, with one arm crossed over his stomach. Around him the field was already blanketed with parked cars and loud laughter. Last Boston College home game of the season. Tailgate parties were bellowing to life.

"Is she coming?" Denise asked.

"Yes."

"You look perplexed."

"Harry Whitcombe is back in Boston."

They'd set up a grill behind the open hatch of their Volvo wagon. Denise put down a pitcher of Bloody Marys, next to a tray of hors d'oeuvres, dip, and a bowl of potato chips. She gave her husband a perplexed look of her own.

"He met Claire this morning, at her hotel," Gallagher explained. "Claire sounded a little…"

"There you are!"

This booming interruption came from Mike Fallon, red-faced and grinning. Though with Fallon, Gallagher and Denise both knew, redness was a matter of degrees. His wife Shannon was more restrained than her husband, but a good sport about pre-game parties. She placed a sealed, plastic bowl of cookies on the table, after which Gallagher gave her a hug---one that grew more from common origins in South

Boston than shared corridors of the *World Tribune*. Fallon did likewise with Denise, then slapped a fleshy hand on Gallagher's shoulder.

"Saw you on the phone, Art...Hope you weren't doing newsroom business."

Denise and Shannon separated themselves into another conversation.

"Well...not exactly. That was Claire. Bradford's widow."

Fallon's head cocked. Management at the *World Tribune* was unsettled and on guard because of Whitcombe's abdication. He looked at Gallagher, expecting more.

"Let me get you a Bloody Mary first, Mike," Gallagher said. He poured two glasses and extracted his cigarettes from his jacket pocket. He lit one for Fallon, and one for himself. Before sipping his Bloody Mary he took a deep drag. "Claire's staying in a hotel," he said finally. "We invited her to dinner tomorrow evening."

"Nathan Frick invited too?"

Gallagher grunted and snorted smoke out his nose, and Fallon laughed. In surrounding parking fields, bellowing and laughing grew louder as more spectators arrived. Barbecue smoke infused the air. Sounds of drums and wind instruments issued from the stadium, as bands warmed up before the game. They glanced up at the changing skies. It appeared that the weather would hold, at least through kickoff.

"Your boy Conley just has to make it to the end zone, Art. No...let's call it the finish line."

"Right. He's almost there. Just another week."

"After that Harry Whitcombe will be back, too. Everything will be normal again."

Gallagher thought for a moment, still puzzled by Whitcombe's early return to Boston. There was no point in informing Fallon for now.

"Let's drink to it," Fallon suggested. He raised his glass.

Gallagher sighed and reciprocated. "I hope you're right, Mike."

"That's the spirit."

Over Fallon's shoulder Gallagher saw Denise signaling toward him.

"Time to light the grill," he said.

CHAPTER 72

For the first time ever Claire ordered room service. Her appetite was so meager that she ate only a few bites of her sandwich and fruit salad, and left plates and uneaten food in the hallway. After lunch she sat in the armchair or paced. Her mood alternated between muddled despair and stubborn determination. During one of the latter she moved a framed photograph of Peter from the nightstand to the desk. Would his image bring answers? None came.

Should she call Uncle Harry and Elizabeth and opt out of dinner? Grapple with this alone? She took a deep breath. Uncle Harry was as distraught as she was. And Elizabeth was understanding, *très sympathique.* They wanted to help her, one way or another. There were no sound reasons to cancel.

As the hour approached she washed her face, re-applied her makeup, brushed her hair, and put on a charcoal gray evening dress and pearls. Uncle Harry sent a car; near six o'clock it deposited her at the side entrance of the Whitcombes' red brick mansion in Cambridge. Harry and Elizabeth were there to greet her. Just inside the foyer, Claire started in surprise. Tracey stood waiting. Was she informed about Peter? Her presence suggested she was.

"We weren't sure that Tracey would join us." " Whitcombe said, helping Claire off with her coat. "Hope you don't mind."

"No. Of course not." Claire tilted her face upward for an exchange of kisses. Tracey displayed her usual long-limbed modesty. Claire had long wondered: did Tracey understand how striking she was? But that was of no consequence tonight...

"There are only four of us," Whitcombe said. "And we're all family. I suggest we have drinks in the library." On the way, Claire noticed there were no servants. Elizabeth explained that she had expected to drive to Loon for the weekend, and had dismissed the cook and maid until Monday. She was preparing dinner with her husband.

The Whitcombes' library was paneled in dark wood and upholstered in burgundy leather. Turkish rugs covered swaths of floor. The house had been in Elizabeth's family for generations and harked back to an earlier epoch, before television and films. Books were numerous enough to require a decimal ordering system. Claire requested scotch on the rocks on the stronger side.

"I think we all need one of those, Claire, after this week," Elizabeth said, tilting her head in shared commiseration.

"I'll join you," Whitcombe responded.

Tracey demurred and chose mineral water. Whitcombe repaired to a small liquor cabinet set among the bookshelves. When they were all seated with drinks Peter and the Swiss bank account hung in the room like a silent specter. Soon Claire realized the aim of this gathering was not endless dissection in the French manner. These old-line Yankees lent moral support through less esoteric means: simply by hewing together. Tonight maybe that approach was probably appropriate. Their careful cordiality reassured her, while the scotch lubricated her throat and disentangled her senses. By degrees she settled back against the soft leather of her backrest.

Tracey mostly listened, perched forward with alert eyes.

After about 15 minutes Uncle Harry and Elizabeth excused themselves to the kitchen. Claire took another gulp of scotch, finishing her glass. Tracey noticed at once and offered to get her another. Alcohol was having an effect. On the other hand, as Uncle Harry said, this was family. And these were special circumstances. Claire looked at Tracey's mineral water.

"Will you join me, Tracey?"

"Well, okay…maybe just one."

Tracey traversed the room to the drink cupboard, a little self-conscious. "I just learned today, Claire."

"Like me then…"

"Yes…" She poured drinks; her own portion somewhat smaller. "…At least my father's behavior now makes more sense. We didn't know what was going on."

Claire remembered Whitcombe's regulated breathing and long strides up the mountainside at Loon. She couldn't say she felt better now, knowing the source of his torment.

After handing her the refill Tracey re-seated herself on the forward edge of her armchair, pressed her long legs together, and wrapped her hands around her glass. "There was a fairly big age difference between Peter and me growing up," she said. "But we did spend a lot summers together. I was shocked. It just doesn't fit."

Some seconds of silence passed. Faint sounds of cookware emanated from the kitchen on the other side of the house. What could she say? This evening was about reinforcement, not explanations.

"You're kind to come tonight, Tracey."

"No need to thank me Claire. I admit…I feel partly to blame."

"You?"

"I thought my father told you at Loon…"

Claire had almost forgotten about Tracey's connection with Conley---obscured by Uncle Harry's bombshell in the park that morning. However that was tangential to their main worry and *très personnel*…

"He did. But really, Tracey…"

"No need to be embarrassed." Tracey paused for a moment, considering her words. She took a small sip of scotch. "How well do you know Steve Conley?"

"Well…he was only in Paris a week."

"Then I want to reassure you."

"Reassure me? About Steve?"

"I can tell you that he means well. Even when he's not really at fault…he'll keep your best interests in mind."

Claire remembered Conley's impulsive, bumbling pass in the corridor outside her apartment, and his subsequent misadventures in Prague and Moscow. Tracey's endorsement of him seemed ambiguous. This scotch was not just relaxing, she realized; it was dulling her mental acuity. She frowned and moved forward on her armchair, gripping her glass hard with both hands. "I'm sorry, Tracey…I don't understand what you're getting at."

"Whatever information Steve uncovers about Peter, he'll be responsible with it."

" 'Responsible?' I don't quite follow…"

"I mean that he'll have some discretion in the way he reports the story. And well…we can be hopeful."

Claire gazed into her drink and fought her enveloping haze. Discretion? That word had never come up before. Tracey opened her mouth to elaborate but stopped when her father's tall frame appeared in the doorway. Whitcombe's preoccupations seemed leavened by the act of cooking. Claire had never seen him wearing an apron.

"We're ready with dinner," he said. "Rather simple. Sometimes, though, simple is best."

CHAPTER 73

Two years earlier the base had served 15,000 to 16,000 Russian border troops. That was now below 5,000, thanks to recent reductions. Who was going to fill the void, Conley wondered? Tajiks?

"There's the nub of the problem," Oleg said.

Depleted or not, by nine a.m. the base was already high gear. Like many military installations it was a self-contained entity, with complex infrastructure. Transport, housing, food, maintenance and training were all in evidence. Individual soldiers---most clad in camouflage---strode between office buildings around staging areas, carrying paperwork, maps or tools. A platoon marched and performed weapons drills. Clerks unloaded a supply truck at an adjacent mess hall. Near a gate a convoy of five armored vehicles queued up with engines idling; *serzhanti* and an officer performed final checks before venturing into rocky flatlands to the southeast. On an adjacent landing pad a helicopter stood with stationary blades. Crates and gear were stacked nearby, prepared for loading. To one side Conley spotted his black hardcover suitcase, surrounded by olive duffel bags. Civilian baggage seemed an incongruous presence, somehow, in this hardscrabble corner of Central Asia.

"There'll be some military personnel along for the ride," Oleg said to Conley. "But this flight to Dushanbe is basically for you."

"Didn't realize the Russian military was so accommodating to Western press."

"Times change."

Nikolai appeared with a steaming pot of coffee and three aluminum mugs, and sat down with Conley and Oleg at a wooden table, situated along a clapboard-sided administrative building. There was bite in the dry air, but no wind. Interrogation of the prisoner had already started. Conley decided to hold that subject for later. "I'd first like to ask about Peter Bradford," he said, pulling out his notepad. Oleg translated his questions about the mission that Bradford had accompanied. Nikolai was complimentary. Bradford had followed instructions without hesitation: no problems at all with the Russian language. Calm at all times, even while lying in wait on a ridge.

"Very professional," Nikolai said. "He knew how to behave."

Conley made a note and underlined it. Bradford had never encountered combat before. Not bad for a blueblood scholar in Slavic studies, who'd spent most of his adult life in lecture halls and libraries at Harvard and the Sorbonne.

Was Bradford disappointed when there were no encounters with smugglers? No, Nikolai answered. Bradford seemed to understand the vagaries of such operations: "It didn't seem essential to him, one way or the other."

What was essential, then?

Nikolai thought for a moment. "Nothing I mentioned about the political situation seemed new to him." Complicity of the Tajik government in the heroin trade? Bradford had listened carefully and taken copious notes. Not surprised, though. More like confirmation. Nikolai called Bradford "a man who came prepared." At last Conley asked about the interrogation. Nikolai shook his head in distaste.

"Same old story. We've caught a half-dozen of this type before."

This particular smuggler was a junior officer in the Dushanbe militia. His job was to make sure the convoy reached destination---a small warehouse near the train station in central Dushanbe---without interference from authorities. Imprimatur for safe transit. Orders? "Right from the top," the smuggler had pleaded.

"What will happen to him?" Conley asked.

"We'll hold him for about a month, then turn him back to the Tajik government."

"Then what?"

"His main mistake was getting caught. So he might spend some time in prison. Symbolic: six months or a year. After that...who knows? He might even be put back in circulation."

"Incredible. Is the Tajik government adversary or ally in all this?"

Nikolai's offered a fatalistic shrug. "That's for Moscow to determine. We're just military. We have to do the best with the orders we're given."

After translating this remark, Oleg injected commentary of his own, speaking less like an interpreter than a spokesperson for Russian interests: "You should appreciate our dilemma here, Steve. Tajikistan is a sovereign country. Root out government corruption? That's not realistic. What's the best we can do? Same we've been doing since the 90s. Reduce heroin going to Russian cities---at least a little bit. Curtail opium going through to Europe. Deprive the Chechens of some income. That's about it." By now Oleg had gotten up a head of steam, to the extent possible for a stoic, careful Russian. "...That's not even our main worry. If Russian troops were completely gone, can you imagine the dangers? Hordes of Muslim extremists flooding in here from Afghanistan? Think it's bad now? It would become a real nightmare."

Conley visualized a map of the region, with various curved arrows pointing north. "I suppose that explains why the U.S. has become engaged." Oleg grimaced. He translated the remark into Russian for Nikolai, who averted his eyes and seemed content to let Oleg respond:

"The U.S. means well. But quite frankly..." He checked himself. "It lacks experience in the region."

"Let's take this prisoner, for example," Conley said. "Interior Ministry. That's part of Shakuri's domain, isn't it?"

"Yes."

"How does Franklin Stanson react to such information?"

"Stanson is more-or-less well-disposed toward Russians and values our recent cooperation. Still, on an institutional level, the U.S. doesn't trust our intelligence. There's suspicion that Russia is...how do you say it...trying to box the U.S. out of the region. Call it residual mistrust...a legacy from the Cold War. That filters out into the field, even to guys like Stanson."

"So Stanson would prefer to trust Shakuri?"

"Shakuri speaks fluent English. That counts for a lot. Stanson says 'Shakuri is a man the U.S. can do business with.' "

Conley glanced up from his notepad and across the compound toward the helicopter pad. Blades on the aircraft remained still but soldiers were now loading baggage and other items aboard. Departure was scheduled in 30 minutes. He turned back again to Oleg.

"Still...my impression is that Stanson is dedicated. This war on terror is important to him. Would you give him that?"

This question was translated into Russian for Nikolai; he kept his hands folded and stared down at the wooden table.

Oleg released a weary exhalation. "Maybe. But good intentions can be dangerous in this part of the world."

CHAPTER 74

Thick fudge frosting and Oreo cookie ice cream, and such portions…Claire couldn't recall last time she'd eaten such abundant, rich dessert. But after this weekend she needed a boost. Not to mention allies. She couldn't turn the Gallaghers down.

"There's more, if you like," Denise said.

Claire hadn't yet finished her first serving. Art was ready for seconds.

"Just a small slice and one scoop, please," he said to Denise.

Cake that Denise subsequently transferred onto her husband's plate was sized…*très généreusement* by French standards. The garnishing of ice cream was by itself…*une dessert propre.* Claire remembered why she'd had trouble staying trim during her sojourn in Boston with Peter. It seemed like such a pedestrian preoccupation now, after all that had happened during the past two months…

"Usually I'm stricter, because of Art's diet," Denise said. "But these last weeks have been stressful…due to Peter, of course, and Steve Conley…and everything else."

Did Harry Whitcombe fall into the same category of woe? Nathan Frick? Claire wasn't sure how to react.

"More decaf?" Denise asked her.

"Please."

Earlier that evening she'd arrived still disoriented; Uncle Harry's bombshell had turned her world inside out. What, now, was she aiming toward? What did she hope to gain from Art Gallagher, if anything? Then there was Tracey's half-hearted encomium to Conley, which had spun her thoughts off in a vague new direction.

But the Gallaghers turned out to be just the rock-solid way station she needed. Sympathetic and involved, like the Whitcombes, but less directly affected. Art's altruistic impulses toward her were now unmistakable. Misgivings? There clearly were some. But both Art and Denise were in her corner. She had relaxed ever so slightly.

During pre-dinner drinks, Gallagher had inquired, with evident circumspection, about Harry Whitcombe's surprise appearance in Boston. "Estate issues," she'd explained. What else could she tell them? Art had adjusted his glasses and flicked a glance toward his wife. "Is he going back to Loon, or staying here?"

"I'm not exactly sure, Art."

Now over dessert Gallagher trod gently back toward the *World Tribune.*" I don't want to discuss the assignment too much on a Sunday, Claire," he said, dabbing his lips with a napkin and reaching for his coffee cup. "But I thought I'd give you some news."

Claire swallowed cake that was in her mouth and washed it down with a gulp of decaf. Another bombshell was the last thing she needed.

"Our Congressional reporter in Washington...Reynolds is his name, as I told you...continues to track that aid bill."

"Something happen since Thursday?"

"Well, yes. The amount of money..."

Claire dropped her fork, which clanked off the side of the dessert plate and onto white tablecloth. The utensil stuck in place because of its coating of fudge and ice cream.

"...Has been increased: from $500 million to $550 million. And the bill now has the votes to pass." While Gallagher paused, Claire pried the fork off the fabric and examined the sticky, chocolate-colored stain underneath. Denise caught her gaze and smiled. "It's nothing," she told her in a polite undertone.

"...Final passage is expected on Friday," Gallagher added.

Claire struggled to appear calm. She replaced the fork on her plate. "Is that good?"

Gallagher took another sip of decaf, then stroked his beard once with thumb and index finger. "Good for Conley, I think. The Tajik government will go out of their way to make sure nothing happens to him this week. The situation should be more controlled. They don't want any last-minute dramas. Too much money is at stake."

Claire's next words were spontaneous, entirely devoid of premeditation. Afterward, she wondered if they were provoked by the high level of sugar in her bloodstream, or by the Gallaghers' cat, which brushed against her shins at that very instant under the table.

"I wish I could be there myself," she said.

At first Art's and Denise's expressions were uncomprehending. Then knowing sympathy appeared, first in Denise's eyes, seconds later in Art's.

"That's a noble sentiment, Claire, after all you've been through," Denise said.

"No. I mean it."

Gallagher contemplated her for a moment, then said, "It's just a matter of days, Claire. Steve will be leaving Dushanbe on Friday." She took another quick sip of coffee while her thoughts raced ahead toward concrete steps...travel...implementation...before hitting a wall and stopping cold. Visas took weeks to process and there were no commercial flights into the country. Her idea was foolish.

"I'm sorry," she said. "You're right."

"It's okay," Denise said. "We've all be under some stress."

Still thoughtful, Art turned his attention to his last bites of dessert, and Claire felt the cat brush her legs again. She lifted the edge of tablecloth to look down around her ankles. The cat stopped and looked back up at her, wide-eyed and intrigued.

Denise smiled. "Her name is Cleopatra. I hope she's not bothering you."

After her gaffe, Claire welcomed such distraction. "No, of course not."

"She's drawn to people with a lot of energy."

Claire took the remark as a compliment. She smiled with all grace she could muster, after the ordeals of the weekend. When they'd finished desserts Denise cleared away plates to the kitchen, declining her offer of help and leaving her and Art with fresh refills of decaf. Claire noticed Art eyeing his cigarettes, which were lying next to an ashtray and lighter on a side cabinet. She remembered him lingering outside the lobby of the *World Tribune* on Thursday.

"I don't mind if you smoke, Art."

"Thanks. I guess more lenient attitudes still prevail in Europe." With exertion he pushed back his chair, then reseated himself with a thud. His first drag was a deep one. Nicotine appeared to crystallize his thoughts.

"I understand you're coming into the newsroom tomorrow," he said.

"Yes...Janet Larson invited me."

Around Gallagher the smoke formed a blue-gray cloud. He shook his head once. "A lot of newsroom politics have grown up around this assignment. But let's try to forget about that this week."

"Okay."

Indeed, politics were now the least of her concerns.

"These next few days, Claire, what can I do to help you?"

"Well...I...don't even know anymore, Art. I just want..."

Gallagher studied her, his concern palpable through the pall of smoke.

The dictum from Voltaire almost caused her to add, *"...the truth."* But she stopped herself. Now she wasn't sure if she meant it.

CHAPTER 75

Cleopatra was already shooting upstairs, sensing the approach of bedtime. Denise paused at the bottom step. "Coming up soon, Art?" From his favorite armchair, Gallagher blew a column of smoke out into the darkened living room. "Just a few minutes, dear."

Trajan sprawled on the carpet a few feet away, eyes half-closed. Gallagher had just taken him out to curbside for the day's final ministrations. A tranquil ritual: Trajan was compliant and predictable when there were no bitches in the vicinity.

Embers glowed in the fireplace. The fire had been largely for Claire's benefit, as they'd settled down for after-dinner liqueurs. Now she'd been gone more than an hour. Her presence, though, still buzzed the house. Gallagher continued to marvel about her. There was no mistaking it; for all her trauma, she was a force. He had strong suspicions that activity in the newsroom---at least that involving Larson, Frick and himself---would revolve around her all week. Whatever happened, she'd be the driver.

Not that that was bad. He'd decided she deserved it.

Moreover these newsroom maneuvers would probably matter little, in the end. Conley would be making his own decisions on the ground in Dushanbe.

There was little choice but to hope for the best.

After a last, deep drag Gallagher stubbed out his cigarette and rose with a half-grunt. He bent over and patted Trajan. Unlike Cleopatra, Trajan was limited to downstairs. "Good old boy," he said.

Once upstairs, he sat down on the edge of the bed, pulled off his slippers and unbuttoned his cardigan. Denise emerged from the bathroom, wearing a cotton nightgown. Cleopatra showed her contentment by brushing against Gallagher's calves.

"I'm glad we invited Claire," Denise said.

"I am too."

"The poor girl seems under terrible strain."

"Yes...Even more than a few days ago."

"Why would that be?"

Gallagher exhaled hard and stretched his arms backward to slip off his cardigan. "Harry's return, maybe. Or those estate issues she alluded to."

"I hope she's not having money troubles."

"Wouldn't think so."

Denise clicked on the bedside reading lamp, turned back covers, propped up a couple of pillows, and climbed in. On her nightstand was a hardcover copy of Norman Mailer's *Ancient Evenings;* her interest in ancient Egypt paralleled her husband's in Rome. She reached for her reading glasses, just as Cleopatra leaped onto the bed, in single, spring-like motion. The cat settled down around her feet. As rituals went, sleep was Cleopatra's favorite.

"Do you think Harry will show up at the *World Tribune* tomorrow?" Denise asked.

"Good question. I don't know."

"Would you be surprised?"

Gallagher sighed. He stood, inhaled, and thrust his chest out. With both hands he reached under his stomach to unfasten his belt buckle. "After the last couple of weeks, I'm prepared for anything."

"This drama is almost over, dear."

After hanging his clothes, he padded across toward the bathroom, clad only in boxer shorts and undershirt. He observed Denise opening her book. Its binding extended up to the plunging neckline of her nightgown, accenting her plump bosom. New and unexpected energy took hold of him.

"Are you going to read now?"

On the bed, Cleopatra raised her head from front paws and opened her eyes, shooting glances at both of them.

Denise looked up at him over the tops of her reading glasses, smiling and a little surprised. "Why do you ask?"

CHAPTER 76

In physical terms Bill Hermann struck Conley as a younger clone of Franklin Stanson: same wire-rimmed aviator glasses and spreading midriff. Otherwise: minus the drawl and unaffected manners. A more explicit offspring of Washington, and of the defense establishment in particular.

When Hermann saw Oleg he stiffened, as if encountering an intruder on a restricted base. It was clear that Hermann did not share Stanson's ease with Russians.

"Peter Bradford came alone," he said.

"Oleg is my translator during this trip," Conley explained, shaking Hermann's hand.

"But our talk's in English."

"Oleg's accompanying me to everything. The more informed he is, the better."

Hermann paused and squinted at Conley and Oleg through his glasses. Conley wondered if Hermann was among those who rejected intelligence from the Russians. Safe bet that he was. Fifteen years after the fact, the Cold War had its stubborn holdouts. When at last Hermann thrust out his hand to Oleg, the movement could have been through barbed wire.

"That's right. Franklin mentioned you."

Oleg's face was impassive, except for a slight curl around his mouth. He seemed used to such treatment.

They settled around a small conference table along one side of Hermann's spacious office. A fourth-floor window opened onto the gray tones of Prospekt Rudaki, the main boulevard of Dushanbe, and was set in a five-story building---seemingly the only modern, post-Soviet office building in the capital. There was a perimeter wall around the edifice and tight security in the lobby. The office was furnished with sleek, new acquisitions: satin-nickel finishes and black-leather. On a side cabinet next to Hermann's desk were a state-of-the-art PC and a full complement of peripherals, including a 19-inch flat-screen monitor. Like Stanson, Hermann didn't seem to lack for funding. The war on terror didn't cut corners.

Hermann spent just half the week there. As usual he'd flown in from Almaty that morning, and would fly back out on Wednesday afternoon. His main office was in the U.S. Embassy in Almaty, which other members of the U.S. mission to Tajikistan also utilized as their primary base.

"Still a bit hairy to live here full-time," Hermann stated in an over-forceful voice. "But we're looking to change that."

His State Department title was "Special Liaison for Anti-terror Initiatives-Tajikistan." His line of reporting was somewhat ambiguous, although he seemed to fall under Stanson's supervision. Was Hermann CIA? Such distinctions were often blurred where terror was concerned. Conley decided to ask.

"The Agency has never had any permanent resources here," the official answered. "So if you're asking if I'm the Station Chief, the answer is no. There's nothing to manage."

Conley didn't understand. If not intelligence, what was his principal brief?

"Planning for this aid grant. Preparing the way for a 'full-court assault' on the terror networks here."

Further questioning revealed that Hermann was the local U.S. interlocutor for Shakuri, at least for three days per week. To Conley's astonishment he admitted he had never ventured outside of the region around Dushanbe, not even south toward Afghanistan, as Conley just had---with Russian troops or without them. The anti-terror effort meant something different in Tajikistan than it did in Afghanistan. Money was the centerpiece, rather than U.S. operatives on the ground. For now the entire initiative hinged on Shakuri. The U.S. military advisors and equipment, if they came at all, would come later.

Hermann read Conley's dismay and tried to defuse it with an awkward nod to nationalism. "You should understand, Steve. The Russkies..." Conley glanced at Oleg, who just gave the official a cold stare. "...are on our side now, at least at the top level. I'll acknowledge that. But down here, there's still the old rivalry. They'll try to shut us out, if they can. Here we have to find our own solutions."

If he was bothered by Oleg's disdain, it didn't show---as if the dynamic was immutable and therefore unsuited to regrets. However Conley's dismay stemmed more from other factors. "With so little intelligence," he asked. "What makes you certain you can trust Shakuri?"

Hermann refocused his hard stare. "I know the rumors about him. That's the sort of thing we hear from the Russians." Conley described what he had seen on the heroin interdiction sortie over the weekend---a smuggler in Interior Ministry uniform. "It's a messy country," Hermann responded. "Dirt poor. There's bound to that kind of thing. Shakuri wants to clean it up."

"With $500 million in U.S. funds?"

Hermann seemed proud of the number. "Actually it's now $550 million."

"Really? As of when?"

"Saturday." Hermann reclined in his chair and crossed his arms. "You know. Peter Bradford seemed to understand all this before he got here."

"Understand what?"

"Our challenges in this country. How terror is priority number one. And maybe most important…that we've got exploit the assets we have."

That led Conley into his next line of questioning.

*   *   *

On the subject of Bradford's murder Hermann adopted a tone of bureaucratic lament. An unfortunate but unavoidable accident in a chaotic region. Collateral damage. "Sad," he said in a more somber tone, leaning forward again over conference table. He interlocked his fingers in a show of fatalism. "But this kind of senseless violence happens in these parts." Conley asked: did Hermann believe explanations from Shakuri and Tajik authorities? Oleg bore in on Hermann with an intense look. This seemed of more interest to the Russian than other matters.

"No doubts at all," Hermann answered.

Even though Bradford was killed by security personnel who worked for Shakuri?

"Shakuri let us know right away. The killers were found and arrested the very next morning."

"And died a few days later in prison," Conley noted. "Before you could interrogate them yourselves."

Though Hermann had his defenses raised he was not the type to be provoked. He sat up straighter, one elbow on an armrest, and studied Conley with a plain expression, ignoring Oleg for the moment. This was one American to another. No concealment behind the big aviator glasses. There was nothing to hide at this outpost of empire.

"Let's review the facts," Conley suggested.

Hermann appeared ready to oblige and reached for a folder. Conley glanced over the exterior of the packet for indications of security classification, and saw there were none.

In slow, methodical, fashion he revisited the crime and reviewed details of the official Tajik investigation. There was an unadorned directness in Hermann's approach that Conley found commendable to certain extent, but also unsettling. For a security operative in a dangerous, convoluted region---an emissary in the war on terror, in effect---Hermann exhibited little fine differentiation. There was no calibrated scale; the war on terror set us against them, forces of good versus forces of evil. Shakuri had joined ranks with the United States; his reliability in the Bradford investigation was assumed.

And if not? The war on terror trumped other considerations.

"One part still doesn't make sense," Conley said.

Hermann listened, still willing to cooperate, to a point.

"Why would the killers assume that Bradford was carrying a large amount of cash?"

"Maybe they'd heard things."

"Like what?"

"I'll be honest, Steve. I mean they'd heard about Americans distributing cash... Stanson and me. Preparing the ground here. We'd visited Shakuri's villa. Details are classified. But you get the picture."

Conley glanced at Oleg, who didn't seem surprised.

"You mean they thought Bradford was working for the U.S. government?"

"Maybe. An easy mistake. Not many Western journalists come through here...They didn't speak English. Maybe they thought he was making the rounds...that Shakuri was just the first stop. I hate to say it. These people are primitive. Who knows what they imagined?"

A half an hour later, when Hermann saw Conley and Oleg off in the lobby, Conley remained troubled by these explanations. Hermann's singular focus and credulity were vexing. Too many suppositions and leaps of faith. Out on the Prospekt he and Oleg walked southward, toward their hotel. Piles of pungent, dead leaves---raked long before and still awaiting collection---lined the sidewalks. They passed Dushanbe's massive, columned opera theater, a relic of Soviet dominion and now in crumbling dilapidation. The main railway station was visible at one end of the boulevard; Conley knew it was the primary transit point for heroin bound northward to Russia. Car traffic was meager. Almost all pedestrians were male, in somber Central Asian garb.

Despite overlapping history, this was a world apart from Moscow.

He stopped, reached into his case and pulled out his camera. At two o'clock they had an interview scheduled with the Tajiki director of drug enforcement, an underling of Shakuri's. That left time for photographs before lunch. Like Bradford, Conley was acting as his own photographer on this assignment. He turned on battery power and examined digital indicators. "Oleg, I'm starting to agree with you in one sense. Stanson and Hermann seem a little one-dimensional."

Oleg raised his eyebrows. "What about Bradford?"

"Not cut from the same cloth. Bradford was different."

He stepped closer to the curb and readied his camera. He had gotten it into his head to take some shots that encompassed the train station. Several passersby gave him suspicious, angry stares. He ignored them.

"Different? How?" Oleg asked, becoming a little on guard because of the attention.

"He was too smart, one would think…to blunder into untenable situations."

Oleg made a quick scan of the sidewalk in both directions. "You're probably right. My impression is…he wasn't the blundering type."

CHAPTER 77

This was precisely what Claire had aimed toward when she'd first come to Boston. Respect from Larson. Support from Gallagher. Placement in the thick of editorial decision-making.

Only now her plan had been turned upside down. What disgraces might Conley unearth about Peter, halfway around the globe? This question kept turning over in her head.

The meeting---late morning on Monday---had been underway for nearly an hour. She was sitting at one end of the long table, opposite Larson---a sign of her new, hard-won status. Frick resided at Larson's elbow, sinewy and alert. Halfway down the other side, Gallagher reclined with his arms folded over his stomach. They'd been reviewing Conley's agenda for the week in Dushanbe. Plans and contingencies. Soliciting her input at every turn. Through it all she was doing her best to stay composed. She kept her hands folded on the table, to avoid shaking. Conscious that tightness in her throat made her speech hoarse. Larson---in her careful, diplomatic way---was finally getting around to what she'd been intent to know from the beginning: whether Claire remained in contact with Harry Whitcombe. "These next issues relate to the aid bill," she said, flicking her eyes down the length of the table over the tops of her reading glasses. "A shame Harry's not here..."

Friday's luncheon maneuvers now seemed like hollow tactical triumphs. Claire told herself to be prudent. To keep Uncle Harry's unscripted homecoming to herself. Nonetheless she struggled to think straight …Gallagher intervened to take her off the hook. "On that note…I've got an update from Reynolds…" His chair produced a metallic squeak as he leaned forward over his notes.

A sudden impulse seized her. She was desperate to break free of this play-acting…to get something moving, even if she didn't know in what direction. She lobbed her bombshell back across.

"I saw Uncle Harry over the weekend," she said.

Larson and Frick froze. Gallagher looked up from his legal pad--- more worried than startled.

"In Boston?" Larson asked.

"At my hotel on Saturday morning. And again that same evening, for dinner in Cambridge."

Larson made on obvious effort to stay cool, though her eyes bore new flickers of trepidation. This kind of chaos was not her strong suit. "Is he still here?"

There was no going back. "Well, yes," Claire blurted. "He called me this morning." At the same instant she felt her cell-phone buzz in her breast pocket, and pulled it out so that the low buzz became audible to everyone, as well as a flashing LED indicator. The display didn't identify the originating caller.

"Only a handful of people have this number," she said, her voice still hoarse. "Could be either Steve Conley or Uncle Harry."

Everyone stared at the phone. Another chirping ring pierced the silence.

"Perhaps you should answer then," Larson said.

*   *   *

Due to the weakness of the signal Conley rose from his shabby, low-slung armchair and walked over to the window. Over a crackling connection, he heard Claire say, *"It's Steve."* There was a pause and sound of a door opening.

"Claire, can you hear me? Am I interrupting something?"

"I was in a meeting...I'm here at the World Tribune. But I'm out in the corridor now."

"Another meeting...?" A burst of static cut him short. He shifted two steps, hoping to mitigate interference. His third-floor room in the *Hotel Tajikistan*, in classic late Soviet style, had a large, drafty plate-glass window, hung with worn, mass-produced lace curtains. Outside, darkness had fallen.

"It's a long story..." Her voice sounded strained. *"I'm involved on this end now. Janet and Art have agreed..."* Another burst of static garbled her remaining words.

In frustration Conley yanked open the threadbare curtain, as if that would improve his reception, and determined that his south-facing direction was the problem. That Claire had insinuated herself into editorial meetings somehow didn't surprise him.

"Where are you calling from?" she asked.

"My hotel room."

"Can't you use your room phone?"

"No...I've been advised not to. It could be tapped."

"Tapped?"

Hermann had given him the warning. For an instant he stared at his own reflection on the blackness of the window holding cell-phone; such advice now struck him as preposterous. He decided not to go into details.

"It's nothing," he said.

Shifting another half step, he found a vector where reception sounded more stable. "It's been a few days since we talked, Claire," he began, before giving a quick summary of his weekend with the Russian patrols. In contrast to earlier calls, she was short on questions, much less insistent. He wondered if it had something to do with her presence in the newsroom. In response to his query about the meeting she belied uncharacteristic hesitation.

"Well, one topic…is whether or not you should go to Shakuri's villa. That is, if you're invited."

"Art and talked about that last week. We agreed that Oleg should go with me."

"Now they don't seem so sure…"

There was a knock on the hotel room door, three quick raps: a code/safety measure he had agreed upon with Oleg. Conley took several quick steps toward the door, unlatched it, and bounded back toward the window. Crackling obliterated most of Claire's words. He glanced toward Oleg, who wore a winter coat and held a fur hat; he made an apologetic gesture, as if to leave and come back later. Urging him to stay, he held out his palm, then leaned closer to the glass.

"Claire, this connection is too erratic. Tell Art I'll send him e-mail later tonight. Tomorrow I'll find a place where there's better reception."

"So you'll call tomorrow, then?"

Her tone, Conley noticed, was more plaintive than resolute. That was a first, since he'd left Paris.

CHAPTER 78

Through his office windows Gallagher spotted Larson, striding along the opposite wall of the newsroom. With one hand she held up her reading glasses, prodding her lips with an ear stem. Even from a distance he could tell she was frazzled. Still off balance after the morning's meeting. It was the first time that had happened since he'd known her. And he had little doubt about the cause.

As if on cue the door to the women's restroom swung open and Claire emerged, while Larson was just a few paces away. Claire's eyes enlarged, and they both pulled up and stared at each other.

Larson lowered her reading glasses and emitted an apparent pleasantry, while Claire, taking a step forward with a stiff movement, clasped her lightly on the elbow. Quick, forced smiles and both went on their way---Claire bound for the water cooler.

Gallagher couldn't foretell how the conjoining would play out. For now Claire enjoyed an exclusive line of communication to Harry Whitcombe---her main card. This week would be an engrossing and unpredictable all around. Not just in Dushanbe.

Whatever happened he re-affirmed his resolution. He would help Claire where he could.

He swiveled back toward his computer screen to re-read Conley's
e-mail. It was long: Conley's first since Moscow. He skimmed over his
long description of the Russian patrol, reaching the part that concerned Hermann:

*...To me, this Tajik Interior Ministry uniform was vivid evidence of corruption.
But Hermann was dismissive: "the sort of thing that's bound to happen in a
dirt-poor country," he said. And that, "Shakuri is trying to stamp it out." He
claims the Russians exaggerate the phenomenon. Old-style geo-political games-
manship. I'm less convinced, so far...*

Gallagher frowned, stroked his beard, and skipped further ahead.
During an afternoon interview with Ibrohom Vokhidov, Tajik drug
enforcement chief, Conley had decided not to reveal his first-hand wit-
ness of the uniformed smuggler. He was withholding this bombshell
for his interview with Shakuri:

*...I won't meet Shakuri until tomorrow morning but Vokhidov seems very much
Shakuri's man: nothing but slavish praise for his boss. And very obsequious to
me, because I'm an American journalist. He doesn't speak English very well yet,
but "is studying with a tutor." Oleg translated. Vokhidov wrings his hands over
the prevalence of smuggling in the south...This aid bill seems to have him sali-
vating. Not that they're strapped; they're already on an American gravy train,
as far as I can tell. Vokhidov was wearing an expensive tailored suit and had
a spanking new Mercedes limousine parked outside...Either through the heroin
trade or U.S. largesse---or both---these guys at the top seem to have tapped into a
gold mine. I never imagined money would figure so prominently in this milieu.
Bradford was definitely on to something...*

Gallagher shook his head, regretful that Bradford's final e-mail had
been so lacking in detail, compared to Conley's disquisition. He
skipped ahead to Conley's last paragraph:

Claire told me on the phone that you, Janet and Nathan have doubts now about the advisability of going to Shakuri's villa. Is that true? I haven't received an invitation yet, but one may indeed be forthcoming tomorrow during the course of my interview. For now I'm planning on accepting, as long as Oleg can come along. If you've decided otherwise, please let me know by e-mail. I'll also try phoning tomorrow, if I can find a location with a reliable signal.

Steve

Some of Gallagher's resolve faltered and his stomach gnawed again. He couldn't accord Conley second priority simply because he was ten time zones away while Claire was here with her own agenda…A sharp tap behind him plucked his anxiety and sent him swiveling 90 degrees. Claire stood in the doorway gripping an empty paper cup with tense knuckles.

"Can I come in?"

"Sure, Claire."

In seconds she settled in the chair across his desk and leaned forward. The cup was already drained. She'd been drinking coffee and water in a steady stream all morning.

"Any news from Steve?" she asked, her voice still hoarse.

"As a matter of fact, yes. Just reading his e-mail."

Dread crossed her face. For a moment Gallagher wondered if her concern about Conley's safety had grown. Then he reminded himself: for her this was still about her husband.

"No bad news. Interesting observations about this aid bill, though. Here. I'll make you a copy."

He clicked the "Print" command on-screen, then labored up from his desk. The printer was out in the newsroom, just a few steps away, and as he stood next to the machine, Frick strode by, taut and observant. He spotted Claire and frowned before switching to a rigid half-grin.

"Art."

"Nathan."

Frick continued on his way, heading toward Larson's office. There was one benefit to the current maelstrom, Gallagher thought. Usual plots were suspended. Subsumed by Whitcombe and Claire. No need for political self-defense.

When he got back Claire was perched on the edge of her chair, paper cup now crumpled in her hand. He watched as she skimmed through the two-page text, wide eyes dancing over the lines. At first she seemed comforted, until she got to the second page and reacted with a slight intake of breath.

Conley's reference to Bradford, Gallagher guessed. He was seized by new pangs of compassion, which impinged upon his parallel responsibilities to Conley. There was no easy way to do both of them justice. His stomach churned as she read through to the end.

"Are you going to approve his visit to Shakuri's villa?" she asked, barely able to get the words out.

Gallagher looked down at his desktop and took a deep breath. "I have some qualms about it. But if his interpreter, this fellow Oleg, goes with him, I'm going to give the green light."

"Are you sure?"

"We've gotten this far, Claire. If possible, we should see it though."

She swallowed hard and became trance-like. Gallagher was surprised. Why wasn't she relieved, as he expected?

CHAPTER 79

Government offices Conley had visited elsewhere---Prague and Moscow on this trip; others during his posting in London---were impressive. Spacious yet understated emblems of state power.

He and Oleg now sat in Shakuri's outer receiving chamber. It was just as large as Vokhidov's actual office, which they'd visited the previous afternoon, and possessed an even greater abundance of Turkish rugs, Italian marble statuary and silk throw pillows. Even relative to previous experience, he was stunned by such opulence. Understatement did not apply.

"I can imagine the President's quarters," he said.

"It's on the floor directly above us," Oleg answered.

"Convenient."

Over dinner the previous evening Oleg had characterized Shakuri as "the President's bagman...at least that's the view of him in Moscow."

"By the Russian government?" Conley had asked.

"Russian media, too."

Double doors opened at the end of the room. A dark, well-manicured man of about 30 approached them. He wore a European suit and a cordial smile. "My name is Usmonov," he said, in heavily accented English. "I'm the Prime Minister's assistant."

Conley and Oleg shook his hand. Usmonov's next statement sounded well rehearsed.

"Pleased to receive you. The Prime Minister is ready."

Usmonov led them through his own office, about the same size as the outer chamber, where Conley glimpsed additional fine appointments. With ceremony, Usmonov opened another set of double doors, stood aside, and beckoned them to enter.

In the middle of a cavernous space, Shakuri stood waiting. As Conley crossed the floor, he registered soft carpeting underfoot and luxuries in every corner. Official photographs of Shakuri now seemed to him not entirely true to subject. Up close and in person Shakuri looked more aging sybarite than virile right-hand strongman: an over-fed, rounded face, framed by receding dark hair and a mustache. His physique was dominated by ample mid-girth.

The Prime Minister's eyes were alert and evaluating, and he contrived a mirthful smile. His handshake was fleshy and warm, and he held the grip a little too long for Conley's comfort.

"You said you were coming with an interpreter. I hope that doesn't reflect on my English."

"Just in case there's a need," Conley replied. He introduced Oleg.

"We didn't meet when you came last year with Franklin Stanson," Shakuri said to the Russian.

"Franklin didn't include me in that particular discussion," Oleg answered.

Shakuri tossed off an apparent joke in the Russian language while clasping Oleg's hand. Oleg smiled just enough to be polite. Message: he was not to be co-opted.

To prepare for the interview Conley had reviewed Shakuri's background. Former young star in the Communist Party. Educated in Moscow at the prestigious Institute for International Relations, including intensive training in English, in preparation for Soviet diplomatic service. With the fall of the USSR, a shift to…a more lucrative stage.

They walked over to Shakuri's desk. The Prime Minister's English pleasantries were free and subtle. The President, by all accounts, spoke just Tajik and Russian. Who better positioned than Shakuri, therefore, to cultivate Stanson and Hermann?

An elaborate, hardwood conference table stood to one side of the office. Conley glimpsed oil paintings, more sculptures, and table lamps with gold adornments. The room was crammed with ostentation. Behind them, Usmonov silently retreated, closing double doors. Conley and Oleg seated themselves on two chairs with carved armrests and silk upholstery, while Shakuri ensconced himself on a high-backed leather desk chair---more throne than office furniture. Conley leveled his gaze across the expansive, polished desk surface.

Shakuri had left his drab Soviet roots behind. His was a relatively novel breed that Conley had read about but never glimpsed up close: Central Asian kleptocrat.

CHAPTER 80

How did a kleptrocrat behave? That depended on circumstances, Conley supposed. And to whom the kleptrocrat was talking. Across the desk, Shakuri adopted a humble posture. Like a merchant beseeching an aggrieved customer. Bowed head. Random and unforeseeable misfortune. Damage to both sides.

"I should first tell you this interview won't be easy for me," Shakuri said, clasping his hands and tilting his head at Conley and Oleg in turn, in a gesture of mutual bereavement. "I couldn't help but feel responsible for what happened. Peter Bradford was a fine man. I was deeply saddened. I still am."

Conley had to admit. Shakuri was smooth. Only his eyes gave him away. Calculating and intent.

Prior to arriving Conley had devised a strategy, consisting of stages. First elicit Shakuri's recollection of Bradford's interview---conducted across this same desk five weeks earlier. Next hew to chronology: dinner at the villa, discovery of Bradford's body, and ensuing investigation. His objective was to draw Shakuri out. Allow him to recount details. Then double back to whatever questions, by Shakuri's account, Bradford had asked about government complicity in the heroin trade.

Had Bradford been focused on this issue? Was he satisfied with Shakuri's answers?

At last Conley would describe what he had seen on patrol with the Russians: the opium smuggler in uniform. Hit Shakuri hard. Try to rattle him. Suggest that Bradford had uncovered dangerous truths--- truths that threatened the U.S. aid bill. Trace a possible connection between these and his murder. Raise doubts about the investigation.

Problem was---Shakuri was alert to his strategy from the outset. Prepared to confront the corruption issue square on. Yes, Bradford had raised allegations that the Tajik government was complicit in the heroin trade. Yes, Shakuri had told Bradford, he was aware of such allegations.

What followed was a more detailed version of Hermann's exculpation. The Tajik government could afford to pay militiamen and soldiers only about $50 per month, while single smuggling operations could earn them $500 or more. Tajikistan was one of the most impoverished republics in the former Soviet Union. Heroin trade out of Afghanistan generated billions. Imbalances were too profound.

"I told your Peter Bradford, 'What are we to do?' " Shakuri said, palms turned upward, an expensive Swiss watch visible under one cuff. "There are bound to be pockets of corruption. I can't fight that kind of temptation." Nearby, on one corner of the broad desk, stood a gold-plated reading lamp. Conley glanced at Oleg. Expressionless: just listening.

Hence the need for the U.S. military aid, Skakuri maintained. At the time Bradford visited Dushanbe, the bill had not yet been introduced to Congress. Still in drafting stages. Had Bradford been somehow aware of the bill, Conley inquired, and asked questions about it? A measured smile crossed Shakuri's face.

"Oh yes. He had done his research. And knew all facts and figures."

"Really? I thought those didn't become public until a few weeks later"

Shakuri shrugged: not his place to explain. Had Bradford obtained this from Stanson and Hermann? Conley made a note to ask them about timing.

"Based on Bradford's questions, one thing was clear to me," Shakuri said next.

Conley looked up from his notes.

"He believed in U.S. policy here. He thought the aid bill was a good idea."

"As simple as that? What about the corruption issue?"

Shakuri hung his head for an instant. When he raised it he oozed regret. "With all due respect to our Russian friends..." He nodded at Oleg. "They have their own interests here. I think Bradford saw through their...tactics."

Conley glanced at Oleg, whose distaste was now more palpable.

"Like that uniform you saw, for example...on the so-called smuggler..."

Conley was stunned. There was no way no way the Russians would have informed Shakuri. That left only Bill Hermann...

Shakuri brought his folded hands up to chin level and regarded him with a serene expression. "I'm not on the side of these terrorists... I assure you, Mr. Conley. My goal is the same as the United States'. Franklin Stanson and Bill Hermann know that. Peter Bradford did, too."

Sudden frustration welled in Conley. Hermann had spoiled his ambush. An edge came through his voice.

"If I may say so, Prime Minister Shakuri, Bradford wasn't representing the U.S. government. He was here to report on heroin smuggling. How can you be sure what he believed?"

"He accepted my dinner invitation. That says something, doesn't it?"

CHAPTER 81

Some of Shakuri's description of his evening with Bradford rang true: French cuisine---at least the Tajik evocation, prepared by Shakuri's personal chef---Russian language, wide-ranging discussion of Central Asia. Consistent with what Conley had learned about Bradford in Paris.

Other elements were less plausible. That Bradford had not asked any follow-up questions to the morning's interview. That he hadn't even taken notes.

"We shared a bottle of fine Bordeaux," Shakuri said. "I saw it as a kind of celebration."

"Celebration?" Conley asked, mystified. "Of what?"

"Of a successful interview. Common points of view."

Without notes? Then why had Bradford taken his laptop along? Shakuri had a ready answer: Bradford didn't want to leave it in his room at the Hotel Tajikistan. Worried about robbery. In solemn, fateful tones, Shakuri proceeded to accentuate the laptop's role in his subsequent detour and murder. From his imperious desk chair the Prime Minister gazed over Conley and Oleg into middle spaces of the cavernous office, as if he were glimpsing a vision:

"If he hadn't brought that laptop case, it all might have been different."

Different, Conley asked?

"Well, you have to understand how simple most of our people are...even those who work for me."

Conley recalled Hermann's commentary, delivered in guileless Rocky Mountain drawl.

"In short," Shakuri continued, hewing the same line. "They thought it contained money."

And why would they think that?

"People visit my villa. Cash is sometimes involved. This is not Washington, Mr. Conley."

" 'People?' People like Bill Hermann?"

Shakuri leaned back. A little arrogance showed through. "I'll let Bill answer that."

There would be time later to get back to Hermann, Conley figured; he contained his frustration and focused on the killers. "Shouldn't these two men have known the difference between a laptop case and a money satchel?"

"These men were drivers, security. They probably had never seen a laptop computer in their lives."

After Bradford left the villa, according to Shakuri's recounting, inordinate time passed before confirmation came of his arrival at hotel. Shakuri, worried about an accident, ordered a search, and police promptly discovered Bradford's body in a clearing off the main road into the city. Within hours the killers were apprehended at a road checkpoint 60 kilometers north, attempting to flee through mountains into Uzbekistan. And the laptop? Thrown out the window as the men fled, Shakuri said. Never recovered, despite "thorough" search efforts.

By time Conley got around to the fate of the two men he could anticipate Shakuri's explanation. Another variation on the poverty theme:

"We can't afford large prisons. All these animals are thrown together. Other prisoners got the idea that these two were rich. How? I don't know."

Stanson arrived that weekend with Hermann. Two days of due diligence: including repeat interviews of policemen, hotel clerks, waiters at Shakuri's villa. Quick stamp of approval. Some feature was discordant...Conley couldn't pinpoint what...until Oleg interjected, leaning forward with the interlocked fingers and unflinching demeanor of a graduate school examiner:

"Did they have an interpreter?" he asked.

Shakuri appeared surprised but recovered himself with a flash of magnanimity toward the Russian. "They used Bill Hermann's interpreter for certain things...a Tajik, one of ours. On loan from our Foreign Ministry. Most of the time, though..." Shakuri bowed his head in another bout of contrived humility before looking up with a proud smile. "...I was able to interpret for them myself."

CHAPTER 82

Claire closed her eyes as warm water massaged her face and slid down her body in soothing, shifting layers. Steam filled the shower, and she drew moist vapor deep into her lungs with slow inhalations. Noise didn't penetrate from the hotel corridor---a welcome separation. She reached for a bar of aloe-based, perfumed soap; with languid, circular movements she lathered the smooth skin of her breasts and stomach. Her sleep had been restless. She needed to rally. These were last moments of refuge before she confronted a new day of tumult and challenges. In three hours she would be implanted in the conference room at the *World Tribune,* in another grueling, interminable session with Larson, Gallagher and Frick.

High-pitched prattle from the telephone yanked her out of her sequestration. Soap slipped from her hand and shot across the tub. She grabbed the lever on the shower control and cranked the water off with such sudden force that valves shuddered in the wall. She spun and flung open the shower curtain.

"Zut!" she shouted. Five or six rings sounded by time she grabbed the handset, alongside the toilet. Her heart pounded with renewed tension. *"Oui?* ...I mean, yes, hello?"

"Claire? I'm sorry. I know it's early..."

"Uncle Harry?"

"Yes…I tried calling your cell phone…no answer."

"Something wrong?"

"Well…I do have some news…" His tone was somehow becalmed, with new resolve. *"I'm still in Cambridge. I'd like to see you this morning, if possible…before you go into the newsroom."*

Would this be another world-shattering stroll in Post Office Square? She didn't think she could sustain another. She took a deep breath, still dripping wet. Was this something he could tell her over the phone?"

"You already know half of it, Claire. Maybe the rest won't be such a shock."

Claire waited, fearful of what he would say next.

"Why don't we meet for breakfast? We can get a quiet table…just have a long talk."

"Here at the hotel?"

"Yes. Can you be ready in 30 minutes?"

Claire's hand shook as she replaced the receiver.

She finished her shower in a hurried, heart-pounding blur. When she blow-dried her hair in front of the mirror, she was unsettled by her own reflection. Her eyes were glazed and haunted. After three days of torment and disorientation, she wondered if she would finally learn the full truth about Peter. Half in a trance, she managed to get dressed, presentable and downstairs to the Café Fleuri at the appointed time. Whitcombe was waiting, at a far table. The waiter ushered her there at once. Another Air France crew was assembling at the usual circular table in the middle of the restaurant. This time she hardly registered glances from several pilots as she passed by. When Whitcombe rose to greet her, she noticed he was wearing an immaculate gray suit, starched shirt and tie---as if prepared for business. He appeared fatigued, but with new purpose.

"Let's order first," he said, after they sat down. "Shall we just get the buffet?"

Claire agreed. Food was her last concern right now. After the waiter appeared, poured coffee, and noted their decision in favor of the buffet, Whitcombe made no move to get up. Claire sat stiff in her chair, almost afraid to speak. He broke the silence.

"We've got time, Claire. I've got my driver with me. We can proceed to the *World Tribune* together after breakfast."

"Together?"

"Yes. I'm going back to work today."

CHAPTER 83

Conley rounded his knuckles and rapped; a blunt *"Da"* sounded within. The latch released and Oleg appeared in the doorway, wearing a tracksuit and slippers. He was holding a book, his place marked with an index finger. Conley apologized for interrupting.

"Phone reception is better on the other side of the building. I want to make a few calls before we head out."

Oleg examined him and thought for a second. "Hang on. I'd better go with you." A half-minute later he'd donned trousers, boots and overcoat, and they were lurching downstairs in a creaky and cramped Soviet-era elevator. Western travel advisories were consistent: Dushanbe could be dangerous for foreigners after dark, even around hotels. Conley and Oleg put on their fur hats before they emerged into the lobby, hoping to avoid attention.

Outside they found a small, scruffy, park-like area situated on the north side of the building. Nearby streetlights were broken or not turned on; the only illumination emanated from an interspersing of occupied guestrooms. However a clear nighttime sky made for decent visibility. Temperatures were just a few degrees below freezing. As Conley examined the green glow of the LCD on his cell-phone, Oleg pulled out a pack of cigarettes and offered one. Conley declined.

"I didn't know you smoked, Oleg."

Oleg lit up and took a deep drag. "I've been away from my wife for a while."

"You mean she forbids it at home?"

The Russian didn't answer. He took another drag, ember flaring in the darkness. Conley found the number he was looking for. His call was picked up after two rings.

"Steve!" Milena answered.

Safety ranked first among her concerns; Conley assured her he was alive and well. However that was not her only priority; there was also the critical matter of his assignment. During Conley's quick summary, her breathless queries suggested that her investment in the outcome had only grown since Prague. Conley attributed that in part to her gunshot wound. He asked about her recuperation.

"It's still healing well. I should be off the crutches in two more weeks."

During ensuing chitchat Milena didn't mention her broken engagement. Indeed her singsong tones implied it was no longer relevant. Conley nonetheless felt guilty, and apologized for various disruptions he had wrought. After the call concluded he stared into the darkness for a moment, his thoughts wandering. Oleg took a last drag and eyed him through a small cloud of smoke.

"I thought these calls were for work," he said, making his dissatisfaction clear.

"Not exactly…my interpreter in Prague."

"Interpreter?"

"Female. It's a long story."

Oleg snorted some last smoke out through his nostrils, then ground the butt into a patch of hard-packed dirt with the toe of his boot.

"Just one more…personal call…if you don't mind, before I call my newsroom," Conley added. "To Lilya."

"Lilya? Can't that wait until another time?"

Somewhat irritated himself, Conley ignored the question. Oleg just shook his head and lit another cigarette. Finding Lilya's cell-phone turned off, he called her apartment, where a male voice answered---her father. English didn't work. Conley passed the cell-phone to Oleg, who engaged in a brief exchange before pressing the "Disconnect" button. His disaffection became more evident.

"She's at the library," he said, half-scoffing. "She'll be home later."

Conley shrugged and took the phone back.

"Don't you get tired of all that?" Oleg asked.

"Of what?"

"Constant juggling? Instability?"

"Sometimes."

"Where's it all going?"

Conley returned an uncomprehending stare, together with another flare of irritation.

"...I mean wouldn't you be better off focusing those energies on just one?"

As he opened his mouth to answer his attention was diverted; a mid-sized German sedan jammed on its breaks on a side street, about 70 meters away. The driver was alone in the vehicle, and eyed them at length through the passenger side window before crawling forward. They could make out just his dark silhouette. Twenty seconds later the car passed the corner of the park area and disappeared from view. Through the darkness Oleg squinted after the vehicle, then took another drag. Conley was now glad the Russian had stayed around.

"Just one or two more calls," he said. "Both work-related." Gallagher's office number fell to voice mail, so he left a message:

"...As expected, Shakuri invited us to dinner at his villa. We accepted. A car will pick us up in an hour. Naturally we're both wary, especially after some tense moments during the interview this morning. But I agree with you. Dangers are low. Shakuri won't let harm come to us with so much riding on this aid bill. In fact he's promised to send two elite bodyguards along with the driver. I'll send an e-mail upon my return, along with details about the interview and dinner. Before I go, I also promised to ring Claire on her cell phone..."

As Conley prepared to redial Oleg observed him. His sarcastic tone became somber.

"Hope your call to her isn't your last, as Bradford's was..."

They both stopped, alarmed again, and looked toward the side street. The same German sedan returned, again at slow speed, the driver's attentions even more flagrant than before. His silhouette showed him to be young and hatless, with short hair. The vehicle vanished again at the end of the hotel building. Engine remained audible.

"I don't like the looks of that," Oleg said.

"Neither do I."

They gazed toward the end of the building in silence. A half-minute later the engine stopped, and a car door opened and closed. "Let's be alert," Oleg said in an even undertone. He threw down his glowing cigarette.

Admonition was unneeded. Conley was already tense.

There was reason to be; an instant later the driver rounded the corner of the building with quick steps. He glanced in several directions, then strode straight toward them. He carried a small case in one hand.

Conley didn't see a weapon but nonetheless considered various quick courses of action. Most obvious was to hustle back into the hotel.

"Hang on," Oleg said, gripping Conley's forearm. "I think I recognize him."

CHAPTER 84

Their chauffeured Lincoln glided from the new downtown tunnel into bright daylight on Southeast Expressway. Morning traffic was heavy, though smooth. The tunnel had mitigated Boston's notorious bottlenecks of past years.

Claire wished her own world were half as well ordered.

Whitcombe sat beside her on the leather-upholstered rear seat, elbow on armrest and gazing toward the Harbor. He turned toward her and clasped his long fingers around her wrist.

"Both of us have to put on brave faces, Claire."

She nodded and fought back tears. They'd reach the *World Tribune* in six or seven minutes, and have to show themselves in the newsroom. How could she face Art Gallagher and Janet Larson after what she'd just learned?

Nothing made sense. Even less now, with stomach-turning new details from Swiss banking authorities. Shakuri, a "two-bit potentate" Uncle Harry had called him…obscure political games centered on the U.S. Congress…numbered accounts…"influence peddling". Peter, her exemplar of a husband! How could it be? What had driven him to this? Hadn't he appreciated how much she loved him, with or without money? She still did! Perhaps only time would help her understand…

Until then, she had to re-orient herself. How remained an open question.

Embellishment of Peter's memory now seemed vain and over-reaching. Most important now was to minimize damage. Rescue his reputation post-facto. This had become a salvage operation.

"Remember the approach we agreed on, Claire?" Whitcombe asked.

"Nothing about this to anyone, at least for today?"

"Right."

Claire couldn't conceal her doubts. Information like this was bound to explode into public domain sooner or later.

"The Swiss banking authorities won't let on," he added. "Nor will the U.S. government…that's for sure."

"What about the longer term?"

"We'll have to react to circumstances."

Claire's mind careened through different scenarios. What would her family and social circle back in Paris think of Peter if all this came out? Her parents would be dismayed…even disgraced. Veronique, Francois and others would remain sympathetic at first, but their recollections of Peter and attitudes toward her would soon tilt toward pity and embarrassment. Those were the last outcomes she wanted.

A revelation hit. Her new direction came into clearer focus. Yes, salvaging Peter's reputation was essential. However…she also had to start thinking about herself. Peter himself would have approved, given the circumstances. She was the one still on the planet, after all. Affirm Peter by saving herself…That principle would also guide her forward, in addition to the first…

"There is one key variable we can't control at this point," Whitcombe added.

Her nausea grew as she remembered Tracey's obscure praise. "I know…Steve Conley."

"We can't blame him Claire. I put him in that situation."

"Do you expect him to find out?"

"It's possible. Who knows what he'll encounter with this Shakuri fellow? Maybe the same propositions Peter did."

"*Mon Dieu!* Conley was supposed to interview Shakuri this morning." She reached in her purse and checked her cell phone. There were no new messages. "And if he does learn the truth?" she asked, half-breathless. "What will the paper do with it?"

Their limousine moved to right lane, preparing to get off at the next exit. Whitcombe gazed out toward the Harbor again, over beaches of the South End, before turning back to her. "We'll have to publish it," he said.

"Even if the U.S. government objects, Uncle Harry?"

"I'm afraid so."

One of Tracey's words came back to Claire as they curved off the highway and down the ramp. Scenes outside her window blurred, but the word rang clearly.

Discretion. Maybe that was her only hope.

CHAPTER 85

"Looks like Usmonov," Oleg said.

"Shakuri's aide?"

Oleg nodded, still squinting into darkness. The figure strode nearer through shadows, making his face more identifiable. Oleg was right.

Conley's nervousness subsided, but seized him again when Usmonov drew up close. The Tajik's eyes darted back and forth and he grasped the case in one hand with a rigid, bare-knuckled grip---as if he were transporting live explosives. Conley peered down and examined the item. This was more than a social call. Neither he nor Oleg could guess its premise.

"I wanted…find you," Usmonov blurted to Conley, in a low tone and with heavily accented English. He glanced toward the building. "Shakuri has…security man in lobby."

Conley shot a glance back at the hotel, then at Oleg. This had veered far outside ordinary.

"I have…tell you something…." Usmonov faltered as his rehearsed English from the office that morning deserted him. His quick breaths produced bursts of condensation in the cold air.

"You can speak Tajik," Oleg said. "Or Russian."

After a second's hesitation, Usmonov responded with a torrent of Tajik.

"We'd better move over there, a little further away from the hotel" Oleg said to Conley, his face intent. He pointed to a cluster of trees that afforded more darkness. The three of them moved across about 15 paces, while Usmonov's eyes continued darting. No other people were visible in the area.

Once among trees, his words gushed forth anew in hushed tones. While Oleg listened, he glanced several times at the case, which he now clutched with both hands. Despite darkness Conley gave it closer scrutiny. It appeared to belong to a laptop computer. Conley thought he heard Bradford's name mentioned. Oleg interrupted Usmonov to translate:

"This situation is dangerous, so I'll try to condense what he's saying. He says that laptop computer is Bradford's…"

"Bradford's?!"

"Please listen…Shakuri had it in his office. Usmonov stole it from a locked storage closet there this evening. He says Shakuri is not telling the truth about Bradford, and the laptop proves it."

"Good God." Conley turned toward Usmonov. "Did Shakuri have Bradford killed?"

Usmonov was agitated. He answered with a shake of his head and an almost desperate shrug. What could that mean, Conley wondered? His rapid-fire monologue resumed, until Oleg interrupted again.

"He says he found Bradford's body in the clearing. Shakuri sent him to search. The laptop was there, too. He doesn't think Shakuri ordered Bradford's murder. But he can't be positive. What he does know is that Bradford didn't visit Shakuri's villa just for dinner. There was another reason."

"What?"

Usmonov opened his mouth to answer but stopped. His eyes widened as he stared over Conley's shoulder. They spun around to see a burly, mustachioed man, wearing leather coat and leather cap, was approaching them from the hotel---without obvious menace but with an intent gaze through the shadows. Oleg muttered under his breath.

"Trouble...looks like one of Shakuri's bodyguards. I saw him this morning outside the Ministry."

Already tense, Usmonov flew into panic. He thrust the laptop case into Conley's hands, then turned heel in the direction of his car, holding up a hand to conceal his face. After eight or 10 paces he broke into a run. Shocked, Conley watched him sprint away.

The bodyguard, apparently confused, also watched Usmonov's hasty retreat, but made no move to follow. Instead he drew up silently, his eyes cold through the darkness. His eyes traveled at once to the laptop case. Seconds passed before suspicion finally rolled across the man's dark features. He responded with an open palm---indicating Conley and Oleg were to remain where they were---and pulled out a walkie-talkie. After brief conversation, his addressed them in tone that was unmistakably aggressive.

"He wants us to go with him to his car," Oleg translated. "It's in the parking lot. Other side of the hotel."

In the silence Conley heard the ignition of Usmonov's BMW, followed by squealing rubber.

"And go where?"

"To see Shakuri."

"We're not scheduled to leave for another hour."

"I don't think we have a choice."

The bodyguard stepped toward Conley with extended arms. A bulge became visible beneath his jacket. There was no need for translation; he wanted the case.

"I would give it to him," Oleg suggested.

CHAPTER 86

Six department editors got up and filtered out; this morning's convocation had been shorter than usual. Larson stayed seated and kept her head down, frowning at notes through her reading glasses. Another meeting was coming up. More important, everyone assumed, given Conley's agenda in Dushanbe.

Gallagher hauled himself out of his chair, and grabbed a late City Edition off the table. Out in the corridor he re-scanned the front-page headlines. An early-morning mill fire had claimed upper placement, but Reynolds's bulletin from Washington occupied prominent side position.

Senate Expected to Approve Military Aid to Tajikistan

Coverage of the bill by the *World Tribune* had been extensive, due to the connection to Bradford and Conley. A sub-headline highlighted the money involved:

Vote scheduled for Thursday
$550 million to battle narcotics and terrorism

Frick almost barreled into Gallagher near the newsroom; only the newspaper prevented frontal collision, and half crumpled in Gallagher's hands. Gallagher couldn't hide his irritation. "No need to rush, Nathan. Our meeting's not for 45 minutes."

Frick's apology was quick and distracted; he obviously had more urgent priorities. He sidestepped Gallagher's bulk and hurried toward the conference room, evidently in search of Larson. Gallagher, throwing a chafed glance after his tense and wiry frame, wondered when these absurdities would finally end. There was enough pressure on everyone this week without frantic maneuvering and furtive one-on-ones. Conley's safety and Claire's continuing trauma deserved primary consideration. He exhaled hard through his nose and shook his head.

Reynolds' story continued on page five of the front section. Opposite, on page four, Gallagher saw the latest installment in the advertising campaign. The same one had appeared in earlier editions. It occupied a full page:

This week __Boston World Tribune__ reporter Steve Conley is in Dushanbe, Tajikistan, investigating the death of colleague Peter Bradford. In parallel Conley is continuing Bradford's efforts to report on the heroin trade in Central Asia.

Few Western reporters visit this remote and dangerous country. Conley's assignment reflects the ongoing commitment of the __World Tribune__, even in the face of tragic loss, to courageous and unrelenting global news coverage.

Full stories to come in December.

Beneath was a file photograph of downtown Dushanbe, one that emphasized the city's more exotic qualities. Further down were the by now familiar twin, head-and-shoulders portraits of Conley and Bradford. Phil Marcello was lingering along Gallagher's path and saw him examining the advertisements.

"Is the campaign going straight through to December?" he asked.

"Good question," Gallagher grumbled. In fact the ads had been on auto-pilot since Harry Whitcombe's abdication. Like many aspects of this assignment, the campaign had acquired momentum all its own. There was nothing Mike Fallon could do. Marcello strolled alongside Gallagher toward the business department. Gallagher snorted and folded the paper. Marcello looked ahead and suddenly stiffened.

"Maybe you'll get an answer today," he said.

Gallagher followed his gaze and also stiffened.

Across the expanse of the newsroom, on the far side, Whitcombe's towering height was unmistakable. He stood erect and well-attired in a cluster of desks, shaking hands with one of the older copy editors. Claire was nearby had her back turned toward them.

"Well I'll be..." Gallagher sighed, trailing off.

He hesitated to guess whether the publisher's appearance heralded renewed stability or another round of turmoil. As Marcello veered off and he drew closer, Whitcombe still looked worn out, though minus his earlier despair. His aura was closer to resignation.

"Hello Art," he said, shaking Gallagher's hand. "I've returned somewhat earlier than planned."

By now Gallagher was inured to this. When he turned to Claire, though, his jaw dropped. Her posture was rigid. Her eyes were glassy. Stress from the weekend multiplied by three. Paternal instincts brought his hand to her shoulder. "Everything's okay, I hope, Claire?"

Whitcombe answered for her. "No crisis, if that's what you're asking." Through his tiredness he gave her a reassuring smile. "Right, Claire?"

"Right."

Her voice was hesitant and high-strung. For whatever reason, she didn't seem overjoyed by Whitcombe's early return.

"I'll explain more shortly," Whitcombe said. "Where's Janet? Ah... here she comes."

Larson approached, Frick nipping behind her. She observed Gallagher, Whitcombe and Claire together, and appeared to flip through a Rolodex of scenarios. Her baseline composure rallied enough for a cheerful greeting. Beyond that she seemed at an uncharacteristic loss for words.

"I suggest we gather in the conference room," Whitcombe said. "The first thing I want to do is clear up any confusion."

CHAPTER 87

The villa's living room was sunken and centered around a massive stone hearth. A large fire was burning and exuded a sweet, pungent odor. Shakuri tended the blaze with a metal poker, endeavoring to quell crisis and play gracious host. His jerky manipulation of the poker betrayed his worry.

"This is all so unfortunate," he said with a strained smile.

Conley and Oleg were seated on a plush, low-slung leather sofa, facing the fire. Décor around them was a domestic variant of Shakuri's office opulence: Turkish rugs, carved end tables and garish lamps. Conley stared at Shakuri, still dismayed. Oleg wore an expression of quiet anger.

Shakuri paused, with a veneer of normalcy that contravened present realities. "You are my guests here. I hope you realize that."

Conley glanced around. A burly bodyguard stood in the front foyer. Another stood with arms crossed, blocking French doors that led out to a patio. "Guests?" he said, unwilling to play along. "We were ordered to come."

Shakuri contrived an accommodating tilt to his head. "I'm not forcing anything on you here."

"Then why take away our cell phones?"

Shakuri didn't answer, and turned to gaze into the fire.

"And Bradford's laptop, for that matter?" Conley persisted.

Another soothing smile. "A precaution, until we sort this out."

"How?"

"Why don't you tell me what Usmonov told you?"

Conley felt a new swell of irritation. "A reporter is supposed to ask questions, not answer them."

"How shall we start, then?"

"You can start by giving back that laptop."

Shakuri sighed and re-extended poker into fire. His movements became more abrupt than before, as if he was growing exasperated. The point of the instrument started to grow red hot.

Next to Conley Oleg sat straight and immobile, arms crossed. His earlier impatience with Conley had long passed, his contempt for the Tajik leader now manifest in his eyes. "You'll never see that laptop again," he told Conley in an even voice, before re-fixing his cold stare on Shakuri.

"Ah…the usual Russian mistrust of us Tajiks," Shakuri said, shooting a hard glance at Oleg before resuming his poker thrusts.

"Experience," Oleg answered.

"Such it has been for centuries. Can it ever change?"

Oleg held his cold stare.

"You know…" Shakuri said, still occupied with the fire and seeming to welcome detour into a more general theme. "…That's one reason we turned to the Americans."

For the first time since the ride out Conley remembered Stanson and Hermann. Their single-mindedness and suspension of disbelief now struck him as more preposterous than ever. Hermann had probably winged his way back to Alma Ata by now, his weekly stint of two days and one night complete. "You mean because they trust you?"

"Yes," Shakuri said.

"And what else?"

Shakuri ceased his poking but didn't answer.

"Money?" Conley suggested.

This word appeared to hearten Shakuri; he took several steps away from the hearth and held the poker and its glowing tip out for inspection. The gesture was more distracted than threatening, as if animated by the imminent and delectable prospect of a half-billion dollars-plus in U.S. largesse. His thoughts appeared to order around a decision, and he stepped back toward the hearth and placed the still-hot instrument in an iron stand. With unhurried steps he crossed the room to sink into in a low-slung armchair perpendicular to the couch.

"The laptop's in the next room, in my study," he said. "I'll be happy to give it to you later." He locked his eyes on Oleg for an instant, in the manner of a debater who has scored a tactical point.

Oleg would have none of it. His only response was a slight, contemptuous shake to his head.

Shakuri crossed his legs and steepled his fingers, still clinging to pretenses of normalcy. "I can guess what Usmonov told you. Probably about some cover-up. About what happened with Bradford. Yes?"

"Never mind what he told us," Conley said.

"Please, Mr. Conley..."

"Let's talk instead about Peter Bradford. Did you force him out here also? The same way you forced us?"

Shakuri brought his conjoined fingertips up under his chin. "I was hoping it wouldn't come to this. But it seems I have no choice."

Some seconds of silence passed---just crackling from the fire. Conley half expected Shakuri to signal to his guards to hustle over and haul them away. Instead Shakuri gazed into middle distance and exclaimed, "I know you're a journalist, Mr. Conley. But please let me talk for a while. You can ask questions afterward."

"We're listening," Conley said.

CHAPTER 88

The thought that Peter had done this for her anguished Claire. If she had known she would have stopped him. One thing was certain; he'd left her in *un gachis terrible*. To salvage his reputation and save herself from scandal she had to act fast. That meant rethinking her venue. Was the *World Tribune* newsroom still the most pivotal location? She had doubts. In Boston she was simply awaiting an eruption. Pre-positioning herself to limit damage. Dynamics had changed.

If an eruption came, she now recognized, it would emanate from Dushanbe. And Conley would be the catalyst. In Dushanbe she could identify a margin for genuine action, thanks to Tracey's observations…She stopped herself again, struck again by her own foolishness.

Visas and time zones obstructed her path. There was no way to reach Tajikistan in a short period.

Whitcombe now stood at the end of the long conference table. Larson and Frick were already seated. Gallagher was the last to arrive, huffing in from the hallway with a notepad in hand and thudding into a chair. The under-support yielded a grating squeak.

"Excuse me…I just got a message from Conley," he said.

This riveted Whitcombe and abruptly refocused attentions of Larson and Frick.

"He and Oleg, the interpreter, were about to head to dinner at Shakuri's villa."

"Is that all?" Claire sputtered.

"He didn't go into detail. I've got my cell-phone here. Please make sure yours is on as well, Claire. He could call at any time."

"When he does," Whitcombe said, his shoulders sagging slightly but his jaw set. "We should try to get him on the speaker phone."

Claire pulled her cell phone from her purse and checked the display. As she slipped the device into her coat pocket, an impulse took hold that was both unsettling and empowering. She hesitated for a moment before acting on it. Then with a subtle movement of her thumb, she switched off the ringer.

If Conley called, she wanted to be alone. Maybe she could mitigate damage. Circumscribe the initial discharge of information back to the Gallagher and others. Engage him one-on-one. Only question was…how to do it. How could she induce the kind of discretion that Conley had shown Tracey?

"Anyway…glad we're all here…" Whitcombe said, taking his seat. Larson and Frick still looked shell-shocked. Gallagher regarded Whitcombe carefully while stroking his beard.

"…Why have I come back early? First and foremost, to be here during this critical week. Granted, the situation became more complex. The aid bill. Growing murk in Dushanbe. High stakes geo-politics. But I over-reacted. I lost sight of my duty. Bottom line is…Conley is in the thick of all this. And he needs all the support he can get. And Claire, too. I wanted to be here with her if any important news came back about Peter."

Whitcombe directed a steady, tired gaze at her, as if to confirm their covert collaboration. Simultaneously Gallagher rotated his head and made eye contact, awash in paternalistic sympathy. So well-meaning, she now realized. If he only knew…

"I realize I was a little too partisan about Peter early on," Whitcombe continued. "That was wrong. I'll try to stay more objective from this point forward."

Trying to appear inconspicuous, Claire reached into her pocket to double-check her cell-phone. The ringer remained off.

CHAPTER 89

Sap ignited and spewed miniature, staccato explosions inside the fireplace. Shakuri waited patiently until the noise subsided. Then he began.

"Right away, during the interview in my office, Peter Bradford was a man I understood. Realistic. Ambitious. And, I confirmed later, family-oriented. In some ways, I might even say, not unlike myself. We came from different worlds. But we spoke the same language. I'm not talking about Russian, English, or whatever. I'm talking about views of life…suitable priorities."

Here was a post-Soviet kleptocrat, Conley thought, feigning likeness to a bookish Yankee blueblood. He found these premises ridiculous, but held his tongue for the moment.

"Therefore, not far into the interview, I wasn't surprised when he made me a proposal."

"He made *you* a proposal?" Conley interrupted.

"Please." Shakuri held up his palm. "Let me continue. Yes, that's right. He made *me* a proposal. He started by making an observation, much as you did today. That my government is mixed up in the heroin trade. Okay, I have trouble claiming total innocence. We didn't want to, we've had no choice. We've had to support ourselves…and our country, somehow."

This provoked what sounded like profanity from Oleg, half-audible and in Russian. Shakuri gave him a smile of false commiseration. "The Russians know this all too well. However if they could send us bigger amounts of money, not just tanks, soldiers and helicopter gun-ships, it might all be different…"

Oleg's eyes narrowed. He contained himself.

"Bradford understood. He understood how important this aid bill was to me…to my country. He also recognized that I am not a terrorist, as I said before. I despise those fanatics in Afghanistan and Chechnya as much as anyone. I am two things. First I am a leader, with the best interests of my country at heart. Second, I am a businessman. I realize that life demands pragmatism…Transactions of different kinds."

Shakuri paused again for effect, rotating his head 45 degrees and scrutinizing the fire over the peaked roof of his fingertips. Conley was finding such theatrics even more insufferable than earlier.

"…And Peter Bradford was ready to do a deal. He proposed that I pay him two and half million dollars. Why? To write a favorable piece…to say that our government is fighting the heroin trade. To play up the anti-terrorism angle as much as possible. The way he framed it, my payment to him would be half of one percent of the $500 million in the aid bill---a reasonable proportion, under the circumstances."

Conley's objection was automatic. This had to be a hoax, part of the cover-up. "That makes no sense," he interjected. "For all sorts of reasons…"

"No? Please let me explain. Bradford knew that he was the only American journalist here in the weeks before this bill was introduced. At that time---in late September---prospects were more uncertain. His story would be picked up by the wire services and published all over. It would be the only independent coverage at a critical stage. His influence could be decisive. I think he planned it that way."

"And then what?"

"I accepted his offer."

Conley's voice rose. "What you're suggesting is the worst sort of corruption…"

"Are you sure? Peter Bradford was simply endorsing the position of the U.S. government. Was that so corrupt? Was it unpatriotic? So what if he made a little money on the side?"

"That's not the way our system works…" Conley decided that an American civics tutorial was pointless. A more unsettling possibility occurred to him, even though he still assumed Shakuri was lying. "…Were Stanson and Hermann aware of this 'deal,' as you call it?"

Shakuri smiled. "Not of the particulars. For obvious reasons, they preferred to look away. But you know how these things operate…" His vagueness seemed calibrated, as if even the hint of complicity would frighten Conley off.

This assumption was foolish and off the mark.

"So…I invited Bradford out to my villa. He came of his own free will. And frankly, I was glad to have him. The deal he proposed made perfect sense. Good business, as far as I was concerned. I did not resent it."

"And then what happened, as you claim?"

Again the gracious host, Shakuri sustained Conley's incredulity with patience. "We talked over details. What he'd include in his articles and what he wouldn't. When we agreed, we shook hands. Then it was time to transfer the money…or half of it."

"In cash?"

"Of course not." Shakuri bristled for an instant before regaining his composure. "We're more sophisticated than that, Mr. Conley. I have an account in Luxembourg. I can order electronic transfers over the Internet. I have a high-speed satellite connection here. Bradford gave me his bank data. A numbered account in Switzerland. I simply got on-line and ordered the transfer."

"What about the rest?"

"To be paid after his articles were published."

Next to Conley Oleg snorted through his nostrils. He was listening closely but stared straight ahead at the fire. None of this seemed to surprise him.

"Do you know anything about international banking, Mr. Conley?"

"Very little."

"How about you Mr. Mikhailov?"

Oleg shot back a look of quiet loathing.

"Normally international wire transfers take two or three days," Shakuri said, a glint of smugness crossing his dark features. "During that period the money is essentially out of control of both sender and recipient. One of the many ways in which bankers make their profits. However for certain preferred clients these times can be reduced. I'm one of those. My bank in Luxembourg executes all transfers within two hours." Shakuri paused, expecting them to be impressed.

"And where does the money in that account come from?" Conley asked. "Stanson and Hermann?"

"They have already been generous with their help. However I also have other sources of funds. Does it really matter?"

Conley didn't answer.

"Two hours," Shakuri resumed. "We had to wait that long for Bradford to check that the money reached his account, using his laptop---and a special interface program he got from his bank. Perfect for dinner. We went to my dining room to celebrate." He gestured toward a threshold to one side of the fireplace, leading into the room in question.

The scene was hard for Conley to imagine. "What did you talk about?"

"As I said…a lot about politics. Central Asia most of all. Bradford was well versed. After a while, and some wine, we talked about our families."

Bradford had struck Conley as the last person to discuss his family with a stranger.

"I think he was trying to justify what he did, especially to himself," Shakuri added. "Not really out of guilt. More of an intellectual exercise."

"Justify? How?"

"He explained he came from a wealthy family...the newspaper, old money on both sides. But he couldn't really take advantage of it. Said all his money was tied up in special funds. Restricted in various ways. I admit, I couldn't relate directly to his dilemma. It's not part of my experience. What I could understand was his frustration. He felt he wasn't doing right by his wife. He and his wife were renting an apartment. Real estate prices had gone up in Paris, like everywhere...They couldn't afford to buy one. His wife's parents had offered to help. Any man would feel humiliated. He felt trapped."

"I'm afraid that doesn't sound like Peter Bradford at all. His family apart, he earned a good salary."

"Really? As a journalist? Please, Mr. Conley. Do you know his wife?"

"Well...yes."

"He said she was fond of fine restaurants. Fancy hotels. Works of art. Stylish clothes. Tennis, as I recall. In Paris and Boston those expenses can stretch a journalist's salary pretty thin. They'd even put off having children. Moreover he wasn't even sure he wanted to stay with the paper and move back to Boston. And these special family funds he talked about compelled him to do that."

"Why would he tell you all this?"

"I understood him. I have a wife. Children, too. I'm also a man who can't wait. And...I'm loyal to my country, just as he was."

Conley raised his eyebrows and shook his head.

"...Still don't believe me? The proof is on the laptop."

"Ah... the laptop." Conley adopted a sarcastic tone. "The reason Bradford was killed, according to you and Hermann."

Shakuri paused again and gazed into the fire over his fingertips. "Not only that. It also had to do with his wife."

CHAPTER 90

Where was Claire? She'd looked more strained than ever, and Gallagher was worried. After the meeting, he'd wanted to invite her to settle in his office for a while, as they awaited news from Conley. Instead she'd beaten an exit and disappeared. With creased brow he stood and scanned the newsroom through his office windows. Still no sign of her. He checked his watch. More than an hour until lunch: the usual juncture for his late-morning cigarette. He hesitated, then grabbed his cell phone off the desk and put on his coat.

At least Harry Whitcombe seemed back in standard form---for now. He half sighed and made his way toward a small corridor that led to an outdoor patio.

"Art..."

He whirled around. It was Claire.

"Where are you going?" she asked in her French accent, before he could speak.

"Outside for a cigarette. But that can wait..."

"I'll join you."

"It's winter weather. You might want your coat."

"It's okay. I seldom get cold."

Gallagher examined her with a cocked eye as they walked along. Her strain had acquired a different aspect. Her face had become flushed. Her movements were quick and electric. He could imagine why. This waiting was bound to stir adrenaline.

The rooftop patio contained a half-dozen picnic tables and over-looked a small parking deck. Route 93 lay just beyond; its never-ending, multi-lane traffic flung off a clamorous hum. Gusts of northerly wind blew from direction of downtown, and compelled them toward a wall for shelter. Claire crossed her arms tight. To Gallagher her gesture originated more from an impulse to expend energy than conserve it.

"May I?" she asked, when Gallagher pulled out his pack of cigarettes.

"Of course." He proffered one. "I didn't know you smoked, Claire."

"Not since university. But the last week has been stressful."

"For all of us."

Gallagher extended his lighter with a cupped hand. Her cigarette shook between her fingers as she tugged at the flame and took a deep drag. Her expression was concentrated.

"At least your uncle's back," he said.

"Yes."

This did not have the reassuring effect he intended. Her gaze roiled, swinging toward highway traffic and back onto him.

"Art…if Conley finds out anything bad about Peter, how would you react?"

"Bad? What do you mean?"

"If Peter made a mistake…did something foolish."

"Foolish? He was over-ambitious, maybe. Too hard-driving. But I never considered him foolish." Gallagher tried for a comforting tone. "I'm sure that any mistakes he made were honest ones."

She contemplated his answer by bringing her cigarette to her lips for another deep drag. The ember flared hard and yielded a long ash. As she withdrew her hand, wind swirled around the corner and knocked the ash away in dust-sized fragments. For Gallagher there was a helpless, susceptible quality in this. He endeavored to reassure her further.

"Your husband was a fine reporter, Claire."

"Thank you, Art..." She exhaled smoke and cleared her throat. Next she looked away; her whole body appeared to shudder. One arm remained wrapped tight against her stomach.

"Are you sure you're not cold?"

"No. It's more nerves."

"Of course. I'm sorry."

On the highway, a tractor-trailer truck roared by and emitted several loud blasts from its air horn. Gallagher took a drag of his own and waited until the harsh noise tapered away.

"By the way. I assume Conley hasn't called?"

Her eyes widened and she reached into her suit pocket. When her hand found the device, she remained immobile for several seconds. She extracted it with a trembling palm and examined the LCD screen. Flush rose again in her face, despite the frigid air.

"No. Nothing."

CHAPTER 91

Shakuri rang a small hand-bell and a maid appeared. She was modest and matronly, a contrast to Shakuri's other indulgences. "Something to drink, before we continue?" he asked. Conley and Oleg looked at each other, dismayed at Shakuri's continuing pretense of hospitality.

"Just water," Conley answered.

"Tea," Oleg said, in a sullen monotone.

The maid disappeared and Shakuri resumed, unfazed. "Once you've heard me out, maybe you'll join me for dinner. My wife and children are away this week..." Vanity flickered in his eyes. "...At our vacation house in the Maldives."

Conley ignored both house and invitation. "You were telling us about the laptop...and about Bradford's wife."

"Yes...the laptop..." Shakuri shook his head, taking pains to show his disbelief. "After dinner we proceeded to my study. A little more private..." He gestured toward the retreating maid. "...And more suitable for such a transaction. He booted up his laptop and got on the Internet. He confirmed that the money was in his account in Switzerland. Lastly he sent a quick e-mail to his banker. Our business was done."

"Then what?"

"A little final celebration was in order."

Conley maintained his skeptical gaze but played along.

"Nothing unusual," Shakuri continued. "Just an aperitif back in the living room. Meanwhile I asked my men to get the car ready."

"What's that got to do with Bradford's wife?"

For the first time Shakuri's affectation fell away; he clenched his teeth with what seemed real regret, even self-recrimination. "What happened next was my fault. I should have known better…" He re-clenched and sighed. "Our chat was pleasant. We were both satisfied. Why not? Our transaction had been profitable for both of us. I congratulated him on his ability to see the big picture, and to take advantage of it…" They were interrupted when the maid re-appeared with a silver tray: water and tea, along with scotch on the rocks for Shakuri. She placed a silver bowl of mixed nuts on a coffee table in front of Conley and Oleg, then stood to one side awaiting further instructions.

"Mehrangiz would like to know if you'll be staying for dinner," Shakuri said.

Oleg didn't waver from his sullen stare. Conley shook his head.

Shakuri murmured an instruction; the maid silently retreated. Dinner now seemed secondary; he had become engrossed in his recollections and impatient to resume. " We got up…While I organized the car, he returned to my study to pack up his computer. When he showed up again in the hallway, I asked him if he had sent an e-mail to his wife. He said his wife preferred the phone. He intended to call her back at the hotel."

Conley startled; this element rang true. Shakuri sensed he'd found resonance.

"…At the door, Mehrangiz helped him on with his coat. I referred to his upcoming stories…he joked that I should withhold judgment until I read them. We shared a laugh. Then I said, 'You do all this for her, don't you?' Bradford asked what I meant. I pointed to his laptop, which he held in one hand, and said, 'This. Your work. Your ambitions. What we did this evening.' He didn't answer but smiled a little. I knew I was right. As I said…we understood each other."

Shakuri smiled for an instant at this particular reminiscence, before his cloud of self-recrimination returned.

"...During this conversation one of my two security men was standing nearby, listening. His name was Nadyrov. Bradford and I were speaking Russian, so Nadyrov understood most of what we were saying. I hardly paid attention to him. You have to understand...He'd been with me for years..." Anger boiled up in Shakuri; he paused to regain his focus.

"Afterward I recalled... that Nadyrov was staring at the laptop. Intent on it. He offered to stow it in the car while Bradford and I said our good-byes. Bradford politely declined. After Bradford was found dead...when we finally captured Nadyrov and his accomplice... the other man I sent that night...we did an interrogation. The picture came together. Nadyrov thought the laptop case contained money."

Conley studied Shakuri, half-stupefied. Oleg sat alongside with his lips pursed, still staring at the fire, surprised by nothing.

"Is that all?" Conley asked. "That's a weak variation of what Bill Hermann told us. You toss off some pleasant remarks about Bradford's wife and Nadyrov thinks the case contains money? It doesn't make sense."

Shakuri leaned forward in his armchair and placed his elbows on his knees. True or not, this retelling was cardinal to him. He was determined to finish.

"That's not all, Mr. Conley. Why don't the two of you come with me."

*   *   *

They crossed the entry threshold. The bodyguard who had ensnared Conley and Oleg at the hotel stood with arms akimbo and feet spread, glaring at them with dark eyes. "This way," Skakuri said, gesturing down a hallway which ran along a grand staircase.

They took a right into the study, which was a smaller and somewhat less garish version of Shakuri's government office. Desk not as outsized; a modest collection of books lined parts of two walls. A big window opened out onto a dim panorama of craggy hillsides. Conley guessed Shakuri's wife had exerted a restraining influence.

"Please, over here," Shakuri said, directing them across a thick rug that embedded under their footfalls.

On the far wall he slid open a door to a closet and switched on a light. The opposite side of the space was lined with shelves; on these were stacked several piles of American newsmagazines, along with an assortment of American souvenirs that presumably originated from trips to the U.S. Shakuri pointed down at the floor.

"I came to show you these," he said.

There, in a neat row, were nine or ten identical black cases. The cases were soft-cover and well crafted: synthetic canvas, treated leather and durable, high-grade zippers. Their pliable handles protruded upward in near symmetry. The entire ensemble appeared spanking new.

"Are these laptop computers?" Conley asked.

"No, in fact, just cases," Shakuri answered.

Conley squinted at Shakuri, uncomprehending. Oleg stood a half-step back, chafing, his mouth curled in sarcasm.

"Take a closer look," Shakuri said.

Conley leaned over and examined the luggage from varying angles. The cases did appear to be for laptops, although their zippers and compartments made them suitable for multiple uses. He reached for one and grasped one pair of handles. It contained no weight and came up easily, feeling empty. Standing again, he proceeded with closer inspection. An imprinted leather brand label read "Tumi." Remarkably similar to Bradford's laptop carry-on, the one he'd held two hours earlier, perhaps even the same make and model. He opened his mouth to speak. Shakuri interrupted.

"I know what you're thinking," he said. "And you're right. It's practically the same."

Conley squinted back at him. "Fine. But what does this prove? And what's this got to do with Bradford's wife?"

"In fact this part has nothing to do with Bradford's wife. It has to do with Bill Hermann." He paused, in the manner of a self-important trial lawyer reaching summation.

"We're listening."

"Hermann has used these for cash during the past eight months. How much? It's not really important. I even lost track. They were short-term payments...unofficial transfers, if you will. To get me by until the aid money came through. I always asked Bill if he wanted the cases back, to use them over again. He repeatedly waved me off. *What the hell,*" he would say---here Shakuri did a passable imitation of an American western drawl---*'Don't bother.'* His budget seemed unlimited. Therefore the cases have been piling up here in my closet."

Conley scanned down the black row. Whatever denominations were involved, total currency had to be a lot.

"...My drivers and security people are not complete morons," Shakuri continued. "They understood what was in those cases. They also saw that Hermann left without them, empty-handed. They correctly surmised that the contents went straight into my safe."

He gestured toward a wall panel adjacent to his desk. The safe was apparently hidden.

"So they thought Bradford was *leaving* with money?" Conley asked.

"Exactly. Bradford came out in here with me in my limousine, after work. My daytime driver was on duty at the time...the other two took over for him. But they never saw Bradford *arrive* with the case. Then there was Bradford's fluency in Russian. Other Americans these men had seen---Stanson and Hermann---spoke just English. Another thing we gleaned from our interrogation. They thought Bradford was some sort of independent merchant...maybe an arms dealer. That made them a little more willing to take a risk. I mean as opposed to someone like Hermann. Nardyrov and his cohort were cunning, up to a point."

"Didn't you tell them Bradford was a journalist?"

"I did, but who believes that, in this part of the world? Most people play multiple roles. Russians certainly do, right Mr. Mikhailov?"

Oleg glowered at Shakuri for several seconds then shifted his eyes back toward the panel that concealed the wall safe.

"I still don't get it,' Conley persisted. "What do your comments about Bradford's wife have to do with all this?"

"They just corroborated what Nadyrov already assumed. People in government or journalism don't have such conversations. Businessmen do. More often than not, they're out struggling for their wives. What other motivation is there? Am I right?"

Conley didn't answer him and pressed on. "After that…did you have those two men killed? Was that story about the prison disturbance a fabrication?"

"Does it really matter?"

"Do Stanson and Hermann know all this?"

Shakuri gave a faint smile but stayed mute.

"What about Usmonov? What's his role?"

Shakuri sighed, as if bemoaning the overreaching of youth. "Yes…When Bradford didn't arrive at the hotel on time, our security people there called me. At first I thought it might an accident. The roads along these hillsides up here can be hazardous. I called Usmonov in the city. Asked him to drive toward the villa, looking for a car wreck. Instead he found tire tracks into the woods. By the time he found Bradford it was too late. I instructed him to leave at once, take the laptop. He gave it to me the next day, and I stored it in a locked closet in my office. I should have known better. I should have destroyed it."

"Where's he now?"

"Usmonov? He won't get far."

Conley glanced at Oleg. His face was stoic, except for a simmer of contempt in his eyes. "Now what?" he asked, turning back to Shakuri. "Are you telling me this so I can publish it? Somehow I doubt that."

Shakuri drew his arms back so that his suit jacket splayed open and his ample midriff protruded forward over his belt. He met Conley's gaze with a smirk. "Let's put it this way, Mr. Conley," he said. "I have an offer for you."

Conley was about to object when Oleg intervened in a caustic tone: the first time he had spoken since they'd entered the study.

"I knew this was coming," he said.

CHAPTER 92

Back in the living room, Shakuri re-stoked the fire before settling again in his armchair. He interlocked his fingers and directed his attention over them at Oleg, who glowered back.

"We're not interested in any offers," Conley said.

Shakuri smiled, clinging to his motif of cordiality. "But you haven't heard my proposal. Please, Mr. Conley…have a little patience."

"You can start by assuring us that no harm will come to Usmonov." Conley demanded. "He was just returning what was ours." Shakuri kept his smile but his voice hardened a bit. "You have your own perspective on that. It was a crude and idiotic stunt…But let's get back to our main business." Conley glanced again at the guards, who remained in place with feet spread and arms crossed. "Is this an offer or a demand?" he asked, sarcasm in his voice.

"An offer."

Getting past the guards and beating an escape into the surrounding hillsides was the only way out. Conley supposed Oleg was thinking along similar lines. However the guards were armed. And there was nowhere to seek refuge after that.

"Okay. Now you know the truth about Bradford…" Conley opened his mouth to object, but Shakuri held up his palm and continued.

"All proven, as I've said...by information on the laptop. Which I'll give you momentarily. So where does that leave us? With an embarrassment. To myself, my country...and, if I may say so, also to the U.S. government. At a moment of great importance for all concerned. Why should we wreck all that because of the stupidity of a couple of bodyguards? Misunderstanding over what was in a ridiculous little case? I didn't commit any crime. Neither did Hermann or Stanson. Bradford proposed our arrangement, after all. Entered it under his free will."

"So that's now what this is about?" Conley asked.

Shakuri returned a pleasant, inquisitive smile.

"...Not derailing the $550 million dollar aid bill?"

Shakuri looked down at the floor. Relish crossed his eyes, as he contemplated vast sums in prospect. "Well, yes. But not just that. What about the reputation your paper, Mr. Conley?"

"My paper has a reputation for truth and accuracy..."

Shakuri affected a slight guffaw. "Okay then, what about Bradford's young widow?"

At this Conley faltered before responding. Did Claire know about the money? Was it now in her possession? These questions had thus far not occurred to him.

"For her and everyone else," Shakuri continued. "What's to be gained from exposing all this?"

"That's not the point here..."

"You'd be doing your own government a favor, just like Bradford was."

"You still don't appreciate the way the U.S. media operate..."

"No? I've been to the States numerous times. I know money reigns supreme. Free press or not. Just like it does in Russia now, too." With a flicker of amusement he glanced again on Oleg, who appeared to figure more prominently now in Shakuri's calculations. Oleg didn't deign to return this particular eye contact. "Or am I wrong?"

Shakuri's question hung in the air. It was rhetorical anyway.

"...And what I'm asking is minimal, Mr. Conley. You can write any-thing you want on the heroin trade. Those stories won't appear until after the vote on Thursday. When they do? Wheels will already be in motion. They'll be nothing but background noise."

Conley waited. He now guessed what Shakuri had in mind.

"All you have to do? Forget what I told you about Bradford. Stick to the current explanation...which, by the way has been seconded by the U.S. government. And..." Shakuri paused for climactic effect. "...Make some money for yourselves in the process..."

Shakuri observed them. His attention fixed again on Oleg.

"The deal? Same I reached with Peter Bradford. Two-and-a-half million dollars. For *each* of you. Yes, my total price has gone up. But...a necessary piece of business, let's say."

Shakuri paused again, with a calibrated grin, studying their faces.

"I'm ready to pay each you of half up front. Tomorrow, even. That would give you a day to set up suitable banking arrangements. Contact lawyers in Europe, do whatever you have to. I'm assuming neither of you has a pre-established Swiss account...like Bradford." He laughed at his own joke.

As Shakuri's laughter trailed off in the cavernous living room Conley experienced neither indignation nor righteousness. More like...detachment. The offer didn't tempt him at all. It was odd. He glanced at Oleg. The Russian, for his part, seemed neither surprised by Shakuri's brazenness nor curious to hear more.

Shakuri noted this and remained focused on Oleg. "Russia may not be down and out any more, Mr. Mikhailov. But $2.5 million goes a long way. In Moscow, just like anywhere else. It's a respectable number by any standard, no?"

Oleg continued staring into the fire.

"Meanwhile...you might even score some points with your friends at the U.S. Embassy," Shakuri added. "Maybe they'll issue you an American passport?" He chuckled again.

Conley thought Oleg might bristle. There was still no reaction.

Shakuri's eyes flitted to Conley and back to Oleg. "Of course the two you would both have to agree. Just one of you won't suffice."

Oleg's contemptuous expression hadn't wavered. Otherwise Conley couldn't tell what the Russian was thinking.

"Mr. Mikhailov...Maybe you could help persuade your American colleague? Tell him his ideals...or his priorities...whatever..." Shakuri chuckled again. "...are all well and good, but...you know..."

Now Oleg locked eyes with Shakuri and gave him a cold stare.

Shakuri's grin faded. "I see...of course. Typical Russian caution. They always suspect dirty tricks."

CHAPTER 93

Even absent his smile, Shakuri didn't appear to lose heart. After a moment he rose again, in no hurry, and walked over to the hearth. Though the fire blazed, he picked up the poker and jabbed out with distracted movements. Conley watched him from behind. Oleg appeared to sink into his own thoughts.

"Maybe you just need more time," Shakuri said, keeping his back to them.

"Time? For what?"

"To consider my proposal." He glanced over his shoulder at Oleg, with an arched eyebrow. "To talk it over."

"Forget it," Conley said. "I thought I made that clear."

Shakuri turned back toward the fire, piercing several glowing embers and sending sparks fluttering up the chimney.

"We'd like to be brought back to our hotel," Conley added. "With Bradford's laptop. Without further delay." Shakuri's profile was visible from rear angle. His mouth and the corner of one eye turned up again in amusement. Conley felt a growing anger. "Are you aware of what you're doing? The course you're embarking on?"

Shakuri stabbed at another ember, provoking a new burst of ascending sparks. "Alas, Mr. Conley. I've already embarked."

Overtones in his voice caused Conley's heart to pound. He nonetheless held firm. "Well then ask your driver to get the car ready."
Conley was about to rise from the sofa when Shakuri replaced the
poker in the cast iron stand next to the hearth. With deliberate
slowness he turned to face them, his amusement giving away again
to regret---the kind he had shown before they'd walked to the
study.

"You know, Mr. Conley, I thought you might be more like Peter
Bradford. Are you married?"

"No, I'm not."

Shakuri clasped his hands behind his back and took several slow
paces across the room, parallel to the sofa. He pivoted slowly, then
stopped to re-scrutinize him. "Ah yes," he said after a moment. "At last
I recognize your type."

Conley couldn't tell if the remark was leading to flattery or something else. He glanced at Oleg, who was watching Shakuri again and
listening with a sardonic twist to his mouth. The latter paced back in
opposite direction, and allowed himself a slight laugh.

"Perhaps if I threw several women into the equation? Most alluring
young beauties in all Tajikistan? The rest of the week with them…that
plus the money?"

Conley just stared, astonished. Shakuri was serious.

"…All these accumulated misfortunes and rough edges…
Bradford's murder, the militiaman…everything…would become less
important…rendered secondary by the sweet thrall and incomparable
release of the female sex. By Friday night you would be here toasting
the aid bill here over dinner with Franklin Stanson and me, with no
burning determination to set this all right…"

"You're wrong about that…"

Shakuri pivoted to face them, his face still showing more regret
than menace. "Am I?" He directed his gaze once again at Oleg.
"Mr. Mikhailov?" Conley looked at Oleg next to him on the couch; the
Russian met his gaze for an instant before looking away, his manner

obscure. All at once Conley lost patience. "All right, this is enough." Abruptly he rose from the divan to a standing position.

With a world-weary expression Shakuri raised his hand in a signal to the two guards. Both advanced several steps, their arms hanging ready at their sides and ready for roughness.

"Wait," Oleg said. He was still sitting.

Conley was startled. "Wait? For what?"

"Maybe we should take some time to talk this over."

"Are you kidding? Anyway this is my decision, not yours."

Oleg's voice was flat, unemotional, his eyes now more pragmatic than contemptuous. "I mean this situation has a lot of angles." Still flabbergasted, Conley glanced back at Shakuri, whose eyes displayed hints of mastery.

"Your Russian friend has a point," he said.

"Give us 48 hours," Oleg said from the couch.

"I was hoping for that," Shakuri answered. He turned to Conley. "Unfortunately you'll have to stay here, at my villa. As my guests, of course."

"Guests?" Conley shot back. "That's absurd...If I don't communicate for that long with my editor and others, alarms will be raised."

Shakuri smiled. "I have a plan for that."

CHAPTER 94

Face and hands crimson from the outdoors, Claire maneuvered through the newsroom maze and ignored lingering glances from scattered male reporters. Already light-headed from nicotine, she nonetheless garnered a second cigarette from Gallagher and returned to the patio an hour later to smoke alone, her back to the wall and one eye on the glass door leading to the newsroom. Twice, in between agitated drags on her cigarette, she punched the speed-dial to Conley's cell-phone---to gain the initiative...to intervene somehow while such possibility existed. And twice she heard: *"Number active but unavailable"* in Tajik, Russian and English.

Now her modicum of control was eroding fast. What if Conley tried reaching Gallagher again? Her only hope was first contact. That one incoming call, if it went elsewhere, could hurtle her world into chaos and scandal.

In Paris she'd recognized that she'd have to depend on Conley. His role was essential, like it or not. But beholden to him to this degree? Now here she was entertaining various wild schemes...Centered around the same womanizer who'd derailed his career over Tracey Whitcombe and who'd risked the same with a bumbling pass at her? The preposterousness of her position only compounded her anxiety.

She made her way back into the newsroom.

"Claire?"

The voice came from behind. She stopped and spun around. It was Nathan Frick.

"We've been looking for you," he said, in an excited tempo.

"Oh, really?"

"Where are you going?"

"To meet Art. We're going to lunch."

He frowned. "I see." With a nervous and deliberating smile, he marched off in the direction of Larson's office. Claire took a deep breath to clear her head and quickened her pace. The last thing she wanted was to be corralled before leaving and subjected to Larson's piercing eyes and measured questions. By contrast Gallagher's interest was compassionate, paternal. If she had to sustain this suspense with anyone, better with him...

She didn't quite make it. Five meters short of Gallagher's doorway, Larson intersected with her at brisk stride. Frick followed at her elbow, like a faithful farm dog.

"Claire, Nathan told me you and Art were going to lunch." Her politeness bore an inquisitive edge. "Mind if we join you?"

"I don't know...I haven't even asked Art where we're going." She glimpsed Gallagher through his office windows, sitting at his desk, gripping his phone with intense concentration. He next hung up in slow motion, appearing stunned, then struggled up from his chair. Larson and Frick turned to watch him emerge, huffing, from his office.

"That was Stanson, the U.S. official in Moscow."

Claire felt her heart skip a beat. Heads of Larson and Frick snapped up.

"Conley's missing. Along with his interpreter."

Claire gasped. She'd been so preoccupied with the risk of exposure that she'd forgotten other dangers. *Mon Dieu...*

"Missing?" Larson asked.

"He was supposed join Shakuri for dinner tonight. He missed his pickup. Disappeared from the hotel, along with Oleg."

"Just disappeared?"

"Last seen outside the hotel in early evening, making calls on his cell-phone. Never returned to his room, Stanson said."

"Did he ever call here again...to either of you?" Larson glanced at Gallagher, who shook his head, then at Claire, who did likewise. Her face became more concentrated. "What time is it there now?"

Gallagher glanced at his watch. "Ten-forty-five. Shakuri apparently started a search at once. About an hour ago he called Stanson in Moscow with the news."

"Does Stanson have any notion what happened?"

"He's greatly alarmed...worried it might be a kidnapping... criminal elements. He's keeping close tabs on the situation through Shakuri."

"What about other U.S. diplomats or officials in Dushanbe? Are there any present?"

"Not right now."

The four of them stood in silence for several seconds. Claire struggled to guess what this could mean. Her thoughts careened through different scenarios.

"We should tell Harry," Gallagher said.

"Right away," Larson agreed.

CHAPTER 95

Conditions of confinement could have been worse: delectable mutton and potato casserole---a traditional Tajik dish, prepared by Mehrangiz, the matronly house maid---coupled with Saperavi wine, a Georgian variety that Conley had never sampled before. Mehrangiz served Conley and Oleg ate at opposite ends of the long dining room table.

Mehrangiz spoke just several English phrases, with a thick accent: "Would you like?" "Please" and "You're welcome." Her manner was sweet and considerate. If she was aware of crisis, curious about Shakuri's absence, or unsettled by the armed guards positioned outside the two doorways to the dining area, it didn't show. Whatever puzzlement she experienced stemmed more from the sullen silence that pervaded the meal. At one point, as she re-filled wine, she paused at mid-table, switching her gaze back and forth between Conley and Oleg, almost willing them to engage in conversation. After she'd gone back to the kitchen, Conley couldn't restrain himself. He looked down over a pair of lit candles, where Oleg was eating with his head down.

"What did you mean by 'talk this over'?"

Oleg looked up, impassive, and with a flat voice answered, "Let's discuss it after dinner."

Still dismayed, Conley resumed eating. Oleg's perfidy aside, there was one small basis for optimism. Shakuri had not yet maltreated them. He was stalling. Reason to hope that he would not go as far as murder. By meal's end it was late: almost 11:30 p.m., or 1:30 in the afternoon back in Boston. He tried to imagine the scene in the news-room…Oleg was finishing a post-meal cigarette when Mehrangiz reap-peared, minus her apron, and made an announcement in Tajik.

"She's going to take us up to our room," Oleg translated.

"Better that than a cell in the basement," Conley answered, getting up from his chair.

Both guards reasserted their presence and they followed Merhangiz out across the living area to the foyer. As they mounted a curving mar-ble staircase, he heard Shakuri's voice behind a closed door, evidently talking on a telephone; the language was English. Upstairs, halfway down a high-ceilinged corridor with marble floor and moldings, Merhangiz opened a heavy door of dark wood.

"You're welcome," she said, beckoning them to enter first. The two guards stayed in the corridor.

They entered an expansive, high-ceilinged bedroom. In the center was a small sitting area with furniture, flanked by twin beds against each wall. Chattering in Tajik to Conley, Merhangiz gestured toward one of beds.

"She offers to turn down the beds," Oleg said.

"Fine."

She turned down Conley's bed then crossed the room and did likewise for Oleg's.

"She says the bathroom is there, near the entry." Oleg pointed toward a door off the entryway. "There are toothbrushes and towels inside. Also bathrobes in the closet."

"We're right at home then," Conley snapped.

His sarcastic tone caused Merhangiz an instant of disappointment, but she beamed another gracious smile as she turned to leave and said, "You're welcome." Before the door closed behind her Conley spotted the leg and shoulder of a guard, positioned across the hallway.

"She's a nice woman," Oleg said.

Conley just grunted. He crossed to a large, two-paned window on the opposite wall, parted the curtain, and looked outside. Below was a small garden, bounded opposite by woods and an ascending hillside. Lights along several walkways provided partial illumination. A guard stood next to a garish fountain, head tilted upward. He tried the handle. It was locked tight.

"Great," he said, releasing the curtains and turning away.

Oleg was already sitting in an armchair. "It wouldn't matter," he said, lighting another cigarette.

"Well, at least we agree there."

The Russian didn't appear eager to press his case. He took a slow drag and exhaled a plume of smoke toward the ceiling.

"Dreaming about new-found riches, are you?" Conley asked.

"No."

"Then what?"

"Analyzing other aspects of Shakuri's proposal..."

"Oh really...?"

"...which you might have been too quick...to rule out."

"Look," Conley said, leaning forward to show his anger. "It's a bribe, plain and simple. And Shakuri is despicable...a dissembling huckster. If you think..."

Oleg winced, held his palm up and shook his head---causing Conley to stop in mid-sentence. He raised his index finger and encompassed four corners of the ceiling with a circular gesture, then held the finger against his ear. His message was clear; the room was bugged.

"What the hell..." This time Conley cut himself off.

"What I'm saying is..." Oleg continued. "...Some of his points make sense. For example...what's to gain from revealing all this?" At this he stuck his cigarette in his mouth, rose from his chair and padded across to a desk near the window. There he found a pen and paper, removed a single sheet, and scribbled a note.

Conley was unsure how to react. "Well, that's..." From the desk Oleg made another circular gesture with his index finger, encouraging Conley to keep talking. "...where you're wrong...But go ahead... We have time...You can at least state your case..."

Oleg was now in front of him, holding out the piece of paper. "Thanks. Okay...Let's start with Bradford's reputation...and his widow..."

Conley took the note. It read: *We're only buying time.* He grabbed the pen from Oleg's hand, took several steps to the desk and scribbled: *For what?* Oleg paused, as if the answer wasn't straightforward. He re-took the pen, leaned over the desk, creases forming between his eyebrows. Before he scribbled again, there was a knock on the door. He stuffed the paper in his back pocket, while Conley crossed and opened the door. It was Shakuri.

"May I come in?" he said.

Conley responded with a sullen nod, then closed the door as Shakuri walked past. In his hand...and impossible to miss...was Bradford's laptop case. Shakuri stopped in mid-room and turned to face them. "Yes, I've brought it," he said.

Conley wondered if Shakuri meant to turn on the device at once.

"You know," Shakuri continued, "you've caused me to do a lot of scrambling tonight. I've been on the phone...mostly with Franklin Stanson but also with my own police officials."

"Stanson?" Conley said. "Good God...is he..."

Shakuri gave an ironic snort and didn't allow Conley to finish the question. "And Franklin has been on the phone back to Boston...to your editor..."

"Art Gallagher?"

Shakuri nodded. "You've been reported missing. Absent from your hotel without explanation..."

"You're insane! Do you have any idea...?"

"Officially I'm enraged...and orchestrating the search." Shakuri paused, letting the words sink in. "If you're not found, well..." He smiled. "Just one more example of the chaos here...And of the need for American aid."

Conley glanced back toward the door and clenched his fists, seized by the impulse to attack Shakuri and at least go down fighting before the guards could intervene.

Shakuri observed his coiled stance and smiled. "Don't worry. There's still time to avoid extremes." He glanced at Oleg. "I'm counting on Mr. Mikhailov...not to mention the laptop."

CHAPTER 96

Gallagher didn't waste critical seconds stepping back into his office. Instead he grabbed a phone from an empty reporter's desk. "I see," he said, in staccato syllables. "How long ago? Thanks." He slammed down the receiver and turned back to Claire, Larson and Frick. "Harry just left for lunch," he explained, backing away. "I might still be able to catch him downstairs."

"We'll come too," Larson said, Frick following a half-step behind her.

Gallagher dodged a desk and glanced back at Claire. She passed the others and drew alongside him, holding out her cell-phone and punching buttons with her thumb. "Don't bother," he told her, starting to pant. "His secretary said he left his phone behind…"

At full march perspiration broke from his armpits, while his thudding strides and trailing cohort activated alarm. Editors and reporters cleared a path. Past newsroom reception he charged down the narrow, single-file escalator, sliding rubber safety railings through both hands. Machinery boomed and shuddered under his mass; over the din he heard Claire's heels clanging close behind. At bottom the steel floor panel came up fast. He grunted as one leg almost gave out.

"Art!" Claire shouted, clasping his shoulder from behind.

"I'm okay…" Back on balance, he whirled, put his head down, and flung open glass doors into the main lobby. In brighter daylight he made a quick scan, then focused his vision through the tall, green-glass atrium facing Morrissey Boulevard. Whitcombe was climbing into the rear of his limousine, one foot still planted on the asphalt.

Before the driver closed the door, Gallagher burst through the entrance, shouted *"Harry!"* and lumbered down the wheelchair ramp. Whitcombe re-extracted his angular frame, swathed in gray overcoat. His weary resolve appeared to mingle with dread.

"It's Conley, Harry…I just got a call…" Gallagher paused, leaned forward with his hands on his knees, lungs heaving. "Excuse me…" he said, straightening. "From Stanson in Moscow…Conley missed his dinner appointment…His interpreter is gone too…"

Gallagher felt Claire's hand on his back: comradeship in crisis. Larson and Frick finally drew up alongside. When his breathing moderated enough for continuous speech he relayed the rest.

"No leads?" Whitcombe asked when he was done.

"None."

"What's Stanson doing in response?"

"Monitoring the situation for now, through Shakuri. He's planning to fly down on Thursday."

"Thursday? Today's Tuesday…"

"Almost Wednesday morning in Tajikistan."

Gallagher felt a chill from the wintry air. Looking down, he realized his perspiration had soaked through his underwear and imprinted foot-long ovals under the armpits of his shirt. Whitcombe considered the situation, squinting toward the harbor.

"We can't stand still," he said after brief seconds.

Larson drew a step closer, intent. Whitcombe glanced at her, noticed Frick over her shoulder, then re-fixed on Gallagher.

"I'd like you to fly there, Art. To Dushanbe…to be on the scene as soon as possible."

Astonished and still panting, Gallagher was at a loss for words.

"Claire, I'd like you to go also," Whitcombe added, turning toward her.

"Me?"

"You're part of this. Probably more than anyone."

Claire's mouth dropped in shock before her wide gaze shifted to Gallagher and another reaction took hold. Gallagher couldn't classify it precisely. Whatever tumultuous forces had unsettled her over the weekend unsnarled and reordered. Hitherto vague notions crystallized. Her eyes seized with re-found purpose. He could feel it, even if the outlines weren't clear to him.

She saw a way forward again.

Expressions on Larson and Frick told a different story. This was thermonuclear. Gallagher finally managed a response.

"We'll get on it, Harry. However there are issues of visas and transport..."

Whitcombe had not lost capacity for command after all and would brook no obstacles. "Art, I suggest you get back on the phone with Stanson," he said. "Have him push necessary buttons. Try to get on his plane from Moscow to Dushanbe on Thursday."

Gallagher made some quick calculations and cleared his throat. "Actually Harry...that could work."

All five of them stood in dazed silence as wind gusted off the harbor, blowing up Whitcombe's salt-and-pepper forelock. It also shot through Gallagher's soaked shirt and undershirt, inducing harsh tingling on the wet skin underneath. This was precisely the outcome for Conley that he had feared. From behind Claire pressed her hand more firmly against the damp fabric on his back. Her touch felt directed now, somehow more resolute. It was also trembling. Gallagher realized she wasn't the only one.

"Art, you're shivering. Let's go back inside. Time is short."

CHAPTER 97

As Shakuri's footsteps receded down the hallway Conley strode over to the desk and tugged open the zipper to the laptop case. Oleg raised his eyebrows, jaded and incurious, and pulled up a chair. With care Conley extracted the device and placed it on the desk. It was a dark-gray, standard-variety Dell. He also unzipped the back side of the case, which was divided into several compartments. Peripherals were well organized; cords and cables coiled.

"A lot neater than mine," he observed.

Next he found a mouse and power cable, which he connected, attaching the latter to an electrical outlet under the desk. Configured and ready, he pressed power on. While the operating system booted they waited in silence, both disinclined for now toward further play-acting. A screen soon appeared with a password prompt.

"Oh no, just what we need…"

Oleg shook his head and reached toward the keyboard. "Here, let me…" His fingers danced across and he hit "Enter." Booting resumed. "Our programmers hacked Bradford's password when he was in Moscow," he explained, leaning back.

Icons materialized on screen and Conley focused. A standard array of applications, installed by the *World Tribune* systems department---nothing unusual. Except one: Hoderer-Feltz Bank, Zurich, an elegant icon that seemed more Old World than New. He clicked, unsure what he would find. To his surprise the application opened at once, no further password required. A custom program, but relatively simple. The main page contained the name and address of the bank in Zurich, along with an account number. There were also three tabs: *Balance, Incoming* and *Outgoing.* He clicked *Balance.* A new window popped up. There was a single, stark figure, denominated in U.S. dollars: 1,250,000. Stunned for an instant, he glanced back at Oleg, whose eyes were also on the number. The Russian showed no reaction.

Next he clicked *Incoming,* popping open another window showing the same number: $1,250,000. Also carrying a transfer date of October 15th---the date that Bradford had interviewed Shakuri and dined at the villa. The originating bank was in Luxembourg. He glanced back again at Oleg and found the same bland stare.

"You don't seem surprised."

Oleg snorted. "Should I be?"

"Fits Shakuri's story. But it might be a ruse. Shakuri could have installed the program."

"And Usmonov?"

"Before drawing conclusions let's look in some other applications."

Conley found Bradford's e-mail client and opened it. There was a message from Gallagher in the *Inbox*---one Conley had already read back in Boston. He clicked on *Sent Mail.* There was a long list of messages, mostly to Gallagher. At top was one addressed to franz.schulter@hoderer-feltz.ch, dated October 15th. Startled again, he clicked on the header:

Franz,

I have confirmed receipt of US$1,250,000 to my new account. I would like to invest half of this amount in six-month U.S. Treasuries and UK gilts, and the other half in high-yielding European corporate debt. Please provide appropriate suggestions.

I expect another $1.25 million transfer in about two weeks.
Regards,
Peter Bradford

"Had his investment strategy all worked out," Oleg observed in a caustic tone.

Conley sat back and crossed his arms, still incredulous. "Such a straight arrow…such a great future ahead. Hard to believe." He looked at Oleg again, who only clamped his lips in distaste. "You seemed to expect it all along, Oleg. Can I ask why?"

For first time all evening, the Russian laughed. "Instinct, I guess. It's not important. The main question is…what are you going to do now?"

"Assuming we get out of here?"

"Of course."

"I'll report what I found. There's no choice."

His smile disappeared and he shot Conley an impatient glance, waving his index finger at the ceiling. Eavesdropping was a new phenomenon in Conley's experience and so bizarre that he had quickly forgotten about it. He recovered himself.

"Well…I suppose we should consider our options…" This came out like a line from a laughable high school drama production. He felt awkward and suddenly tired. "…Bradford profited, and…"

"Why shouldn't we?" Oleg suggested.

"Yes…perhaps."

"I suggest we…you…sleep on it."

"Not a bad idea." Conley looked over at one of the beds and noticed a clock on the nightstand. The time was nearly one a.m. What he needed most now, he reckoned, was a good night's rest. The next day promised to be strenuous, no matter how it developed. He stood up, wondering if Mehrangiz had supplied toothbrushes in the bathroom.

"Think about Bradford's wife," Oleg added, irony in his voice.

Conley managed a beleaguered laugh.

"Right. I'll do that."

CHAPTER 98

Conley awoke with a restive jolt. The room was dark and the only illumination came from moonlight filtering through the curtains. He reached over and rotated the clock on the nightstand. He had to squint to read the time: 5:17. His nervous system was taut. Not from instincts toward self-preservation---though these would have fit the circumstances. More from everyday compulsions.

Here he was in grave, even mortal, danger---held incommunicado as part of a blundering, high-stakes geopolitical game---and all he could think about was...the female sex. He rolled over and drove his stiff appendage into the mattress...Just before waking he'd had a dream: A frenetic maelstrom in Moscow. Claire, Milena and Lilya in provocative mien. Irregular outcomes. Details were already slipping away...

Across the room Oleg was snoring. As Conley listened as the Russian mumbled and stirred. He wondered if he was having a nightmare. About Shakuri? About Stanson's collusion? The huge sums of money wasted, in such a corrupt region of the world? Maybe all these together...

He rolled onto one side, then onto the other, trying to subdue his energies before making out the laptop through the darkness, still set up on the desk. In response he ripped off his covers, swung his legs out of bed, and tugged on his socks. Recalling that Mehrangiz had mentioned bathrobes in the closet, he crossed over and pulled one on, then cinched the belt, walked back to the desk and sat down. The computer was still on and had had gone into dark-toned screensaver mode. When he hit a key he got a password prompt.

"Damn!" he muttered. He glanced toward Oleg's bed: unsettled but still sleeping.

Half out of frustration, he tapped in the first possibility that came to mind: *Claire1.* To his surprise the screensaver vanished, re-displaying Bradford's message to the Hoderer-Feltz Bank. He clicked back to Bradford's *Sent* File in the messaging application, and scanned down through the list for September and October. There were no messages to Claire, just as she'd indicated. Most were to Gallagher---others that Conley had also read when he started the assignment. Some additional messages related to Bradford's appointments in Prague and Moscow. He clicked on a half dozen of these, paying special attention to messages to Stanson. Nothing unusual: dates, times, preliminary queries.

Scrolling further back into September, another message caught his eye: to Harry Whitcombe. The destination address was private: not bearing the publisher's *bostonworldtribune.com* suffix. With slight hesitation, he clicked to open it:

Uncle Harry,

Enjoyed seeing you and Elizabeth and the rest of the clan for sailing last month, when Claire and I were Stateside. The clambake was also delightful. Sorry my work prevented me from joining you for golf in subsequent days.

For some months now I've had some issues I wanted to discuss about the trust, but decided Marblehead in August wasn't the right time or place.

Since I turned 26 my income from the trust has been $150,000 per annum. Coupled with my salary from the paper, that leaves Claire and me a substantial base of support. ...even though Claire has been unable to gain any traction in *her career and contribute. But Paris, as you know, is an expensive city. And U.S. and French taxes together swallow nearly half our inflow. Travel expenses have eaten into the rest. Claire's parents have offered to help us buy an apartment here, even with skyrocketing prices. But I've held them off until now and we've stayed with a rental.*

Still, that leaves us in a bind---barely breaking even. My question is this: given my intention to make a career at the World Tribune, and to meet the requirements specified by the trust, might some of this income be accelerated? As I understand I will receive $350,000 annually-- at current distribution levels---if and when I move up to the Managing Editor position. I could really use some of that in Paris just now.

On a related note, any chance that Art Gallagher might be encouraged to retire sooner rather than later?

Respect and affection,

Nephew Peter

Conley stared on screen and shook his head---uneasy that he was delving into private correspondence but also dismayed that Bradford had trouble living on such an income. How much did two people need, even in Paris? In both London and Boston Conley had managed fine on his salary; he'd even shaken off the decimation of his savings by the Nasdaq meltdown in 2001. During the past year he'd been helped, perhaps, by Jenna's insistence on sharing their restaurant and vacation bills...Curious about Whitcombe's answer, he switched to Bradford's incoming folders, sorted by date, and found what he wanted:

Peter,

I sympathize with your dilemma. I know Paris is expensive and that Claire is accustomed to living well.

However great-grandfather Whitcombe was a stern master. We're still abiding his rules today. I'm afraid my hands are tied; there's no choice but to wait.

Art Gallagher? Art has been a faithful servant to the paper for more than three decades. We haven't even broached the subject of retirement yet, although he's approaching his mid-sixties. I've assumed this is still two to three years out. I'm waiting for his initiative.

Janet Larson has lately suggested---in her typical subtle way---that Art should be nudged aside. Seems she has one of her protégés in mind, as a way of consolidating her grip and also heading off your ascendance. She's astute in many ways, but this isn't Minnesota. She's got a lot to learn about the way we operate here.

My advice for now? Have a talk with Claire. Convince her to keep her spending down. And hang in there.

In love and support,

Uncle Harry

P.S. - Enjoyed your piece last week about tensions in NATO over the European Expeditionary Force.

All of a sudden Conley noticed the room had grown quiet; Oleg had stopped mumbling and thrashing. He glanced over at the bed and saw Oleg lying on his side with eyes open, staring back.

"Bad dreams?" he asked.

Oleg didn't answer. He swung his legs out of bed and sat with his elbows on his thighs. After a moment, he looked up.

"Anything interesting?"

"Well…more substantiation of Shakuri's story."

Oleg clamped his lips again. His eyes were bleary but still not surprised.

Conley summarized what he'd read, highlighting Bradford's financial strains. The Russian shook his head.

"Poor guy. A common problem."

"Bradford? A poor guy? With trust fund income…and a good salary besides?"

"I mean with such a wife."

"Claire? She's from a well-to-do family, as far as I gathered."

Oleg was still bleary. "I don't mean just money."

"What, then?"

"I've understood she's attractive. Right?"

"Well, yes…"

"Ambitious?"

"I don't know. In her own way, maybe."

"Determined? Always wanting to go forward?"

Conley paused and recalled his week in Paris in more detail. Claire's parting stipulations at Charles de Gaulle Airport were most vivid.

"I guess I'd have to say so."

"It can be difficult to refuse such women…to slow them down."

With effort Conley tried to reconcile the picture. "I can appreciate that to some extent. But to make the choice that Bradford did? To compromise himself in this way? And with a repulsive kleptocrat like Shakuri?"

As if reprimanding a careless child, Oleg held up his index finger again and pointed at the ceiling----another reminder about listening devices. This caused Conley to expel a long breath, chafing anew at the limitation. The Russian resumed.

"We don't know. He might have been under her sexual thrall. Sometimes guys like Bradford…straight arrows, you call them?…are susceptible to that."

"All because of sex? That's a bit extreme, isn't it? In my case, I'd never…" Conley stopped himself. His thoughts muddled.

Oleg was insistent.

"It happens all the time."

CHAPTER 99

The bellhop at the *Langham* waved goodbye, unsure whether to smile. Claire's departure was premature and sudden, and the faces of Gallagher and Denise were lined with worry. Out of polite reflex she waved back. Denise edged the Volvo away from the curb, checking traffic on Franklin Street in the rearview mirror. Gallagher, sitting beside her in front, placed his hand on her backrest and twisted his neck and shoulders.

"Looks clear," he said.

Lights were red at the intersection with Congress Street. From the backseat Claire directed one last half-dazed glance at the hotel. Gallagher examined her with concern. "You're sure about this?"

She met his gaze and tried to appear calm. She'd asked the concierge to return her rental car, in order to save time.

"…You can still get off in Paris. Forget about going on to Dushanbe."

"I'm sure."

"Okay, Claire. We're in this together."

The previous afternoon and evening at the *World Tribune* had been a whirlwind: emergency visa arrangements for Russia and Tajikistan, orchestrated by Stanson from Moscow, flight reservations, a flurry of meetings with Whitcombe, Larson and Frick. Even a direct phone conversation with Shakuri---middle of the night in Tajikistan---broadcast on the conference-room speakerphone.

"You have no idea why they disappeared?" Gallagher had demanded---still disheveled from his frenetic rush downstairs to Whitcombe's limousine. He'd leaned onto the conference table with straight arms, one shirttail hanging down under his paunch.

"None." There was static but Shakuri's voice had resonated with sympathy and shared vigil. *"But we've organized an all-out search around Dushanbe."*

"And what if they've been taken elsewhere?"

"I am considering all possibilities, Mr. Gallagher."

Now Claire took stock. She wanted to be in Dushanbe, on hand if and when the situation broke. But what if she never saw Conley again? Broader issues aside, this was a real possibility; at intervals it made her nauseous. She remembered Uncle Harry's harried one-to-one discursion in the corridor, between sessions.

"I'm as shaken as everybody else," he'd said. "We can only hope Conley hasn't come to harm." Above his crossed arms he'd kneaded his chin. "Is this somehow connected to Peter? We have no idea yet."

"When I get there, Uncle Harry, what do you expect me to do?"

"Art is acting on behalf of the paper...looking out for Conley. As far as I'm concerned you're representing the family."

She'd given him a quizzical stare. His interests here were not entirely consistent with her own.

"...Most of all Peter's memory, Claire."

"Assuming Conley is okay...do you want me somehow to...*intervenir*?" Her English had deserted her. "I mean so that...bad things aren't published?"

"No...If the truth comes out, we shouldn't suppress it."

"What then?"

He'd re-kneaded his chin and looked down at the floor. "Just keep it all as dignified as possible. Yes...dignity, Claire. That's all we can hope for."

She'd considered his exhortation, about to object. Dignity for whom? Then Frick had poked his head out of the conference room and they'd re-entered the whirlwind...Now Denise finished navigating the maze of downtown Boston and entered the Ted Williams Tunnel. The new asphalt gave a smooth ride, and white lights lent a surreal quality to the interior of the vehicle. Once settled at cruising speed, she glanced in the rearview mirror, eyes awash with compassion.

"This has got to be as hard on you as anyone, Claire."

Claire examined her reflected image, unsure of her meaning.

"Because of the parallels..." Denise continued. "It's like we're re-living everything that happened a month ago."

"Yes...I suppose you're right."

"And you just saw him in Paris...Conley, I mean."

Claire swallowed hard. Conley *was* well-intentioned, as Tracey said, despite his base impulses. Very human, after all.

"Let's not take the parallel too far," Gallagher interjected solemnly. "Conley is still alive, as far as we know."

Denise reached across put one hand on her husband's knee. "Of course, dear. That's what I've been praying for these past 24 hours." He looked down and placed his hand over hers. In the mirror Claire could see tears well in Denise's eyes.

"...You'll look out for each other, won't you Claire?" she said into the mirror.

"Of course, Denise."

Claire felt tears of her own. Gallagher struggled for a sober tone.

"We'll fly to Dushanbe on a U.S. government jet, and be with Franklin Stanson," he said. "There will be American security personnel. All possible measures. We'll be safe. Conley is our main concern." He twisted back again. "Right, Claire?"

"Right."

Claire almost choked on her response. Would Conley's discretion even be relevant, at this stage? There was a real chance he'd be killed, if he hadn't perished already. Now some of her earlier thinking seemed so selfish...Daylight broke at tunnel's end and they entered the complex of ramps and roadways connecting different parts of Logan Airport. Denise and Gallagher turned attention to signs that would lead them to Terminal E for Air France. Still taut in the back seat, Claire re-adjusted her vision and clutched for lucidity. Art was right. Conley's survival *was* now paramount.

She couldn't forget that as this crisis unfurled.

CHAPTER 100

After lunch Conley and Oleg had suspended their play-acting, fed up with the artifice. Now the room was quiet, except for faint noises from elsewhere in the villa. Oleg reclined on his bed and stared at the ceiling, while Conley lolled on an armchair. Their inertia, as far as they knew, stood in bizarre contrast with the world outside. Reverberations from their disappearance had spread to distant corners: Boston, Washington and Moscow, not to mention Tajikistan.

Most bizarre of all was that Art Gallagher and Claire would wing their way to Dushanbe on Thursday, according to Shakuri. Aboard Stanson's government Learjet, no less. Gallagher's intervention was understandable. But Claire's? Conley didn't know to make of it. He remembered Shakuri's snide suggestion:

"Wouldn't you like to tell her what she wants to hear?"

The Prime Minister had summarized his wider deceptions as if they were marks of self-importance. Expansion of the search to include the entire western half of Tajikistan, "at the request of your newspaper and of the U.S. State Department." A press release from his own office----Conley and Oleg were described as a "Boston-based journalist and his Russian interpreter"----which declared their disappearance "likely connected with terrorist and heroin smuggling elements operating in Tajikistan." In Washington: official consternation. The Administration, Shakuri claimed, was even exploiting the event to advance the aid bill. A Senate vote was still planned for Thursday.

"You see," he'd said, stubborn in his confidence. "You have nothing to gain by refusing my offer. Everything will go on as before."

Somewhat to Conley's mystification, Oleg's gambit had actually bought time. "And what if we do accept now?" he had asked. "How would we explain our disappearance?"

"We'll cook something up, don't worry."

Today Shakuri had been absent since morning, in his office in the city. On the phone, conspiring with Stanson and Hermann to contain the crisis? By now Conley supposed the two American officials were involved, on some level. Only the degree of their complicity remained to be determined, if he and Oleg ever exited this alive.

Restless, he stood and approached the window. Out in the garden area the exterior security guard remained, bundled in winter clothes and bouncing on his feet to stay warm. The other kept station in the corridor, his occasional coughs and shuffles audible through the door.

Pacing back across the room, Conley re-analyzed the situation. After some moments he stopped and addressed Oleg.

"Shakuri's painted himself into a corner."

Oleg rotated his head on the pillow. "Meaning?"

"He's detained us. And now he's issued false press releases."

Oleg raised an index finger toward the ceiling in yet another reminder, but went along. "So?"

"One way or another, there's no going back."

"True."

"Then what's the point of his 'offer'? Why the stalling?"

"He may be corrupt, but he's not a killer," Oleg said, his tone reverting to graduate school pedantry. "He's giving us a chance. Groping for a way out. Just like we are."

Conley clenched his hands, paced back over to the window and leaned forward onto the sill. Hard truth was settling in, and made this play-acting too preposterous to sustain. He straightened abruptly.

"At this point, he can't let us out of here alive. Can't you see that, Oleg? He wouldn't risk it."

"We won't know for sure," Oleg answered, eyes flashing irritation but voice even. "...Unless we agree to his proposal."

Conley glanced at his watch and confirmed that it was already late-afternoon. Oleg was getting on his nerves again. "Our 48-hour clock is almost half-gone," he shot back. "Are you suggesting we just wait here until time's up, sticking with this charade?" Through walls he heard sounds of two or three cars, pulling into the house drive-way. He assumed Shakuri had returned. Oleg ignored the sound and acquired another sarcastic edge.

"What else do you have in mind?"

Instead of answering Conley scrutinized ground directly below the window. It was a long drop; still, about one meter out from the wall was a cluster of low-lying evergreen bushes which appeared relatively soft---a gentler landing surface than in Argenteuil. He was suddenly grateful for that bizarre and painful experience. This time he would do it right...

The windows were heavy double-paned glass, but without exterior grillwork. Each half was about twice as wide as his shoulders---more than ample clearance. He glanced back at two armchairs alongside the sitting table. Perfectly sized battering rams. He walked across, picked one up, determining the weight was just right, while Oleg watched, curious. Conley ignored him for now and visualized a plan. One key would be to wait until the guard was directly below. Then if he and Oleg got running starts and broke through each window simultane-ously, they could fly down from above with the advantage of surprise. With luck they'd land on the evergreens, compelling the guard to jump out of the way. Between them, they then stood a decent chance of overpowering him and wresting away his gun

"I have an idea," he said.

Still stoic, Oleg didn't move. His eyes flitted to the chair that Conley still gripped with both hands.

"What are you going to do?" Conley's voice rose. "…Just sit here waiting to die?"

Still no response.

"All right, Oleg. Suit yourself. I'll do this alone if I have to…"

Shouts erupted outside, interrupting their exchange and fracturing the quiet. These were followed at once by staccato bursts of automatic weapons fire. Within the span of a second, Oleg jackknifed up to a sitting position, intent and alert. Conley put down the chair and gaped across at him.

"What the hell is that?" he said.

CHAPTER 101

The Air France jet ascended through clouds northeast of Paris and settled at cruising altitude; Moscow was almost three hours away. With a slight grunt, Gallagher unbuckled his seat belt, snapped open his *International Herald Tribune,* and reread the front-page headline.

American reporter disappears in Tajikistan
Apparent abduction

The previous day the *Boston World Tribune* had published a brief story on page one, with initial, scant information---and this in turn had circulated on wire services. Today Conley's disappearance had become a major global news item, in part because of the aid bill pending in the U.S. Congress. More details were emerging, including a statement from Shakuri and comments from the White House.

In the next seat Claire sat taut and engrossed in the morning's edition of *Le Figaro,* which contained a lengthy, page-three article on continuing developments. On the *International Herald Tribune,* Gallagher scanned down to Conley's photograph: same one employed in recent *World Tribune* advertisements. With a hollowed-out sensation he re read the text:

...This is the second disappearance by a World Tribune reporter in Tajikistan in little more than a month. Peter Bradford, a World Tribune correspondent based in Paris, was murdered under mysterious circumstances on October 15th. Both Bradford and Conley traveled to the remote, little-known region of Central Asia to investigate the heroin trade out of Afghanistan, a major source of financing for international terrorist organizations...A spokesman for the White House called the abduction "alarming, a situation we are monitoring closely." The official asserted that "such lawlessness highlights the need for a greater American security presence. Terrorist elements behind Conley's disappearance should know that this Administration will not be dissuaded..."

Gallagher leaned his head back on the seat rest and exhaled hard through his nostrils. The all-night transatlantic flight had been taxing, as always. And on this onward leg dozing was out of the question. Claire was now absorbed in *Le Monde*, which also had page-three coverage. Its pages quivered slightly in her hands. Gallagher knew enough French to understand the headline:

Un deuxième journaliste américain disparu en Tadjikistan
La Maison Blanche promet la fermeté

"Anything beyond what *Le Figaro* reported?" he asked her, startling her out of her concentration.

"Same, more or less. This article mentions me, like the other one."

French media apparently did not yet know she was bound for Tajikistan. Thus far she had not been mentioned in American reports.

"Reporters are calling my parents in Paris," she said, referring to her quick phone call to them from CDG Airport.

"How do they feel about this?"

"My trip?"

"Yes."

"They doubt it's a wise idea. They're extremely worried."

Gallagher winced. Back in Boston he'd been through two agonizing phone calls with Conley's parents. They also were distraught, quite understandably. Claire observed his pained expression.

"This isn't your fault, Art."

Before he could object a stewardess pulled alongside with a beverage cart. They both ordered coffee. Taking a sip, he said: "It still doesn't make sense."

"What?"

"That Shakuri would allow this to happen, with so much at stake."

The pilot came over the address system with customary remarks, first in French and then in English. Smooth flying was expected, although a light snowstorm was underway in Moscow.

"...When we land there I'll have some pointed questions for Franklin Stanson," he added.

Claire nodded, though her expression became distracted; Stanson seemed of little consequence to her---as if Conley's safety was now foremost. Gallagher hoped she was realistic about her ability to affect the outcome.

"We should remember, Claire. Our influence may be limited."

She thought for a moment.

"Maybe not, Art. If we're with Stanson, we'll also be close to Shakuri, right?"

"I would think so."

"Good. That means we'll be right in the center of things."

CHAPTER 102

Gunfire lasted all of five seconds. There were shouts outside---some barked like commands, others shrieked like pleas of capitulation. Conley continued gaping across at Oleg. He asked him if the shouts were in Russian.

When Oleg looked back and didn't answer, Conley walked back to the window and peered outside, cautious. The scene in the courtyard took him aback.

Four Russian soldiers in special operations gear surrounded Shakuri's guard---a couple of whom Conley thought he recognized from the smuggling patrol. The Tajik's hands were atop his head. One soldier had relieved him of his pistol. Another was patting him down for additional weapons.

Another ruckus erupted downstairs---what sounded like a group of soldiers bursting through the front door. More shouts, in both Russian and Tajik. Rapid footfalls receded down the corridor: their guard abandoning his position. Shakuri's voice was distinguishable in the downstairs din, in frantic Russian. Conley shot another question at Oleg, who was still sitting on his bed.

"Can you tell me what's going on, for heaven's sake?"

"Let's just stay put."

Still stunned, Conley moved toward the middle of the room. There was a thundering of soldiers up the stairs, then more harsh commands. He stared at the door, unsure what to expect. Within seconds a soldier hammered on the door.

"*Vee, Oleg?*"

Oleg stood up and shouted back. "*Da.*"

"*Kto drugoi?*"

"*Tolka Conley.*"

Splinters flew and the door ripped from its hinges. A Russian soldier hurtled into the room, and crouched with weapon at the ready. Two others followed, weapons also leveled and scanning all corners. Behind them, standing in the doorframe, was Nikolai, wearing special operations gear like the others. He made eye contact with Conley, and then with Oleg. There was a flicker of acknowledgement, but no smile. He made an abrupt movement with his hand toward the corridor.

"*Davaitse!*"

"The laptop!" Conley blurted, turning back toward the desk.

"Get it fast and let's go," Oleg said, in the same commanding tone as Nikolai.

Conley yanked plug from socket, then jammed cord, mouse and laptop into the case and zipped it up. When he looked up Oleg was already beating a headlong exit. Nikolai---bulk augmented by gear, was poised with wide stance and flexed knees, impatient and ready to hustle Conley away at full tilt.

"*Davaitse!*"

Grabbing the handle, Conley ran across and into the corridor. Halfway down the stairs---behind one soldier at full rush ahead and Nikolai propelling him from behind---he heard the pulsating chop of a helicopter nearing the villa.

Two soldiers were half-carrying Shakuri out the front door, one at each elbow. Shakuri muttered a stream of protests, and what sounded like Russian epithets. On the way through the foyer, Conley caught a glimpse of Mehrangiz standing by in befuddled alarm. "Wait!"

he shouted, halting Nikolai's impatient momentum. He and Oleg snatched fur hats and overcoats from the hall closet, throwing them on in half-stride. He had an ill-placed impulse to say goodbye to Merhangiz, but there was no time in any case...Outside, in front of the villa, the helicopter had landed---blades idling.

"Davaitse!" Nikolai shouted again.

Shakuri was hauled onto the aircraft like a sack of over-ripe potatoes, and Oleg jumped after him. Nikolai directed Conley up under the moving blades and Conley scrambled aboard, where a soldier pointed him to a bench next to Oleg. Across the helicopter Shakuri was already strapped in, lashed so hard against the interior fuselage that his face had gone red. He directed a bug-eyed, angry gaze at Oleg.

"I should have known..." he spat in English, gritting his teeth. "The Russians can't do this anymore...Franklin Stanson will hear about this."

Oleg ignored him as remaining soldiers scrambled aboard. Engines revved for liftoff and the aircraft shuddered aloft with a thumping roar. Fifty meters up it banked away hard, inducing Conley and everyone else to flail for handholds. Bracing cold wind blew in through the side hatch. Once on a straighter course, Conley caught glimpses of rugged hilltops, passing underneath at high speed.

"We're heading for the Russian air base," Oleg explained.

Holding ceiling netting for stabilization, Nikolai approached them from bow end, automatic weapon still slung over one shoulder. He reached into his jacket pocket and pulled out two cell-phones, then presented them on his meaty palm. His comment came---at last---with a half smile.

"These were in the villa," Oleg translated.

Uncomprehending, Conley took his phone back.

"That's how they found us," Oleg added. "Triangulation."

"Does that mean you're...?" Conley stopped himself and decided to save that question for later. He looked down at the display. They were close enough to Dushanbe---and high enough in the air---that he appeared to have reception. His first reflex was to call Gallagher. Maybe reach him while he was still in Moscow and figure out what to do next. However Gallagher didn't have a European cell-phone. That left Claire...

Watching Conley, Nikolai's smile faded. His remark carried a harsh tone again---more like a command.

"Better wait until we get to the base for phone calls," Oleg translated. "We should be there in about five minutes."

As the helicopter continued its fast trajectory over the hilltops, Conley tried to comprehend the wider picture.

"Do you think Stanson knows about this operation?" he asked Oleg.

Oleg didn't bother asking Nikolai.

"Not yet. This is where real complications begin."

CHAPTER 103

This was Claire's first visit to Russia, and despite her strains, the country stirred stronger sensations than most others. Similar to visceral reactions she'd experienced on early trips to the United States. She supposed foreigners felt the same arriving in France...though of course she was French.

Although her knowledge of Russian history was sparse she could divine reasons for the aura. Russia was a country that mattered. A place of earth-shaking events---a nation with capacity to surprise. Peter had tried to communicate these features on a few occasions. Then, they'd seemed abstract, remote. Now they were palpable. Why did she sense that something important would happen to her here? On this journey she was just passing through to Tajikistan...

Amidst a bustle of arriving passengers at Sheremetyevo-II airport, most bundled in winter coats, she and Gallagher approached passport control---a more imposing checkpoint than most others she'd encountered. Stanson was supposed to meet them here---accompanied by a Russian customs official, so visas could be issued on the spot. After customs clearance he would then accompany them to another Moscow airfield, a smaller one, for onward departure to Dushanbe.

Assessing the queues, and with Stanson nowhere to be seen, Gallagher excused himself to visit the restroom.

While Claire waited for him to return, she scanned the line of booths, looking for someone resembling an American government official. Stanson had her cell-phone number, she remembered, in case there were problems. The cavernous terminal at Sheremetyevo was chilly, which kept her alert in spite of her jet lag.

Then she spotted him---it had to be----at the end of the line of booths: swelling midsection under a too-tight overcoat, mostly bald and wearing gold-rimmed aviator glasses. He reacted with a folksy wave, removing any doubt. His lopsided grin was muted---this was a crisis, after all. There was a Russian customs officer at his side. Stanson gestured for her to wait., then stepped into an adjacent, windowed customs office.

Her phone chortled and she straightened with a sharp intake of breath. Apart from Stanson, she wasn't expecting any calls. Stanson was visible through glass; he was not holding a phone. With a trembling hand, she pulled out the device and answered.

"Claire?"

"Mon Dieu! Is that you…?" She sputtered. "Steve?"

"Yes. The first news is that Oleg and I have been rescued." Conley was speaking English. *"We're now at a Russian base. We're safe."*

"Thank God. Who…what…?"

"It's a long story. There's not much time. Where are you now?"

"Moscow airport." She could barely get the words out. Her first reaction was relief. Conley was alive. Moreover he'd called her first.

"Is Art with you?"

She cleared her throat. "Yes…but he's gone to the toilet."

"Are you with Stanson?"

"No, not at the moment…" Her head spun. "…But he's here to help with our visas." She looked toward the passport office. Stanson was emerging with the Russian official, who carried documents in hand. "Wait…he's coming over now."

"Still no sign of Art?"

She shot a glance in the direction of the restrooms.

"Not yet."

There was a brief pause on Conley's end.

"Don't tell Stanson yet that I'm free. I want to talk to Art first."

"Why? I don't…" Stanson had covered about half the short distance now, and was glancing around the terminal, curious why Gallagher was not with her.

"…It's complicated. There's no time to explain. Clear passport control. Then play along as if nothing has happened. I'll call back in 15 minutes."

The connection went dead and Claire stood frozen for several seconds, holding the phone near her ear. Stanson and the official were almost upon her.

"Claire?" Stanson asked, with a distinct drawl.

"Yes…" Just before he drew up she replaced the phone in her coat pocket.

Stanson observed her quivering hand and re-assumed an air of sympathy as they made introductions. The Russian official spoke English but was all business. Claire had trouble looking the American in the eye. Conley's warning had unleashed wild speculations. Why such caution? With a U.S. official, no less? Her throat became dry and tight. Conley was safe. But this was another wrenching twist. She would have to think on her feet.

"Here comes Art," she rasped, relieved to see Gallagher striding back from the restroom.

CHAPTER 104

There hadn't been time for a final restroom visit onboard the plane. Now Gallagher felt better. Ready to bear down on Stanson. He had some hard questions.

Through the moving thicket of arriving passengers, he spotted Claire, standing with two men. One wore the uniform of a Russian customs officer. The other, he presumed, was Stanson. In foreign locales he could usually identify his countrymen.

Stanson's official status did not reassure him. Gallagher had entered the journalistic profession during Vietnam, and the epoch had imbued him with baseline skepticism toward the U.S. government, especially when it came to foreign policy. Bradford's murder had been appalling enough---attributable perhaps to the hazards reporting from an unstable part of the world. But Conley's abduction bordered on bizarre. Something was out of whack. His latent mistrust from decades earlier had re-wound to full.

Claire didn't appear at ease around the American official either, which made him even more vigilant. After quick introductions, he demanded an update.

"Unfortunately there are no new developments," Stanson drawled.

"Nothing?"

"I've kept in constant contact with Prime Minister Shakuri."

"And?"

"And the search continues."

"Shakuri's your man, isn't he?"

"Well, yeah…"

"Is he going to be answerable this time around?"

Stanson rocked back on his heels and swung his arms up slightly from his sides, as if surprised by an unruly animal in the wild. Gallagher also noticed Stanson's winter boots, under his suit cuffs, which appeared incongruously large. A closer look revealed the reason. Their soles contained lifts, which gave him extra stature that he didn't really possess. Gallagher wasn't at all surprised.

"I'll fill you in the car, Art," the official answered, struggling to maintain his rangeland cadence. "But first I reckon we'd better get these formalities out of the way."

As they followed Stanson and the Russian customs officer, Claire flashed Gallagher a rattled look, followed by a glance at her watch.

"Remember, Claire…"

Her wide eyes turned back toward him, in stride.

"…We're in this together."

She responded with a stiff nod.

The Russian official excused himself briefly at the checkpoint, and the visas took just minutes. Out in baggage claim, Gallagher and Claire took position near a moving carousel, with Stanson standing beside them. Other arriving passengers on *Air France* were mostly middle-aged French and Russian businessmen. Many of these, Gallagher noticed with slight irritation, directed discreet gazes at Claire. An *International Herald Tribune* tucked under one man's arm made Gallagher remember the aid bill.

"You up to date on the vote in the Senate today?" he asked Stanson.

"Sure."

"Well?"

Stanson glanced at his watch. "Oh, it's still on…in six hours or thereabouts. Around the same time we'll touch down in Dushanbe tonight."

A sharp intake of breath emanated from Claire. Gallagher glanced at her. Her eyes remained fixed on the carousel.

"No postponement because of Conley?"

"Well no…You have to remember, Art…there are broader issues involved here."

Anger welled in Gallagher. He'd heard that line before. "Wait just a minute, Franklin. You mean to tell me that a reporter's life is…" He stopped, alarmed. Claire was breathing hard, almost hyperventilating. Despite chilliness in the terminal her overcoat was unbuttoned, as well the top of her blouse. Her face and the exposed skin above her breasts were crimson.

"Claire! Are you okay?"

"Uhh…just a little warm. There's my bag." She pointed at the carousel.

Gallagher looked over and found most male eyes in the vicinity fixed on Claire's partly open blouse. His glower compelled them to look away.

"I'll get it," Stanson volunteered, stepping toward the carousel.

"Mine's right behind it," Gallagher said.

A beefy man with a crew cut and goatee materialized out of nowhere, whom Gallagher took to be a plainclothes security guard---American. He helped Stanson with the bags while Gallagher guided Claire to a row of chairs outside the nearby Air France baggage office. Stanson issued an instruction to the guard, who carried the two suitcases outside, the stepped away to a quiet corner and pulled out a cell-phone.

Once seated, Claire remained flushed and panting.

"Claire is there anything I can…?" Gallagher began.

Her cell-phone chortled, cutting him off. She pulled it out, not bothering to look at the display, and handed it to him while it was still ringing, in a quavering hand.

"It's Conley."

"Conley?" Gallagher was confused for an instant before his hopes surged. He took the phone and flipped it open. "...Steve?"

Their ensuing conversation came in quick bursts and was the most staggering in Gallagher's 40-year career in journalism. Abduction, attempted bribery, high-stakes geo-politics...even a daring military rescue. And these were just the highlights. Some details, Conley insisted, weren't suitable for the phone.

CHAPTER 105

Claire tried to regain her composure and listen. The gist of the call was unclear. She couldn't hear Conley's end, and Gallagher mainly asked clipped, intermittent questions. A few passing references to Peter caused her heart to skip. Whatever Gallagher heard didn't appear to surprise him---or even more important--- provoke rueful glances in her direction.

When the call was over he snapped the cell-phone closed and slumped back in his seat, holding the device on his stomach. "Thank God…" he muttered, appearing both stunned and relieved. For some seconds Claire couldn't get a word out.

"So where…?"

Stanson's large boots appeared *tout direct* in front of her. Her eyes traveled up. The official was still gripping his cell-phone in one hand. New twin creases had formed above the nose-bridge of his aviator glasses. He didn't ask her how she was feeling. "Strangest thing," he drawled, half to himself. "I can't reach Shakuri."

"Is that so?" Gallagher responded, crossing his arms over his belly and tightening the fabric over his overcoat around the shoulder.

"Yeah…And none of his folks are in his office."

Gallagher stroked his beard with one hand, his manner more aggressive. "What's next then?"

"Well..." Stanson continued. "Guess we should get going all the same. I can try Shakuri from the car before we get airborne. Are you ready?"

"Our bags in the car?" Gallagher asked, getting up from his seat.

"Yeah...all set."

"Take them out. We won't be flying to Dushanbe."

Stanson's eyebrows rose, shifting the creases to his forehead. "What?"

"We're heading into the city instead. We're staying in Moscow."

"I don't understand..."

"Conley's been rescued."

"Rescued...?"

"By Russian troops."

Stanson went rigid.

"And I can tell you why you can't reach Shakuri, Franklin. The Russians have taken him into custody."

Horror spread across his face.

"It was Shakuri who abducted Conley."

On television or otherwise, Claire had never observed a government official---French, American or any other---subjected to a world-upending experience. For Stanson this was just such a tornado: one that smashed long-held assumptions and sent them spiraling into the air like clouds of debris. Months of planning and organization tumbled up and away before his eyes. With fascination she watched him: wide stance, chest heaving and speechless in the face of the devastation.

"Sir?" The young plainclothes guard asked, returning to Stanson's side.

More chest-heaving silence.

"...Sir, I called ahead. Your plane's waiting."

At last some ingrained adaptability in Stanson seemed to come back to the fore. One that derived from untamed spaces, Claire supposed. Yes, an unexpected obstruction from a harsh natural order. But there was no point in commiseration. There might still be time to rise and regroup. Stanson narrowed his stance and raised his head.

"Cancel the plane," he told the guard. "I'm going back into the city." He gestured at Gallagher and Claire. "So are they."

"Sir?"

"And get a line open to the White House. We've got to decide what to do about this aid bill. I've also got some things to hash out with my Russian contacts." The guard pulled out a walkie-talkie to transmit instructions to someone outside. Stanson turned back toward them; behind the aviator glasses his eyes were now on automatic. "Can we take you in, Art?"

Gallagher took one step closer to Claire: a protective move. He glowered back.

"Never mind. We'll take a taxi."

CHAPTER 106

Thrust from the twin jet engines was sudden and powerful and pressed Conley against the backrest. He reclined his head and relaxed his neck, accommodating the force. The Tupolev 104 surged down the runway and lifted off in a smooth, roaring arc. At 300 meters and still ascending, the aircraft banked hard left. A gaping downward view opened on the floodlit perimeter of the airbase. Gripping both armrests, he peered out his window.

Below he spotted the main gate, in bright illumination. There were two vehicles parked outside---big SUVs. Several human figures stood nearby and although they were already in miniature their faces were tilted up at the plane.

"Probably Hermann," he remarked over the engines.

"Sure you did the right thing?" Oleg responded.

"There was no time."

The plane came out its bank turn and rose into low-lying clouds, leaving just darkness out the window.

"You could have stayed."

"No thanks."

After an initial plea Hermann had called again---the ring came on the stairs the plane. Conley had turned off his phone. The sooner out of Tajikistan the better, he'd decided.

Now Moscow was less than three hours away. A full speed flight plan, Oleg had indicated, with a light load---Conley and Oleg were the only passengers in a modified commercial liner that seated 30. Suitcases three rows back amid empty seats, snatched by the Russians from their hotel in downtown Dushanbe. How? Conley couldn't imagine. His laptop was stowed in an overhead bin. So was Bradford's, inside a Russian military-green duffel bag which he'd requested at the base.

In terms of efficiency and coordination the Russian rescue operation had been flawless. Subsequent preparations at the base had lasted just 90 minutes. This dedicated jet---described by Oleg as a "special government plane"---was further evidence of priority treatment. Now Conley was ready to pose the obvious question. He waited another few minutes until the aircraft reached cruising altitude, then fixed on the translator's profile.

"Come clean, Oleg. Are you a Russian intelligence agent?"

Oleg didn't bat an eye. "You mean FSB?"

"Or SVR...whatever. Initials aren't important."

When there was still no reaction, Conley pressed further:

"My suspicions began on the patrols. When Shakuri took us prisoner, you expected a certain outcome...confident the whole time. The airbase was the clincher."

Indeed, during more than half of their 90-minute sojourn at the base, Oleg had been away for undefined "consultations." Now the Russian stared forward and didn't answer. By now Conley had gotten used to this.

"And what about this plane?" He swept an arm toward the empty rows of seats. "A special jet for an obscure American reporter and his humble Russian interpreter? I mean, come on!"

This comment prompted only a sardonic half-smile. After a moment Oleg finally answered.

"Would it really matter, for purposes of your story?"

"Maybe not. One part I can't figure out, though. I understand the stakes for Russia. But why involve me?"

Oleg chose his words with care. "A lot of intelligence is just being on hand when important things happen."

"Fine. And the rescue? The timing seemed too good to be true."

Oleg pursed his lips in a show of disappointment, and finally turned his face toward Conley. "You're a smart guy. Internet intercepts...a few bugs in the villa. It's not difficult."

"You mean you...the Russians...knew what happened with Bradford all along?"

"The bribe? Yes. The rest was logical deduction."

"Then why not tell Stanson and Hermann?"

"We couldn't hand over recordings. After all we'd recorded Stanson there, too. That e-mail was circumstantial. We just conveyed our 'interpretation.' "

Various elements came together..."I see..."

Oleg gave a slight nod.

"Think Shakuri informed them about our apprehension, while it was in progress?"

"I doubt it. That was just bluster." Oleg shook his head with an air of lament. "Never thought I'd be excusing America to an American. Blame Stanson's behavior on cold war reflexes...or on his overriding focus on terror. Or on..." He trailed off.

"Incompetence?"

"That's probably too strong a word. Better to call it lack of experience. At least in Central Asia."

Conley started to laugh, but his smile faded when he remembered the $550 million of U.S. taxpayer dollars involved. This was one expensive bungle.

"I can only imagine what's going on with the aid bill now. Think Stanson flew to Dushanbe by himself?"

"No."

"So he might be waiting for me in Moscow?"

Oleg raised his eyebrows: a clear affirmative. Conley didn't ask him how he knew.

"Great. Just what I need."

"That might be the least of your challenges," Oleg observed.

"Are you referring to Felayev?"

"No…though speaking of incompetence, there was no excuse for what happened last week when you were in Moscow. It shows that we… Russia…are also susceptible to our own missteps. Just like Stanson and Hermann. However before we arrive I can assure you. There will be no repetition of that fiasco. Felayev's lawyer has been detained. And Felayev himself has been put in strict isolation."

"That's good to hear. What are you talking about, then?"

"A different kind of challenge."

Oleg's omission took several seconds to register. "Damn. I'd started to forget…" Conley reclined his head again on the backrest and stared up at the overhead bin, where Bradford's laptop was stowed. The duffel bag was meant for concealment from inquisitive eyes---Claire's, above all.

"I'm not looking forward to that;" he said. "Lord help me."

"What are you going to do?"

"The first thing I'm going to do is talk to my editor."

"Art Gallagher?"

Conley gripped the armrests and released a long exhalation.

"Yes. Before I see Claire, I hope."

CHAPTER 107

With an irritated movement Gallagher ground out another cigarette in the floor-post ashtray. Through wafting smoke he squinted across the lobby bar of the *Radisson*. To his dismay Stanson had materialized. Near the lobby's artery the U.S. official paced with wide gait and cell-phone to his ear, pleading in over-audible down-home vernacular to a Russian government contact named Vasily for confirmation of Conley's touchdown at a Moscow airfield. Claire circled close-by: arms coiled, shooting wary glances at him and steeling an eye on the automatic doors of the main entrance. Her excited mid-body squeeze swelled her bosom, her tight dress amplifying her curves.

This had become an overcharged welcoming party.

Coming down with her in the elevator, after they'd both checked in and gone to their rooms, Gallagher had also caught a subtle scent of fine perfume. He understood that French women tended to present themselves in exquisite manner on important occasions. And Conley's liberation truly was exceptional. This had to be a relief to her, for obvious reasons. Why did Stanson have to interfere?

Rounding out the contingent was one of Stanson's goateed, beefy private security escorts, standing at semi-attention with face fixed forward---and eyes flitting inexorably and intermittently to Claire.

To Gallagher, her wariness of Stanson was more than appropriate. He'd guided her husband and then Conley into the clutches of Shakuri---a figure proven corrupt and duplicitous beyond even Gallagher's rather extreme speculations. And there were plenty of other troublesome questions that lacked answers.

When Stanson snapped his cell-phone shut, the device rang again within seconds. He answered and made a few glum acknowledgements. Collapsing the phone again, he strode straight toward Gallagher in the lounge area.

"Just got confirmation from Washington," he drawled, sidling up. "The Senate vote's been postponed."

"Postponed?" Gallagher growled. He had been on the phone with Reynolds in Washington. "I heard that the bill was dead."

"Well...that depends."

"Depends on what?"

Stanson hesitated, as if on another tornado watch. Gallagher clambered up from his upholstered armchair with a snort and stood face-to-face, letting him know he wasn't in the mood for evasion.

"Well..." A pained expression crossed Stanson's face. "The main problem is Shakuri."

"You don't have to tell me that."

"He didn't just let us down. He also embarrassed Rahmonov, the president of Tajikistan. And maybe cost his country a half billion dollars. Shakuri is through."

"Then how can the bill still stand a chance?"

"Rahmonov is putting forth another Prime Minister."

"Quick as that?"

"Younger guy, named Usmonov. Supported by the Russians. We don't know him well yet, although he does speak some English..."

Stanson trailed off, his head pivoting toward the middle of the lobby. Gallagher's gaze followed; he assumed Conley had arrived. Instead two long-legged young, women sauntered through, wearing elaborate, expensive fashion, including fur coats. Two somewhat older men, presumably their husbands, trailed behind, smoking cigars. Just back from a concert or expensive dinner, Gallagher guessed. So called "New Russians," radiating prosperity. Claire caught the women's attention. Admiring glances at first...until they noticed an absence of male attendance. Their expressions became wary and territorial. They assumed Claire was a hooker. A threat.

The scene ratcheted up Gallagher's anger even further.

"If I were you, I'd be a little more worried about Claire, and a little less worried about the bill," he said.

Stanson looked dumbfounded.

"...Do you realize what she's been through? If it hadn't been for Shakuri..."

"Art, please."

Gallagher glowered at him.

"I'm sorry about Bradford, but there are bigger concerns here."

"I'm telling you Franklin, if I hear that line one more time..."

Their exchange was broken when Claire's heels went snapping away from the lounge area, toward the front door. She had a full head of steam. "Probably Conley," Stanson declared, spinning away with no apology and striding off after her. Gallagher snorted, then huffed along behind.

As Stanson passed his American security escort Gallagher heard him mutter, *"It's always the French."*

Now Gallagher's blood was really boiling.

CHAPTER 108

Fresh snow dusted the ovular drive. The driver steered the Volga into a controlled skid on the slight incline, overcoming limitations of rear-wheel drive. Car and driver were courtesy of an unspecified branch of the Russian government.

"What the hell...?" Conley said, gripping ceiling handle in the back. A massive, dark-blue SUV hulked atop the rise, near the Radisson's main entrance. Just like Hermann's in Tajikistan. A driver was silhouetted behind the wheel.

"Diplomatic plates," Oleg answered. "American."

"Uh oh."

As the Volga passed the SUV the driver raised a walkie-talkie to his mouth.

"Damn...just what we need," Conley said.

The hotel's revolving glass door opened just before they pulled to a stop. Instead of Stanson, however, the figure of Claire launched toward them with quick steps, arms wrapped tight and eyes blazing with energy. Her tangent brought her to Oleg's side of the car, which was closest.

"Claire?" Oleg said, eyebrows up and sitting a little straighter.

Conley nodded once.

"Wow."

Outside Claire was introducing herself to Oleg when her eyes found Conley over the Volga, while behind her, half in a blur, Stanson emerged with a single-minded look. As Conley rounded the back bumper she shot toward him, arms outstretched and skidding on the snow with her high-heeled shoes. And into clearer focus: with make-up, despite her long journey. To keep her balance, she reached forward and clasped his shoulders, then kissed his cheek in greeting. Inadvertent closeness brought contours and discharges of perfume. He sputtered half-coherent gratitude before she withdrew.

She looked overwhelmed, even more than in Paris.

At last Gallagher appeared, shouldering past Stanson and snorting condensed air out his nostrils. He brightened only when he gave Conley a handshake and a tug on the shoulder.

"You can't imagine how relieved we are Steve," he said.

They were interrupted when the Volga's trunk sprung open with a creak. Before the driver could reach inside, Conley grabbed the duffel bag, along with his own laptop. Stanson drew up a few paces away.

Conley adjusted his grip on the items, keeping careful distance, while Claire hovered at his shoulder, her wariness palpable. Gallagher's glower revived. The cause was unmistakable now.

"Look Steve," Stanson drawled. "It went wrong for all of us."

"Us, Franklin?" Conley answered. "You weren't abducted. We were."

"I know."

"So?"

"Shakuri let us down."

"Is that all?"

"Not by a long shot. Our effort there is in ruins."

"Really? Can't say I feel any sympathy."

Stanson did not bristle. Instead, looking hard-hit and numb, he extended his hand. Reluctantly, Conley put down the duffel bag and shook. Incompetence was forgivable, he decided. It did not equal conspiracy.

Gallagher's was not going to let Stanson off that easily.

"Let's get inside, Steve," he said, putting a hand on Conley's back. "There's no need for this out here."

A beefy young American with a goatee showed up alongside the car; Conley took him for contracted security. The duffel bag was still on the ground, and now gained everyone's attention, including Claire's. It was clearly not full, with just one item inside. Oleg stepped forward and picked it up before anyone got ideas. An instant later a hotel porter also materialized, and offered to help with their suitcases.

"I know it's late, Steve," Stanson said. "But maybe just a few questions…"

This really set Gallagher off.

"You've got to be kidding, Franklin. We're the ones with questions for you."

Stanson reared back, as if encountering a rattlesnake. His eyes gravitated again to the duffel bag.

"And we have a deadline to worry about tonight," Conley added.

The official's reaction looked just short of desperation.

Claire and Gallagher nevertheless left him behind, standing on the cold sidewalk in the company of the stern-faced security guard. Oleg pulled up the rear with the duffel bag. Conley tried not to look at Claire. His first order of business was to talk to Gallagher---alone.

"Where are you going?" she asked, still close, in a tremulous voice.

"Right now…to my room."

The entrance door revolved and conducted them to more comfortable interior temperatures. She took his arm---a gesture he could have done without. This time, he knew, his resolve would have to stick. The next 24-48 hours would demand a clear head. He modified his earlier maxim somewhat, to suit these more acute circumstances.

Not Claire. Especially not now.

CHAPTER 109

Claire sprayed another wisp of perfume on her throat and smoothed her dress along her hips and thighs. Then she inhaled and inspected her image in the full-length mirror. Her hemline bordered on *risqué*. Such an approach was manipulative, she knew. She wasn't proud of it. But other options had run out. Now she had to maneuver along less demure borders.

All she needed was Conley's attention. She would proceed from there.

What had he learned about Peter? That would be her first order of discovery. If he knew what she supposed he knew…well, then she faced a challenge of persuasion. She had to nudge him toward concealment. Or at least toward circumscription of the most shameful details. Play on his sympathies, without becoming suggestive. Redirect his impulses toward benevolent ends. Tap into the discretion that Tracey had described.

That was, as long as she still had time. Deadlines were coming into play.

"Call me when you're ready," Gallagher had told Conley as they'd stepped off their elevator, about ten minutes earlier. "We have nine time zones in our favor. No extreme rush."

"You won't be asleep?"

"Let the phone ring if I am."

Her room was on floor six, across the hall and three doors down from Gallagher's. Conley's was below on the fourth floor; she'd memorized his number. In front of the mirror she took one more deep breath to steel her nerves, and ventured out. She closed her door with care, minimizing the latch-click, then padded down to Gallagher's door, where she paused and listened. Just quiet tapping on a computer keyboard---fine so far. Because elevators lay further away than the stairwell, she opted for the stairs. Time could be critical.

On the landing between the sixth and fifth floors, out a low-slung window, she glimpsed the Moskva River, illuminated along both banks. Visible to the left were top floors of *La Maison Blanche de la Russie,* or Russian White House, where she knew that Boris Yeltsin had stood atop a tank during the 1991 coup attempt by Communist retrogrades---last, wheezing gasps of Soviet power---and ushered in a new age. This fleeting panorama stirred sensations like those she'd experienced at the airport that afternoon. Russia was a land of pivotal events, earth-shaping changes. Through no choice of her own it was turning out that way for her…She tried to control her breathing the rest of the way down.

More than 30 hours had passed since she'd slept; she was now operating on adrenaline. In the curving hallway on the fourth floor, she had trouble registering the numbers. Yes…ascending like the eighth floor…Conley's room #454 was about halfway to the end. Her breathing quickened again as she approached his doorway and stopped. She lifted her arm to knock, but paused in mid-air.

Her hand was shaking. Not just trembling. But really *shaking…* more than at any time since Peter's funeral. She lowered her arm and filled her lungs with a slow, deep breath, sensing she had to compose herself.

Again she smoothed her dress and looked down the length of her figure, from cleavage to tapered ankles. Her figure gave her confidence.

If she couldn't command a few decisive minutes---especially with some-one of Conley's susceptibilities---who could? All of her tribulations and efforts on behalf of Peter, it seemed, had come to this. Her goals were different than at the beginning, but stakes were never higher. Paris, New Hampshire, Boston...interviews, phone calls, travel...all that was behind her. And what better venue now than Moscow? It seemed fitting.

She raised her hand. This time she brought her knuckles down and knocked.

She waited, expecting the door to open. Instead...nothing. She bent forward and listened: total silence. Alarmed, she knocked again. From within: more wrenching silence.

Her mind revved as she wondered where Conley could have gone in such a short span. She'd never seen Stanson leave the hotel. Maybe he'd hung around and telephoned Conley from the lobby...prevailed upon him to come downstairs, intent above all on that damned aid bill...*Ras le bol!* Chest heaving, she turned heel and strode toward the elevators. If Conley was indeed down with Stanson, there might still be a chance for preemption...

At the elevator bank she stabbed the *Down* button, and crossed her arms. One compartment was descending. Taking forever. When its doors opened there was single occupant...one of the goateed American guards, standing straight-backed and startled against rear wall. Issuing another expletive under her breath, she stepped on board, arms still crossed and in no mood for standard pleasantries. Then jabbed the button for the lobby---already illuminated---and whirled on the American. His face flustered.

"Don't tell me you've taken a room at the hotel!"

"Well, ma'am, I..."

"Is Steve Conley downstairs?"

The guard's eyes widened. As the descent resumed, he pulled a walkie-talkie from inside his coat.

"Is he with Franklin Stanson?" she demanded.

"I'm afraid I can't answer that, ma'am."

That particular form of address made her ready for battle.

When the bell dinged and doors opened she stormed straight into the lobby, and in full stride she scanned the armchairs and couches before pulling up with a sharp breath. There was Stanson, hunched forward on a couch and talking into another walkie-talkie. Conley was nowhere to be seen.

Stanson caught sight of her. Surprised. Then puzzled. He glanced over her shoulder. Claire spun around. The guard was coming up behind her, his own walkie-talkie to his mouth. He made a hand signal which confirmed her suspicion.

They were also looking for Conley.

She stared down at the floor to think clearly. If Conley was absent from his room and wasn't with Stanson, where could he be? This was Moscow. She'd gained an inkling he'd met a girl here. A rendezvous would be in character…his usual misplaced priorities. The hotel bar… She spun again, finding her coordinates and spotting it off to the right of the atrium…Then set off again, heels snapping and determined to hold the initiative over Stanson. The bar adjoined the lounge area and busy with a late evening crowd. She marched straight to the heart of it, near where a jazz pianist was playing. The eyes of the musician and those of some of the clientele flitted over to her, curious. The space was sprawling and dimly lit. She scanned low-slung leather arm chairs for Conley…in discreet *tête-à-tête* with a young woman.

Nowhere in sight.

Her chest heaved again when she realized she'd left her cell-phone back in her room. *Non! Comment-est-il possible?* She marched back out into the lobby, where Stanson and the security guard remained, still in battlefield surveillance mode.

Her next thought was the hotel entrance---that Conley might be awaiting an assignation outside. She snapped across the lobby and out-side with such impatience that she almost clipped the sliding doors.

A few taxis…Stanson's SUV…*quel monstrosite.* But no Conley.

The next idea that occurred to her was the shower…She hadn't heard running water but maybe he'd had the bathroom door closed. Back across the lobby an empty elevator was poised with open doors. She hit number four and then the "Close" button, before the guard could make a move to follow her. Up on the fourth-floor she scrambled down the corridor, ready to abandon all attempts at decorum.

This time she pounded on Conley's door.

"Steve, are you in there?"

Silence. She pressed her ear to the painted metal surface. No murmurs of running water.

She pounded again. More jarring silence.

Had he deliberately eluded her?…Taken an elevator to Gallagher's room? She darted to the stairwell, prevented from bounding the steps in pairs only by her skirt and high heels. Her clattering echoed up and down concrete walls, abating abated only she attained carpeting on the sixth floor corridor.

Fresh panic gripped her and brought her foot speed under last-second control as she approached Gallagher's room, worried that she was too late. She padded forward as if in a trance, quiet except for her heavy breathing. Nearer…a murmur of low voices turned panic to dread… She stopped outside. The voice inside was Conley's, in purposeful narration. How? Almost gasping for air…unable to get enough oxygen…she bent closer. Gallagher was now posing a question, in a tone serious and full of consequence.

Abruptly their conversation stopped. Claire guessed her labored breathing was audible, and she was seized by a flight impulse. In a blur she scampered down and across the hallway to her door, number 657. She fumbled with the key card that she'd clutched in one palm during her entire foray, now slick with perspiration and difficult to manipulate. It shook in her hand…she couldn't insert it. She shot a panicked glance over her shoulder…The card finally slipped in and out, unlatching the lock. She lunged inside and brought the door closed.

She listened. There were no untoward sounds from the corridor.

The room spun around her. She needed the embrace of gravity. Her feet brought her to the bed, where she collapsed, face upward. Both Peter's legacy and her own future were being defined across the hall. After weeks of planning...yearning ...struggle...Moscow had yielded forces beyond her control. There was nothing to do but wait.

One way or another, she was sure that life would be different in the morning.

CHAPTER 110

By Gallagher's reckoning a daily newspaper was compelled to cover the sweep of human existence: the whole mixed bag. This included, by unfortunate necessity, the repellent and disruptive---crime, catastrophe, armed conflict, disease, corruption. The less agreeable aspects of life on the planet.

Reporters, at least those on his watch, were supposed to be the detached chroniclers of this malady and chaos. Not the propagators, as beset by avarice and delusion as everyone else.

Maybe recent turmoil with Whitcombe should have inured him. The mystifying and unexpected could come from anywhere, even closest proximity. He leaned forward on knees and stroked his beard.

"So you're telling me Bradford planned this all along?"

"Sure looks that way," Conley said.

They sat in two cylindrical chairs upholstered in bright fabric, situated before wide, plate-glass windows in Gallagher's room. Curtains were open. Snowflakes fluttered down outside, glittering with refracted light from the hotel entrance driveway six floors below. Beyond was a background panorama of the river and nighttime Moscow. They hardly took notice. Conley was also leaning forward on his knees, appearing overcharged rather than fatigued by his recent ordeal. Earlier he'd placed the empty duffel bag aside. Now he pointed to the laptop case, lying on the small circular table between them.

"It's corroborated there."

"Corroborated or confirmed?"

"Not quite confirmed, but almost. Consistent with everything Shakuri claimed."

Conley had already filled out the whole story: kidnapping, surreal purgatory at the villa, Oleg's presumed links with Russian intelligence, the stunning rescue by Russian *Spetzsluzhbi*. Gallagher had listened with rapt attention, injecting occasional queries---an editor intent on details. He'd also listened with the stupefaction a man in his 60s who has encountered most of the gamut but is surprised to learn there are yet more bizarre and unimagined permutations. Human capacity for folly and self-ruin was remarkable indeed.

"I suppose Bradford was always something of a cipher to me," he said to Conley.

"I never knew him as well you did."

"So gifted. So privileged. Why would he do it?"

Conley thought for a moment. "More than just money, it seemed."

"What then?"

"Shakuri kept emphasizing Claire."

"Lots of men are devoted to their wives. But why such recklessness? Loss of judgment?"

"I've wondered about that."

"Any theories?"

Conley hesitated, then leaned back and ran a hand through his hair. His cheeks inflated as he exhaled, as if he was fighting some interior pressure. At once Gallagher guessed what that was.

"Have you told anyone else this?"

"The only other person who knows is Oleg. And now you."

"I appreciate that. Why?"

Elaboration didn't come easily to Conley. "I haven't worried about the reputation of the paper, to be honest."

"Well…it's a blow. No doubt about that."

"I'm also not worried about the impact on U.S. foreign policy, either. I mean the ramifications for the aid bill. That strikes me as a three-ring circus anyway."

Gallagher shook his head and grunted, remembering Stanson's fatuous oversimplifications.

"Claire, on the other hand…" Conley didn't finish.

Gallagher reacted with a similar drawn-out exhalation, and also reclined in his chair. He then stroked his beard, raked by disquiet of his own. Claire's presence across the hall was a palpable reminder of what had become his parallel priority with this assignment. Conley was safe: most pressing priority accomplished.

"Do you mind if I smoke?" he asked.

Conley seemed glad for the interruption.

Gallagher used a matchbook provided by the hotel. During his initial drag Bradford's laptop was next to the tabletop ashtray, mute and inert but inviting contemplation.

"In normal working order?" he asked.

"Yes." Conley shook his head, showing regret but not spelling it out.

The subtext was clear to both of them. If the computer had been destroyed as Shakuri had intended, or had never been found, Shakuri's claims could have been dismissed as the eleventh-hour rants of a desperate charlatan. His incriminations would have been almost impossible to investigate, and unsuitable for publication. As it was…

Gallagher took another deep drag, squinting at the machine.

"Do you think Claire knew?" he asked Conley.

"In Paris, I was pretty sure she didn't. After that I can't say."

Gallagher experienced a sudden onrush of connections. Events of the previous two weeks tipped in relentless, interlocking sequence and created a pattern…Whitcombe's mysterious disintegration…Claire's abrupt journey to the U.S. over "estate issues"…their urgent consultations in New Hampshire…Followed by her rush back to Boston and frantic involvement in newsroom affairs. Whitcombe had run across the money, he guessed, even if its origins weren't clear. Then passed that information on to Claire.

"Why don't we just ask her?" Conley volunteered.

"Let's not rush...and reduce our options. We want to handle this as best we can."

At first Conley appeared puzzled, then...buoyed...as if he'd spotted an exit marker. An instant later his expression became more guarded. These were forbidden waters.

Gallagher studied him, taking another drag on his cigarette. The contrast with Bradford was heartening. Here was conscience, even if pulled in two directions. As for the rest...Conley's supposed predilections were proving inaccurate. No way they applied here. Not after the crushing blunder he'd perpetrated just last year with Tracey Whitcombe.

Moreover Claire was not that type of girl.

In this case a different impulse manifested itself. The sort of virtue Gallagher thought had disappeared from the last generation or two. Sometimes gallantry came from improbable quarters.

"Don't get me wrong," he said. "I'm not trying spare the paper here. Or even Harry Whitcombe, for that matter."

Conley studied him in return.

Gallagher believed some of Whitcombe's tribulation was deserved. Claire, on the other hand, was different. An unimpeachable casualty of her husband's greed and overreach. In broader sweep, even a collateral victim of the war on terror. Her visit to Belmont the previous Sunday already seemed like ages ago. Since then his sympathies had deepened, due perhaps to his reflexes as a father. Her struggles had become his own.

Not that he would compromise truth...He hadn't done that in his entire career. They just needed to delete one small part while retaining essentials. Edit out one component without damaging the whole. Spare Claire without sparing Stanson. And the risks, if there were any?

Larson had him in her crosshairs. Frick was insufferable. And absurdities of previous weeks made retirement look like an improvement.

"Let's consider some different approaches," he said, before taking another drag.

Conley raised his eyebrows.

"Hypothetical ones," Gallagher emphasized, exhaling gradually and squinting at Conley through the smoke.

Conley brightened---a ready and reliable participant.

"First, the evidence," Gallagher continued. "Do we know for sure this money was a bribe? That there was quid pro quo?"

"No. Not absolutely."

Gallagher paused, holding his dwindling cigarette near his lips. Was he going too far? For an instant he wondered if his judgment had been befouled by jet lag. With a decisive movement he stubbed out the butt in the ashtray. No, he determined. The fault lay with this assignment. It had been dubious from the beginning. And evolved into fiasco.

Now was time to find a redeeming outcome.

"Okay, then," he said. "Let's talk this through."

CHAPTER 111

The digital bed-clock read 12:51. Conley double-checked it against his watch. The hour was suitable. More nocturnal the better. He hoped Gallagher was right. Their plan was already in motion. There was no space to backtrack.

Two floors up, Gallagher was writing an initial bulletin to send back to the *World Tribune*. Within minutes of transmission wire services would pick it up. Reports and commentary would cascade across far corners of the globe. Swift and indelible consequences in Boston in Washington. Convulsions in politics and diplomacy here Moscow and back in Dushanbe. Conley took a deep breath, smelling the odor of Gallagher's cigarettes on his clothes. Finally he stood, wrapped his scarf around his neck and buttoned his overcoat. He considered telephoning Oleg for help, but decided this was best done solo. Time was short, and the fewer complications the better.

He *really* hoped Gallagher was right.

Bradford's laptop case lay on a luggage platform by his closet; Conley grabbed the twin handles and slung the strap over one shoulder. In his other hand he clutched his fur hat, exited the room, and closed the door with as little noise as possible.

An instant later the hotel phone rang from inside, its two-tone electronic sound resonating up and down the quiet corridor. Acting upon his first instinct, he re-inserted his key-card, jump-stepped back inside, and shut the door. Had Gallagher developed second thoughts? Stanson, in a last-ditch scramble to shape the outcome? He decided there was no choice but to answer, in case the caller was Gallagher. On the third ring he picked up.

"Steve, this is Claire."

She was speaking fast. Her voice was strained and excited, even more than earlier.

"I've wanted to see you. Were you up with Art?"

"Well, yes, for a short talk…"

"Can I see you now?"

"It's late, Claire. I suggest we wait until morning. Art and I are meeting downstairs for breakfast at 7:30. We're going to review everything…"

"Steve, I really can't wait. I'll be right down."

"Claire, I…"

She hung up.

Conley thought fast. He considered stowing the laptop in the closet, or exchanging a few words with her before leaving. It was impossible… Claire was not the type to be sloughed off. Within seconds he spun heel and bolted back out of his room.

Not Claire. Especially not now.

His door closed with an overloud thud, making him wince. He glanced toward the elevators---and wary of intersecting with her---clasped the laptop to his hip and sprinted toward the stairwell. Behind him he heard the bell ring and the doors slide open. As he reached the stairway exit he yanked down the lever and pivoted inside, grasping the interior handle and releasing it with as much delicacy as he could.

The click was muted but audible. Leaving no time to linger. He lunged down the stairs and grappled the tubular railing, taking steps two at a time down through the third and second floors. Ten seconds later he burst into the lobby, heart pounding, and slowed his pace. There were still dozens of people present despite the late hour, and among them, in the lounge area, he spotted one of Stanson's security detail rising to his feet and raising a walkie-talkie. Eyes forward, he traversed the open area near reception with a swift, controlled stride. At the entrance the sliding glass doors opened in quick sequence, and once outside he veered to his left, where several taxis were waiting. Halfway down the U.S. Embassy SUV remained parked in the fluttering snow. He jumped inside the first taxi in line.

"Just go!" he half shouted to the driver, pointing two fingers toward the avenue.

The middle-aged driver was alarmed but nonetheless started up and roared down the drive. Passing the front entrance Conley caught another glimpse of the lobby. No sign of Claire. He sighed with relief, then looked back. The SUV had illumined headlights and was following about 15 meters behind.

"Idiots!" he said in a loud voice.

The driver startled and apprised him in the rear view mirror.

"You speak English?"

"A little."

At bottom the driver merged onto the riverside boulevard, where the late-night traffic was moderate and fast-moving, and snowfall only a minor impediment to visibility. Conley looked back again over his shoulder. The massive grill and multiple headlights of the SUV loomed behind. The security guard was keeping close contact, preventing other vehicles from interposing themselves in the lane.

"Can you lose that SUV?"

The driver examined his mirror again. "The truck?"

"Yes. That's the one."

The driver didn't answer but stepped on the gas and shifted lanes, shooting several cars ahead of the SUV. Within seconds the guard adjusted and re-closed the distance. They were now sweeping down the river at considerable speed. Much faster and this escapade would turn dangerous.

Stanson's single-mindedness had gone way too far.

"Where?" the driver asked, looking at Conley with a furrowed brow in the mirror.

"There." Conley pointed ahead. "Take a right on that side street."

The driver abruptly re-shifted lanes and did as instructed, compelling Conley to grasp the seat back as the Volga rounded the corner. Conley glanced again over his shoulder. The SUV's chassis tilted as it hit the turn, before its grill and headlights popped back on course. Feeling a ripple of dismay, he swore. He was a U.S. citizen, a journalist engaged in private activity, not a terrorist or criminal. ...The situation was devolving into the bizarre. He examined the street through the windows: quiet, with darkened residential buildings. Parked cars and snow-banks were tight on both sides, forcing the driver to moderate his speed.

"There," he pointed. "Back toward Kiev Station."

The driver did as told, then looked in the mirror. In his growing alarm he blurted a question in Russian. Conley guessed its meaning.

"Then take the bridge...Let's get to the other side of the river."

Around the station they veered around scattered pedestrians and circumvented several parking areas. The SUV did likewise and stayed tight behind, its massive grill looming even closer through the illuminated snowflakes. The taxi driver kept one eye on the mirror as they ascended a ramp toward the bridge. Halfway across Conley's cell-phone rang from his coat pocket, giving him a start He extracted it from his coat pocket. The number on display was Claire's---the last distraction he needed at the moment. He turned off the ringer.

"Where now?" the driver asked as they reached the opposite embankment.

This couldn't go on, Conley decided. It was preposterous. An idea hit him, drawn from one of his taxi rides with Oleg the previous week.

"Church of Christ the Savior. You can drop me off there."

The driver look perplexed for an instant, but appeared to understand. Most of all he was relieved to hear an endpoint.

"Just at church?"

"That's right. And you can take it at normal speed on the way."

At the next intersection they turned right up a wide boulevard, heavily trafficked despite the late hour, and cruised down the middle lane until they re-approached the opposite loop of the *Moskva*. Now certain of their destination, the driver remained wordless as he changed lanes, exited a down-ramp and turned left at a green light. On the ensuing riverside thoroughfare the illuminated spires of the Kremlin loomed up off in the distance, while the SUV remained hard on their bumper. Conley turned around in his seat and made out its massive grill-work and rack-headlights, tempted to throw a finger. He now regretted cutting Stanson some slack earlier in the evening. Even more, he wished he could describe these ridiculous excesses in his upcoming articles. Under the circumstances, however, he knew he'd have to refrain.

The church came up fast along the embankment, and the driver exploited a break in oncoming traffic to perform a sharp, illegal left-turn. The SUV promptly followed suit with screeching tires, tilting on its chassis again and provoking loud honks from onrushing traffic.

With the taxi in the lead, they entered a well-lit drive which appeared to lead to underground parking beneath the church. "Here," Conley pointed. "Near the bottom of those ramps." He glanced at the counter, doubled the amount and hastily retrieved necessary rubles from his wallet as the driver pulled to a stop. "...*Spasibo*," he said, before grabbing the laptop case and flinging open the door. Out on the pavement he saw the SUV already halted, just two meters back. The guard emerged from the driver's side door and stepped around front, crew-cut and goateed like the other one---an overweight thug. Conley was half-inclined to pause and give him a dressing-down, a verbal thrashing. Even better an actual one. Instead he kept it short, making sure he was heard above the nearby traffic.

"You guys are out of control!" he shouted.

With a stone face the man stared back.

An instant later both of them caught sight of a police car about 30 meters away, parked under a concrete awning closer to the church. Two Moscow cops were visible inside, wearing their trademark fur hats. Seeing them, Conley didn't hesitate, and turned and bolted toward the ramps. Upon reaching the first one, he looked back. The guard obviously wanted to follow, but was preoccupied instead by the police car, which had turned on its headlights and advanced out from its original position. To minimize further attention to himself, Conley slowed to a fast walk. From the second and third ramps he verified that he was proceeding alone.

At the broad stone terrace which surrounded the church on top, he performed another scan, finding the area deserted and coated with new snow. The church in its nighttime isolation presented a striking, even peaceful, tableau, but he beheld it for just a few seconds before turning right toward the connected footbridge. Its span was also empty. Part way out over the river, he cast another look back at his drop-off point. The two policemen had now exited their squad car, while the American guard remained in place, talking into his walkie-talkie but unable to abandon his own vehicle.

When Conley reached the middle of the bridge he gazed out over the railings. Jagged platelets of ice moved past in the current below: new since his sojourn a week earlier. Ahead, through the fluttering flakes, a factory district came into view on the opposite bank. It also appeared devoid of people and activity at this hour, but he hoped he could find a taxi stand somewhere beyond.

By now Gallagher had probably filed the initial report. At last the way was clear...for the other component of their plan.

CHAPTER 112

The structure was massive and darkened. The only illumination issued from surrounding street lamps.

Lilya was to thank for this particular venue. Conley spotted an access point. It was closed to motor traffic by metal barriers but penetrable on foot.

"Stop here," he said.

The driver was older than the first one and appeared confused by the unorthodox destination. This was middle of the night in winter. And his passenger was a lone foreigner. Conley re-donned his fur hat and decided not to wrestle with language barriers and the return journey. This task could take a while. The driver accepted payment without a word, and once Conley had exited the vehicle, gunned his vehicle back toward the center. Sound from the engine receded in snow-bound quiet, leaving just a muted hum of traffic from the expressway several hundred meters back. Light snowfall had stopped, replaced by a clearing night sky.

Inside the complex was a wide parking lot, plowed and hard-packed underneath the new dusting. Conley crossed it to a cast-iron fence, found the main gate locked, and peered through the iron bars. His destination hulked unlit and empty under its white half dome vacated of events and spectators in the winter months. Surrounding grounds and roadways were deserted. *Luzhniki.* Lilya had also noted its former Soviet appellation: Lenin Stadium. Built at the zenith of Soviet urban construction in the 1950s. Later employed in the ill-starred 1980 Olympic Games. Lenin's statue still towered out front: gaze fixed on an idyllic future, overcoat billowing.

Just the setting Conley wanted. He found an open secondary gate and entered the grounds. A park area to the left was lined with bare trees and blanketed by white; he traversed it on a curving walkway. His feet squeaked on the fresh, light layering of snow. There was still no one to be seen.

The southernmost loop of the *Moskva,* he knew, lay just ahead.

Through tree branches he glimpsed the terraced hilltop campus of Moscow State University, high on the opposite bank. Lilya was likely asleep in her family's nearby apartment. His ruminations next returned to Gallagher, who had been to Moscow once before but not to this particular bend.

"Will the laptop by itself ever prove anything?" he had asked.

"Not by itself."

"Could we investigate this further, through other avenues?"

"We can try," Conley had answered. "Tough, though, given Swiss banking laws."

At last the riverside promenade came into view. Stone slabs lined water's edge; along one section was a balustrade with iron railings. Lighting was bright and would make him visible in wide vicinity. He looked left, remembering his earlier late-night survey with Lilya. Several hundred meters up-river was a metro station, suspended under a bridge, its plate-glass windows still brimming with light. But its enclosed platform looked empty. Moscow metro had closed more than a half-hour earlier, which decreased the likelihood of casual observers.

Though he wore gloves the hand in which he held the laptop case grew a little numb. He flexed his fingers several times around the twin handles.

"...And that would mean dragging Claire into it," Gallagher had continued, more statement than question. "Right?"

"Unavoidable."

Gallagher had taken another long drag on his cigarette; by this time the hotel room had grown thick with smoke and shared purpose.

Conley crossed a stadium roadway that and reached the promenade. He stopped and glanced in both directions. The entire river-bend was bright and open. Still devoid of people. His final steps to water's edge were slower---he didn't want to appear frantic and attract attention, just in case. His measured footfalls squeaked in the silence. Through dissipating clouds a half-moon filtered through and cast a faint light on the river---wider at this point than at others in Moscow. An irregular patchwork of black water and white ice fragments drifted in a gentle current. Opposite banks were steep and forested, rising up into Lenin Hills. He balanced the laptop case on the iron balustrade. This was the last chance to take stock.

"Is the part about Bradford's action essential to the rest of the story?" Gallagher had asked.

"Not to the heroin smuggling. Not even to my own abduction, when you get down to it."

Gallagher had studied him, although he appeared to know the rest.

"...Really just the tribute angle."

"That's it?"

"Yes."

"Right. So that's where we are."

Now it was Conley who waited for a cue. Gallagher had taken another long drag on his cigarette.

"Let's ask ourselves, Steve. What's to be gained?"

It hadn't seemed appropriate at that juncture to mention Versailles...the rainstorm...even if that was where some of the dynamic had originated, at least for him. Since then, he'd convinced himself, other impulses had taken over. Baseline compassion. Considerations of fairness. His motives had become more enlightened...Hadn't they? He'd taken a deep breath. Anyway the question that Gallagher had posed was valid and more immediate.

"I just want to weigh the overall situation," he'd finally answered.

"And?"

"Make the best choice. Do what's right."

Now Conley re-scanned river waters and weighed the case in his hand, wondering if the nylon shell would provide unwanted buoyancy. There was also the risk of suspension on an ice patch. He decided these were minimal. Extra battery packs, portable surge protector and power cords---still stored in the zippered side compartment---added more than enough density. And he could aim for open water. He stepped back from the railing and swung the case backward, estimating how far he could hurl it with a locked sidearm. Advantage could be obtained from the flexible handles. Release would be critical, much like a hammer throw.

He stopped and stood still---one last fit of contemplation. The snowbound quiet was almost total: disturbed only by murmur from the river and distant, faint din from the expressway. Jenna's stinging denunciation re-crossed his memory. Here he would exercise different reflexes. More justifiable ones. Even if they required a stretch.

"Women---at least certain ones, under special circumstances---can move our boundaries," Gallagher had said, just before Conley had gotten up to go. "That's just the way we're constituted."

Conley ventured one more glance around the area---still white and lifeless---then heaved in several lungs-full of cold air. Out on the river a sizable patch of black water had formed among the ice flows, 20 meters straight out from his position on the balustrade. He tested his footing. New snow helped, affording additional traction on the hard-pack. Seeing no sense in agonizing further, he took two more quick steps away from the railing and swung the case around and behind his body in a deliberate half-circle. At maximum extension he cocked his back knee, then exploded forward with short, hop-steps and hyperventilating breaths. Just short of the balustrade he snapped his shoulder forward and reversed the arc, rising to the balls of his feet and propelling his arm forward. The case ascended above eye level; he raised his chin and extended his fingers. At the instant of release he grunted, delivering the object up and out into darkness.

Trajectory was perfect.

He stood with feet splayed, hands on thighs and watched; moonlight provided just enough illumination. The case re-acquired gravity and carried out dead center into open water. There was a white splash, muffled, like everything else, by the snow.

For several seconds…five, ten…the case bobbed on the surface. Like some abortive flotation device. Conley stood up straight and leaned out over the railing, squinting for better visibility.

At last water permeated zippers and nylon and the weight of electronics took over. The case sank by rapid, inexorable degrees and disappeared with a gurgle.

CHAPTER 113

Helplessness had spun into despair, and three hours of fitful sleep hadn't slowed her spiral. Questions had tormented Claire all night long. Why were Gallagher and Conley boxing her out? There could only be one answer. And it wasn't in her favor.

Conley's behavior was most maddening. Running off for a late-night rendezvous just when she was most desperate for information. Eluding her…Not even bothering to answer his cell-phone. Couldn't his Russian girlfriend wait? Yet that shouldn't have been a surprise. Same self-absorption she'd witnessed in Paris.

First let down by Peter…the man she loved. Now forsaken by Conley and Gallagher---her supposed collaborators in an undertaking that would define the rest of her life. *Le caractère masculin* was just as inconstant and unreliable as she'd suspected during certain low points before her marriage. American besides; that could only exacerbate the syndrome. Possessed by cold agendas. Inaccessible, devoid of compassion…

Claire poked the "L" button on the console with a feeble finger. Her hand drooped back to her side and she glimpsed herself in the elevator mirror: ashen face. Eyes without the usual tense determination. Spent. Defeated. Humiliated.

Near ground level she closed her eyes and sucked a deep breath. *Bien*…her fate was decided. She'd tried to salvage Peter's reputation, and her own life. But what more could she do? A merciless new reality awaited her. She should at least grasp a strand of dignity and maintain her self-control. That would be something. By time the doors opened she had squared her shoulders and raised her chin, ready for the worst. In the hotel restaurant Gallagher sat alone at a big table along one wall. He raised his hand to get her attention, then huffed to his feet. His courtesy seemed hollow after last night, along with his paternalistic air. After they sat down he waited for the waiter to pour her coffee.

"Steve called me. He's upstairs in his room with Oleg. Said they'll be down in about 10 minutes."

"Oleg? I thought he was coming later."

"We wanted to speak to him before Stanson had a chance."

Another furtive conclave, she thought. These men and their maneuvers, their puerile political games…Of course she'd been shunted aside. It was all too late now, anyway.

"Claire, I can guess what's foremost on your mind. The best way to start is to read this."

Gallagher slid a single sheet of paper across the table. It was a computer printout: page one of the *Boston World Tribune's* on-line edition, dated that day. Claire's fingers trembled much more than usual as she picked up the sheet. Headline was huge:

Conley freed in Tajikistan by Russian troops

World Tribune Wire Reports - *World Tribune reporter Steve Conley, who disappeared on Tuesday while on assignment in Tajikistan, was freed from captivity Thursday in an extraordinary helicopter-borne rescue operation by Russian Special Forces.*

Conley and his Russian interpreter were abducted Tuesday from their hotel in central Dushanbe on orders from Tajik Prime Minister Shimon Shakuri, and subsequently held in forced seclusion at Shakuri's residential villa outside the city. Shakuri orchestrated the abduction in an apparent attempt to conceal damaging information about the murder of World Tribune reporter Peter Bradford, who died while on assignment in Tajikistan on October 15ᵗʰ.

Russian forces tracked Conley through his cell-phone and staged a surprise assault on the villa.

Until Thursday Shakuri was the main U.S. liaison in the Tajik government for a proposed $550 million U.S. military aid package. The fate of the aid package is now in doubt. (see adjacent story)

Conley, 30, a five-year veteran of the World Tribune news staff, was in Tajikistan in part to investigate Bradford's death, which occurred under circumstances which the World Tribune believed had never been adequately explained.. Conley had interviewed Shakuri early Tuesday.

Within hours of their rescue Thursday Conley and his interpreter---a Russian citizen named Oleg Mikhailov, aged 32--- were flown out of Tajikistan by Russian military air transport. Both are now in Moscow and report no injury.

In the course of the operation Russian troops apprehended Shakuri. Russian military authorities later turned him over to the custody of the Tajik government. Shakuri has been relieved of his responsibilities and is now in Tajik prison awaiting trial on kidnapping charges.

Timing of the abduction, according to Conley, was connected with a vote in the U.S. Senate on a military aid bill for Tajikistan, originally scheduled for Thursday. Shakuri served as the main U.S. liaison in the Tajik government for the aid package, which has been motivated by the war against terrorism. The Senate vote was postponed when news reached Washington that Shakuri was responsible for Conley's kidnapping.

Bradford, 28, was murdered under mysterious circumstances after a dinner at Shakuri's villa on October 15th. Two of Shakuri's bodyguards were charged in the killing, but died in a prison disturbance before they could be tried in court.

During the course of his two-day captivity Conley elicited additional information from Shakuri about Bradford's death. Shakuri claimed that he attempted to bribe Bradford during Bradford's visit to the villa, to dissuade him from reporting upon Tajik government complicity in heroin smuggling.

Bradford refused, though the two bodyguards assigned to transport him back to his Dushanbe hotel believed he had accepted, and killed him en route on the mistaken assumption he was carrying a large amount of cash.

"We'll never be able to confirm Shakuri's explanation," Conley said in Moscow. "It's plausible, but it doesn't mitigate the tragedy and senselessness of Bradford's death."

Shakuri offered similar bribes to Conley and Mikhailov, $2.5 million dollars each, Conley said, which they refused. Their refusal prompted Shakuri to detain them at the villa....Russian troops sustained no casualties in the rescue operation. Russia has based 20,000 troops in Tajikistan since 1995. A phased withdrawal from border areas began in March 2004...

Claire didn't bother reading the rest. The sheet continued trembling in her hands, for different reasons now. "So that's all Steve learned about Peter?"

"Inadequate, I'm afraid. It leaves a lot of questions unanswered."

"Will there still be an article?"

"You mean about Peter?"

She nodded.

Gallagher studied her for a moment and stroked his beard. "Of some kind. But the focus may shift. More to Steve's abduction. A lot will depend on Harry Whitcombe."

Claire's heart was pounding...Deliverance. A benevolent quirk of fate. Maybe God himself had even intervened to spare her...

"Less than you wanted, I know."

"No, I...I mean I..."

"Good morning, Claire."

She looked up and saw Conley standing next to the table, Oleg at his side. He looked worn out as they sat down, no doubt from his late-night assignation. That hardly mattered now. Gallagher told them he had just shown her the story. While the waiter reappeared to pour more coffee for everyone, she couldn't contain herself. Her English became jumbled, a little euphoric.

"Don't think I'm disappointed, Steve. I wanted more answers. But you and Oleg got out from there…that's first of all…"

She realized Oleg was observing her. The Russian looked away and took a sip of coffee, wearing a half smile, and over his cup cast a sympathetic glance at Conley, who frowned, as if warning him off. Conley then made quick, indecipherable eye contact with Gallagher.

Puzzled, Claire stared at all of them in turn. A tenuous silence fell over the table. Relieved as she was, she was gripped by new curiosity. What exactly had gone on last night?

"Guess it's a buffet," Gallagher said, suddenly pushing back from the table. "We should get breakfast. We've got a full day ahead."

CHAPTER 114

Whatever misgivings Gallagher retained dissolved as he watched her. Across the breakfast table Claire appeared unburdened and rejuvenated. Animated in a way he remembered from brief encounters before Bradford's death---as if she could now get on with the rest of her life.

This made all his recent trials a little more bearable. Absurdities less acute.

He was convinced. He'd finally struck the balance he'd sought at the beginning.

"Usmonov provoked the crisis," Conley explained to Claire, re-tracing the prelude to the abduction, finger hooked in his third cup of coffee. Oleg was in on the narration and eager to participate. "Right. Because Shakuri couldn't leave us with the laptop."

"Why not?" Claire asked.

"It showed Shakuri had orchestrated a cover-up," Conley answered.

Claire frowned for an instant. *"Comment...How?"*

"Skakuri told Stanson and Hermann that the laptop was never found. This was reported in the official Tajik and American investigations. It was a lie."

"Once we got the villa, we never saw that laptop again," Oleg added.

"What happened to it...finally?"

"Destroyed," Conley said. "Shakuri didn't want to make the same mistake twice."

They were nearly an hour and a half into an exhaustive review of Conley's ill-starred days in Dushanbe. This exercise was intended partly to log and synthesize facts for Conley's future articles in the *World Tribune*, with questions from Gallagher and observations from Oleg, while the Russian's input and recollections were still available. But it was also a summary presentation to Claire. Modified and abridged, of course, just like the accounts that would appear later in the paper.

It was proceeding well. With one caveat, Gallagher noted. Relieved as she was, Claire detected missing elements. Her body language became a little restive. This left him more convinced than ever that she had learned something about Bradford's misconduct in New Hampshire and Boston. How else to explain her distress over the weekend? Gallagher's thoughts were interrupted when oversized boots appeared alongside the table. They were Stanson's. Higher up, the official displayed red-rimmed eyes behind his aviator glasses. Like Claire, he also appeared unburdened, compared to the previous evening.

"Look, Steve. I'm here to apologize..."

With his mind on other matters, Conley was slow to react. He had told Gallagher by phone about the erstwhile car chase, a stunt beyond the pale---almost astonishing in the retelling. His face soured, while Gallagher's own ire re-boiled; Stanson seemed to expect this.

"To you too, Art."

"Apologize? As damn well you should. What kind of nonsense was that?"

"It was a tense night. Our guys just went a little overboard."

"Overboard?" Conley said at last. "To say the least."

"There are no excuses."

"You better believe it," Gallagher shot back, glaring. "We're of a mind to write that that up for tomorrow's paper."

"Will you, if you don't mind my asking?"

It was almost certain that Stanson's security detail had seen Conley return to the hotel, minus the laptop. For several seconds Gallagher didn't answer. Conley's distaste turned to unease.

"I know...Not my place," Stanson drawled, with an inflection that carried a little too much inside game.

Claire's ears raised in full alert, her gaze darting back and forth across the table.

"We're busy here Franklin," Gallagher snorted. "What do you want?"

"Look...we took our licks yesterday in Washington. Mostly deserved. I saw your story this morning...and connected it with every-thing last night. Just want to say...you could have gone harder on us." He directed a benign glance at Claire. "Whatever your reasons...well, we appreciate the way it came out. You've left us with a chance to sal-vage something."

Gallagher snorted again. "That wasn't our intention."

Stanson thought for a moment.

"Fair enough. Can I give you a ring later?"

"Maybe after lunch."

Gallagher was eager to get rid of him.

They watched Stanson amble out of the restaurant, pulling his cell-phone out as he went. Silence at the table elongated past a com-fortable threshold...Gallagher stroked his beard. Conley gazed into his coffee. Claire's eyes were narrowed; as if she was entitled to answers.

"Actually I have a few calls to make also," Oleg said. "I'll excuse myself for about 10 minutes."

Oleg pulled back his chair; Gallagher and Conley watched him march past the buffet counter. The shine in Claire's eyes grew more intense.

"Maybe a good time for a break anyway," Gallagher suggested.

"I agree," Conley said.

The two of them took last gulps of coffee and transferred napkins onto the table. Claire's eyes narrowed further; she evidently wasn't pleased with this evasion. "Okay, as you wish." Without pause she bolted up and strode away, parting the mostly male clientele with quick, headlong progress. Her eyes were on Oleg's back as he exited into the lobby.

"Uh oh," Conley observed. "She's identified a soft target."

"I hope he's ready," Gallagher answered.

CHAPTER 115

Claire lost visual contact. By time she emerged into the lobby Oleg was nowhere to be seen. She scanned back and forth before spotting him at a coat check counter. Why was he going outside? Snow was piled a half-meter high and temperatures were well below freezing. And it was supposed to be a short break. This Russian really was inscrutable. Tightly contained. She wondered if she could breech his sealed façade.

Still, he was alone. Split off from the pack, while Conley and Gallagher maintained closed ranks back in the restaurant. She didn't hesitate. She was halfway across the lobby, heels snapping, when he began buttoning his coat.

He raised his head and his austere expression vanished at once. Replaced by one she didn't expect: both intimidated and gentle. He made eye contact with a hapless half-grin.

"Claire…"

"Going outside, Oleg?"

"Well, yes…I need some fresh air. And the lobby's noisy."

She crossed her arms and took a step closer. He stiffened, holding his half-grin. Her position blocked his path.

"I wanted to ask you a few questions," she said, slowing the tempo. "While I had the chance."

"But we're going to start again in 10 minutes."

"I know."

"And I need to make a couple of calls."

"I'll go with you. I could use some fresh air myself."

"They're sort of…private."

"I don't speak Russian, so I won't understand anything."

"Hmmm…of course…" He nodded once, defenseless. "Wait…what about your coat?"

"It will be short. And I seldom get cold."

He looked at her again, before nodding in surrender.

"Okay."

Claire fell in step beside him, her arms still crossed tight. At the sliding doors, Oleg put on his fur hat, his gaze reserved, aimed down. Something about his manner struck her. She performed a quick re-assessment. In one sense the Russian resembled Conley. Beholden to the female of the species. Though minus Conley's rash, uncontrollable impulses. Here was the civilized variant. She liked her chances.

To obtain what was another question. She'd gotten what she wanted. Why did she remain dissatisfied?

Mid-morning sun was relatively bright, with little wind. Still, the temperature contrast was bracing. As they crossed to a small terrace that jutted out onto the snow-covered front grounds of the hotel and drew to a stop, her receptors notched even higher.

He pulled out his cell-phone but didn't punch any buttons. First privilege, as she anticipated, fell to her. From the other side of the hotel she heard a train, departing Kiev station. She locked eyes with him while remaining polite.

"Oleg, please tell me what's going on."

"With what?"

"You, Steve, Art…You're not telling me something."

"About what happened in Dushanbe?"

"About what happened to Peter in Dushanbe."

He reacted with an anguished expression, glanced sideways at her, then gazed out toward ice flows on the *Moskva*.

"There is something, isn't there?" she persisted.

His mouth opened as if he wanted to ask a question. He stopped. Claire kept a civilized distance, arms crossed. No advantage in moving closer. Oleg was not Conley.

"Let me put it this way, Claire," he said at last, choosing his words with care. "Steve made a hard choice."

"What kind of choice?"

"To withhold certain…information."

"What, exactly?"

"You're putting me in a difficult position, Claire…Aren't you cold out here?"

Claire had hardly noticed. Her curiosity now consumed her. This lack of confirmation was intolerable. She re-tightened her crossed arms and stared at him, not moving. Oleg continued after a reluctant pause.

"Let's put it this way…Some unpleasant facts emerged. Not things that happened to Peter. Things that he did."

"What things?"

"Claire, please."

"Peter was my husband. Don't I have a right to know?"

Instead of answering he studied her for a moment---discerning, circumspect---then turned his eyes downward onto the paving stones of the terrace, from which snow had been brushed away. His cell-phone hung at his side in one hand: calls forgotten.

She waited. Civilized or not, he was not going to get off the hook. When he looked up his eyes were more decisive; his words came in a purposeful stream.

"I won't tell you what those facts are. That's not my place. You'll either have to find them out for yourself, or someone else will have to tell you. What I can tell you is this. Steve didn't make this choice for selfish reasons. Or for the sake of the paper. Or because of Art… although Art was part of the decision. He made it for your sake."

"Me?"

"What your husband did in Dushanbe was...embarrassing. Disgraceful, truth be told. You would have been ashamed. Steve recognized that and tried to spare you. With Art's consent, of course."

"But for me? Why?"

"He said he'd added to your distress in Paris, and that he didn't have the heart to do it again. He also mentioned something about redressing a wrong he'd committed last year with his publisher... though that part I didn't understand."

For a fleeting instant Claire thought she saw moistness form in the Russian's eyes: a glimpse into a deep well of sentiment behind the controlled exterior. He promptly re-contained himself, and resumed.

"I'll be direct, Claire, if I may. Steve hardly knows you, really. Nonetheless he's tried to undo damage that your husband did. And he's taken great risk in the process."

This comparison to Peter rattled her; in a way she didn't expect. Her eyes also grew moist.

"I would say you're lucky...lucky that Steve was the reporter on this assignment."

She felt disoriented all of a sudden.

"...If I can give you any advice, Claire, it's this. Don't press Steve about this. That would just add to his challenges. Especially today. He's got stories to file. And he and Art have to contend with Franklin Stanson. Just accept that he's done something good for you. And stand by in quiet appreciation."

"Stand by...?"

Her voice was hoarse and trailed off. Moscow seemed to shift and undulate underfoot. Snow and sky became an unsteady kaleidoscope of blue-grays and indistinct horizons. Her interior coordinates also loosened: a spontaneous re-ordering. Since New Hampshire and Boston she'd lacked a satisfactory focal point; self-preservation wasn't enough...

"Claire, are you okay?"

Crystals tumbled into place. New colors and alignments emerged---ones she never anticipated. In them, Conley evoked not qualms and apprehensions but …gratitude. And to think she'd flogged him forward through trials he might have avoided on his own…Here in Moscow even contrived to exploit his susceptibilities. Her own egotism appalled her. How could she have been so oblivious? Francois had been right. She *had* gone to excess. She bent forward slightly to bring more blood-flow to her head, and took several deep breaths. When she stood straight Oleg eyes were infused with sympathy.

"I'm sorry Claire. Maybe I went too far."

"No, Oleg…you were right."

They stood in silence for a long moment. Claire continued her regulated ventilation. Gradually the snowbound cityscape stabilized. At last Oleg appeared somewhat reassured. Then something caught his attention across the hotel drive.

"Lilya!"

The salutation caught Claire off guard. Oleg waved to a young hatless woman across the drive, about to enter the hotel. She stopped and looked back: tall, slender and with a shy smile. About 20 or 21, Claire surmised, and bearing an extraordinary resemblance to Tracey Whitcombe. Though probably Russian.

The young woman hesitated for a moment, unsure whether to interrupt, and greeted him. "Steve's in the restaurant," he said in English, loud enough to be heard above nearby traffic. "…I'll be there in five minutes." The girl smiled again and continued into the hotel. Her gait was long-legged. Claire watched her disappear.

"Who's that…?

"Oh…just a girl Steve met here last week."

"I'll let you make your calls, Oleg," she said suddenly.

He looked at her, appraising the change.

"Thank you for everything."

Before Oleg had a chance to utter another word she turned heel and strode back into the hotel.

CHAPTER 116

Conley observed Gallagher at the buffet, surveying the pastry selection through his bifocals. At peace, it seemed. All they had to do now was stymie Claire's curiosity through the afternoon, and file a follow-up bulletin back to the paper, which would lay groundwork for later feature articles. Conley was confident about Oleg; the Russian was the epitome of restraint.

He did a double take and put down his coffee cup.

Lilya had entered the restaurant. When he stood and waved, she located him and came over, grabbing attention from several quarters, more exceptional even than he remembered. Tall and flawless. Like Tracey. During his week in Dushanbe she'd become almost an abstraction.

"I got your phone message when I was in class," she said. "Maybe I should have called first."

Conley deflected her apology and gave her a hug, surprised to see her so soon---especially when her returning embrace became tender and prolonged. Inhibitions from their previous encounters seem to have melted away. He was not complaining.

"I was following everything on Russian news," she said.

"Well, it turned out okay."

"I was worried."

"Thanks, Lilya…"

While they were still standing close he glanced over her shoulder and trailed off. Claire was marching past the maitre d', a new kind of urgency in her step. Her inquisitive cast was gone, replaced by a look of gratitude…and something else. His first concern was that Oleg told her more than he should have.

Gallagher returned with his plate and introductions followed. As everyone sat down, Claire took the chair next to Conley, leaving Lilya across the table and looking a little uncomfortable. Conley didn't know what to make of the situation. Hadn't he relieved Claire of those pressures? Done his duty?

"You actually came at a good time, Lilya," he said, trying to put her at ease.

"I'm not interfering?"

"We were on a break."

No warning signals showed in Oleg's eye when he rejoined them. Instead a glimpse of deep emotion---a facet of him Conley had not seen before. Had Claire gotten to the Russian? Her inflection suggested that she had.

"Finish all your calls, Oleg?" she asked him.

"Yes."

Gallagher took a bite of pastry and wiped his beard with his napkin. He appeared to appraise the new dynamic, and wasted little time.

"Shall we get started again?"

"Sounds good," Conley answered, reaching for his notepad. "I suggest we review details of the rescue operation. Okay with you, Oleg?"

"Fine with me."

Lilya asked them if it was okay if she stayed. Conley saw no reason why not.

"Of course. You're a journalism student. You might benefit."

She hesitated. "Okay."

He flipped to a fresh page. At Luzhniki Stadium he'd made a vow. This was going to be a different kind of release. Different from the one he'd envisioned at first. That meant avoiding Claire in the aftermath. Not revisiting impulses from Paris.

Maybe Lilya offered a way out.

"This part should be more straightforward," Gallagher observed as they re-started their review.

Conley hoped that would be true.

CHAPTER 117

In the retelling, Conley and Oleg had just lifted off from the Russian air base, bound for Moscow. Gallagher assisted their reconstruction---and their omissions---by asking suitable questions. Now the narrative was winding down. So was Gallagher. His jet lag was finally hitting him in earnest, despite countless cups of coffee. A cell-phone rang at the table. It was Claire's. She looked confused as she answered.

"It's for you, Art," she said, handing the device over.

He listened briefly, issued a slight grunt, excused himself and walked out to the lobby.

The caller was Reynolds, from Washington---well before dawn East Coast Time. In the face of dismay in Congress and outrage in the media, the White House had decided to withdraw the aid bill. No vote rescheduled. Conley's kidnapping and Shakuri's disgrace had done too much damage.

Gallagher smiled as he snapped the phone closed. Satisfaction lightened his step as he re-traversed the restaurant. He and Conley had achieved a worthwhile final objective in this long ordeal; their plan had come off. They'd spared Claire without sparing Stanson.

American taxpayers would not squander $550 million on an initiative born of zealotry and incompetence.

Truth had been edited only at the margins.

Some follow-up would be necessary during the remainder of the day, including an interview with Stanson---more tolerable now that outcomes were known. Conley could file a second bulletin back to Boston. Maybe there would be a low-key celebratory dinner. After that Gallagher was looking forward to telephoning Denise and getting to bed early.

When he returned to the table he announced the news.

"That's great," Conley responded, looking distracted. Eager to get up.

Reaction from Oleg was more enthusiastic. If Oleg was indeed an intelligence operative, preferences of the Russian government were plain.

"You're sure?" he asked. "Completely withdrawn?"

"Seems that way."

Gallagher had decided not to press him about his true role in all this. At least for today. Oleg had been a party to the plan; he deserved his due. "I suggest another break," he said, reaching for his cigarettes. "Before Franklin Stanson hunts us down."

"No arguments here," Conley said, closing his notepad. He glanced across at Lilya, who had followed the review with quiet attention.

"I should go back to my classes, Steve."

"I'll walk you out."

As Conley pushed back, disappointment seemed to fall across Claire. She asked him how long the break would be. He cleared his throat and glanced at Gallagher. "What...ten minutes, Art?"

"Make it twenty. I'll call Stanson. We'll get that over with before lunch."

Gallagher lit a cigarette and remained seated, watching Conley and Lilya make their way toward the lobby. Exhaling a plume of smoke, he realized Claire's gaze was fixed in the same direction. He turned and examined her profile. Glints of curiosity were gone, supplanted by a new expression. Gratitude, or even tenderness?

Did she know?

He decided it didn't really matter. Her burdens seemed lifted. That was what he wanted most of all.

And this was almost over.

CHAPTER 118

On the way out Lilya re-established her earlier distance. Conley walked alongside, matching her long gait, dodging a couple of waiters, wondering if he'd be able to revive the openness he'd glimpsed in her when she'd arrived. He hoped she hadn't misinterpreted Claire's presence. They drew up at the coat-check counter.

"Can we meet this evening, Lilya?"

"What about everyone else?"

"Well, we are meeting for dinner…a kind of celebration. But you can join us."

Hesitation crossed her face. "I don't know, Steve. I feel out of place."

"You're not."

"It just seems like there's still a lot going on. Your editor's here. Claire also, who naturally has a strong interest in this…I'd just be a distraction."

"How about tomorrow?"

She considered the proposition, and said, "Maybe the best thing to do is wait a few days, until your situation settles down."

"Really, I'll have time."

"I think it's best, Steve. For now, let's just stay in contact by phone."

Her mind appeared made up. "I should probably get to back my classes," she concluded. She gave him an amicable smile and resumed stride across the lobby, buttoning her coat as she went. There was no confrontation involved. No shyness, either; she was just trying to be sensible. Outside, they moved a few paces from the entrance and stopped. Her posture reminded him of their walk at Moscow State University. Before he could formulate further objection she pecked him on the cheek, gave him a light hug, and strode away down the curving sidewalk. He took a deep breath, watching her go. She was probably right.

Back inside, halfway across the restaurant, he spotted Claire talking into a cell-phone. The phone was his; he'd left it lying on the table. When he got closer he discerned her end of the conversation, in French.

"No, Steve is fine…I'm making sure of that…I also felt you and I had established a bond when we talked by phone two weeks ago. It was almost instinctive…"

Conley drew up to the table and remained standing, trying to figure out what was going on.

"Oh, here he is now." Claire smiled and handed the phone up to him. "I answered for you. It's Milena."

"Milena?"

"I'm calling from Prague…" She now spoke English. *"I've read the news on the Internet…I wanted to call you as soon as possible."*

Nearby Claire remained tuned in, as if following an exchange of joint interest. With his usual tact, Gallagher smoked and directed his gaze elsewhere. Conley sidled to an inactive corner of the restaurant and sat down at an empty table.

"I've been terribly worried."

"I appreciate that, Milena. But the reports are correct, as Claire just told you I'm fine."

"In fact I've wanted to see you as soon as I can. That's why I applied for a Russian tourist visa."

This was like a bolt from the blue, and especially welcome after Lilya's retraction. Conley's hopes swelled and elongated.

"Unfortunately they turned me down because I'm still on crutches."

Deflation occurred just as quickly. On her end, Milena did not sound disappointed.

"I was pretty down about it, until I called your cell-phone and Claire answered. I had no idea she was there. I just spoke to her. Talking to her, I realized it was probably for the best that I didn't come."

"What? No...I would have been glad to see you..."

She interrupted him.

"Steve, that's the same selfless quality that drew me to you in Prague. But you've got your stories to write. And now Claire's there...and no doubt wants to hear more about her husband. I could hear the excitement in her voice. She deserves your full attention."

Conley tried to object again, in vain. The rest of the conversation ran its course. In cheerful, singsong tones, Milena declared that further postponement of their incipient romance was in both their interests; she was, after all, still dealing with the after-effects of her broken engagement. In a final, unconventional postscript, she revealed that she and Claire had exchanged phone numbers.

After the call he sat for a moment: legs wide and elbows on knees, staring at the cell-phone in his hand. He looked up. Across a half dozen other tables and too far away to have heard the conversation, Claire gazed back. She had the same look of gratitude in her eyes---the one that had started after her talk with Oleg.

He tried not to let it affect him.

Then out of the corner of his eye he caught Stanson making his way across the restaurant. Conley supposed he was back for his interview.

CHAPTER 119

Gallagher was not pleased to see Stanson coming. On the other hand, he wanted to get this over with.

A well-dressed young Russian strode along at Stanson's side. When the two neared the table, Gallagher noticed his breast-pocket name badge: hotel management. The Russian's expression was harried. Stanson appeared back on edge. Something was up.

"Excuse me, Mr. Gallagher?" asked the manager, in correct English.

"Yes?"

"There are two television crews outside the hotel."

Gallagher glanced toward the lobby. Indeed, some sort of commotion seemed to have started. Elevated noise. Hints of bright light.

"Television news?"

"One from CNN, one from a Russian station. They've learned that Mr. Conley is here."

Conley re-approached, still clasping his cell-phone. His face was perplexed, and became more so as he caught these last sentences. Stanson addressed him, with a nervous, momentous aspect to his drawl.

"They want interviews, Steve."

"Now?"

"Well…those folks don't like to wait."

Gallagher made eye contact with Conley, whose thoughts appeared to run in multiple directions. This was not what they needed just now. The manager re-addressed Gallagher.

"Others have started to call, from newspapers also…From different countries."

"Many?"

"Ten or twelve. Maybe more."

Gallagher frowned. For all the respect he retained for his profession, he knew that reporters in a pack, on pursuit of a breaking story, could become wild and obnoxious. Television journalists were the worst. He visualized a daylong media circus. All at once, his anger re-boiled. He glared up at Stanson.

"Are you behind this, Franklin?"

"No…believe me, Art. These hyenas corralled me when I went to the embassy this morning. I couldn't get rid of them. They followed me back here."

"Great. Thanks a lot."

Gallagher punctuated this with a snort. Stanson was supposed to at least be adept with logistics. Couldn't this would-be rancher get anything right? Clamor from the lobby grew. He stroked his beard and took stock. Timing was inopportune. Still, he and Conley had to pass this hurdle sooner or later.

"Have a seat, Steve," he said. "Let's talk this over."

The closest chair was the same Conley had occupied all morning: other side of Claire. As he re-seated himself, her features became more alert. He resisted looking at her.

"Well, what do you think?" Gallagher asked him.

"This is kind of sudden, Art. But I suppose I can do the TV. At least give a statement."

"And say what?"

Conley appeared to struggle to order his thoughts.

"Review the story you filed last night. Maybe add a few facts that we discussed this morning."

"Will you take questions?"

Conley thought for a moment.

"Guess I'll have to."

Gallagher felt a jolt of apprehension. Enormous outcomes were now riding on this exercise, for better or worse. They'd embarked upon a hazardous course. From this point forward there could be no missteps.

"Sure you're up to it, on so little sleep?"

"Yes."

Stanson and the hotel manager were still hovering over the table. Gallagher stared down into his empty coffee cup and re-stroked his beard. "He'll be right out," he told the manager, who hurried away. Turning again to Conley, he said, "After your TV appearance, Steve, I suggest you get out of here for awhile. Get some fresh air."

"Leave the hotel?"

"We want to break the rest of this story ourselves. Better to avoid further TV appearances until things have settled down."

"And the print reporters?"

"I'll handle them. I'll also finish up here with Franklin."

Conley took a deep breath and rose to his feet. He continued to look distracted, and to Gallagher's concern, didn't immediately step away from the table, as if doing battle with interior imperatives.

"I'll prepare the statement in my room," he said. "Also brush my teeth. I'll be back down in about 20 minutes."

Claire also stood, with a purposeful aura. She spoke next.

"I'll go with you, Steve."

CHAPTER 120

Up in her room, Claire re-touched her makeup and pulled herself together in minutes. Vanity was an indulgence; Conley took priority. Taking the stairs, she clattered down to the fourth floor and rapped on his door. He took a while to appear. In one hand he clutched pen and paper.

"How's it going?" she asked.

"Almost ready."

To her Conley looked somewhat unfocused. She began to worry about his capacity for orderly presentation in the face of such a media frenzy.

"Just a few more minutes," he said.

"Shall I wait out here?"

"What for? Come on in."

Before stepping across the threshold she gave him another examination. His eyes rambled down to her middle curves. She flushed, remembering where she had seen that before. In her apartment building. After Versailles.

"Better I wait out here. I'll just distract you."

His gaze left her with reluctance; he shut the door and returned to his sequestration. Claire paced a short distance down the hallway and back. Some of her nervousness came back. Would he pull through? Missteps here could undo everything. Her heart was thumping and her breath was short by the time he re-emerged, wearing overcoat and scarf. One sheet of paper was folded in his hand.

"Have your hat?" she asked.

"For the press conference?"

"No, Steve. We're leaving right afterward. Remember?"

Absent-mindedly, he went back inside and grabbed it. Had he already forgotten Gallagher's plan?

When the elevator doors opened downstairs, five reporters waited. Hotel security had been able to ward off only the cameras. Claire locked her arm through Conley's as they stepped out.

"We're all set up outside," one reporter said, in a Russian accent.

"I'm ready," Conley answered, leading Claire forward through the group.

Dense light penetrated the lobby. Through plate-glass windows Claire glimpsed the scene outside. Light snow was falling. Four or five tripod-mounted lamps formed an impromptu stage on the front steps of the terrace, throwing snowflakes into stark illumination. Other TV crews appeared to have joined the original two. There was a throng of print journalists. One of the reporters had fallen in next to Claire.

"Can you say who you are?" he asked, in an American accent.

"Claire Bradford."

"Peter Bradford's widow?"

"Yes."

The reporters scribbled on their pads. One spoke clipped syllables into the mouthpiece of a headset. Claire felt under assault, and locked her arm tighter. Fate had thrown her lot together with Conley's. It was too late to backtrack.

"I'm Lyle Higgins from CNN," said the reporter with the headset.

"Yes?" Conley answered, not breaking stride.

Their gaggle was now approaching the sliding glass doors.

"We're breaking into our main coverage."

"You mean…"

"Yes. When you come through those doors you'll be live."

Claire's heart slammed several beats.

"Good God," Conley said.

Claire re-tightened her arm and tried to speak with a steady voice. "You'll do…fine, Steve."

In seconds they were through and outdoors and staring across the hotel drive at a disconcerting multi-tier of lights, lenses and indistinct faces. A racket erupted: questions and instructions, mostly in English, along with pings and whirs from digital cameras. Claire noticed four or five large-diameter TV lenses: all aimed at her and Conley. Among these was one from TV2, the French station. How many were live feeds? It was surreal.

"Let's go," Conley said.

They crossed the entryway to the front steps of the terrace. He drew several lungs-full of air. Snowflakes accumulated on his eyebrows.

"Here, give me your hat."

Claire was barely able to get the words out. She took his fur head-piece and separated herself.

Cameras stayed on Conley. He took position near the top step, where a bank of microphones had already been set up, and held out his single sheet of paper. When he looked up the throng fell silent; only noise came from traffic on the boulevard below. For a long moment he appeared mesmerized by the lenses. Seconds passed as snowflakes fluttered down and Claire felt her knees grow weak: a terrifying help-lessness. To waver now would be catastrophic. Her new appreciation for him aside, Conley could be a stricken fool on occasion; she knew that firsthand.

However in the next instant he became straight and focused. Wayward currents that gripped him at other inopportune moments appeared checked and re-channeled. He began in a deliberate voice.

"As has been widely reported, I went missing in Dushanbe, Tajikistan on Tuesday, along with my interpreter, Oleg Mikhailov.

This happened while on assignment for my employer, the *Boston World Tribune.* We were investigating the heroin trade, as well as the death of my colleague Peter Bradford, who perished in Tajikistan on October 16th while on assignment there. In fact, as my paper reported last night, we were kidnapped and held in forced custody by Shimon Shakuri, the Prime Minister of Tajikistan. This was a misguided attempt by Shakuri to cover up incriminating details of Bradford's death. We were rescued late yesterday afternoon by Russian special forces, who invaded Shakuri's residential compound by helicopter. The main elements of the episode are described in today's report in the *World Tribune.* I am making this statement to confirm that Oleg Mikhailov and I both came to no harm, thanks in large part the professionalism of the troops involved. We are both in excellent condition."

A tumult exploded. Claire couldn't make out any individual questions. Conley raised his voice to finish.

"I will provide further details of my experience in an upcoming series of articles in the *Boston World Tribune.*"

He took a step backward and toward her, but before he got further the reporters swarmed around him. They were like pack animals. Cameras whirred and clicked anew.

"How much did Shakuri offer you?"

"What exactly did Shakuri want you to do?"

"Are you sure Bradford wasn't bribed?"

At that Conley stopped. The unruly chorus subsided, lenses still trained.

Claire held her breath. She had half an impulse toward consolidation. To lead him away before this spun in dangerous directions. However when he answered, his words came out with extra conviction, as if animated by a primal force.

"Yes, I am. Peter Bradford was not bribed. He was just doing his job, and pursuing a story. For that he sacrificed his life."

His tone carried impact. Uncharacteristic silence fell on the throng, even if just for a brief moment.

"...We should accord all possible respect to his memory."

The chorus erupted again. This time Claire didn't let Conley linger. "Let's go, Steve," she said, pulling him away by his elbow and up onto the hotel drive.

There was a line of five taxis further down the curve. Several reporters and two cameras were keeping pace with them. "Better that one," Conley suggested, pointing further down then opening the rear door when they reached his intended vehicle. He seemed to know the driver. Once installed in the back seat Claire was still panting. Lenses still seemed everywhere, aimed at her through the windows. However the test had passed. Relief began to take over.

"Where to?" the driver asked.

Claire figured Conley should decide. He had certainly earned the privilege.

CHAPTER 121

At first the taxi made slow, fitful progress. Gallagher could not see Conley or Claire in the backseat; thickets of bodies around the vehicle were too dense. Shouts from reporters shrilled the air. Oleg nodded toward the commotion.

"Satisfied, Art?"

"Couldn't have gone better," he answered.

They'd watched the brief press conference from the hotel's blanketed front lawn, back some yards from the cordon of media personnel. Snow beneath their feet had already been kicked up and trampled over by assorted news crews. Gallagher thought for a moment.

"What about you, Oleg?"

"Me?"

"Shakuri's out. The aid bill's been derailed. And your man...I mean Russia's man...will be the next Prime Minister."

Oleg looked back, impassive except for a raised eyebrow. He still wasn't letting on.

"Russia did get what it wanted," he acknowledged. "All the same, I wouldn't go too hard on Franklin Stanson. His intentions were good. And we're basically working toward the same goals there."

To Gallagher this was far too generous. He said he was inclined toward less leniency.

"Actually, that wasn't what I was thinking about, just now," Oleg continued.

Gallagher eyed him.

"I was thinking Steve and I turned down two-and-a-half million dollars each, for something we ended up doing anyway."

Gallagher snorted, with a faint smile. He hadn't thought of that.

"Any regrets?"

Reporters, photographers and cameramen had finally and grudgingly given way, and the taxi was proceeding less tentatively. Oleg waited some seconds as the ruckus de-intensified.

"No. Money was never a motive for me in any of this." He paused for an instant. "And I don't think it was for Steve, either."

"What was it, then?" Gallagher asked him.

"For Steve?"

"Yes."

Their gazes gravitated back to the taxi, now descending slowly between snow-banks along the curving hotel drive. Through the rear window, Conley and Claire were now visible, in apparent conversation. Several cameramen and photographers still jogged alongside. Oleg considered and opened his mouth to answer. He stopped when a uniformed concierge materialized, holding a portable phone.

"Mr. Gallagher?"

"Yes?"

"You have a call. A Mr. Harry Whitcombe."

"Can I take it out here?"

The concierge handed the phone over. Oleg took a couple of polite steps back. Gallagher held up a gloved hand, gesturing for him to stay, and spoke into the device. The connection was clear. Below, he saw the taxi turn on its right blinker, waiting to merge into boulevard traffic.

"Harry?"

"Art...I wanted to reach you earlier, right after you filed your story..."

Whitcombe's voice shot with elation. He sounded more alive and confident than he had in weeks. Gallagher checked his watch. It was just after 3:30 a.m. in Boston.

"And, I just saw Conley on CNN."

Had the stalwart publisher regained his old form? After a delay, Gallagher recognized why. There had been several by-products to this. Winners and losers. He'd almost forgotten: Whitcombe was one of the former.

"Congratulations are in order, Art. Conley's safe. Although nothing is definitive, we gained some more clarity about Peter. And this has turned into the kind of big story that I imagined at the beginning. We'll give Conley's articles top play. This truly stands to energize the paper."

Gallagher thanked him. There could be worse beneficiaries from this than Whitcombe.

"I also want to tell you, Art...There are some issues I've got to sort out with Janet...Some things I haven't been pleased with. Let's just say I want you to play an even more central role when you get back."

Another by-product that Gallagher hadn't intended. He did not object.

"Is Conley there?"

Gallagher turned again down the drive. The taxi was gone. Cameramen and photographers who had followed the vehicle down to the gate were already walking back up toward the hotel.

"I'm afraid you missed him, Harry. He and Claire have just left."

Other journalists and news crews milled nearby, appearing unsatiated. A couple of reporters recognized Gallagher, and began heading his way. Others paid attention. Oleg gave Gallagher a cautionary glance.

"I may have to sign off soon, Harry," Gallagher said. "A stampede is coming."

"Just one more thing, Art. I know you recommended Conley for this assignment in the first place. And I had some doubts, based on my personal experience..."

Gallagher waited, wondering what was coming.

"But maybe those also told me, deep down, that he was right for this."

Gallagher glanced again toward the boulevard.

"I would agree, Harry. Your instincts were correct."

CHAPTER 121

At the gate Conley looked over his shoulder. Last foot-bound pursuers from the media contingent drew up and watched, still not satiated, as the taxi turned onto the boulevard. No vehicles gave chase.

With the furor behind, Claire appeared relieved, redirected. As though she'd re-claimed core certainties. She scooted closer. Nothing suggestive; she just looked grateful. He belatedly recognized that much of her behavior the evening before---and even earlier that morning---had been a function of stress.

"You did well, Steve."

"Well enough, I guess."

"No. *Incroyablement.*"

"Thanks."

Their taxi fused into traffic. They were moving southwest along the *Moskva*: the first riverside route Conley had attempted night before. Luzhniki Stadium lay further around the wide bend, on the opposite bank. Unrecoverable distance, it seemed to him, had opened between that expedition and the present.

"Guess that's it, then," she said.

"Not exactly, Claire. I still have my articles to write. Probably the most important component of all this."

"Of course. Any second thoughts?"

Conley gave her a quizzical look. As if to release him from responding, she smiled. Rush from the media spotlight was still strong; she had an effect. He had to fight it. There would be no replay of Paris. Even if Lilya and Milena were for now out of the picture.

Observing his unease, Claire became contrite.

"I'm sorry, Steve. I don't want to press you. It's just that these last days have been very emotional."

"I understand."

"And turned out better than I could have hoped…"

She paused. Their driver reversed direction at an intersection and re-traced the river. Snowfall remained moderate, though enough to lend indistinct, otherworldly qualities to central Moscow.

"I know, Steve," she said at last.

"You do?"

"Yes. The laptop…everything. I put it all together."

"And…?"

"Yes." She nodded. "I know what Peter did."

They crossed the Kutyzovkski Bridge. The Russian White House loomed along their left. Claire fixed her eyes on the landmark a moment, as if making broader associations.

"Since when?"

"Since last week. Thanks to Harry Whitcombe."

Conley examined her, wondering how to respond. Her next move was to sit straighter. Fabric from her overcoat went tight along her arched spine. Her haunches jutted in a familiar way.

Not aimed at him, as far as he could tell. Just a return of confidence. She remained close. He was trying to tamp down his sensations when she jolted him with another question.

"What made you do it, Steve?"

"It wasn't just me. It was Art, too…" he said.. "It's no so important… Is it?"

She looked at him for a few seconds.

"Yes it is. You did the right thing. At least by me."

River now behind them, their taxi split the bookend skyscrapers on Kalinin Prospekt. Traffic along the wide boulevard moved in forceful flux, unhindered by the snow. Her palm came to rest on his knee.

His reaction was immediately palpable. She pulled back her hand and folded it with the other on her lap.

"Again, forgive my emotions, Steve. It's just that…this is the best I've felt in six weeks, since Peter's death. Like I can start to return to normal."

Conley nodded and inhaled. In minutes they pulled up at the destination he had specified, the first that had come to mind: Red Square.

"Better put your hat on," she said.

"And you?"

"I won't get cold."

They emerged from the taxi onto a sloped plaza, fronted by a deep-red, pre-revolution-era building, and made parallel tracks along snow-coated cobblestones. As they mounted the gradual incline the GUM shopping complex became visible on their left. Snowfall dwindled: just intermittent, fluttering flakes, and by increments the square came into full view, bordered on one side by clock spires and towering brick walls of the Kremlin. The immense space was mostly empty of people: an expanse of new whiteness and muffled tranquility. There was no obvious path to follow.

Just past the edge of the square Claire drew to a stop. Conley did likewise and turned to face her. She brushed snowflakes from her face and her hair to one side. Her hand was trembling less than before.

"How long are you staying in Moscow, Steve?

"Probably about a week."

Her eyes held no implication---just her own next steps. That was enough. Conley resorted to direct appeal.

"Claire, please remember. I've tried to do this for the right reasons."

"I know. That's why I'm not eager to leave."

ACKNOWLEDGMENTS BY THE AUTHOR

Because this was my first novel, the help I received from a small circle of volunteers, friends and conscientious readers was particularly invaluable. Their balanced commentary, constructive advice and general encouragement through various stages of research, writing and editing were vital to the final result.

Dr. Dmitri Galenchik tutored me on fatal gunshot wounds and human responses to imminent mortality. Thibaut Behaghel provided insights and suggestions on French social nuances and specific locations in Paris, as perhaps only a Parisian can. Ann Johnson, Chris DiNapoli and Stephanie Weaver were intrepid enough to plunge into my first complete draft, and their forthright reactions highlighted the many elements that still needed work. Through numerous redrafts Marina Telen, Elizabeth Boluch Wood, Dave Johnson and Irena Farino rendered further diligent and generous assistance that helped propel the manuscript toward finished form. Bethany DiNapoli, Evgeny Tribuloff and Roger Moore contributed additional time as I reached conclusion.

To all of them, I am forever grateful.

NOTES BY THE AUTHOR

Most of the locations I have employed in this story are real, and may be recognizable to readers who have inhabited or traveled to the cities in question. However for narrative convenience I have occasionally altered details or created composite settings, particularly in cafes, office buildings and outlying areas, so my descriptions should not be treated as travelogue.

I have taken somewhat greater liberties with geo-politics, particularly recent U.S. and Russian policies toward Tajikistan. That said, I have drawn my narrative from actual developments. Since 2001 heroin smuggling northward out of Afghanistan has constituted a significant, large-scale problem for the world community---particularly for NATO forces battling anti-Western insurgents in the region, and for countries in Europe and the former Soviet Union where the heroin is distributed and sold. And Tajikistan, while not the only central-Asian state through which this smuggling occurs, is situated at the nexus of interdiction efforts. My disclaimer relates to specifics; the characters in my story are not based upon past or present real-life political figures in the Tajik government, or upon representatives of the U.S. and Russian governments engaged in the region. And of course the specific events I describe are entirely my own creation.

The Boston World Tribune, likewise, is a fictional news organization.

ABOUT THE AUTHOR

Eric Almeida was born in Ithaca, New York in 1962 and raised in Rhode Island. He attended Tabor Academy and majored in History at Brown University, where he also competed on the rowing team. Upon graduation in 1984 he worked as a Sports Writer at *The Providence Journal* for one year, then resumed his education at The Nitze School of Advanced International Studies (SAIS) of Johns Hopkins University, receiving an M.A. in International Affairs in 1987.

From graduate school he detoured into business, working as international sales manager for an American high-technology company for five years, primarily in Europe. He proceeded to co-found a software-development venture based in Belarus, France and the Netherlands, for which he also served as President from 1996-2001.

Soon thereafter he returned to writing, his core interest. He currently divides his time between Ukraine and the New England coastline. For more information about Eric Almeida and his books please visit www.ericalmeida.com.

www.ingramcontent.com/pod-product-compliance
Lightning Source LLC
Chambersburg PA
CBHW051430260626
47162CB00001B/30